I0714274

THE WARDENS OF TERRA

BOOKS 1 - 4

C.D. GORRI

The Wardens of Terra
Books 1 - 4
Paranormal Romance
by C.D. Gorri
Edited by Book Nook Nuts

STOP
If you want to hear more about C.D. Gorri's books, sign up
here:
Https://www.cdgorri.com/newsletter

Or

GRAB THEM IN AUDIO HERE!

Copyright 2019, 2021 C.D. Gorri, NJ

This is a work of fiction. All of the characters, names, places, organizations, and events portrayed in this novel are either part of the author's imagination and/or used fictitiously and are not to be construed as real. Any resemblance to any person, living or dead, actual events, locales or organizations is entirely coincidental. This eBook is licensed for your personal enjoyment only. All rights are reserved. No part of this book is to be reproduced, scanned, downloaded, printed, or distributed in any manner whatsoever without written permission from the author. Please do not participate in or encourage piracy of any materials in violation of the author's rights. Thank you for respecting the hard work of this author.

WELCOME TO THE WARDENS OF TERRA, AN ELITE GROUP OF SHIFTERS DESTINED TO SAVE HUMANKIND!

The Hounds of God have been disbanded by the Catholic Church, leaving a terrible void in the fight to save humankind. As a result, a much older organization returns to power and takes up the reins to fight to save the Earth from the evil that stalks it.

They are the Wardens of Terra, an elite force of Shifters each with a defining power to aid them in the never-ending battle against the forces of darkness. Alone they are fierce warriors. Once they've found their true mates, they become an unstoppable force.

These are their stories.

***

BOUND BY AIR

USA TODAY BESTSELLING AUTHOR

C.D. GORRI

Bound
BY AIR

Instant attraction won't stop him from doing his duty, but there are some things a shifter just can't fight!

Troy Waman is a Thunderbird Shifter, bound to the sign Aquarius, and a Warden of Terra. He is sent to upstate New York to investigate a disturbance in the balance of magic and nature. His job is to decipher whether the sudden string of winter storms is natural or the work of darker forces in the area.

Andrea Kristos' estranged great-aunt recently passed away, leaving her a house in Shadowland, New York. The novice Romani Caster moves into the ancient house hoping to learn more about the parents who left her long ago. During her search, she discovers that some things are better left undisturbed.

Just when things couldn't get any worse, a huge, devastatingly handsome stranger shows up at Andrea's door in the middle of the night and puts her in handcuffs!
How will she get him to believe that she is innocent?

PROLOGUE

Present day, Roanoke, North Carolina.

"*It is time,*" the gravelly voice resounded off the exposed brick walls of the darkened room. The Twelve had resolved to meet there each month since they'd moved their headquarters to the New World in the late 16th century.

It was the same site where some of their ancestors had met like clockwork on each eve of the New Moon. Though, truth be told, the building itself had changed many times, having been burnt down, rebuilt, and renovated with the many advances in industry and technology over the centuries. Still, it was new compared to the thousand-year old structures they still owned abroad.

"*Aye. 'Tis time.*"

"Agreed."

"Si."

"Aftalt."

"Dogovoren."

So, on it went. Each of the *Twelve Heralds of Terra* consented in their native tongue. The sounds of the streets beyond the small, dank room were drowned out by the pounding of their fists on the large wooden table where they'd gathered. It was unanimous.

The eldest among them stood and spoke to the group. His skin was spotted with age, his long hair hung down his back like a white river that reached almost to his knees. His once great height was severely diminished as he stood before the other members of the twelve with his back stooped over and his gnarled hand resting heavily on an aged oak cane.

"I have walked *Terra* for more than a thousand years waiting for this day. It has taken an age to emerge, and yet we have no time to learn to crawl before we walk. Darkness is enveloping our beloved Earth. We must fight it," he exhaled and raised his cerulean eyes to meet those of everyone at the table. The herald was old, indeed, but power was still heavy with him.

"We have trained our *Wardens,* waiting for this time to arise. It has been a long time coming, but now, we are called back to our rightful positions as Guardians of this planet. We Heralds must do our jobs to ensure each Station Master receives their orders correctly."

"Why, *capitaine,* do we not lead them ourselves?"

"Because, my Russian friend, that is not our place. We are the watchers, comrades. We have waited for the right time to come, now we must announce it to all of the supernatural world. The Wardens of terra are back."

"I see."

"Good. Now, the Station Masters will hand out assignments amongst the Wardens, this is the way it has always been."

"And if the *Hounds* re-emerge?"

"Then we shall work with them as we should have been allowed to do from the beginning, but now is not the time to rehash old quarrels. The *Wardens of Terra* are needed again."

CHAPTER ONE

Troy Waman looked down at his smartphone to the little red arrow blinking on his map app, indicating he had reached his destination. He frowned pensively before shaking his head.

"What a fucking shithole," he murmured to himself as he exited the nondescript black SUV his Station Master, Rex, had given him for the job.

"Try not to scratch it," the tough Bear shifter had said with a barely contained growl after their meeting the day before last. After a thousand years of waiting, The *Wardens of Terra* were being called to duty and this was Troy's first assignment.

It took him a day and a half to make his way to Shadowland, New York from the little suburb in Virginia Beach where his Station was located. There were dozens of them across the continental United States and even more overseas, though he'd rarely been out of the county himself.

Troy rolled his shoulders and exhaled. He was the first from his Station to be called to duty. A fact that left him both proud and humbled at the same time. He'd trained damn hard since he was a child waiting for such an opportunity. Now he had it, and it was almost too much to bear.

Fuck and damn. It's time Troy, get your ass in gear. That was all the sympathy he had for himself. Why the hell should he have any at all? Troy Waman was no tenderfoot normal. He was a Warden of Terra. He didn't need to remind himself of the honor and duty that went along with his position.

The *Wardens of Terra* were an ancient group of elite warriors. All of them Shifters. Identified in their youth and trained throughout their preternaturally long lives, they were guardians as well as fighters. *Station Masters* led teams of Wardens across the planet.

Though they'd been deactivated sometime in the last millennium, Wardens were born, chosen, and trained every day with the distinct knowledge that someday, they'd be called upon to defend the earth. That day was here.

Troy Waman had been trained as a Warden since before he learned how to spell the word. His heritage was a mix of Anglo and Native American. His father's blood was a mix of tribes including Algonquin, Lenape, Cherokee, and a few others. He hadn't stuck around long enough for anyone to learn the rest.

He supposed he could get a DNA test, but that might raise too many questions with the normals. Especially in this day of advanced technology in biogenetics.

Besides, it was quite common in today's world to find Native American peoples descended from multiple tribes. Troy Waman was uncommon for an entirely different reason. He was a Shifter, a special race of dual natured beings with one foot in the supernatural world and one in the human. Troy was a *Thunderbird Shifter* to be exact. Something unique even amongst Shifters.

He stretched his long, lithe body as he stepped away from the vehicle. It was already dark out despite it being fairly early in the evening. *Daylight savings my ass.* He sniffed the frigid air. The unusually high winds made the cold seem even more bitter. The street lamp stuttered on the corner, a rusty fence squeaked, and a black cat crossed the street, ducking under some parked cars. Troy's frown deepened.

It looked like the setting of a B-horror flick. All it needed was some half naked co-ed to run down the street with a masked bogeyman stalking behind her, traditional blood-coated knife in hand. *Oh yeah.* They might call it *Shadowland Nightmare* or something equally cheesy.

He stopped his musings and used his heightened senses to take in the downtrodden area around him. It would seem upstate New York wasn't all orchards and sprawling suburbs. He smirked as the "I love New York" song ran through his head. *Yeah, right.*

Apparently, parts of the Empire State were as fucked up as the street where he was born in Newark, New Jersey. He'd visited that shithole back when he was in his teens just out of curiosity. What a mistake that had been! He'd left almost as soon as he'd arrived. His extended family had been, shall we say, less than welcoming.

His gray-haired grandmother had screamed and crossed herself when he stepped over her threshold. He was what they called a *skin walker*. They feared and loathed him as something evil. Him evil? Like he was the motherfucker who knocked-up some unsuspecting normal and left her ass with a Shifter baby.

He was not evil, but he was something they did not understand. He'd been angry and ashamed that day. He'd crashed through his grandmother's kitchen to hitch a ride back down to his Station in Virginia Beach.

In his youth it was more like a military training camp, but it was all he knew of home. After all, it was where he'd lived his entire life. He'd made his peace and settled fully into his life there.

The incident with his grandmother had happened over a decade ago, when Troy had stolen his records out of Rex's office. Still, the memory remained fresh in his mind as if it were only yesterday. The fucked-up street where he was standing only brought back the painful reminder that he'd come from the same kind of squalor. *Fuck this*, he thought.

The pungent scent of despair washed over him. *Reminding him.* A young man with a hood pulled up over his head, eyed him from the street corner. *Drug dealer. Shadowland* indeed. It was an apt name for this shamble of a neighborhood.

The young man continued to stare until Troy allowed his beast to shine through. His golden eyes pinned the errant youth through the inky darkness of the night. Startled, the kid dropped the bag he was holding and ran down the alley.

Punk. Troy walked over and picked up what he had so hastily left behind. A couple of grams of crack cocaine and heroin, *probably cut with Fentanyl.* There were also various sized baggies full of what smelled like some below average marijuana and half-rotted psychedelic mushrooms.

Just your garden variety of illegal substances to be found on most street corners in neighborhoods like this one. *Fucking normals.* He frowned and dumped the still sealed contents down the closest storm drain. He sent a quick text to Rex earmarking the location.

Rex would make sure the local police department got an anonymous tip to retrieve the narcotics before someone got hurt. Recreational drug use, mainly the opioid epidemic, was wreaking havoc amongst the humans with more and more of them succumbing to their addictions.

It was troubling, but not Troy's problem. Shifters were extraordinarily hard to kill. Most human drugs had little to no effect on supernatural beings. *Normals,* he growled the thought, *such weak creatures.*

To be fair, Shifters had vices too. He just had little

experience with it. Cecil, a Station-mate of his, had an adrenaline addiction. He was always putting himself in dangerous situations, even during simple training exercises. Fernandez, a Jaguar Shifter, was always trying to get into some chick's pants. *Sex addict.* And he knew of others who channeled their energies into ways he considered to be mostly unproductive.

His opinion, for sure. He'd always been something of a loner by nature. There weren't many Thunderbird Shifters around. Hell, he was the only fucking one he knew of in this part of the world.

He didn't blame or judge his Station-mates for their proclivities. Most of the Shifters he knew had large appetites which included food, exercise, and sex.

Troy had certainly explored that part of him. He wasn't a man-whore or anything, but he'd had his share of women. None of them mattered to him. Just a means to satisfy the occasional itch.

Troy was determined to live his life as a Warden of Terra alone. He never expected to find anyone willing to share what was a potentially deadly existence.

Those who followed the Darkness and evil were always looking for ways to gain the upper hand and it was his job to stop them. The way he saw it, it was an honor and a duty to serve.

He shared this great responsibility with the entire organization. The core belief of the Wardens was based on one indisputable fact Shifters had walked the earth since the dawn of time, even before humankind; therefore, they were responsible for the well-being of the entire planet and all its inhabitants. Especially those who were inherently weaker. Mainly females and *normals*.

There were other supernaturals who believed humans, or normals as they referred to them, were a blight on the planet. Those creatures wished to destroy them and take over.

Demons, Dark Witches, and a whole plethora of evil beings sought the destruction of the normals and the world they lived in. *Idiots! Did they even realize if they destroyed the world, there would be nothing left? Where the fuck would they live?*

Of course, the supernatural world had many agencies that worked towards the common goal of saving the planet. The *Order of the Guardians,* for example, were responsible for policing the various factions of supernaturals.

Shifters generally tended to ally themselves with the Guardians. Sure, there were *bad* Shifters, but he'd never come across any willing to follow the Dark. Simply because most agreed the destruction of the world could not be allowed to happen.

Different Packs and Clans, etcetera, of course, had different ideas. Some wanted to remain secret, others wished to come out, and other still wanted to rule the weaker humans. It was a whole fucking thing, and they argued about regularly.

Troy didn't know from any of that. He spent little time in the human world. His efforts better spent making himself worthy of being a Warden. Training, exercise, and following orders. That's what Troy lived for, it was why he was chosen.

Thunderbird Shifters were very rare. *Special*. He scoffed at the stray thought. But no matter what way he looked at it, Troy was indeed unique. In more ways than one. He was born *marked* by the stars. A *Shifter of Terra*.

From infancy, he was told he carried the power of his sign within him. *Aquarius* ruled his destiny and it would aid him in the never-ending battle against the forces of darkness.

Every single Warden he knew was a Shifter like him. They were the fiercest warriors on the planet. Like many others throughout the last thousand years, Troy, *a Shifter child who was marked,* was taken from his parents and trained by his Station Master until the time when he would be called into use.

All that time, he thought, *and here I am.* He tried to ignore the pressure building inside of him. He felt anxious. His animal pressed against his psyche, comforting him with his presence.

The significance of the moment was not lost on him. The Wardens had waited a millennium to be called to act. *He* had been waiting his entire life.

"Do not fear the future, Troy," the Herald who had visited his Station said to him when he'd brought word that they had been activated, *"Your destiny awaits."*

Troy wondered if the old man referred to the Wardens finally being called to act, or if the elder spoke of yet another legend. Troy had been shocked to say the least when the Herald had entered their tidy little Station in Virginia Beach with his flowing white hair. After he told them the news, he turned to Troy and recited another old tale.

"Young Thunderbird, you are the first to return us to Terra. Do not doubt your worth. Your destiny has been written in the stars since before you were born, Troy Waman. Remember, a Warden discovers his true measure when his fated mate is thrust upon him."

Whatever the fuck that meant. Troy looked down at

his phone, then to the street sign on the corner, and finally, to the faded numbers painted on the mailbox in front of the ramble of a house his map app had brought him to.

Fuck, am I thinking? Fated mates are myths. Stories made up so orphaned Shifters would sleep through the night. He scoffed at the thought. Memories of tales the head nurse, Sr. Maria, had told him at the training camp he'd called home for years invaded his brain.

Memories were pesky things. Sometimes eternal, and always fucking portable. But he was no longer a child. *No more stories, Sister. Now, I act.*

"A thousand years we've waited, and I'm walking into a fucking scene from a bad episode of *Hoarders*," Troy shook his head and frowned at the decrepit house that sat a few hundred feet away from him.

It was cold as fuck outside and his leather jacket did little to warm him. Avian Shifters did not carry around the same bulk as other types of Shifters. He ran hotter than normals, but the single digit temperature froze him to the bone.

True, he wasn't beefy like some of his fellow Shifters, but he was just as incredibly strong, and he was wicked fast. Much stronger than any average male. He paused briefly gauging the atmosphere.

There was something off about the place. He scented *Magic* and something else. His Bird bristled beneath his skin. *Easy now.*

Lightning flashed in the darkened skies, allowing him to see the worn shingles, and cracked siding of the beaten-up colonial in greater detail. More than one window had been smashed and boarded up with cheap plywood.

If anything, it enhanced the creepy haunted house feel of the place. The porch sagged dangerously. He wondered how the place had managed to not be condemned by the town. One thing was certain, it was an ugly little turd of a house.

Who the hell put gray siding on their house anyway? Maybe it wasn't always that color. Maybe the owner liked gray. *Whatever.* He couldn't give two shits about the siding.

His only concern was the increased supernatural activity in the area over the past two weeks. Ever since the owner, a *Mrs. Renalda Curosi,* passed away. *A haunting?*

A creaking sound floated up to his ears and he stilled his movements. The sound developed into more of a *moaning* noise. An unearthly wail. It grew louder as the lightning continued to flash in the sky.

Troy had never seen a ghost. True, there were a

lot of things in the universe he had never seen nor heard of, but that didn't make them any less real.

If ghosts were real, and they made noises, he imagined that pitiful wail was damn close to what it would sound like.

No such thing as ghosts. Yeah, well, most people had never heard of Shifters either. And yet, there he stood.

His Thunderbird shifted once more beneath his skin, the beast flexing his senses as the lightning in the air drew him to the surface. *No.* He told his other half. His human needed to be in control now. He walked across the street, keeping to the shadows.

Something was indeed off about the creepy old house. He inched further to the black door. The knocker was in the shape of a face or mask. No discernible features, just a vague impression of eyes, nose, and mouth. *Shadowland indeed.*

He listened with his enhanced hearing and frowned. There was a distinct voice somewhere beneath the moaning and creaking. A *female* voice. His curiosity was piqued.

From what he'd seen in her file, Mrs. Curosi was ninety-seven when she passed. Her closest living relative was a half-sister, a *Magdelena Kristos*, and she lived over three hours away in New Jersey. The half-sister was cut from Mrs. Curosi's will recently. She'd bequeathed her entire estate, house, bank account, and all her earthly belongings, to someone named *A. Kristos. Another sister? Maybe.*

Troy hadn't given it much thought until now. A crash sounded from inside the house. He perked up as the feminine voice he'd thought he'd heard earlier screamed in pain. *Time to act.*

CHAPTER TWO

"You've got to be fucking kidding me!" Andrea Kristos was trapped.

She should never have come here! *Stupid frigging binding spell drawn right in the middle floor*! She twisted her body in an attempt to free herself of the heavy magic that kept her lying flat on the cold, unfinished plywood that acted as a floor covering for the entire attic in her recently deceased aunt's house.

The black leather-bound book she'd accidentally opened floated above her. The tome glowed a sickly yellow color as its pages flipped wildly in the supernatural breeze it'd summoned. *Fucking malaka!*

She cursed herself for the idiot she was. Walking

into a strange Romani Caster's house! Relative or not, she should've cased out the place first!

The Romani people, such as Andrea and her family were proud to call themselves, were notoriously cautious and secretive. The house of her dead relative was certainly going to be protected from the likes of any stranger who'd dared to enter. *Yes*, this was her Aunt Renalda's home, but Andrea was a stranger, nonetheless.

The book groaned as it tried to draw in more power. "Oh, crap, this is bad," Andrea gasped as sizzling little zaps of energy licked along her skin. They were hot and malicious like a thousand little daggers. The power coming from the book was most assuredly designed to harm, but what the heck was it doing here, she wondered for the umpteenth time.

Five years away from home and the sweet little old lady who was her great-aunt had turned into some kind of Dark Caster? *Heck no!* She didn't believe it for a second. Something was going on though, and she had the welts to prove it.

"Oh, this is so not good. Ouch! Dammit!"

A sudden pounding noise reached her ears. *Now what?* Andrea wanted to scream. The knocking continued to grow more insistent. Whoever it was seemed pretty determined to get inside.

Good luck, pal! It wasn't like she was able to do anything to help the person get in! Seeing as how she was stuck under the weight of some pretty pissed off magic and all. *FML.*

Friggin' superstitious old Romani biddy! A flash of power zapped her right in the ass and Andrea screamed in pain. *Yikes! Apologies, auntie,* she quickly bit off a small prayer to honor her deceased family member. She knew better than to piss off the dead.

"Look, you're better off staying out there, dude," she yelled over the howling wind and the eerie scream-like sounds coming from the ancient tome.

Oh, Aunt Renalda, what were you into? Puri daj must be nuts sending me here! She wondered just what her grandmother or *Puri daj*, better known as Madame Magdelena Kristos, matriarch of the Kristos Clan and one of the most formidable Romani Casters in the world, was doing when she'd told her granddaughter to go up to this godforsaken place.

So, what if she'd been avoiding all family business the past five years while she backpacked her way across the globe? She was still a Kristos, blast it all!

The nomadic lifestyle was in her blood for Pete's sake. She wasn't going to apologize for something that was basically her birthright as a Romani!

Of course, just lately she'd been feeling a pull to return to the country of her birth. Hell, she'd left right in the middle of a star-studded party weekend on Mykos to come back to this frozen dump of a state. *And for what?* That's exactly what she'd like to know!

When she'd finally landed, she was shocked to be greeted by her illusive grandmother. Andrea should have known then, it was bad news. She hadn't exactly been close to Aunt Renalda, but she remembered the old woman who wore her hair in a severe bun and smelled faintly like the spices she used to cook her famous *spanakopita*.

The woman hand rolled her own phyllo dough for the delicious spinach pie Andrea couldn't get enough of during family gatherings. It had hurt to learn of her passing. Especially when the news came from the iron-willed woman who was her grandmother.

Her *Puri daj's* eyes hadn't teared up or grown misty when she'd told Andrea. Her stylish hair remained untouched, make-up perfect, and her posture as unyielding as ever. Andrea supposed the matriarch needed to be tough as nails. Especially when faced with the death of a sister, no matter how estranged they were. The weirdest thing was that

Aunt Renalda, for some unknown reason, had left all of her worldly belongings to Andrea.

The bank account sum wasn't a fortune by any means, but there were more zeroes than Andrea had imagined. Not only did she leave her all of her money, but her house and possessions as well. *WTF?*

Now, she knew why her great-aunt had done so. The woman fucking hated her! Her sweet great-aunt and loving grandmother obviously wanted her dead or maimed. Vengeance for her leaving them maybe. She didn't know and was unlikely to find out in her position.

Andrea hadn't practiced casting or conjuring in years and now she was faced with magic the likes of which she'd never experienced. Her grandmother's parting words filled her mind, *"Remember who you are, little Andrea. Remember what training you've had, granddaughter. Do not falter, the time for you to use it is near. It seems your destiny is calling."*

Her *training* consisted of no more than a few months with some pretty nutty cousins abroad. Andrea groaned, she should have been a better student.

When she was younger, she'd been impatient to see the world, to get away from her strict Romani upbringing. The clan was grossly old-fashioned, even for having a woman lead them. She'd been severely limited in what she was allowed to do and whom she was allowed to do it with.

Living in her maternal grandmother's clan had its advantages though. When she was fourteen her father had drawn up a marriage contract between her and a boy from his old clan, but *Puri daj* had forbidden it.

She was grateful for her grandmother's interference, but her father had been furious. Always cursing her when she was near to the point where she hated being home. Her mother had died when she was little, and though her parents were married in the eyes of her people, they'd never legally tied the knot. Therefore, Andrea remained a Kristos, ignoring her father's name as she ignored his wishes.

Her father, Hugo Constantine, was a small man. Thin and angry, he'd soon taken to slapping her around whenever she'd displeased him. The clan knew, but for some reason they didn't interfere. She even went to *Puri daj* one day after school in the tenth grade. She'd been late getting dinner on the table and her father had attacked her with his belt. She'd had bruises on her back and legs. It was all she could to get to the six blocks to her grandmother's house.

It had taken all her courage to tell her grandmother about the abuse, but the woman had only dressed her wounds, given her some tea, and then sent her back home. *To him.* Andrea left the next day before dawn, her father's snores echoed from his prone position on the couch.

She pretended it didn't bother her, but the truth was it had hurt. She stayed out late that night, afraid to go home. Finally, a cousin had found her in the local park and brought her to her grandmother's house. There she told Andrea the news. Her cruel and bitter sire had drunk himself to death that very afternoon.

Andrea was finally free. Sure, she had to deal with overbearing uncles and aunts, and a whole swarm of cousins. She'd done that for most of her life anyway. Besides, it was better without Hugo Constantine's presence.

She'd often questioned whether his timely death might have been engineered by her *puri daj*, but she'd never had the guts to ask. Afraid of the answer, she supposed.

When she was old enough, she made plans to go abroad. She'd only been allowed to leave home under the pretense she'd be studying with some cousins. It sure beat sticking around and waiting to be married off!

After spending one year in the small mountain village that wasn't on any map she'd ever seen, somewhere in the wilds of Albania, Andrea took off like a thief in the night. And she hadn't looked back.

A fact that was now biting her in the ass. *Literally.* She gasped at the pain shooting up her backside and her spine. Her eyes rolled towards the back of her head as the book's pages slowed their turning only to zap at her again. White hot agony, unlike anything she'd ever experienced, coursed through her body.

"Fuck!" She yelled as her back bowed underneath the weight of the magic. Thunder sounded outside, lightning struck, and a strong wind rattled the few remaining window panes. The knocking from outside grew louder.

"Ugh, go away!"

Andrea closed her eyes in a desperate attempt to recall something, anything, that would help her battle the Dark magic coming from the book. She struggled to move out of the salt circle, to no avail. She should have been looking down!

There was no way out now. Not without someone from the outside breaking the circle. It had probably been drawn and cast by Aunt Renalda to hold the magic that she'd inadvertently released. She'd knocked the book off its pedestal and out of the binding pentagram.

Now she was trapped, having replaced the book with herself. *Shit.* This was so not good.

As if things couldn't get worse, Andrea heard what sounded like the front door breaking down. *What the hell?* The noise was soon followed by heavy footsteps thudding their way towards her.

Oh, shit! If a normal were to walk in on her, she'd been in all kinds of trouble. Not to mention, he or she could die.

"Hey, back off! Seriously, don't come in here!"

A deep voice cut through the howling wind sending shivers down her spine. He spoke two words and that was enough to send Andrea's heart thudding in her chest.

"Too late."

CHAPTER THREE

Troy felt the power of his sign reverberate throughout his entire body from the second he stepped over the threshold of the wreck of a house he'd been sent to investigate. His Thunderbird hummed beneath his skin.

Something was not right in this place. He tensed as he tried to take in everything about his surroundings. It was cold. *Duh.* But on second glance he realized the coldness seemed to come from upstairs. And it had nothing to do with the weather. *Focus, fucker.*

He didn't have time for second thoughts. The Wardens of Terra were back in play, and this here was his big debut. He was alone in this place. Though it was only a couple of states North from where he was raised and trained, it might as well have been on another planet.

For the first time, Troy was on his own. Far away from Rex, and the other Shifters from his station. They weren't a Pack per se, but they were the closest thing he'd ever had to family. He was not scared, he was anxious. To prove himself and to prove to the Heralds that, yes, the Wardens were indeed ready for this next step.

"It's our time now, finally. There's been a lot of activity up north, Waman. Disturbances in nature attributed to Dark magic. We've pinpointed it to this locale, I want you to go in, neutralize the target, and if he or she remains alive, bring 'em in for questioning. Now, this is the first time I have ever uttered these words outside of a drill, son, I don't need to tell you how important this is. Will you, Troy Waman, protect Terra?" Troy trembled with eagerness at the behest of Rex's deep voice. The huge Bear Shifter sent shivers of anticipation along Troy's spine with his directive. Not that Troy had told the fucker.

He heard himself now as he'd answered Rex in the words, he'd been taught so many years before, "I am a Warden of Terra. Protecting this world from evil is my sacred duty and honor. I will execute my orders to the best of my ability or die trying, sir."

"It's about fucking time, Warden."

That was all he'd said to him. His Station Master did not utter another single word as he'd handed him the plastic keyless remote. He'd sent the necessary coordinates to Troy's GPS without even looking up.

Troy shook his head. The big ass Bear Shifter had turned his attention back to the tablet in front of him. Effectively dismissing Troy from the Station. No words of encouragement or concern, not even a wave goodbye. Not that Troy expected any.

It was simply the way Rex operated. He was cold as ice. Troy wasn't exactly drowning in friends, but his Station mates were cool people, though a little rowdy at times. Perhaps that was why he felt drawn to Rex. His standoffish behavior was something Troy totally comprehended. *It's not easy being the boss,* he smirked thinking how odd it would have been to hear any sappy shit from the tough as nails Grizzly.

Nah. He liked things just the way they were. Troy appreciated Rex's gruff demeanor. It simply wouldn't do for an elite team of Shifters to snivel all over each other on their very first assignment. So, he'd simply turned and walked out of his Station, determined to make his first mission a success.

No fucking way am I gonna mess this up. He had a job to do and he wasn't about to let anything fuck it up. He sniffed the air, his head tilting back as he took in the charge in the atmosphere. There was definitely nothing natural about the sudden drastic drop in the temperature since he'd exited his vehicle.

He'd cased the street from the SUV for over an hour before he'd climbed out into the street. The cold had seeped right through his clothing, biting at his skin. The smell of rot and mold increased in the air and the wind seemed to pick up in speed and frequency.

Whatever was happening inside the house, it had Dark magic written all over it. This was exactly the type of thing he'd been training for. He shook off his nerves and proceeded. The sky flashed with lightning and his Thunderbird stirred. For whatever reason, Dark magic always affected the weather, and that was his domain. His Air sign made it natural for him to look to the skies for any hint of what it was Troy was about to face.

He narrowed his eyes as the sounds coming from the upstairs of the house grew louder. *Time to do this.* The door flew apart under the strength of his shoulder. *Fuck,* he hadn't meant for the thing to explode, but that's what usually happened when he put a little muscle to anything.

He was a Shifter after all. A *Warden* to be exact.

His abilities were above the usual range for supernaturals. It wasn't his ego talking, it was simple truth. His Thunderbird was powerfully built as was the man. Tall and muscular on any given day, but with the sun in Aquarius during the winter months, Troy was even more so. He practically buzzed with the increased strength and energy of his sign.

Adrenaline pumped through his veins. He was ready for this. Troy felt the boost in his powers and noted with satisfaction the steady stream of magic buzzing and humming from the small symbol that marked the skin of his right palm.

The two zig-zagged waves symbolizing his place in the Wardens marked the sensitive skin of his hand. It was his birth sign, Aquarius, the *water-bearer*, was actually an air sign and Troy had been honored, or rather *deemed*, a retainer of Aquarius since birth. He'd been taught to honor and appreciate the extra gifts he'd been given since he was very young.

Shifters whose gifts were enhanced by astrological signs or other ethereal occurrences were rare, as were Thunderbirds. His heritage was as unique as it was mysterious. From his coppery skin to the blue-black hair that fell to his shoulders, Troy looked the epitome of what any romance novel cover would feature as the Native American hero.

He was aware of his attractions. He wasn't bad looking at all, and his ethnicity made him something of an oddity to some normals. If only they knew what he really was. Not that he cared.

He was too focused on his duty to take any serious interest in some female. Sure, he had his share of one-night stands, but he wasn't cut out for the rest.

No matter what the Fates had written in the stars about Shifters, Troy was not interested in finding a mate. Fairytales aside, he was all about his duty. He inhaled deeply as he entered the strange place. The subtle fragrance of caramel reached his nostrils.

Every nerve ending in his body seemed to go on instant alert. He felt his Thunderbird take notice. His unique brand of Shifter magic pulsed under his skin. Some Shifters denied magic, but not those marked by Terra. He understood too well, that magic was woven throughout every thread of the universe.

The sweet smoky fragrance grew stronger, touching someplace deep and hidden inside of him. For some reason, at that moment, he recalled the story he'd been told as a young boy. One every young Warden had heard back at the Station for as long as he remembered:

Before a Shifter is born, he or she is chosen to be a

Warden, selected and blessed by his or her own unique circumstances. It is then that the Fates determine the other half of the Shifter's soul, the one true mate for each Warden designed specifically to balance the Shifter. Their all-encompassing love written in the stars, destiny engraved in the heavens and never to be thwarted. When the soulmates meet, the Warden will know, and when the claiming is complete, strength will overflow in the veins of the Shifter and he or she will be bound for eternity in the warm embrace of the powers of their anima magicae.

It was a fairytale. One served to comfort lonely little Shifters who'd been taken from what he'd always assumed were the usual loving families. *Not like his.* No, Troy was different, and not just because of his heritage. Sex was sex. Nothing more to it than that.

He'd scratched his itch when the occasion allowed, but he wasn't looking for happily ever after. Hell, he didn't believe in it. Troy learned to ignore the stares and blatant invitations of the *normals*, that's what Shifters generally called humans, around him. It was easy, considering he was not usually around them.

Up till then, his time had predominantly been spent at his Station with the other Wardens. His long drive to Shadowland, NY tested his slowly built-up patience and tolerance for humans. Curious fuckers with no common sense. Hardly new a predator when they saw one.

Didn't they know he was a raptor capable of slicing and dicing them as quickly as he looked at them? No. Of course not. They also had no idea he would risk his life to save them from destruction.

He shook his head and forced himself to pay attention to his surroundings. Why the fuck had he taken that little trip down memory lane anyway?

Fuck if he knew. The scent of caramel grew stronger and his dark brown eyes glowed gold with the power of his beast. He took notice of the malevolent charge in the atmosphere inside the house.

His feathers bristled under his human skin. The bird inside of him unusually attentive. *What was with that scent? Caramel and something else, something spicy and feminine.*

He stepped over the debris from the door with the keen intent of a man on a mission. Unwavering in his concentration to find the source of the commotion and, if he was being honest, the tantalizing scent that had him hardening in his jeans.

What the fuck? This is no time for a fucking boner, man. He took the stairs two at a time until he reached the creaky attic door where a sickly yellow light oozed from the gap between said door and the rickety looking floorboards beneath it.

The house was old as fuck. Rotting floorboards, cracks in the walls and ceilings, obvious signs of water damage. It was badly in need of a little TLC. Or maybe a few swings from a wrecking ball. The woman who'd lived there was elderly, perhaps that was why she'd allowed her home to fall apart.

Not surprisingly, the attic door caved in as soon as he pressed into it. The splintering wood made a cracking sound lost among the increasingly loud howling noises coming from beyond.

Troy blinked against the dust particles and the unearthly glow only to stop in shock once his eyes refocused. The sight that greeted him was astounding to say the least.

A *grimoire,* or book of spells, floated above the unfinished floor of the attic. Its pages whipped to and fro in the unnatural breeze that flitted through the stale room. Above the mildew and dust, was the distinct odor of Dark magic, sickeningly sweet like rotting corpses.

Even more alarming was the aroma beneath it all. Troy inhaled, the intoxicating scent made every hair on his body stand up. *Like caramel and whiskey, sweet and heady at the same time.*

He looked down to the floor and was stunned to see a mane of curly brown hair surrounding a face so pale and fair with glowing green eyes, like some kind of angel staring back at him. *Shit. The glowing eyes. Was she a Witch?*

His Thunderbird screamed in his mind's eye. Troy wanted to cover his ears, but it would do no good. *Fuck.* His beast was already taking control. He looked down at his half-turned hands and tried to shake off the *Change*.

His beast screeched and screamed in his mind's eye. His steps slowed, they felt heavy as he stared down at the luscious body on the floor. Ignoring the shock in her bright eyes, he breathed deep and swayed slightly on his feet. *Mine. Mate.*

"Oh shit," he said aloud.

"*Don't come in here!*" She'd said right before he entered, but how could he have stopped himself?

"Run," she mouthed, unable to do more than that.

Troy was stunned. *His mate. Now? Here?!* It didn't matter. Not if she'd been caught practicing Dark magic. Not one bit. Troy wanted to scream his rage. What the fuck were the Fates thinking? But he didn't have the opportunity.

The dark-haired beauty laid out before him like some damn sacrifice, arched her back and cried out.

Her lush body writhed on the litter strewn floor in pain, eyes wide open, yet sightless, pink lips parted while she yelled. Whatever was going on, she was being hurt. *Hell no.*

Troy reacted immediately, as he'd been trained to do. Anger and fury that she'd somehow been injured on his watch filled him. He did his best to temper his warring emotions. The space was small, but the attic ceiling was high enough.

Unusually so. About twelve feet or more. He did not think, he simply acted, switching skins to his enormous Thunderbird. He tore through his clothing without a care. He needed to help her. *Now.*

Blue-black feathers covered his wings, a stark contrast to his white underbelly. He stood on powerful legs ending in huge, claw-tipped talons. His Thunderbird took in the yellowish green Magic that flowed from the book like a sickness. He knew instinctively what had to be done.

Troy allowed his beast free reign, trusting in his other self to do what was needed. Opening his wings to span almost seventeen feet, which was practically the entire length of the room, Troy carried himself above the plywood floorboards.

Intuition and extensive training took over. Troy assessed the situation instantaneously. He needed to stop the spell bleeding Darkness into the land from the pages of that book.

He opened his large, hooked beak and released a powerful battle cry. Instinct rode him hard. Troy used his beast's eyes, rotating them in his head to quickly take in the scene. His three-hundred-forty-degree vision when used with the power of his sign, gave him a unique view of the scene before him.

The woman, *his mate*, seemed to have trapped herself in some sort of spell. She must have done so while using the ancient grimoire, which as far as he could tell, was inherently evil. *But thy?* He shoved the question to the back of his mind.

All that mattered right then was stopping the book. The stink of garbage and rotting flesh increased as did the raging winds and dropping temperatures. It was like a fucking blizzard inside that attic, sans snow. *Fuck and damn.*

His supernaturally enhanced eyesight picked up every nuance in that small space. He'd been trained for this and with some effort, he was able to put his rage at his mate's injuries aside. He concentrated instead on containing the situation.

Troy opened his beak wide and released a deep, barking cry. It was the signature call of his Thunderbird, and he reveled in its power as he cried into the air.

Both his mate and the book shrieked and bucked wildly against his unique brand of Shifter magic. The grimoire pushed back against him. The powerful odor of rot filled his nostrils, but he was more determined than ever. He wielded his song like a sword. Brandishing each note with deadly accuracy.

Unlike regular Shifters, he held the power of Aquarius within. He had special access to the sign and usage of his element, the *air*, to access that magic. Luckily for the universe, he'd vowed to use said powers for the forces of good.

Troy had been trained well at his Station to do just that. He opened his beak and struck another chord. This one higher than the last. He needed to quell the book's power. The evil coming from the pages grew desperate. Its magic stunk of rotten flesh and a vileness that he'd yet to name.

Yet underneath it all, he found the smoky-sweet caramel whiskey scent of his mate. Almost too faint, but not quite. She needed him, and he was powerless to do anything but heed her call. *Mate. Mine.*

He struck his wings together, the mighty clash sending waves of his power through the air. Blue and white light shone from his wings, his power worked to fend off the inky darkness that emerged from the book like a slew of rats bent on escaping a sinking ship.

With the strength of Aquarius pulsing through his veins, Troy thrust his wings together again and again. He managed to weave his unique brand of Shifter magic through the stale air of the attic. The book howled furiously, sending wind and then flame whipping through the air. Troy batted both back with each stroke of his magnificent wings.

His dual nature made him stronger than most. The darkness shrank back as his beast screeched loudly and continued to beat his wings against its wrath. His mate cried out again, eyes closed, chest heaving with each breath she struggled to take.

Troy hated that he was hurting her, but damned attraction or not he must persevere. It was very possible she was his enemy. Okay, it was pretty obvious. *Fuck.* Mate or not, she must be stopped, and it was his job to do so.

No hurting her, she is our mate. Mine. His Thunderbird growled the words in his mind's eye. He couldn't refute the beast's claim, but he'd sworn an oath.

Torn inside, he fought the Dark magic with his

growing rage. He watched the smoky darkness of the book diminish with each note he struck. The bright blue and white magic of his Thunderbird's song wrapped around the sickly yellow aura of the grimoire, blanketing the evil in light.

His call grew stronger and each time he struck out with his wings, beating them in time to his song, the evil tome shuddered and croaked. Troy fought fiercely.

His mate's weak groan almost made him lose his concentration. Pain radiated in his chest. Their bond had already begun, yet, as much as it hurt him, he knew this was the best way to help her.

With one final cry, the book shook and closed, finally dropping to the floor with a heavy thud. It pulsed near his now unconscious mate. The woman was slumped over on her side curled into an almost fetal position. *She could've been killed,* his chest rumbled at the thought.

Never. She is mine.

CHAPTER FOUR

Messing with Dark magic was not something he'd ever been foolish enough to attempt, but Troy knew some who'd been persuaded to try it out. *Seduced by the Darkness,* as it were. In Troy's experience, it always ended badly. *Fuck and damn.* He wanted to hit something.

Why would the Fates have chosen her? It must be a mistake. He shook his head, but his Thunderbird pushed against him. *Mate. Mine.* There was no mistake, she was his.

He growled and paced the room. Logic and instinct were having an all-out brawl inside of him. *Protect her!* Troy stopped pacing and rubbed his forehead. His bird had issued the order with more power than he'd have thought was necessary. And yet he wanted to kick himself for dallying.

Any Shifter worth his salt would protect his mate first, ask questions later. For a Shifter, that instinct was pretty much gonna be on overdrive for the duration. *Move already,* his Thunderbird screamed. He was pretty fucking pissed at his human half.

Troy stopped second-guessing and used his senses to seek out anything else in the attic that might be harmful to his small mate. He needed to ensure that she was safe the way he needed air to breathe. For the first time since the book had stopped wailing, Troy noticed the temperature inside the house had started warming up.

The room had lost its frigidity. Good thing too, since he'd shredded his clothes with his shift. Last thing he needed was anything vital freezing the fuck off. *Fuck and damn again.*

He looked down at the still form of his mate. Concern marred his face. She was so small compared to him. Curvy and voluptuous, but she was still a good ten inches shorter than him. Her eyes were closed, but she breathed evenly. His heart squeezed inside his chest. She looked sweet and innocent. *Like a soft summer breeze,* he thought idly.

His Thunderbird bristled with unease. Was she

okay? His beast sent the message to Troy that he was pissed the woman was injured loud and clear! Much as he hated it, and himself right then, Troy had a duty to perform. He needed to turn his attention to the still pulsing grimoire.

Dark magic oozed from the pages, literally. A thick, oily substance covered the tome, the stench of overripe garbage coming from it was as distinct as it was disgusting. Studying and training had nothing on actual fieldwork, that was for damn sure. He shook his head and took shallow breaths while he secured the book.

He shuddered at the thought of the damage this type of artifact in the wrong hands could do! Sort of like the kind of havoc he'd been dodging the entire trip up north in the form of erratic and increasingly dangerous road conditions due to the weather! He shook his head grimacing. Dark magic upset the balance of everything around it, not just the supernatural plane.

Crops, animal behavior, and most noticeably, the weather were all greatly affected by any disturbance caused by Dark magic. It was as unnatural as silicone and as addictive as cocaine. He growled in frustration. *What was she doing here? What was her part in all this?*

He glanced in his mate's direction and at the salt circle she seemed to be caught in on the floor. *Probably meant to contain the grimoire.* If he wasn't mistaken, the curly-haired beauty was trapped in a mess of her own making.

Fuck and damn. Regardless of the circumstances, he had no choice now. She was his prime suspect. He'd have to bring her back to the Station. Despite the unholy fit his Thunderbird was throwing inside of him, Troy would do his duty.

He clenched his jaw as he lifted the book of Dark spells by one creased corner. His Thunderbird pushed at him to get the vile thing away from his mate. The man agreed. He was careful to avoid letting the goo touch his skin, as he walked over to where remnants of his coat lay on the floor.

Fuck, he'd liked that jacket too. He found what he was looking for. After some careful maneuvering, he thrust the grimoire into the special binding bag he'd retrieved from the tattered coat pocket.

The bag was commissioned by the Wardens, *bespelled* by White Witches, to aid them in their work. It acted as a neutral zone and deafened the powers of the Dark artifacts, like the grimoire, till they were practically nil. After his task was complete, Troy looked over at her.

The air surrounding the unconscious woman was smoky and sweet. *My caramel and whiskey mate.* He bit his lip to stop the groan that fought its way to the surface. Thoughts of running his hands over her luscious body consumed him. It was all he could do to keep himself from molesting the poor unconscious woman.

All he wanted to do was taste her sweet lips and gauge her flavor. Beads of sweat broke out over his forehead as he struggled to keep himself from burying his nose in the crook of her neck. He wanted to breathe her in and keep her there inside of himself. *That'd be fucking great,* her waking up to him sniffing her! She'd think he was a fucking pervert!

He'd been alone so fucking long; the very idea of a mate scared the shit out of him. *What if he fucked it up? What if she rejected him? What if he went fucking apeshit afterwards and they made him leave the Wardens?* He frowned even harder.

Fuck and damn again, Troy. How the fuck am I going to explain to Rex that this Witch is my mate? His bird bumped up against his subconscious. He knew the beast was mad as fuck at him for thinking ill of her. There was no way in hell his sweet mate was a Dark Witch. Her scent alone suggested otherwise.

He'd always associated a Dark Witch's scent with cough syrup, but this woman, *hell*, she smelled like temptation personified. Just thinking about the smoky whiskey and sweet caramel aroma imbued in her skin made him hard as fuck.

He wished he still had his jeans or at least his underwear to cover him up as he bent and lifted her still frame off the hard, plywood floor.

He walked her over to the far side of the room where an exposed pipe ran along the wall only to disappear beneath the floorboards. He actually fought with himself to release her, gently and slowly, back onto the cold floor.

His Thunderbird barked at the indignity of it. Damn beast was more than a little possessive of her already. Troy couldn't blame him. She deserved to be on silks, not some dusty and cracked floorboards. *Fuck.*

His beast twitched and growled beneath his skin. *Get a fucking grip, bird. We need to finish our mission.* His Thunderbird fought him for control, the need to protect and provide for his mate almost overwhelmed the need to claim her.

Get the book away from her. The evil inside of it is tainting the very air. Troy narrowed his eyes at the grimoire. He shook off the mating instinct and focused on his job. He needed to bring the book down to the secure box in the trunk of his SUV, but he couldn't leave the luscious female unattended for long.

His Thunderbird barked and clawed beneath his skin. Troy wanted to kick his own ass for having to do it, but he had no choice. From the second he'd lifted his sweet-smelling mate off the floor, he knew he was fucked.

He'd noted the pentagram had been drawn on the floor with salt, chalk, and ash. She'd trapped herself. *Hmm. She must not be a seasoned Witch to have gotten herself stuck like this.*

That could be a good thing. He shook his head as he took a moment to savor the feel of her in his arms. Not wanting to be inappropriate in the least, he placed her gently near the pipe before taking her wrists in his hands.

Fuck. Fuck. FUCK. She turned her head, burrowing her nose into the rough skin and smattering of hair covering his chest. A soft moan escaped her pretty lips and she exhaled, calm once more. His mate sought comfort in his nearness, a fact that made his chest swell with pride. He looked down at her perfect face, tracing every line with his eyes. He froze as his gaze met her emerald eyes, now wide open.

"Who are you?" She murmured just as he clicked the cuffs in place.

The woman screamed and struggled, and Troy stood up. His lips made a thin line as he waited for her to cease her movements.

"What the fuck are you doing, mister? And why are you naked?"

"Stop screaming."

"*Stop screaming.* Are you insane? Who the fuck are you, buddy?"

"Relax. You are in my custody now."

"What? Why? Are you some kind of naked neighborhood police?"

He frowned and lifted the grimoire in his hand, noting her shocked eyes. She struggled against the pipe where he'd cuffed her. The scent of her fear and anxiety filled the air.

Not good. He didn't want her afraid. It agitated him. A low growl erupted from his throat.

"Look, I don't know who you are, but first, you need to drop that book inside the circle with the star in it that's on the floor over there. Then you might want to get some clothes on, okay?" Her wide green eyes flitted from the book, to him, and to the floor.

She bit her lips nervously, her eyes unable to remain downcast, she lifted them only to peak at him. Troy bit back his grin. So, his little mate liked his body. That was pretty fucking okay with him. He stood taller.

"The grimoire has been contained. What is your name?" He kept his voice even as he spoke.

The last thing he wanted was to cause her anymore anxiety or grief. His mate was fierce, he'd give her that, she continued to struggle against the reinforced handcuffs when she remembered to stop ogling him. *So damn cute*, he thought.

"Please, sit still. You will injure yourself."

"What do you mean contained? Seriously, don't you have underwear at least?"

A deep frown marred her otherwise perfect face and Troy stopped breathing as he finally got a good look at her. *Oh damn.* She was beautiful.

At five and a half feet tall, he'd guessed her height when he'd held her in his arms, she was short compared to him. Not that he minded at all. He liked her height.

Not to mention, her body. She was deliciously curvy, with tempting dips and valleys her clothing failed to conceal. He couldn't wait to explore every single inch of her.

Her skin was fair, the palest ivory he'd ever seen. Blemish free and smooth as silk. He wondered how it would look up against his much darker, coppery skin tone. The mental image made his mouth water.

It burned in his mind as he took in the rest of her. Her hair was thick and glossy, a riot of dark girls hanging past her shoulders. He wanted to tug on a lock just to watch it spring back up again. But it was her eyes that truly captivated him. They were like emeralds. A true deep, green that sparkled in the dim light. *Fuck and damn.* She was absolutely gorgeous.

"I said, what the fuck are you staring at? Uncuff me!" She narrowed her eyebrows and he wanted to grin as her lower lip jutted out slightly from the top one. He practically drooled, wanting to test their softness.

"What is your name?"

"I'm not telling you shit."

"Your name?" He used his sternest voice and almost grinned when it looked like she'd curse at him again.

Instead, she rolled her eyes like a bratty teenager and held her head up high when she answered, despite her position handcuffed to a pipe amidst the remnants of whatever Dark spell she'd been trying to perform. Troy sobered at the thought.

"Andrea. Andrea Kristos," she murmured, clearly disgruntled at the entire situation.

"Sit still, Andrea Kristos. I'll be back as soon as I can."

Troy tried to ignore her voice as she called him any number of names. It was deep and sexy. He needed to hear her scream his name in that husky little voice. *What would she look like in the throes of passion? Oh great, now I'm hard again.*

He grabbed an old afghan off the couch and draped it around his hips as he walked into the cold night air to his car.

He hated that he left her handcuffed to that rusty old pipe in the attic. *Fuck and damn,* he growled as he stomped over to his SUV. He used the key fob to unlock the vehicle and opened the trunk.

First, he placed the contained grimoire into the magically enhanced lock box that was hidden under the carpet in said trunk. Rex had made sure each Warden had one installed in their vehicles. Just in case they needed to transport magical items or arti-facts. As Wardens of Terra, they were trained to handle most any event.

Except meeting your mate, he thought wryly. He

grabbed his duffle bag and an extra pair of boots. He slammed the trunk closed. The SUV barely moved under his strength. Damn thing was a tank in disguise. Lucky for him, it had an extra passenger row. He'd need it since he was bringing someone back to his station.

My mate. No, a prisoner. Fuck and damn again.

Troy cursed and stomped back to the house. As he dressed, he pictured her upstairs. *What kind of mess was she involved in? What were the Fates thinking?*

The woman inside, *Andrea Kristos*, drew him like a moth to a flame. He'd never felt anything like it. The *mating pull* was a fucking force and a half.

Sure, he'd had several casual encounters with the opposite sex before, but they were forgotten the second he scented her. She was everything.

The need to claim her was all-consuming. From the top of her curly head to the bottom of her tiny feet he wanted to hold her, touch her. He *needed* to, like he needed air to breathe.

Fuck, but she's my enemy, he wanted to scream in frustration.

You don't know that, his beast argued.

CHAPTER FIVE

Duty first. He'd scope out the rest of the house. Make sure it was contained from any and all Dark magical presences. Then, he'd get her back to the Station and figure everything else out later. *Solid plan.*

Troy stomped around inside the house. He ignored the sounds of his mate from up in the attic. He knew she was safe up there since it was the only room he'd fully checked out.

His hearing picked up on the various ways she'd like to inflict pain on him and he winced. *Balls in a vice grip, huh?* She was sassy that was for sure, a damn viper.

Well, at least he'd never get away with anything

around her. His personality, like his other half, was strong and dominant. Troy wouldn't be able to stand it if his mate was a simpering female who'd spend all her time flinching around him.

No need to worry about that. From what he could hear, she wanted to kick him in the balls about a thousand different ways. *Ouch.*

He decided not to prolong her confinement to the attic any more than necessary. In other words, he hauled ass and quickly and efficiently searched over the house from bottom to top.

"It's about time you came back! And goody, you found some clothes! Now, can you please take these off me?" His mate bristled.

"No," he decided to keep it brief. The first thing he needed to do was get an explanation. Though duty called for him to contact Rex immediately, his beast and his heart demanded he hear her out first.

"No? that's it, just no?"

"Look, Ms. Kristos-"

"By all means call me, Andrea. I insist that all the men who handcuff me get to use my first name."

"Excuse me?" he growled the question in a voice too low for a normal to hear.

Jealousy crashed over him like a fucking tsunami.

The thought of his beautiful, dainty mate with another man made him want to rip the dick off of every fucking guy who ever looked at her. *Mine.*

"Look pal, I damn near crashed through these fucking attic floorboards while you were gone, and it stinks in here like garbage! Uncuff me. Now."

"We'll be leaving in a minute, but I need you to answer some questions first."

"Like what?" Patience was not his mate's strong suit. Fuck and damn. He was in a ton of trouble. *I'll never be bored that's for damn sure.*

"I've found all manner of evidence the elderly woman who lived here was something of a hoarder. A number of items in this place are under suspicion of belonging to a Dark practitioner and will need to be catalogued and removed-"

"Are you kidding? So much for my fucking inheritance! And I thought my *Puri daj* forgave me for leaving! I swear I'm never going back there again!" She went on a bit of a tirade for a few minutes before he butted in.

"Wait, you're not a Witch then?"

"Who? Me? *A Dark Witch,*" she spat the word at him.

"Uh, yeah."

"You think I'm a Witch? Wait, *what are you?*"

"Do not play games with me, Ms. Kristos, *Andrea.*"

"Oh, sure, cause I'm the one playing games! It is obvious from your glowing gold eyes, you're some kind of Shifter. But you're different than the others I've met, I can sense your magic. It's, it's-"

"My name is Troy Waman. I am a Shifter."

"A what?"

"More later, now it's your turn. What are you if not a Witch?"

"Well, I'm technically a Romani spell Caster, but I don't really practice."

He eyed the magical paraphernalia scattered amongst almost every square inch of the attic. He raised one eyebrow in astonishment. The place was as stuffed and messy as the rest of the house. Whoever *Renalda Curosi* was to his mate, the woman clearly had a thing for magical relics.

Romani were notoriously secretive and, though the Wardens were kept up to date on many super-natural cultures, that one was grossly misunder-stood. The fact that Andrea's own clan might have put her in harm was deeply troubling.

One thing was certain, Troy was becoming

increasingly more concerned with the welfare of his mate, than with his job.

"I mean it, dude, I don't *cast*. I haven't even been here for twenty-four hours yet. I just got in from Greece, for God's sake!"

She seemed rather affronted when he didn't verbally agree with her. She wasn't lying. *Well, not exactly*, he amended. Something was off with her story. A quick inhale told him she was holding back.

His chest squeezed at the thought of his mate possibly practicing Dark magic. Logic warred with instinct. He seemed to simply know she was not evil. *But what was she doing if not casting?* He exhaled slowly.

"I need you to be honest. Lying won't work with me."

"What? Look, I am not lying! I've been away for a few years. You know, backpacking across Europe, meeting my extended family, sowing my oats, you know, having a freaking life that didn't involve my crazy clan and family!"

"You left your family?"

"Well, that makes me sound shitty, doesn't it?"

"Uh, no, I didn't mean-"

"Look, I just didn't want to end up in *Puri daj's* kitchen, like my other cousins. Just another one of my grandmother's devoted lackies, you know? I have my own dreams," she looked down and he felt like a complete *POS* for putting that look on her face, but he had a job to do.

Fuck and damn.

CHAPTER SIX

"**W**hat *dreams* landed you here, in Shadowland, New York? And why the hell are you fucking around with a book that screams Dark magic?"

Andrea bristled at the questions the man hurled at her. No, not man, *Shifter*. Not just a Shifter either. What did he say he was? Oh yeah, a *Warden of Terra*.

Well, in her years of study with her illuminous Kristos Clan, Andrea had never come across such a thing. Maybe he was nuts. *Great*, she thought, *I'm stuck with a crazy, though sexy as hell, Shifter*. This was so not the welcome home she expected!

"My dreams are mine. I'm not sharing them with you, whatever the hell you are? *Warden of Terra*? What does that even mean?"

She watched as he unfolded his arms and stood to his full height. Holy shit. The guy was more than imposing. He was obviously packing some serious muscle, though not like one of those veiny body-builder types.

No, his body was naturally muscular and toned. *Long and lethal. Yeah,* that was how she'd describe him. With long, straight, blue-black hair that fell to his shoulders in a thick, shiny curtain. He looked like some kind of out-of-time warrior.

A light dusting of facial hair covered his rough features. She totally loved that on a man. *Yum.* He had deep set eyes, the color of chocolate. Not that cheap grocery store junk, his was like the *good stuff,* you know the kind. About six bucks for a bar of seventy-five percent pure cocoa. *Yum.*

Andrea wouldn't mind a taste of him. He smelled like rain and ozone, clean and fresh, strong and light. Like walking through a misty morning in Ireland, across green fields and rocky hills. *Fuck,* what was she crazy?

She was daydreaming about some nutty fucker who had her handcuffed to a freaking pipe! Maybe she was still suffering from jet lag? The long flight to New Jersey from where she'd been staying in Greece was bound to catch up with her eventually.

That was it! Her mind had finally snapped. She was hallucinating and would wake up any minute. She closed her eyes, mumbling to herself.

"Come on, Andrea, get up. Wake up! You're still on the plane, this is all a dream!"

"I'm sorry, Andrea, this is no dream and you are in serious jeopardy here," the *Shifter* crouched down and tilted his head as if he thought she'd lost her mind.

He stood back up and ran a hand over his head. His eyes lightened to gold when he focused them on her. She watched him carefully. Sure, he was hot as Hades, but he still never answered her question.

"Okay, I'm not sleeping. So, without the sass, can you tell me exactly what a Warden of Terra is?"

She sucked in a breath when he turned and smiled at her, surprise lighting his handsome face. Her heart quickened and for some reason she found she couldn't breathe. Ruggedly masculine, with hard lines and deep-set eyes, he was gorgeous. And she'd seen some seriously beautiful people over her lifetime, but *no one,* not a single one of them, compared to him.

"You know what *Shifters* are?" She nodded, and he continued turning to fix his dark chocolate stare on her.

"All Shifters are men and women who share their soul with their animal, most common are Wolves, Bears, and various Big Cats, though there are other kinds. As you can tell, I am of Native American descent, that said, my animal is something other than the norm."

"Really?"

"Yes. I am a Thunderbird Shifter," he nodded at her when her eyes met his.

From what little she knew about Native American history from the odd college course many moons ago, Andrea understood the Thunderbird was a part of native American folklore. *Holy shit! They are real. I mean, he is certainly real.* She had so many questions, but she didn't want to interrupt him.

"My dual nature is not the only gift the Fates have bestowed upon me, you see, I was marked as a child with the sign of the Wardens. Given the ability to use the powers of Aquarius to be exact-"

"An air sign? That makes sense. Thunderbird and all," she nodded for him to continue.

Andrea was amazed by the way he cocked his head to the side and watched her with an unflinching stare. Sort of how a bird of prey might do while hunting.

Was it wrong if that solemn stare of his made heat pool low in her belly? Too bad. It was a reflex she couldn't control. Despite everything, she wasn't sure she wanted to. *Sigh.*

"Yes, an air sign. Well, Andrea, Shifters that are doubly blessed with both our dual natures and with the powers of our sign are marked by the Fates and selected to be Wardens of Terra, it is our job to fight evil," he watched her as he spoke, his gaze unwavering.

Andrea nodded encouragingly. She was fascinated by the big man. He was so virile, larger than life, and for some reason she couldn't fathom, he was speaking to her as if she were important to him. *Amazing.*

"You see, I can tap into extra reserves or powers to help aid me in my duty. My organization is as old as time itself. The Wardens of Terra have not been active for centuries, but we have been called to duty now. It is my job to battle the evil that is constantly trying to take a foothold on this earth," he held up his hand.

Andrea noted a shape much like a tattoo inscribed on his skin. She recognized the symbol on his palm. Two zig-zagged lines marked the soft flesh there. The symbol of the water-bearer in astrology.

"I recognize the symbol. A *Warden of Terra? Puri Daj* told us stories of them when my cousins and I were children, but I thought it was a myth."

"Like Shifters and spell Casters?" He smirked as he said it and she was powerless to stop her responding smile.

"Can I ask why are you telling me all this if you think I was practicing Dark magic? Wouldn't I use it against you?"

Oh crap. Why did you have to go and say that? Andrea scolded herself as he crept over to her. She directed her scowl to him. *How could he believe such a thing? And why would he set himself up by telling her his secrets?*

She sucked in a breath as he leaned down in front of her. His handsome face was so close to hers, Andrea could see flecks of gold highlighting his impossibly dark eyes. *Why does he have to be so good-looking? Damn.*

"I am telling you all of this, my little Romani Caster, for one very good reason. *You. Are. Mine.*"

He leaned over her and for a split second she thought he was going to kiss her, but instead he reached for her hands. She could only stare at the hard lines of his mouth while his callused fingers worked to release her. *How would they feel on her skin? Rough or soft?* She was vibrating with the need to know.

The cotton of his shirt brushed up against her thinner one and they both stilled. The slight contact made her body hum with desire. She wanted more. *More contact, more skin, more him.*

With a resounding *clink*, he unlocked and removed the handcuffs. He took her wrists in his large hands and brought them to his mouth. She gasped when he kissed both sides of each hand, his eyes never leaving hers as he massaged her sore skin with his clever fingers.

Andrea swallowed. Tiny jolts of electricity ran up and down her body, all from the slight pressure of his hands on her bare skin. *WTF?* Self-preservation told her to ignore the heat pooling in her stomach and the moisture dampening her panties. The guy was a Shifter. They oozed sex.

Besides, he'd just had her handcuffed to a fucking pipe. *Um. Hello? Not exactly romantic, Andrea. Wake the fuck up!*

"Look, Um, Troy, is it? Well, Troy, I will tell you everything I know about this place, but I am not yours, got it?"

"Yes, *mate*. You will tell me everything, because you and me, we are fated."

"I don't think so."

"Andrea, I must do my duty as a Shifter and a Warden of Terra, but I will always put you first. I apologize if I lost sight of that when we first met, I admit I was stunned to find you. I thought the whole story of Shifters and their true mates was a fairy tale, but tell me you can't feel this?"

He pulled her hand up to his chest and pressed it there. Little sparks of awareness travelled up her arm. Her eyes met his and suddenly everything else fell away.

She wanted to tell him to go to hell. To stop imaging things. She really did. Andrea wanted to deny the sudden insta-lust that burned through her body. But, how could she?

The soul deep attraction was making her dizzy. She swayed towards him, her body recognizing what her mind didn't want to accept. *Get a grip.*

She wanted to ignore the crazy pounding of her heart every time he touched her skin or looked into her eyes, but she was never one for lying. Still, this was all a bit fast. Even for her.

"There is no *this*, Troy. Now, my Aunt Renalda,

the woman who owned this place, just passed away. She left everything in her estate to me. I don't know why. We weren't close."

"Then why are you here?"

"My Grandmother, we call her *Puri daj,* contacted me and told me to come home. I hopped on the first plane."

"If you weren't close, why do it?"

"We always try to honor the wishes of the dead in my Clan."

"Okay, and you have no idea why she would leave this place to you?"

"No."

"It's strange. I mean this place is full of magic and mischief. Can't you feel it?"

Andrea shrugged. *How to say this without embarrassing herself? Shitty, shit, shit, shit.*

"I, uh, I never officially finished my Caster training. I mean, I uh, sort of left my family's home in Europe after like one measly year."

"Okay, well how long were you away?"

"Um, five years?"

"What were you doing wandering around Europe for five years?"

"Um, everything. I don't know, I wanted to try it

all. I studied music and painting. I went swimming in every river, lake, and sea I came across! I went sky diving, sailing, hiking up mountains I never thought I'd see. I ate all sorts of weird food, tried everything I could. It was a blast for the most part. I guess I was trying to find myself."

"I see. And when you came back? What happened then?"

"I missed the funeral," she said in a small voice she hardly recognized. She hated herself for being weak.

"I, uh, *Puri daj* was angry with me for missing it, but I didn't find out about her death in time to make it. I came here as soon as I could."

She took a turn around the room. She needed to dispel some of her nervous energy. *Why so anxious? Could be the hot as hell Shifter who was watching her like a hawk! Or rather, Thunderbird. Snort.*

"So, I was snooping around, taking a look at my so-called inheritance and I found the book. I recognized it as a grimoire and, I knew then that I shouldn't touch it, but I assumed the protection spell inscribed on the floor would hold. I didn't realize it was a trap. Well, you know the rest."

Andrea bit her lip and looked up, trying to gauge his reaction. For some reason it mattered to her, what this stranger thought. She'd never sought approval from anyone before. Looking into Troy's eyes, she knew she wanted his. And more. She wanted *him*.

"I see," he answered in a soft, deep voice that made her toes curl.

CHAPTER SEVEN

Andrea needed to put some distance between them. His whispered *I see* trembled through her body. The timbre of his voice made her aware of his closeness, and the annoying fact that he was still too fucking far away. She wanted to climb him like a tree.

Uh oh. Andrea had always been a free spirit. Live and let live, but she was cautious too. She was no virgin, but she tended to give her heart away to men who serially used her. Despite what this man said, she didn't believe forever was in the stars for someone like her.

"No, you don't see, Troy! I am a fucking failure! I left my family. I neglected my training. I ignored my own damn calling, and you, you think I'm some sort of Dark Witch-y person! *Argh,* I just want you to leave!"

Andrea could not believe the last twenty-four hours! Oh, why did she ever leave Mykos? The lifestyles of the rich and famous on that island were beyond fabulous! She'd been invited to party after party for the month she'd been there, and it had been a blast!

Well, then again, she hadn't especially liked the booze or the drugs or the copious amount of sex her friends were having with just about anyone who asked. Not that she was judging them, hey, whatever floats your boat. But Andrea had never been promiscuous or loose with her body.

That included ingesting poisons, which is what most drugs essentially were. Who was she kidding? She'd spent the first couple of years away burning off her never-expressed teen angst and running amok. But the last two years, she'd been hedging.

She'd been homesick and lonely. Uncertain of the welcome she'd find back in the states, she chose the coward's way and stayed in Europe.

Her parents were long gone. She had no siblings. Just an abnormally large array of cousins and aunts and uncles. And then there was her grandmother, the matriarch of her Clan. Her *Puri daj.*

Madame Magdelena looked surprisingly modern for the head Romani Caster of the Kristos family, but anyone who took her at face value would be seriously underestimating the woman. She was more than the soft grandmother who sang *brigaki djilia* around the campfire. The songs of the hardships of their clans were treasured by her people.

Madame Magdelena was the strongest Caster Andrea had ever seen. Not cruel, exactly, but hard and demanding in her expectations of her clan. Everyone followed the rules or suffered her wrath. Everyone but Andrea. *Good move, she gave you a house filled with Dark magic artifacts, idiot!*

To top it off she had a Shifter here claiming she was his mate. As if she was anybody's mate. *Puhlease!* Andrea turned to find the bane of her problems following her down the stairs.

"*Ugh*, I said leave."

"Not happening. Even if I wanted to, which just to clarify, *I don't*, you, this house, are all under my purview. I've been given this assignment by my Station Master, and I am not leaving until I finish it."

"But why?"

"I am a Warden of Terra, Andrea," he said and looked at her as if she should know what that meant. *Whatever.*

Andrea groaned as she continued to stomp her way down the stairs. She forced herself to ignore the incredulous look that had appeared on Troy's ridiculously handsome face and turned away from the temptation he posed.

Her body tensed with each step he took behind her. She listened to the thud of his boots down the rickety old steps. The noise made her tremble in anticipation. *Stupid house. Stupid inheritance. STUPID ME!*

Why couldn't her aunt had left her a cookbook or a shawl or something? Oh no, not her. Her life would never be that simple! Guess it was time to pay the piper! Five years of freedom and now she was back home to find her whole life completely upside down.

Andrea sighed and stopped when she reached the first floor. *Damn, here goes nothing.* She turned around, hands on her hips, leaving no space for him to step down. *Oops.* That left Troy hovering over her on the last step. *Uh-uh. That ain't gonna work.* The gorgeous Shifter was already too damn tall.

She gritted her teeth and forced herself to prepare to ignore the tingling sensation that ran up her and down her body whenever she had come into contact with Troy's skin. Without any hesitation, she grabbed his hand, pulling him off the step.

Of course, he'd complied with her tug otherwise she'd have been unable to move him. Great, big beast that he was. She smirked when she thought how to even the odds and wound up standing on that last step herself. Pleased with the height it gave her, she looked up, right into his face.

Her inner feminist wanted to stick her tongue out at him for simply being taller and stronger than she was, but that was probably not a good idea. Especially when his dark eyes practically ate her up on the spot. Yeah, um, no sticking tongues anywhere. *Yet.* No. Never. *Uh-uh. Yeah, right.*

She shook her head to shush her inner dialogue and narrowed her eyes. He stood there with a silly grin on his face that made a dimple pop on his left cheek and for some reason, Andrea got even angrier. *Idiot. Why did he have to look so damned good?*

"Look, I don't care what you think about me, *I* know I am not a Witch, Dark or otherwise."

"I believe you, you're not a Witch-"

"Don't interrupt! So, my Aunt Renalda liked to collect things. She was eccentric, not evil! *Puri daj* might be pissed at me for wandering the globe the last couple of years, but I'm sure she didn't know that some Warden of Terra would be here to hand-cuff me!"

"In my defense, you looked like you were performing a Dark spell-"

"I said no interruptions," she stomped her feet and pointed a finger at him, "Look, buster, this is my house now. You said you believed me, so get out! Leave. Now."

"That may be, Andrea, but you do understand we can't just let these artifacts sit here like this. Can't you feel the vibes around this place? The magic is leaking, for lack of a better word, and it is attracting notice."

She frowned thinking back on how the locks to the doors appeared tampered with when she'd first arrived. There'd also been evidence of animals or something scratching at the windows. She really hoped it was the former and not the *something else*. *Shit.* He had a point.

"What is going through that pretty head of yours?"

She bit her lip and told him what she'd found upon entering the house the night before. She left out the fact several of her aunt's wards had been broken as well. *Fucking amateur, Andrea! Why didn't you put two and two together?*

"You stayed here alone and didn't call for back up?!"

"I've been stuck upstairs the whole time. Besides, I don't know what you want me to do about any of this," she grunted her reply.

Frustration and embarrassment radiated off her. She must look a mess! Stuck upstairs for more than twenty-four hours, she was only starting to feel the wear and tear of what she'd been through.

As the adrenaline wore off, she realized she'd had nothing to drink in all that time. Her throat was dry, and her bones felt stiff. She slumped forward, her knees giving way, but before she could hit the floor Troy swooped in and lifted her off her feet.

She gasped at the contact. It was like little jolts of electricity danced along her nerve endings, not painful, but certainly *aware*. She could not believe she freaking swooned like some damsel in distress. *Snort. Yeah right.*

He lifted her as if she weighed nothing, a fact she knew was a total lie. Andrea loved her body, but she was no waif. She liked food and she didn't believe in denying herself one of life's pleasures.

Not that he noticed. He walked to the living room with her in his arms, his breathing even, his grip unyielding. He sat her down, taking a moment to check her pulse and, yes, she noticed the extra attention he gave her body. Though he'd meant to only check her with his eyes and hands, he couldn't seem to help the sensual turn his investigation took.

"Hey!"

"I am not molesting you, I just want to make sure you are uninjured."

"I'm fine! And in no way were my hips and breasts in any danger!"

"Okay, my bad, but you have to understand my beast wants to claim you. I won't until you say the word, but Andrea you're not okay. You've been running on adrenaline. When was the last time you ate or drank some water?"

When she faltered, he rolled his eyes and removed his cell phone from his pocket. She saw he was using a restaurant app, searching for twenty-four-hour restaurants in the area. She bit her lip and blushed furiously as her stomach growled in anticipation of a meal.

"What do you like on your pizza?"

Ah, the test of all tests, let's see if he could handle this one, she thought.

"Pineapples, bacon, onions, and jalapenos," she smirked anticipating his look of disgust. When he grinned instead, she was damn near shocked.

"Sounds awesome, mind if I double the jalapenos?"

"Um, no?"

"Good and done! It will be here in thirty minutes," he looked into her eyes and she found herself unable to break the spell of his gaze.

"Thanks."

"My sweet mate, don't you realize I am here to help you?"

"It's not something I can just take your word on, you know. Besides this whole thing with the house is a mess."

"Don't worry, mate, we'll get through this together."

"Stop calling me that," she mumbled as she settled deeper onto the sofa.

"What? *Mate*? But that is what you are. I promise not to rush you, Andrea, but make no mistake, you are mine."

CHAPTER EIGHT

Troy wanted so badly to reach out and grab his mate in a desperate soul-searching kiss, but he forced himself to remain on the opposite couch as he sent a quick text off to Rex informing his Station Master of the situation.

Within the few seconds it took him to update Rex, his mate snuggled down onto the cushions, which were in pretty fair condition given the shape of the rest of the house. She'd closed her brilliant green eyes and sighed contentedly. Clearly, all the excitement was catching up with her.

Poor little one. For all her curves and snarky attitude, she was tiny and petite. Upstairs and imprisoned in that bind for over twenty hours, she had every right to be exhausted. He frowned, angry with himself for taking so long to free her.

Not your fault, you secured that hateful book and the house first, his Thunderbird spoke to him in his mind's eye and Troy immediately felt better. The raptor was a true predator, but as Troy's other half, he was supportive as always. One thing they both agreed on was he would never endanger their mate.

Troy listened to his Thunderbird's words and heard the truth in them. He frowned thoughtfully, yes, he supposed he'd had to make sure the grimoire was stopped before he could tend his mate. He'd done his duty on both counts.

Troy exhaled slowly. He'd never imagined he'd find a mate. Never mind locate his one true mate destined by the Fates to complete him and his beast during his first ever mission for the Wardens. *Fuck and damn.*

A blessing for sure, but unbelievable at best. He stood up to cover Andrea's sleeping form with the handknitted afghan he'd used to cover himself earlier. She sighed and snuggled into the soft mate-rial and he quickly dropped a chaste kiss to her forehead. *So beautiful.*

While she napped, he'd see about securing the house, and then he'd feed her. Somehow being responsible for her nourishment filled him with pride and purpose. All Shifters were driven by instinct and a deep-seated need to see to their mates' well-being and Troy was no different.

To say he was surprised by his feelings was a gross understatement. The strength of the mating call was beyond anything he had ever imagined. His cock throbbed in his pants with the need to claim his sweet, sleeping mate, but that wasn't the strangest thing. It was the tight squeezing inside his chest that was giving him pause. *What the fuck was going on?*

Sex was one thing. He understood the need to lay claim to the one woman the universe had created for him alone with his body, but where were all these protective, not to mention possessive, instincts coming from? He'd be damned if he knew.

He gazed at his mate longingly. His eyes glowing gold with the power of his Thunderbird. *Mine*, the bird crowed in his mind's eye. He wanted to possess her from the top of her dark, curly head, to her tiny little feet. He loved her spunk and attitude and the way she didn't cower in front of him. She was a spit-fire and she'd definitely keep him on his toes.

Fuck me. Troy laughed and shook his head. He closed his eyes and readjusted himself in his jeans. As if that would somehow stop his raging emotions.

His life had completely turned upside down in the span of a few hours.

His phone buzzed, and Troy looked down. He grimaced. It was from Rex. He rolled his eyes as he read the terse message. His grouchy-as-fuck Bear Shifter boss hated texting. *Must be important.*

Call. Now.

Troy lifted the phone and pressed the green button dialing his Station Master. This was going to suck. It rang twice before Rex picked up. Troy waited, but as usual he was the first to speak.

"This is Waman."

"Why are you still there?"

"Like I said in my text, I've run into a complication."

"Like what?"

"A woman."

Rex grunted his reply. The man had little use for women unless they were Wardens in his care. Troy used to feel the same way, but not now. His Thunderbird pushed at him, the mating instinct making him bristle at the older man's response. He burned with the need to claim his mate and resented the negative tone in Rex's voice.

"If the woman is the complication, lock her in cuffs and get her ass back here. The weather has calmed noticeably according to our sources. A clean-up crew is being assembled and will be there within forty-eight hours to strip the house of all Dark paraphernalia. You've spent too much time there, *Warden*."

Troy growled deep in his chest. When he'd sealed the grimoire in the binding bag, he should've checked the effects on the atmosphere immediately, but he'd been preoccupied with getting his mate to safety. He knew all too well, after years of arduous training that once the offending artifact was neutralized the effects would be immediate.

Now that Rex had said it, he realized the howling winds that he'd walked through to get to the house had stopped their vicious assault. The air was calmer, though still cold since it was still winter. Still, all in all, he'd succeeded in what he'd set out to do.

Instead of feeling good, Troy grimaced. He had yet to deliver the news. *He'd met his mate.* Knowing Rex, he'd scoff at Troy and suggest he use the handcuffs to bring her in. The Bear Shifter simply did not believe the old stories.

"I said, you are to return now, *Warden*, with your prisoner fully secured and in tow."

"I can't."

"Excuse me?"

"She is my mate."

Silence reigned for a long while. Troy tensed, uncertain if his hardhearted boss was still there. Then he heard his Station Master exhale slowly.

"Say that again."

"The woman is my mate."

"And she is your prisoner?"

"No, yes, I mean," Troy growled, "it is not as cut and dry as all that. You have to trust me, Rex."

"Fine, get both your asses back here pronto. Got it?"

"Yes."

The subtle *click* told Troy that he'd hung up. He looked down and was met by emerald eyes with a concerned look in them.

"Was that your boss?" She said as she slowly sat up.

"Yes."

"What did he say?"

Troy ignored her, reaching for the bottle of water he'd snagged from the small cooler inside of his car and handed it to her.

"Here. Drink this."

She sighed and put the bottle to her lips. He'd never thought he'd envy a piece of plastic. Her plump lips wrapped around the rim of the bottle as she drank greedily *Fuck and damn.* He should have taken care of her thirst earlier.

"That's good," she sighed as she handed him back the bottle with less than a sip left. He smiled and put it down on the table.

"So, what's the plan?"

"Plan?"

"Yeah, I mean, I only heard one side of the conversation, but I'm sure your boss there had something to say to you about me, right?"

"Yes."

"Well?"

The doorbell rang, interrupting them. Troy nodded towards the door and headed to get the pizza he'd ordered.

He'd much rather feed his mate and get to know her than think about what it was he had to do. He was a Warden. He had a duty. But she was his mate and his loyalty was to her first, wasn't it? *Fuck and damn again.*

The Wardens of Terra had been on the sidelines for a thousand years. Troy was the first Shifter in his Station to be given an assignment. An honor, for certain. Was he truly willing to risk it all for a woman?

More than a woman. My woman. Mate. He didn't need his Thunderbird whispering those words in his head to know what was what. The answer was pretty fucking obvious.

Anything. Everything. He'd risk it all for Andrea Kristos. She was his. *My fated mate.*

CHAPTER NINE

Andrea inhaled slowly. There it was again, the freshly fallen rain scent that was all him. She breathed deeply, wanting to bury her nose between the crook of his neck. What the hell was wrong with her?

She tapped her short fingernails on the arm of the couch. For all intents and purposes, the living room wasn't in as bad a shape as the rest of the house. The walls looked freshly painted and every-thing from the shelves, to the sofa, to the floor, seemed clean and well-cared for.

She didn't know her Aunt Renalda all that well, but it wasn't unusual. Her Romani family was as big as it was notoriously secretive. *Go figure.*

The magical artifacts she'd seen when she first

entered the house had caused her mouth to drop open. And that was just the stuff on display for all to see, she'd yet to tell Troy about the others.

The items she'd discovered in the attic were priceless to say the least. More troubling than that, several, such as the infamous book that landed her in this mess, had obviously belonged to Dark magic practitioners. Romani Casters could be either White or Dark, but Andrea was a rank amateur. She'd never chosen a side, but if she did, it sure as fuck wouldn't be Dark!

Those sick fucks perverted the very concept of magic with their blood sacrifices and malintent. She sneered at the thought. Her *Puri daj* would've excommunicated her sister for even thinking of dabbling with the black arts. *Hmm, maybe that is why her grandmother refused to enter this house?*

Her thoughts ran away with her for a moment, but quickly went back to the elephant, or rather, giant sexy bird man, in the room. Holy crap! Her mouth watered just picturing him the way he looked upstairs without an inch of clothing to cover the hard planes of his enormous body. And she meant enormous. *The guy was huge.*

Her pussy throbbed just thinking about being filled with his well-endowed manhood. She was no virgin, but Andrea had admittedly never seen a male specimen as perfect as Troy. He was like a living and breathing work of art. She itched for some charcoals to draw him with.

That was something of a passion of hers. Art, not ogling nude men. Though for him she'd make an exception. She'd spent a lot of time over the course of her travels sketching and capturing the things she'd seen in her notebooks.

She'd love to draw him. *Hell,* she'd love to do anything with him. Andrea knew about Shifters and some, though not all, of their legends. The idea of being fated for one another was something out of a fantasy. She didn't know if she bought that. But instant lust, well, that was something she did understand. As it was, the sexual tension in the air was so thick she'd need a chainsaw to cut through it.

The image caused Andrea to giggle as she bit into the steaming slice of pizza her "mate" had handed her. *Mate? Yeah, right.* She thought back to what she knew about Shifters, it wasn't much, but it was something. The idea of her, little Andrea Kristos, being this man's *mate* filled her with something besides desire. It filled her with hope.

But what if he wasn't being completely honest? From what she understood, it was more legend than anything else. The idea the Fates had designed one person who was perfect for you in every way was completely foreign to her. *I mean, really?*

Andrea Kristos was no one's idea of perfect. She was too short, her hair was way too curly, and she had one too many rolls to have anything other than a chubby figure.

Not that she cared about her weight. She'd spent the last month in a string bikini cruising over the Mediterranean with a group of friends she'd acquired over her years in Europe.

She was not self-conscious, but she wasn't delusional either. Perfect? *Nah.* Cute? *Maybe.* It all depended on who was looking. She took another bite of pizza and stopped mid-chew as the sound of rumbling stopped her.

Whoa. Troy's eyes glowed gold as he watched her take a bite. The Shifter in front of her certainly looked as though he liked what he saw. She licked her lips, self-conscious of the pizza sauce she knew was there and his rumbling grew louder. *Oh boy.*

She pressed her legs together, trying to stem the sudden wetness that she felt in her panties. He was so gorgeous. She had to admit, she was doing more than her own fair share of looking and fantasizing.

"So, tell me about yourself?" His sudden question threw her off guard and she frowned.

"Uh, there's not much to tell."

"Are you kidding? You've been in Europe for the past five years, I am sure you have plenty of stories," his eyes lit up with real interest and she found herself responding to his curiosity.

She talked about her travels and the people she'd met. Her favorite places and the times she'd wished she'd never left home. It felt strange and yet as natural as breathing, telling him all about her trip. She felt an instant sort of kinship with him.

"The truth is, I've been wanting to come home for a while now, but I hesitated," she looked down at her hands as she spoke. The idea that she'd been waiting for a reason to come back haunted her. She hated that it had to be her great-aunt's death.

"It's not your fault, you know, that your great-aunt passed. All the reports indicate she died of natural causes, there was nothing your being here could have done," he whispered.

"Thank you for that. I was worried for a minute that her dabbling could have gotten her in trouble."

"Do you know why she had all this stuff?" he asked.

"No, I don't. To be honest, I was never a good

student. And no one would accuse me of being an obedient granddaughter or grandniece. I've had very little contact with my family or my clan over the past five years," she murmured.

"Why is that?"

"I don't know. I guess I never felt like I belonged. You know they arrange marriages; most Romani clans do."

"What?" Troy's eyes glowed with his Thunderbird.

She smiled at the incredulousness of it all. *He was jealous.* Simply incredible! The more she talked to him, the more she wanted to open up. It was as if her soul was begging her to lay itself bare in front of him.

"Were you engaged?" His words were deep, as if he was more Beast than man in that moment.

"Actually, I might still be, and I think the word is technically *betrothed.* The guy is like a distant cousin of mine, gross if you ask me," she said thinking about the last time she talked to her *Puri daj* about the so-called betrothal.

"What's his name?"

"Why?"

"Why? So, I can fucking wipe him off the face of

the planet," he spoke as if it was a perfectly reasonable response to her question.

"A little extreme, no?" She joked. Andrea was surprised to find humor in the situation.

"Hell fucking no. You are my mate," his growl sent delicious shivers down her spine all the way to her heated core. She bit her lip nervously, aware of his sudden focus.

"Troy, you don't even know me."

"I know you, baby. I know everything that counts," he leaned forward, nostrils flaring.

He'd scented her arousal. Something she knew Shifters to be capable of. Andrea stopped breathing.

He wiped a speck of sauce she didn't know was on her chin with his callused thumb in an oddly sweet gesture. Then he put his thumb in his mouth and she gasped. *Who knew talking and eating pizza could be so sexy?*

How long had they been talking? A couple of hours? More than enough time for a spark of interest to sizzle between them. But this wasn't an ordinary flirtation.

Troy's declaration was something beyond her comprehension. Andrea turned her head away from the intensity of his gaze. She reached for her water bottle.

Troy's eyes smiled at her as he leaned back in his seat and grabbed his own drink. The Shifter was something to behold. Tall and muscular, but not overly so.

She wanted to run her fingers through his gorgeous black hair. *Would it be soft as it looked? Like a waterfall of midnight silk?* His dark eyes lightened to gold whenever his beast was taking a peek. *Just like now.*

She pressed her knees together once more. As if that would stop him from scenting the physical proof of her desire. Not even the hearty smell of hot pizza in the air could cover up what she was feeling. She watched as his nostrils flared again, noting the growl that began deep in his chest. *Busted.*

"Can I get you anything else?" His deep voice cut into her thoughts.

"Wh-what?" Andrea wanted to crawl under the couch! She thought she'd die of humiliation when her voice cracked.

"I said, is there anything I can get you, Andrea?" His deep voice was right next to her ear and she startled at the sound of it. *Holy crap*, he moved fast when he wanted to.

She turned her head and met his glittering eyes.

Licking her lips to stave off the dryness, she forced herself to answer his question.

"Uh, I'm fine, thanks."

"I'll say," he murmured as his head dropped suddenly.

She felt his breath fan her face and she tensed. *Oh damn.* He inched closer, giving her all the time in the world to back away. But Andrea didn't want that.

She found herself leaning forward. Her eyes were riveted to his mouth as it neared hers. He was going to kiss her, and she couldn't wait.

Suddenly, she raised her hand and reached around his neck. Andrea pulled him down. She slammed her lips to his own, eliciting a groan from the formidable Shifter. *Not just Shifter. A Warden.*

The second his lips touched hers, Andrea felt as though the entire world tilted a few degrees. A fire began in her blood making her dizzy with need. Andrea wasn't a Shifter, but she had magic. Right then that magic was calling for him with a yearning so strong it left her gasping for air. *Mate. Mine.*

His kiss was firm and demanding. She may have initiated it, but there was no doubt who was in control of it now. His strong, callused hands pulled her closer to him until she was astride his lap.

Andrea moaned as their tongues tangled, teeth

clashed, and lips met in the fiercest kiss she'd ever participated in. Wild and rough. Yes. She loved every second of it. She wanted him so badly.

Andrea moaned, shivering with her increasing hunger for this one man. *Never before,* she thought as his fingers lit fires under her skin. Her entire body shaking with desire for him. *Yes,* she thought.

She'd never been one to cow to society's rules or expectations. Hell, she'd spent five years on her own, globe-trotting and simply experiencing life. But nothing in those five years compared to this man's kiss. Andrea sighed and moved her body closer to his.

He wanted her too. The steel rod that was pressed up against her from their positions on the couch was evidence of his feelings. Troy Waman was no slacker in the junk department that was for damn sure.

She'd had her share of disappointments with the opposite sex, but she knew instinctively that he would never disappoint her in that way.

Her body burned for him. *His scent, his taste,* he was absolutely delicious. His beautifully bronzed skin was hot to the touch.

Firm and tight, his muscles bunched as he moved against her. It was so damn sexy Andrea couldn't help, but steal a taste here and there with her lips, tongue, and teeth.

She lifted when he tugged on her shirt and soon, she felt the cool air on her sensitized skin. He did the same to his shirt, and her bra, until they were both nearly naked and making out like a couple of sex-crazed teenagers.

"You okay?" He asked, his voice deeper than before and tinged with desire.

"Yes," she sighed and moved her head farther back to give him better access.

His hard, tanned body looked so enticing pressed against her softer, paler skin. He seemed to be equally fascinated by it, if the way he reverently molded his hands to her every curve was any indication. His indescribably soft lips followed his hands, kissing her skin as he whispered soft praises between teasing nibbles and licks.

"*Sweet mate*, I want you so fucking bad," he ground out as his hot mouth closed around one full breast. Andrea screamed as he sucked on her pebbled nub and tugged it with his teeth. The sting of pain only added to her pleasure.

She couldn't take her eyes off of him as he flicked his tongue around her areole and back to her nipple. He turned and gave her other breast the same treatment, causing her pussy to drip with anticipation.

"Troy!" Andrea gripped his long hair in her hands as he made his way down her body. *He must be a mind reader,* she thought absently. She wanted him stamped all over her. Imprinted on her body the way he was on her heart. *It's too fast,* she told herself, but was it? She'd never thought much about what others expected. He was a Shifter and she was a Romani Caster, practicing or not. They were not *normals* and didn't need to pretend to move with conventional society. *Not with each other.*

Besides, this felt so fucking good. He travelled down her body, kissing and nibbling her soft skin until he reached the trimmed curls that covered her dripping sex. His grin was almost feral as he lifted her big thighs and draped them over his muscular shoulders. He urged her legs further apart and spread her nether lips with his long fingers.

"You smell so good, *sweet mate,* like caramel and cream," he pressed his face into her folds and sucked in a breath. *Goddess help her,* she creamed a little more.

"*Mmm,* that's so good. You're ready aren't you, mate? I want that too. I want to taste you, feel you clench and quiver as you come on my tongue," his voice was so deep Andrea thought he sounded barely human. She trembled with need, the anticipation alone making her drip for him.

"Please," she whimpered. She was shocked at how much she needed him. Her body was so tense she craved release, satisfaction only he could give her.

Golden eyes met hers as his long tongue snuck out of his mouth, licking her slit up to circle her clit, and then back down, all the way to her forbidden hole. His Beast growled, and her pussy throbbed in response. *Did birds growl?*

That thought and any other she'd had fled her mind as his lips clamped over her clit. He sucked, *hard.* Stars burst in front of her eyes.

Andrea bucked wildly, hips thrusting and channel clenching, seeking fulfillment, but Troy held her down with a firm, yet gentle hand. He licked and sucked in earnest. Bringing her to peak and teasing her until she thought she'd die from it.

Finally, he pressed the flat of his tongue against her bundle of nerves and growled. The vibration sent Andrea flying straight into paradise.

"Oh yes! Fuck! Troy! YES!"

She writhed under his mercilessly sensual assault. Her body throbbed, heart pounding as she tugged his hair tighter, loving the way he punished her for it by sucking even harder.

She could hardly contain her feelings. Her Romani magic pulsed under her skin, alive and unleashed for the first time in her life. She embraced that side of her and felt the responding delight all around her. She screamed his name as she shattered underneath him.

Troy.

CHAPTER TEN

"**T**roy! Yes!"

Pride swelled through Troy as he continued to lick and suck his mate's honeyed sex, urging her to ride out her orgasm on his tongue. Both man and beast lovingly sucked down every single drop of her cream as she spasmed around his fingers and mouth. *Holy fuck!* His mate was sexy as hell!

Responsive and receptive to his ministrations. He growled and pulled her closer to the edge of the couch. He needed inside of her, now. Troy's Thunderbird cawed and crowed in his mind's eye. His beast more than onboard with that idea!

"I need you, Andrea, please," he begged unashamedly.

"Yes, oh yes," she answered and gripped his hips with her hands.

He placed the head of his cock at her swollen entrance. Her emerald eyes peered at him through her heavy black lashes. The moment seemed frozen in time. Troy held her gaze as he pushed forward, slowly filling her heat until he was balls deep inside of his mate's lush body.

They both groaned the very second, he was fully seated in her. *Just like heaven*, he thought as he waited for her to adjust to his size and girth. She was so tight and hot. He'd stretched his little mate until she was pulled taut around him.

His Andrea was all wet-heat squeezing him to bursting. *Fucking perfect*, just like he knew she would be. He couldn't stop the huge smile and the bark of laughter that erupted from his chest.

Her answering smile hit him right in the stomach. Love for her blossomed from deep inside of him. He felt the power of it surge throughout his body and soul. Then he poured all those feelings into her. All of his savagely raw emotions erupting from him like lava from a volcano.

His fingers gripped her thighs as he pumped his hips. Her body fit his like a glove. He thought he'd die from the pleasure. But first, he needed to make her come. Troy swirled his hips, hitting that sweet spot inside of her that made her channel flutter wildly around his shaft.

"You're so perfect and *mine*," he growled as he pulled almost all the way out. He slammed back in and began to move his hips urgently.

"*Troy*," she mewled as she grabbed onto him, her small hands gripping his ass and hips as he pounded into her.

Troy fucking loved every bit of it. Even as her short nails bit into his skin. *Yeah, especially that.* The idea that she'd marked him even in that small way was so fucking hot.

"YES! Mine, all mine, sweet mate, say it, tell me," he growled his request as he fucked her, driving balls deep into his mate's sweet pussy.

She was his every fantasy come to life. Soft and supple with warm skin pale as cream and smooth as silk. He loved the way it contrasted against his own darker, rougher skin. She was rounded and supple as a woman should be. *His woman.*

Her dark, curling tresses were warm and glossy, he loved how she flung them back, away from her beautiful face while he loved her. *Yes,* it was loving, he knew it down to the depths of his soul as those emerald eyes focused on him. They were glazed over in passion and he decided he'd put that look on her face every single day for the rest of his life.

"Love, mate, so good," he groaned as he plowed into her heat.

"Troy? Oh goddess, yes, do that again," she called out to him. He eagerly obeyed her command. Greedy for more of that shocked little moan that left her throat. It was music to his ears as he swirled his hips and hit that spot again and again.

His chest swelled with pride. He knew how to make her moan now. He worked his cock in and out of her heat, rubbing her inside, hitting that one secret place that made his mate's pussy clench tightly around him.

"Like that, love?"

"Oh, yes, yes," she moaned.

"Tell me you're mine, Andrea, tell me now," he said as he flicked her clit with his thumb, loving the feel of her pussy as it convulsed around his shaft. If possible, he felt himself grow even harder inside of her.

"Yes, yours, only yours," she moaned, and he leaned down and captured her lips with his own.

He drove his tongue in and out of her mouth, mimicking his dick as he pushed in and out of her sweet hot sheath. Passion tightened his stomach. *Not yet.* He needed her to come with him.

"Mine," he growled as he moved rougher, wilder over her. *Mate.* His beast drove him to claim her. *Now.*

He licked her neck, pride filled him as she instinctively dropped her head, giving him better access. He felt his teeth lengthen and just as her orgasm began to surge through her body, he struck.

Darkness overtook the edges of his vision as he pounded into her, draining his cock of every last drop of his seed.

He felt the warmth of their bond settle over them and, suddenly, it was as if he could feel everything she was feeling. *Awe. Satiation. Tenderness. Desire. Love.*

"Wow? Did you experience that too?" She asked, wonder in her voice.

"Yes," he murmured nuzzling her neck, "We are connected now. Forever."

Mine.

CHAPTER ELEVEN

Andrea rifled through her suitcase for something suitable to wear. Unfortunately, winter in New York was vastly different from her recent address in Mykos. *Oh well, no more strappy sundresses and flip flops till June!*

"You'll need something warmer than that," Troy said as he saddled up behind her and wrapped his arms around her waist. He was grinning at the silky thong she held in her left hand and she felt herself blush at his soft teasing.

His hair was still damp from their combined shower and it tickled her skin where he nuzzled her shoulder with his lips. *Mmm.* He knew just where to touch her, how hard and how long. Like she was an instrument and he a master conductor. Just thinking about it gave her goosebumps.

He was a sublimely skilled lover. Observant and thoughtful, tender and rough all at the same time. But there was more to him than rugged good looks and a skillful body, he was funny and smart.

He said the sweetest things. Things that made her fall even more in love with the big Shifter. Her entire body felt swollen with need just from looking at him.

"Well, I can wear this pair of jeans and I think I have a thermal shirt in here somewhere. Do you have an extra sweatshirt I could borrow?"

"Of course, but you'll still need a coat. We can get one on the way."

"I'm sure, I'll be fine," she said thinking about the meager savings in her bank account.

She'd spent quite a bit of money on the trip back to New York. Airfare was expensive when you needed it immediately. She bit her lip, unaware of his intense stare. Troy walked in front of her and lifted her chin with one long finger. She whipped her eyes up to meet his.

"It's nineteen degrees outside. You *need* a warm coat. I am more than able to take care of that,

Andrea. You don't ever have to worry about money," he said.

"Of course, I worry about money. I've been living off what I've earned selling sketches in the towns I've visited all over the world. I had a meager savings before I left, but it's gone Troy, and I don't want to-"

"Hush, baby, listen," he said, placing his hands on her bare arms.

The silky bra she wore felt too tight all of a sudden. She exhaled a ragged breath, hypnotized by the feel of his callused fingertips. The soothing circles he was making on her skin were tempting and oh-so-sweet.

"It is my pleasure and my privilege to provide for you. I know you're an independent woman, and I respect that. I am not trying to take that from you, but this is all about being practical, okay? You need a coat, I'm gonna get you one, alright?"

"Alright," she mumbled, though she wanted to argue some more.

She sighed when he leaned down and kissed her, tempting her mouth with his. He brushed his lips lightly over hers, the tension in the room near to bursting. Heat from his body seeped into hers making her tingle all over. *Who needs a coat when I've got you?*

"Mmm. You've got me alright, baby, but you still need a coat," he laughed and kissed her nose.

"Hey! I was only thinking that!"

"I guess I'm a mind reader then," he winked, and it made him look younger, carefree.

She hated it when he made more sense than her! *Okay, not really. LOL.* She watched him turn around to pull an extra black sweatshirt out of his duffle bag. The play of muscles across his back made her mouth water. She couldn't believe he was hers.

He handed her the sweatshirt and she laughed. The thing was huge, but soft and warm. Best of all, it smelled like him. Ozone, freshly fallen rain, and the masculine musk that was all Troy Waman.

He'd already explained about his position with the *Wardens of Terra* and his need to get back to his Station. Andrea was eager to leave Shadowland. The house and all the mess Aunt Renalda left was a mystery to her. She wanted no part of it.

Her head throbbed and for a moment Andrea felt a little bit dizzy. *Whoa.* Odd since she was never sick. She tossed it up to her rather strenuous night of passion with her new mate. Also, she'd only eaten two slices of pizza in the last forty-eight hours.

Andrea had always loved adventure and she was about to embark on the biggest one of her life. Troy had explained what mating meant to him and she'd jumped right on in wholeheartedly. She'd never felt as if she belonged, but she did now. *To him.*

"Are you sure you are okay coming back with me?"

"Of course," she'd replied instantly.

"Cause Andrea, all I want is you."

"Troy, I want you too. Your duty as a Warden of Terra is an important one. I would never take that from you."

"You're incredible, sweet mate."

Of course, that conversation led to another round of lovemaking that had left her breathless and satiated. She felt him in her heart, in her soul. It was all part of their mating bond, he'd explained after he'd claimed her with his bite during their first of many times making love the night before.

Andrea felt as if she'd been reborn. In the normal world, they were strangers. It was way too soon for love. But in the supernatural world, one she'd been born into, she knew it didn't always work like that. The Fates didn't follow the same rules as normals.

They'd chosen her for Troy and vice versa. Whether she'd known him for one hundred years or one hundred seconds, it would not change this one fact, she loved him. *I've known him all my life.* She smiled at the realization.

It was true, regardless of how fantastic it might

sound. She'd always been secretive and quiet around outsiders, but last night she'd talked to him for hours. Spilling all her secret dreams, with no fear of repercussions. He'd taken away all her defenses by simply being there. *Fated mates indeed.*

Andrea revealed stories of her youth she hadn't spoken about in years! He listened too, without judgement or pity about how she'd had no real home or relationships. She'd been wandering the globe for the past five years, and before that, she'd been orphaned and mainly unwanted in her huge family.

Only as a bargaining chip. Her ridiculous betrothal lasted about as long as it took her to say the guy's name, *Manfri Durrekin Pipindorio*. It was a mouthful and a half. She'd only met him once and he was short, bald, and smelled distinctly like rubbing alcohol. *Blech.*

Andrea had no desire to be *Mrs. Pipindorio*! She'd left him, her clan, and her family behind. Betrayed and hurt by *Puri daj*'s insistence she marry the man. She only wanted to join the Pipindorio clan to the Kristos clan through Andrea's marriage bond.

No way. It didn't matter now anyway. She was mated to a Shifter and in love for the first time in her life. She bit her lip and frowned. She hadn't said the words, neither had Troy, and though she felt his feelings for her loud and clear she'd have liked a declaration all the same.

It's early days, she chided herself. Don't borrow trouble. Her head throbbed again as she followed her new mate down the stairs.

"You okay?" He asked, concern showing in his dark brown eyes.

"Yeah, I think I need some food," she said, "I'm just gonna see if there's any aspirin in the kitchen."

"Alright."

She smiled as he went out the door of her great-aunt's house. She turned into the kitchen and rifled through the mandatory junk drawer every old woman in her family had. Her head throbbed harder as she closed her hands over a bottle of aspirin and Andrea sat down hard on a stool.

For some reason, her eyes kept going to the cabinet on the left. She shrugged her shoulders, unable to quell the need to go to the cabinet. When she opened the door, she saw a few jars of spices and dried herbs hanging from nails that had been hammered on the inside of the door.

She frowned ad moved things until she came across a little salve jar. She opened the jar and inside found not the usual gunk, but a small rounded pendant on a leather thong.

She smiled recognizing the small iridescent stone as an opal. It shimmered in the dim light showing off its blues and golds. *Like fire,* she thought and smiled again as the stone warmed in her hand. She sighed and placed it over her head, shoving the amulet under her shirt. Whatever the necklace was, Andrea thought it was beautiful and Aunt Renalda did leave her the house, so therefore, it was hers.

Her headache now gone, Andrea dropped the aspirin bottle and ran down the steps to meet Troy. She kept her eyes trained on him as he locked the door and handed her the key. She smiled as he bent down to kiss her briefly before they headed to his car.

Yes, she thought. She'd made the right decision. Heck, the only decision for her really. Troy was taking her to meet his Station Master. He'd said they would live in the single-family home that each Warden was given upon reaching adulthood.

He'd assured her that she was the only female he'd ever brought to the house. A confirmed bachelor, she understood through their new bond, he was telling the truth. Lying was pretty much impossible for Shifters and most shied away from the practice. She knew instinctively he would always be truthful with her.

She thought about last night and the many ways her life had changed in such a short amount of time. It was incredible to think she'd met her *fated mate* under such circumstances. It was as if the two of them had built a little world of their own over the past twenty-four hours and in it they'd lived with each other for a lifetime.

"What are you thinking?"

"About how much my life has changed since yesterday!"

"Tell me about it, mate. I am so blessed to have found you."

"Hmm, you thought I was practicing Dark magic when you met me and now look at us?"

He frowned, and she felt their bond squeeze her chest. But not in an altogether good way. It was new and strange, being able to sense someone else's emotions, and she was very new to it. But if she wasn't mistaken, something was wrong.

"You know, Andrea, it's okay, I would understand if you were just being curious about some of things in the house or whatever it was your aunt was doing with that book-"

"What? Wait a second, are you saying that after everything we did last night, you still think I was after Dark magic?"

"No! Um, look, I'm just saying you can tell me anything, sweet,-"

"You don't believe me! You think I was looking for some dark and nefarious spell? What the hell, Troy?"

Fury and hurt warred within her and she felt something shut off inside of her. Troy looked miserable and pain seemed to radiate off him as he placed a hand over his chest.

"Andrea, listen, I didn't mean-"

"Save it!" She huffed out a breath and tried not to allow her growing panic to overwhelm her.

Oh no. How could I have made such a mistake? He doesn't trust me, and I don't even know him! This is my fault!

"Look, your family obviously has history with this stuff. It's only natural for you to be curious-"

"You know what, we're going to have to make a little detour," she started typing an address into his GPS.

"We need to get to the Station-"

"No, we're going to my grandmother's house. Now or I swear to God, and the Goddess, and whoever the heck else is out there, I will leave this car and you will never see me again!"

Troy growled as his eyes turned bright gold. His

words were barely discernible through his Beast's fury. Foolish as it might be the possessive display appeased Andrea's bruised heart and pride.

"No. Stay," he grumbled.

"Okay, then drive."

CHAPTER TWELVE

The drive to Newark was long and silent in the dark SUV. Andrea sat with her body angled towards the window as far away from Troy as she could get, he thought angrily.

His irritation was not directed at his luscious little mate, but more at himself. Why the hell had he spouted that shit to her? Even if it was true! He honestly didn't know if she'd been looking for something specific in the book nor did he care.

Andrea was the other half to his soul. She made him, and his Thunderbird complete in ways he could not even comprehend. The simple act of being near her, even when she was pissed at him, was infinitely better than life without her.

Fuck and damn. He really messed up and now he

had to prove it to her. He wasn't the judgmental asshole she thought he was. Troy wished he could go back in time to amend his mistakes.

She was so angry and with every right, but it was the hurt on her beautiful face that nearly did him in. He'd stopped earlier in their trip and pulled into the parking lot of a strip mall, one of several they'd passed along the way, to get her a warm coat.

She wouldn't even get out of the car. It was as if she hated him. A thought that seized his heart in his chest. *No. Please don't let it be too late.*

He went into the store alone and picked out the warmest coat they carried for her. When he handed her the bag, she tossed it into the back seat, refusing to even look at the gift.

Discomfort settled around him like an unwanted blanket. Troy tried to ignore the tension in the suddenly too small SUV. The mating bond that had felt like pure heaven the night before, was shriveling inside of him. He felt angry and cold. *Fuck and damn again.*

Troy had no idea how to make this right. His Thunderbird barked and shrieked inside his mind's eye, furious with him for not taking better care of his mate. At least she'd accepted the bagel he'd gotten for her, he reminded the beast. That seemed to slightly mollify him.

His cell buzzed on the console and he ignored it. He knew who it was from. Rex was gonna be pissed as hell, but Troy didn't give a damn. He used the power of Aquarius to send a mental image to his Station Master, pulling on his sign for personal reasons wasn't exactly forbidden, but it was not encouraged either.

He felt the Bear Shifter's answering snarl and knew he'd have a lot to explain. For some reason Troy's hand, the one that bore the symbol of the water-bearer, was tingling and itching like crazy. He tried to ignore it, but it was difficult since there was nothing to occupy his mind other than his mate's rigid posture and unyielding attitude. *Fuck and damn,* he'd have to try again.

"Andrea?"

She flicked her emerald gaze to his then turned away, her luscious lips pursed in displeasure. *Shit.* He hated that he'd put that look on her face. But didn't she understand. He was trying to tell her he didn't care what she was doing in that attic. Even if it turned out she was guilty, he wouldn't let the other Wardens lay a finger on her. He'd protect her with his life!

"Andrea, whatever this is, it will be okay. I swear, I'll never let harm come to you."

"Is that why you think I'm angry? You think I'm afraid?"

"Andrea, I-"

"Are you kidding me? Stop the car. We're here."

Troy looked around and frowned. They'd turned onto a dank alley off some fucked up looking street in downtown Newark. The place made Shadowland look friendly not to mention affluent.

He jumped out of the SUV before Andrea had time to unlock the door and held it open for her. He'd managed to snag the bag with the coat from the backseat and stopped her with a hand before she stepped out into the biting wind. *At least she'd kept his sweatshirt on.*

"Here, *please*," he held the black ski jacket open for her and was pleased when she stepped into it.

"Thanks," she said tightly and stepped away from his body.

He missed her warmth immediately. *Fuck and damn.* Her caramel and whiskey scent drifted into his nostrils and he bit his lip. He wanted his mate with a fierce need he didn't quite understand, but one thing he did know, this rift between them was killing him.

Before he had time to adjust to his environment, she'd stepped through a hidden doorway among the garbage cans and fire escape ladders. Anxiety rushed through him. Troy frowned and went after her.

"Andrea, wait up." He followed her through the open door only to be stopped by a six-foot tall three-hundred- and fifty-pound man with the face of a bull dog.

Magic singed the air, it wasn't evil per se, but it was *different*. Hostile and aloof. *Romani Caster*, he discerned. The man scowled and blocked Troy's attempt to go around him. Troy growled.

"Get out of my way, *Fido*, or you're bound to lose something you'd rather keep."

"Is that so, *xenos*," the man said in a deep heavily accented voice, "I am five times heavyweight champion in the state and 6th level Caster of the Kristos Clan. No, *Shifter*, I do not think you will get by me easily."

"Move. Now."

"I don't think so. You hear me correctly, yes? I am Romani Caster, so save yourself some trouble. You will not scare me with your growling."

Troy recognized the distinct smell of the man's magic growing stronger. *Fuck and damn.* He had no wish to use what little magical stores he had against this mountain of a man who was more than likely related to Andrea. Still, the fucker was in his way.

Troy sighed and looked past the man to where Andrea walked through a pair of hanging curtains into what his nose discerned was a kitchen. Maybe he could just hit the guy and sneak past?

He was a big fucker, but so what. From the smell of things, he was arming himself with shielding wards and perhaps some increased strength too. *Fuck and damn again.*

"Puri daj! Where are you?" Andrea's voice distracted him for a split second, but that was all Fido needed to throw a cast that sent Troy hurtling out the door.

"What the fuck?" He growled and leapt to his feet.

Troy heard squeals and the sound of his mate yelling in what he thought was a mixture of Greek and Romani. *Hell no!* The brute had his mate in there.

Troy growled and grabbed the door, ripping it off its hinges. He pushed past the surprised man who was attempting to hold onto his mate by her fragile arm.

"Get your fucking hands off her!"

Troy saw red. The fucking fuck had his fucking hands on his mate! *Hell no!* He allowed his Thunderbird to show through his eyes and the beast was pissed. Troy growled, the scent of ozone grew strong in the air. He felt the muscles in his body half-shift, a state he'd never achieved before.

Claws replaced fingers, his muscles bunched. Troy opened his mouth releasing a battle cry, his eyesight that of his Thunderbird.

The stupid fuck still had his hands wrapped around Andrea's arm. Her mouth hung open in shock, but Troy was solely focused on the Caster.

"I said, let her go," he said in a barely human voice before he planted his fist in Fido's face.

An explosion of blue and white light flew from his half-Changed fist to the man's face. A satisfying crunch sounded, and Troy knew he'd broken the Caster's nose. *Fuck if his face didn't feel like a brick wall!*

"Andrea, you okay?"

"Oh, my God, you hit Rolf!"

"He touched you!"

"He's my cousin, you dope! And he's one of the strongest guys I know!"

"Shouldn't have touched you," he growled even as his body changed back to his human form.

"Troy, he's a sixth level Caster! He's part of *puri*

daj's personal security detail! I mean, how did you do that?"

"I don't know, I mean I am a Shifter and a Warden of Terra."

"Yeah, but you shouldn't have been able to do that!"

"I've been meaning to install a steel door for some time, but I guess it will be sooner than later," a heavily accented voice met his ears, "Don't worry, Andrea, your cousin will be fine. Now, come and sit at the table with your new mate, and maybe you can explain how he got through the only man in our clan to reach the sixth level of spell Casters?"

Madame Magdelena Kristos, matriarch of the Kristos Clan and the most powerful Romani Caster he'd ever heard of, walked down a set of carpeted stairs into the foyer. He stood taller, itching to get Andrea behind him. His protective instincts were working overtime.

She barely looked at her nephew-guard as she stepped over the downed man. Troy cringed at the mess they'd made, but she didn't even seem to register the damage to the room as she passed through.

He noted Andrea's posture went stiff at the sight of her grandmother. He moved slightly in front of her. Something the older woman noted with humor if the wry smile on her face was anything to go by. She looked thoroughly modern and nothing at all like how he expected the leader of the Kristos clan to appear.

She had long dark hair with silver streaks in front that she wore in a complicated up-do. She looked neat and tidy in her pantsuit. *Expensive, crisp, and efficient.* She wore tiny stud earrings and minimal makeup to enhance her flawless, olive toned skin.

She was attractive for a woman her age. He could see where Andrea had gotten her poise, though their coloring was not the same. She was much more powerful than she seemed.

Dangerous too. He didn't need his Thunderbird's voice in his head to tell him that. Magic seemed to pulse all around her as she led them both into her kitchen.

There was a pot bubbling on the stove and the scent of meat and spices drifted into his nostrils. His mouth salivated. He hadn't had a homecooked meal in an age, but he was wary of the Romani matriarch.

"Come, sit, we shall eat together to toast the return of my wayward granddaughter, and of course to discuss your mating, *Warden*," Madame Magdelena lifted a large wooden spoon and stirred the pot while adding a few more spices and reducing the heat.

"It seems you two really jumped the gun, am I correct?"

"Yes, *puri daj*," Andrea answered in a small voice.

Her response disturbed him. He knew in his heart she was his fated mate, but she was no Shifter. She wouldn't feel it the way he did. *Was she regretting their mating? Fuck and damn.*

She moved about the kitchen retrieving dishes and utensils, setting the table as she must have several times in her youth. Troy felt his expression soften as he watched her move about the room.

He couldn't help himself. She was the embodiment of every dream he'd ever had. *Sweet Andrea.* His mate was absolutely beautiful wearing his sweatshirt with her dark curls pulled away from her face.

He'd watched her that morning put on some face cream, mascara, and pink lip gloss. He'd told her he didn't mind if she chose not to wear makeup, but she'd replied she was wearing it for herself not him. He'd laughed and tickled her until she couldn't breathe.

"Did he bite you?" her grandmother's voice seemed

far away, but he kept track of the conversation even as he watched Andrea. *Mine.*

"Yes."

"He asked permission?"

"Yes."

"You gave it then? So, it is not forced. I thought not."

Troy growled. Of course, he didn't force her. Who would do such a thing? But before he could answer, Andrea was there defending him. *She still cares. Thank the goddess!*

"No, certainly not! I wanted him as much as he wanted me."

She ignored his stare and poured glasses of what looked like iced tea and set them on the table. His Andrea was quick and efficient, but she was not entirely at home. He remembered the things she'd shared with him and his heart hurt for her.

No, she is not at home here, but she could be with me. He could almost imagine her doing such small, domestic things in their house and his heart thudded. He wanted that. He wanted her in his kitchen in his life, forever. He needed to fix this.

The three of them sat down with steaming bowls of what he'd learned was lamb stew and began to eat. Flavor exploded on his tongue and he didn't miss

Andrea's soft sigh of satisfaction. He made a mental note to make her repeat the sound *later*.

"Well, granddaughter, you are back now, and you've seen the house Renalda left you."

"Yes, *Puri daj.*"

"And?"

"And? Well, let's see, *grandmother*, it seems you had me come back here from Greece where I was having the time of my life partying with a bunch of gorgeous guys and beautiful women-"

Troy growled at her words and she shot him a dirty look. He silenced his growl, but he was jealous. *Fuck and damn.* He felt like ten times an idiot. He'd done nothing but fuck up since he met her, it seemed.

Jealousy was not his thing, but he was practically green with it. He was doomed to make a fool of himself again if she kept talking about other men. But she continued to speak as if he wasn't in agony sitting there! *Fuck and damn again.*

"To come look at some dilapidated pile of junk I inherited from my great-aunt who I don't even remember! Then while I'm trying to figure out how to get the heat to work, I stumble over a binding circle and I released some damn grimoire and then, this idiot over here comes stomping in and hand-cuffs me-"

"You handcuffed my granddaughter?"

"Yes," he growled. He was alternately embar-rassed and uncomfortable.

"Then he goes on to tell me I'm his mate and-"

"And the two of you fucked like rabbits if those *mating marks* on your neck is anything to go by. So, Andrea, so tell me why then are you here?"

Troy grinned as he looked at Andrea's bright red face. She was so fucking adorable. He didn't think she'd imagined her grandmother using that language, regardless of how apt the imagery might be. If he'd thought anything about this situation as funny, he'd laugh, but as it was, he simply sat there on needles and pins.

"Well, we are here because I want this, our mating undone!"

"NO!" He roared and stood up, knocking over the chair he'd been sitting on in the process.

"Yes! You big stupid jerk! You still think that I had something evil in mind when I tripped over that book and got stuck in the binding circle! I don't want to be stuck with someone who thinks I'm capable of that!"

"Think of how it looked-"

"Think of how it looked? All I've been doing is thinking of how amazing this connection between us is, but apparently I'm the only one who feels that way!"

"That's not fair!"

"Not fair? You think I was practicing Dark magic! How is that for not fair?"

"We just met! How the hell do I know what you're capable of!"

"Well that's great isn't it! You had no problem licking me from head to toe and marking me with your bite, but you still think I'm practicing Dark magic! Well, fuck you very much, Troy Waman!"

"Oh hell, I didn't mean it like that! Andrea, you are *my mate, mine*, there is no going back!"

"Actually, there may be a way," Madame Magdelena sat back in her chair ignoring the overturned chairs and bowls of stew after Troy and Andrea began their tirades.

The atmosphere was so tense you could hear a pin drop. Troy's Thunderbird roared in his mind's eye. The beast was ready to rip out the throat of the Romani Spell Caster who was threatening to take his mate away.

The power of Aquarius flashed through him. Troy's muscles tensed, and his skin beaded with sweat. The urge to Change into his other skin almost overpowered him. Troy clenched his jaw. He needed to remain human to talk his mate out of such a thing.

"What did you say, *Puri daj?*" Andrea turned to her grandmother and for the first time, Troy noticed the tears streaking her face. The bitter tang of misery and sadness overpowered her usual sweet and smoky scent.

Oh no. He'd done that. He put that sorrow on her face. How the fuck could he do such a thing? Pain lanced his chest he dropped to his knees in the middle of the Romani matriarch's kitchen. His matebond shriveled even smaller and coldness seeped into his bones. The power of Aquarius quaked within him, shunning his already made decision.

"Andrea, oh no," his voice was hoarse and aching.

He was sick with grief, "please forgive me, mate, I am so sorry. I never meant to cause you any pain."

"If you wish to stop harming my granddaughter, *Warden,* then you know the way to end a mating, don't you?" Madame Magdelena's voice was loud in the small room.

"Yes. If that is what she wants, then I will submit."

"I suggest we sleep on it tonight. Andrea, you

may have your old room. Your cousin, Melinda, has been using it, but she is away tonight."

"Okay, thank you. I'm going to go up now. I need to think," Andrea left the room in a rush.

Troy hated the tears he saw visible in her emerald eyes. He put them there. *Fuck and damn.* He turned to find Madame Magdelena's dark stare riveted to his face.

"I don't imagine you will require a bedroom?"

"No, thank you. I doubt I will sleep tonight," he sighed running his hand over his face. It was early in the evening yet. But he knew the time would tick by slowly.

"You understand what I meant when I said there was one way to break a bonding such as yours?"

"Yes. I have heard stories, but if you doubt my resolve let me say out loud to you that I would gladly give my life for Andrea."

"I thought you might say that, but we shall see. Excuse me," she left without a backwards glance.

Troy stood and walked to the living room. The giant man whom he'd learned was Andrea's cousin Rolf was sitting on the floor wiping up blood with a bucket and warm water.

"Uh, suppose I help you clean this up?" Troy asked.

The man looked at him and grunted before nodding towards the remnants of the front door.

"You clean up that mess. My cousin is bringing a new one now. We will put it up. Then we will get drunk and I will figure out how you bested me."

Troy nodded. It wasn't how he'd have preferred to spend his evening, but beggars and all that. *Fuck and damn.* His Thunderbird cried in his mind's eye.

The sorrowful song was enough to break Troy's heart, but he silenced the beast with a strict command. He couldn't fall apart now. He needed to see her safe first.

Troy woke up the next morning with a dry cottony taste in his mouth. That was the last time he got drunk with a bunch of Romani Casters! Damn bespelled ouzo was enough to knock any Shifter on his ass for an hour or two. The amount of it he drank would've killed a lesser man. Shifter or not.

He sat up and grabbed the glass of water he'd left on the coffee table. The sound of snoring made his head hurt. Rolf was face down on the opposite sofa, a line of drool hanging from his crooked lips. Fucking guy was alright.

They'd spent the night bullshitting and drinking. Rolf had been in love once, but the woman dumped him for a richer man. He'd been avoiding females ever since. His story was sad, but it had nothing on Troy's tale.

Fuck and damn. He'd met and lost the one woman the Fates had created for him alone in the span of twenty-four hours. *How's that for fucking up your life?*

He felt better once he'd finished his water and stood to use the restroom. Once he was finished with the new toothbrush and other toiletries he'd found, he stepped back into the living room right into a cloud of smoky caramel sweetness. *Andrea.*

She must have walked past while he'd been busy. He followed the scent to the kitchen and found her busy over a pot of coffee. She looked beautiful. He drank up the sight like the first rain fall over a desert.

"Hi," his deep voice cut through the silence, but she kept her head down.

Before he could say anything else, Madame Magdelena entered. She wore a casual pantsuit with her hair coiled on top of her head.

"I have the necessary ingredients for the breaking of the bond, if you are ready-"

"Wait a minute-"

Troy sucked in a breath. Andrea had interrupted her grandmother, but could it mean what he hoped it did?

"You've spoken your mind, Andrea. You wished to end this mating. Perhaps you should have stuck to your training child? Then you would know the ways of such things, wouldn't you? Now, show me what you have taken from Renalda's house."

Troy didn't have it in him to respond to the odd request. As far as he knew they'd taken the book and nothing else. He was surprised when Andrea reached into the simple black shirt she was wearing.

When she pulled her hand out, she held a small amulet. *She'd kept that from him.* He'd never felt so hurt and miserable in all his life. He sank to his knees beside her and dropped his head too ashamed to meet her eyes. It didn't matter. It would all be over soon anyway.

"The opal is your *soul stone*, then?"

"I am so sorry, Andrea, for what I said, how I behaved," Troy spoke, but the women ignored him.

"It is a sign of her power. Powers that have been awakened just recently. This called to you, Andrea?"

"Uh, I don't know, I just had a headache and was looking for aspirin, but then I had the urge to check behind the cabinet and found this. It was pretty, and my headache went away, I just figured-"

"So, you took an enchanted amulet and put it on

without a single thought in that curly head of yours, didn't you? And do you want to know why?"

"Well, I-"

"Child, you are drawn to this amulet because it is a manifestation of your gifts. It will help you to focus your budding talents as a Caster. Being near your fated mate allowed you to see the way to your path."

"I thought since I neglected my studies that the magic would just, you know, go away?"

"That is not so, child. Your *mate* here has awakened your magic, but if you no longer want him-"

Startled green eyes zipped from Troy to Magdelena and back again. He couldn't begin to hope, wouldn't allow himself to. Before he could understand what was happening, the sounds of heavy footsteps and loud voices reached his ears.

"Get the fuck out of my way and get me my Warden now, fucker!"

It was Rex. *Fuck and damn.* Troy sighed and moved to stand, but the Romani matriarch stayed him with a wave of her hand.

"In here, *Station Master*. I have been expecting you."

CHAPTER THIRTEEN

Rex entered the small kitchen with his Bear hardly contained. His eyes glowed blue with the power of his Grizzly. He was definitely pissed.

Fernandez, his Station mate and Jaguar Shifter, came in behind him. The smooth as silk Latino winked at Madame Magdelena before raising an eyebrow at Troy.

"What the hell are you doing on the floor, man?"

"Uh-" before he could answer Andrea jumped in front of him. His fierce little mate looked ready to take on the tall Jaguar Shifter, eyes blazing.

"Back off, buddy! Look Troy, obviously there has been a misunderstanding, and we really need to talk, but I'd feel a lot better if you'd stand up now that these, uh, *gentlemen* have invaded my grandmother's house."

"Uh, it's okay," Troy's lips turned up into a brief smile.

His heart was still breaking, but he admired her fearlessness. She stood toe to toe with two of the biggest bad asses he knew, and her only thoughts were for him. He touched her shoulder and placed her behind him.

Sparks sizzled between them, but he ignored them for now. What was he to do? She didn't want him. And he would always want her. That was a fact he would have to live with for the very short time he had left.

He knew what the old woman had in mind for him. The only way to break a new mating. Right then death was something he'd welcome gladly if it would bring his mate joy.

I have completely fucked up my life, but if I can bring her any peace I will. He nodded at Fernandez and lowered his gaze in deference to Rex's dominance and position.

"Hey," he said.

"You've disobeyed orders, Warden. You were to return with this person of interest in tow ASAP. What the hell happened?"

"Excuse me, Station Master, are you saying my granddaughter is a suspect, in what exactly?" Madame Magdelena's anger was tangible.

"And don't bother with denials, I know who and what you are. Your *Herald* has eaten at this very table! It is about time the Wardens were called back into play, the Kristos Clan have been your staunchest supporters for centuries! Don't even think about feeding me a line or I promise I will make you regret it."

"*Puri daj*, please, let's hear them out."

"Magdelena Kristos, matriarch of the Kristos Clan and one hell of a Romani Spell Caster," Rex recited as if he'd memorized her file. *He probably did, the fucker.*

"I am not at liberty to discuss Warden business with you, ma'am, but if you wouldn't mind, I need to take your granddaughter in for questioning."

"*No!*"

"*I'm not going anywhere with you!*"

"*Over my dead body!*"

The sounds of protest from Troy, Madame Magdelena, and Andrea overlapped one another in a cacophony of voices loud enough to make every Shifter in the room cringe. Troy vibrated with anger.

She may not want him, but his Thunderbird still

held a claim on her and there was no way in hell he'd allow her to be taken from his side by anyone other than her. Hers was the only voice that counted with him.

"Sit! All of you," Madame Magdelena's order was obeyed by all.

Much to his consternation, Andrea settled between her grandmother and Rex, leaving him next to Fernandez on one side and Madame Magdelena on the other. *Fuck and damn.*

"I know who you are, *Wardens of Terra,* and I know the legends. Tell me, have you studied your history?"

"How is that relevant, ma'am?" Rex's cold tone was oddly polite, but still, Troy cringed. For some reason, he felt protective of the small, though formidable woman.

"*Shifters,* such as yourselves, are rare quantities in the universe, *Rex Bastian,* Grizzly Bear Shifter, retainer of Taurus, and most dominant in your Station. You all have travelled alone and unpaired for eons, but your time is here. The universe and the Fates have joined to offer you the blessing of a mate. With that mate comes strength, unity, completion, and power beyond what you have each attained."

"That's just myth-"

"Is it, *Bear Shifter*? Take a look at your friend here. Troy Waman, bearer of Aquarius. He has found his mate and in the last twenty-four hours, he's claimed and almost lost her. Look at him, his hollowed cheeks, the despair in his eyes, the resignation in his posture, you see my granddaughter here has denounced his claim."

"*Puri daj*, I didn't mean-"

"Hush, child, I know what you meant, and despite the bonding that has begun between you there is one thing you have neglected."

"*Huh?*"

"*What?*"

"Quiet and listen! You missed a step in your mating! It isn't all rough sex and biting you know!"

"Puri daj!" Andrea blushed furiously, but for the first time since the old woman spoke, Troy felt hope.

"However, you must be certain, for once this vow is spoken, there is none that can break it. Not even Death himself. Now, Rex, you and I and your Jaguar Shifter here, are going to leave the room for a few minutes. We are going to let them talk. And, granddaughter, this time do not speak foolishly."

Hope blossomed within his chest. Andrea's green eyes met his from across the table and he saw his feelings echoed there. The time since last evening, ever since she'd spoken her doubts, had been the most awful of his life. And that was really saying something.

He stood up and moved towards the sink in an attempt to give her room. He didn't want to crowd her. The fact was he could hardly get within two feet of her without growing hard and giving into his sexual desire for his delicious mate.

"Troy, please look at me," Andrea's soft voice reached his sensitive ears and he turned to face her. He exhaled slowly and shoved his hands in his pockets. He wanted to reach out and grab her, pull her close to his body and kiss the breath out of her, but he didn't dare.

He did not want to seduce her into staying with him. He needed her to make the choice freely. It was the only way they could build a future together.

Please say yes. Say you will stay mine, sweet mate. Mine. He repeated the mantra like a prayer over and over again in his mind's eye. Beast and man trained on her entire being. Looking for signs.

CHAPTER FOURTEEN

Andrea could not believe what had just happened. She'd made Troy drive to her grandmother's house with the intention of simply proving to him that her clan did not practice Dark magic and in fact, forbade it.

However, she'd always been a passionate person and her rather big, unfiltered mouth had been known to get her into trouble time and again. She didn't know exactly what she'd done, but apparently it was serious. Her chest ached, and she couldn't breathe, but before she could take back her hasty words, two huge Shifters barged into her grandmother's kitchen.

What was this a freaking free for all? What did a woman have to do to get some alone time to talk to her man? Apparently, she needed her grandmother to get it for her. Ugh. Another thing she'd owe the old lady. One thing Andrea knew, was that nothing came free in the Romani clan.

"Troy-"

"Andrea-"

She smiled, and he ran a hand through his long dark hair nervously. *Shit.* This should have been easier. She exhaled and focused. *Time to put on my big girl pants.*

"Troy, the other night was the most incredible night of my life."

"Mine too," his voice was deep and thick with emotion. She wanted to reach out and press herself against him, to smooth the worry-lines that she'd put on his forehead and kiss away his frown.

"I guess we sort of rushed things, being a Shifter and all, I imagine you couldn't help it," she smiled, and he nodded his agreement.

"I knew you were mine the second I scented you. I've wanted you every second since, Andrea."

"Me too. I was hurt and angry that you didn't believe me."

"I am sorry I didn't let you explain. And it's not that I didn't believe you, I just figured the easy explanation was the answer. I was so intent on letting you know I was okay with everything and anything you did, I forgot to listen. I am so sorry. I meant it, you know?"

"Meant what?" She asked, stopping directly in front of him.

Her green eyes ate him up, traced him lovingly from the top of his head, to the toes of his boots. Energy and longing vibrated between them like something tangible. She was desperate for him. *Does that make me a fool?*

For some reason she didn't think so. Wasn't it the ultimate trust to surrender to someone out of love? She wanted to surrender to him, to submit to his will. Pride had no place between them.

"I will consent to the breaking of our mating bond, if that is what you want, Andrea."

She frowned. She didn't want that. Not at all. She wanted him. Stupid jerk that he was. How could he think she wanted to live without him? *Because you let him, idiot.*

Andrea frowned. She'd been a loner, a traveler, an independent woman living on what she'd earned or the kindness of others. She was Romani. A natural born nomad indeed, but for some reason she felt different now.

Ever since she'd laid eyes on his imposing figure

in her aunt's attic, something had changed. Her whole life seemed to have been building for this moment.

No more running away from who and what she was. Andrea was ready to embrace her heritage and her place now. She felt as if she'd finally come home.

"Andrea?" His anxious question shook her out of her thoughts.

"No, Troy, I don't want that."

"What do you want?"

"I want *you*. I want *us*."

"You do?"

"Yes," she said reaching out for him with her hands. That was all the invitation he needed. Her Shifter swung her up in his arms and squeezed her while she giggled like a schoolgirl.

His mouth crushed hers in a soul-searing kiss that left them both panting and breathless for more. She felt her skin blush under his heated touches. Her nipples hardened, and her stomach clenched.

She'd never wanted anyone like this. Finding herself sitting on the countertop with her legs wrapped around her man's waist while he plundered her mouth was not exactly how she wanted her grandmother to find them. But then again, it was better than what she would have seen, had the older woman waited another ten minutes. *Grrr.*

"Enough, children, please you are not alone now!"

"I love you," Troy said against her mouth and picked her up off the counter, making sure she touched every inch of his body as she slid down to the floor.

A huge grin split his handsome face from ear to ear, Andrea found herself answering with a similar expression. Her heart soared.

Their fragile matebond had been bruised by her callous words and his mistaken beliefs, but now it pulsed between them with renewed hope and love.

"Do you feel that?" he asked with one hand pressed against his chest.

"Yes, I do. Puri daj?"

"Ah, I see the reparations have begun. First, let me ask you, have you decided that the Fates have not made a mistake after all, granddaughter? You wish to stay mated to this Thunderbird here?"

"I do," Andrea's voice rang with certainty and Troy squeezed her hand and dropped a soft kiss to her temple.

"Okay, then with your permission, I will ask Troy's Station Master and the other Warden to witness what I want to share with you," she pulled a long wooden staff out from thin air and with it an aged scroll.

Troy nodded. Rex and Fernandez appeared in the room beside them. He kept his arm wrapped around Andrea's waist the entire time she spoke.

"I have been keeping this scroll safe for over a hundred years. It was passed down to me by my father, as he'd received it from his father before him," the entire room seemed to shimmer with magic as the Romani Caster unraveled the scroll and read the inscription.

"Heed me, you Shifters of Terra, we are the Parcae, the three sisters whose needlework determines your lifespans.

We, the Fates, have halved your souls, the missing piece of each of you lies within your one true mate.

The Wardens of Terra have been thusly designed with the intention of balancing your powers and focus.

You have been truly blessed above all others. Your fated mates have been written in the stars. Your destiny spelled out across the heavens.

Follow your path to your other half for you will not know truth until that mate is found. Your strength as Shifters of the Terra will increase when the claiming is complete. Power will flow in abundance in the veins of you Wardens, and your mates shall bask in the glow of such strength.

You have only to speak your vows aloud and ask us for blessings, if granted you shall be bound for eternity. Stake your claim, but strike with care, for once complete, none can destroy your matebond.

Blessings to you who embrace the powers of your Shifter soul and the one true mate fated for you.'"

Silence reined for a few moments after Madame Magdelena finished reading. Troy's eyes were locked on Andrea's and she gasped with the intensity of his gaze. Her chest squeezed tightly as the precious bond that had been formed between them pulsed again with new life.

It was as if the rest of the room faded away. She vaguely heard the kitchen door closing as Madame Magdelena shooed Rex and Fernandez into the other room with her. Andrea's entire focus was on Troy.

Her giant of a man smiled at her with sparkling eyes that shifted from the darkest brown to the light gold she recognized as his Thunderbird. His hands held hers as he dropped to his knees for a third time in that kitchen, only now his whole face was alighted with happiness. Anticipation clenched in her belly as she watched his chest rise and fall with each breath.

"Andrea, sweet mate, I ask you and the Parcae in the heavens to hear me," his voice was deep and husky, a sweet note of love in every word, "Will you do me the honor of accepting my claim?"

"Yes, I will," she answered, and for some reason, she sank to her knees in front of him, laughing at his confused frown.

"We begin here both of us, together, on equal ground. Lovers, friends, mates, destined by the Fates, my love," she spoke the words from her heart, tears spilling from her eyes as the feeling of his love wrapped around her entire being.

"Yes, my sweet mate, I promise to cherish you, to honor and protect you, to listen to you and to let you into my heart where only you and our children will reign. We belong to each other as only the Fates can foretell, it is a bond that none can break, no man or woman, not death, space, nor time."

"Not death, space, nor time, Troy," she answered pressing herself as close as she could get to him.

She smiled through tears as she felt the warm embrace of their love thrumming through her body. Devotion, happiness, desire, respect, and adoration all poured into her. It was him, her mate, showing her without words how he felt.

She moaned as his lips met hers in a heartbreakingly tender caress. His fingertips held her head gently in place as he brushed his lips over hers again and again in soft, arousing touches that made her blood burn for him.

"I love you," she whispered into his mouth.

He growled and lifted her to him, passion overwhelming tenderness. Not that she minded.

She could've cursed when the door flew open again.

CHAPTER FIFTEEN

After obtaining the scroll from his new grandmother-in-law, who also informed him and his new mate that Andrea would be more receptive to Magic now that they were mated, he packed up the SUV and got ready to head back to the Station.

It seemed that now that she'd found her *soul stone,* Andrea would be even more of an asset to Troy in his hunt for those who practiced the Dark. Andrea had raged at her grandmother for all of three seconds about having to go to that dilapidated house in Shadowland in the first place, until she'd realized what going there had meant for her.

"I'm sorry, *puri daj,* I know you would never have put me in harm's way intentionally. I guess I needed to follow my path to *him,* my mate, and it was worth every single step," she looked at Troy at the end of her speech.

It humbled him beyond any ability to answer coherently. She saw her journey to meet him as something not only necessary but blessed. *How did he get so lucky?* He kissed her. Something he didn't see himself tiring of ever.

They drove all the way to his Station in Virginia, listening to her preferred rock stations while he anticipated getting her alone. He couldn't wait, but first they needed to check in with everyone.

The Wardens of Terra, Virginia Station was set up like one of those exclusive gated communities. Because of all the training exercises that were constantly going on and the amount of supernaturals in the area, they'd decided about two hundred years ago to section off huge parcels of land for their use.

Troy pulled into the main building which to a normal appeared like a regular community center. Of course, once you went down a level it was like something out of a comic book or sci-fi novel. Shifters and other supernaturals roamed the area. They had state of the art computers, an entire room devoted to arms and ammunition, not to mention the various magical artifacts that helped them determine and identify which areas to search.

That was where Rex and the rest of the Shifters and supernaturals in their Station congregated to dole out assignments. Only now, instead of training assignments, they were being given real ones.

"Well, well, well, the conquering hero returns! And who is this gorgeous creature?" Cecil greeted him with his usual bro hug, his stark white eyebrows arching as he looked over Andrea.

"She's mine," Troy growled, unable to help the possessive words that flew out of his mouth.

"Yes, baby, I'm yours," his mate pressed her hand across his chest, soothing the beast and wrapping him up in her smoky sweet scent.

"It's nice to meet you, please excuse me if I don't shake your hand. We are newly mated," she smiled softly, and her face seemed to glow. Troy echoed her expression, his chest swelled with pride. She was outstanding.

She blushed prettily, and Troy growled again. This time for a totally different reason. He needed alone with her now.

"No problem, man, Rex gave us the heads up. Congrats you two!" Cecil walked away laughing and Troy still wanted to throttle the idiot.

Rex strolled in a half a second later and stopped in his tracks.

"What the fuck are you two doing here?"

"Well, I thought I needed to discuss, you know, the mission?" he ended up asking it as if it was a question because of the incredulous look on Rex's face.

"Are you nuts? Get the fuck out of here until you two have completed your, uh, *mating*."

"But?"

"Look, Waman, I've been reading through the *Scroll of the Parcae* while Fernandez drove and that possessive instinct your feeling? Well, it's only gonna get worse, like until you start ripping heads off."

"What?" Troy had been getting more and more antsy the longer they stayed in the Station with all those unmated males around his Andrea. He thought he was imagining it, until now.

"That's why you were able to put her cousin through the door. It's all part of the mating instinct, until the bond is complete, your beast is gonna want to fucking kill any male that gets within thirty-feet of her."

Troy growled, then nodded. What Rex was saying made sense. His Thunderbird was cawing loudly in his mind's eye. He could feel the ripple of his feathers just under his skin, the beast wanted her. Now.

"You know, her cousin, he was a class six Caster man! No way one Shifter alone could have done what you did without the increased power of finding your mate. She's something isn't she?" Rex asked with something like wonder in his voice and Troy felt his jealousy rage again.

"We need to go, now," he said to Andrea.

"Right," she said and grabbed his hand.

He couldn't keep it together a second longer and before he knew it his beast burst through his skin. Skin turned to feathers and clothing flew all around them. He screamed into the air and Andrea seemed to understand, jumping onto his back and clinging to his powerful body with her arms and legs.

Rex yelled orders to someone and within seconds an escape hatch opened, and Troy flew straight out and into the night air to his home which was a three-minute flight from the Station.

As soon as his talons hit the tiled terrace floor, Troy switched skins. He turned his mate in his arms, increasingly aware of his stark-naked state. He used his claws to rip off her clothes, the two of them uncaring of the bitter night air as they struggled through the door that led to his bedroom.

Andrea moaned as he pressed her against the wall, his tongue dueling with hers in the warm caverns of her sweet mouth. Troy growled loving the feel of his lush mate's body, her soft, pale skin against his darker flesh made his mouth water. He wanted to lick her like cream.

He shoved what was left of her panties off her legs and lifted her back up. His hands full of her rounded ass, he walked with her backwards until he hit the bed. She straddled him with one leg on either side of his hard body. His cock throbbed between her slick folds and they both moaned at the contact.

"Not yet," she whimpered, pushing him down flat and using her palms and knees to move down the length of his body.

He tensed as her heavy breasts brushed against his skin. *Fuck and damn.* She was so incredibly sexy. She looked at him with passion glazed eyes and licked her pretty lips before opening them around his swollen head.

She massaged the throbbing vein beneath the head of his cock with her skilled tongue. The sounds of her sucking his dick made Troy growl as he pulverized the blanket beneath his claws.

She hummed around his cock, her cheeks hallowing with every dip of her gorgeous head. *Oh fuck,* every moan and slurp of her wet, hot mouth against his member brought him one step closer to coming and he was not about to let that happen.

He lifted her up and kissed the disappointed look off her face before lifting her body further until she straddled his shoulders. He wrapped his arms around her perfect thighs and growled deep.

"Fuck, mate, you're so wet and hot for me," he parted her lips with his fingers before he buried his face into her slit. He breathed in her scent and growled before teasing her slit with his tongue.

"Mmm, you're dripping, mate, what is it you want?"

"Lick me, Troy, make me come on your tongue," she moaned and rocked her hips, but his strong hands held her still.

He couldn't deny her, fuck, he didn't want to. He dove in, using lips, teeth, fingers, and tongue to drive his little mate wild. Her hands slapped the wall as she thrust her hips in time with his movements.

He couldn't wait until she exploded on his tongue. He doubled his efforts and was rewarded when she went taut over his mouth.

"Oh Goddess, yes, Troy!"

"Easy, baby, that's it, love," he said as she cried out.

He flipped their positions, bringing her down to the bed as he hovered over her. He smoothed his callused hands down her soft body as he brought her down from one height only to send her to a new plateau. He was not finished with his mate, not by a long shot.

He traced the lines of her body with his lips from the hollow of her throat down her long graceful neck. When he reached her cleavage, he licked a trail from one breast to the other using his fingers to knead and tease the sensitive mounds.

Her nipples grew hard under his skilled fingers and still he caressed her. He wanted nothing more than to drive her mad with wanting. *Yes*, he thought as she moaned his name. Troy savored every moan, he etched every curve, every dip, and valley of her form into his brain.

"Mine," he growled as he licked her navel and caressed the soft skin on the inside of her thighs.

She opened her legs for him, wiggling in an attempt to move him, but he wasn't done yet. He parted her lips with his fingers and looked at her.

"You are so pink and perfect," he murmured petting her pussy with his long fingers.

She blushed prettily from her cheeks down to her breasts at his praise, but still he continued.

"You taste like heaven on my tongue, mate, and I can't wait to have you there again, but I need you now. I need to claim you, my Thunderbird demands it," he growled the last and felt his beast flash in his eyes.

The heady scent of her arousal filled the bedroom and Troy growled as he knelt between her prone thighs and gripped his thick cock with one hand. He stroked himself once, then twice, his eyes glued to her pussy as it dripped in anticipation of his imminent invasion.

"Troy?" She squeezed her eyes closed and groaned. He understood. She needed him too.

"Yes, mate?"

"Take me, fuck me, make me yours, now."

He lost what little control he had over himself with her whispered plea. He placed his swollen head at the entrance to her slit, and leaned down, using his body to caress hers.

"Andrea Kristos, mate, mine, I love you," he groaned as he pushed into her welcoming heat.

He felt her then, in every single part of his body. In his heart, his mind, and his soul. She was his everything. *Andrea,* he sighed her name in his mind's eye. *The most beautiful name in the world,* he thought as he pushed in and out, loving her with every inch of him.

Yes, Troy, you feel perfect inside of me, he heard his mate's voice and almost lost himself completely.

"Is that real? Is that you?" he asked aloud.

She only smiled. *Yes, Troy, I can hear you in my mind, and you can hear me too,* her mouth was closed and yet, he'd heard it again.

This is real then, we are blessed by the Fates. I love you so much, sweet mate, I will hold onto you forever.

As will I, her sweet voice echoed in his brain.

Their bodies seemed to move in tandem. Thoughts flowed over their minds the way their hands smoothed over one another's skin. He plunged deeper as she arched her back, lifting to meet his every thrust. Troy rotated his hips, hitting that special place inside just as his pelvis rubbed over her sensitive bundle of nerves.

So good, almost, yes, her mind screamed into his. Troy moved his body against hers, the tips of his fingers digging into her ass, he lifted her higher. Her channel squeezed him, and he inhaled sharply.

In unison, they sighed and groaned as they satiated their love and desire for each other. Then with one final, hard thrust, they both cried out in unison, achieving release together as they never had before.

It seemed to take forever, but eventually they came back down to earth. Wrapped round each other in a cocoon of love, Troy slowed his movements and eventually slipped out of her.

"How do you feel?" he asked gathering her close and kissing her lips.

"I feel wonderful, I feel loved," she smiled and lit up the whole room. Troy touched her face and rubbed her swollen bottom lip with his thumb.

"You are loved."

"Yes, but for the first time I feel connected to someone, Troy. I feel connected to *you*."

"Me too, sweet mate. Our bond is incredible. Strong and pure, like our love for each other."

EPILOGUE

"So, Troy Waman, you have the honor of being our first mated Warden. How does it feel?" The ancient Herald of Terra looked at Troy with something akin to mischief sparkling in his nearly white eyes.

"Well, it feels great," Troy answered honestly. He didn't need to feel his mate's gaze on him to know she was intent on his answer.

"Ah, and your strength, has it changed?"

"We've tested Warden Waman and have found his overall strength has increased by more than thirty percent, as for the magical effects, we don't yet know," answered Phoebe Bright, the new Junior Station Master.

The spunky little Witch was quickly becoming

his mate's confidant and Troy was fond of her himself. He was glad that Andrea was settling into the little community he and the other Wardens had made for themselves. Of course, there'd been only a few female Shifters in residence as most Shifters tended to be males.

He'd worried about Andrea and how she'd do on her own when he was out on assignment. As it was, she'd been great. He'd converted one of their extra rooms as an art studio for her and she'd taken up her passion for drawing and painting and had even made some sales off commissioned pieces through a nearby art gallery.

He had plenty of money saved, but she was determined to do something while he worked. He was just glad that it was something she loved. She no longer worried about having money of her own since her grandmother had bought her Aunt Renalda's house from her for market price.

The only condition the Romani matriarch had was that the Wardens would strip the place of any illegal Dark magic artifacts. Something Troy and Andrea saw to personally.

When they'd returned back home, they celebrated with pizza and a six pack of her favorite German grapefruit beer, Schofferhofer. Afterwards,

Troy indulged in his caramel scented mate for dessert. His Thunderbird cawed at the memory.

He smiled as he stood before the Herald with his mate's tiny hand in his. He'd never felt stronger, prouder, or more complete as he had since they'd found each other.

"That is good, young Warden, you will need the strength of your mate in the battles to come. We were fortunate this encounter was not more disastrous, but the book is secured now?"

"Yes, we've sent it to the compound, Herald," he answered.

"A most excellent and successful first assignment! I will record your names in the ledger," the Herald lifted a giant book encased in gold leather and lifted his hand, without seeming to touch the page he spoke, and the words inscribed themselves on the pages, "Warden Troy Waman, Thunderbird Shifter and retainer of Aquarius, Status, Mated to Andrea Kristos, Romani Spell Caster of the Kristos Clan. The two of you have been bound by air as the Fates have determined eons ago, never to go asunder."

"Thank you, Herald."

"My pleasure. Many blessings to you both."

Later that night...

Troy lay with his mate secure in his arms as he

kissed her head and sighed contentedly. He noted the small changes in his bedroom and smiled. She'd brightened the place up. A pillow here, a painting there. She'd made it a home. *Their home.*

"What do you suppose he meant by that?"

"Hmm? What?" he asked his mind still whirling after the love they had just made.

"He said we were bound by air as the Fates determined eons ago," she said as she traced small shapes on his stomach with her long fingernails.

"I think it means that I love you, Andrea Kristos, and I always will. You're mine, mate," he growled softly and captured her lips, determined to savor his sweet mate this time around.

The end.

STAR KISSED

USA TODAY BESTSELLING AUTHOR
C.D. GORRI
Star
KISSED

WARDENS OF TERRA

Second chances weren't on Isabella's agenda, but when she's faced with one, the Fox Shifter has a tough choice to make.

Sexy Fox Shifter, Isabella Fuente has spent years learning to harness the powers of her sign and trying to forget *him*, the man who broker her heart.

A chance reunion at the Wardens of Terra Centennial Convention has brought Luis Fernandez, Jaguar Shifter, and retainer of Aquarius, in her path once again. This time, he is not about to let her get away!

A Tarot reading from an unusual fortune teller leaves them both shaken. Will Fate finally have its way with the two wayward lovers?

PROLOGUE

"Luis?" Isabella hurried through the forest behind the weathered *finca*. She smelled rain on the air, but that was hardly unusual for this part of the world.

Ecuador's coastal towns often endured the heat of the tropical sun followed closely by light to thunderous showers on any given day. The farmhouse or *finca* was as old and stately as the Station Master who ran it.

Armando Fuente had been Station Master for near on three decades. He was an Andean Fox Shifter and also uncle to Isabella and her older brother Marco. He'd been named their guardian when their parents died in a tragic car accident years ago.

She hardly remembered them anymore. Isabella relied on Marco to tell her about the way her mother smelled of roses and her father told lousy jokes to bolster her few memories. Life on the *finca* was hard and rigorous, but she loved it.

She loved her Tio Armando too. Well, as much as he allowed. He wasn't exactly the warm and fuzzy type. He'd raised his niece and nephew in the same way he did the other young Shifters in his care. With education, instruction, and rigorous training.

She looked down at her wrist where the symbol of her sign sat etched into her skin since birth. *Almost like a tattoo.* Except every now and then it pulsed and hummed with the magic of her sign.

The glyph symbolized the maiden and her bundle of wheat, an earth sign, representing purity and innocence. She scrunched up her nose at that. It was her hardworking nature and analytical mind that drew her to the sign, rather than her purity.

She'd often wished for another sign, Taurus perhaps. Like Marco. But that kind of thinking was beneath her. She was a Virgo and proud of her sign.

Still, it was an honor to be marked. Chosen by the *Parcae,* the three sisters who wove the fates of those who inhabited the planet Earth.

Isabella understood from a very young age that

she was special. Wardens of Terra were almost never female, and those who had the powers of their astrological sign such as she, an elusive retainer of the powers of Virgo, were exceedingly rare.

Marco on the other hand was everything a firstborn son was supposed to be. Born with the mark of Taurus on his arm, he was a brave, rough and tumble sort. Four years older than his little sister.

Isabella was younger and smaller than most Shifters at the *finca*, but she worked twice as hard. Both Fuente children lived at the Station year-round with their uncle.

The other young Shifters who were trained there came and went regularly. As they had for hundreds of years since the last time the Wardens of Terra had been called upon to defend the earth from darkness.

Serious minded as ever, Isabella understood her role and reveled in the fact that she was one of the chosen few. Despite Marco treating her like porcelain, she always managed to prove her worth in the practice rings and in the classroom.

Along with him. Images of a certain young man with dark hair, and impossibly darker eyes, filled her mind. Heat flushed her rounded cheeks and made her belly tighten. She moved faster, panting with the effort. *Tonight was the night.*

The familiar smells of wet earth, heavy air, wild grasses, and the occasional farm animal reached her nostrils. *Good.* She wasn't too late. *He* hadn't made it that far yet.

Isabella moved silently, a part of the night that swept over the land like a blanket. Underneath the smells of the farm and forest, Isabella found his scent. It tickled her nose and warmed her stomach. *Like always.*

On two legs, he smelled fresh and clean. His scent drew her to him then, but as his Jaguar it was that much more potent. She caught stronger whiffs of that musk that was all male, *all him,* with a hint of wild cacao and the *Tocte* nuts that grew in the forests around them.

It drove her Fox crazy. Her beast panted after him. The beast pushed harder, demanding she find him. One word repeated over and over in her mind. *Mine.* She took shortcuts through the brush, paths his fur had recently tread over.

Luis was part of the land as no other. He carried its flavors on his skin. Flavors Isabella found herself more and more desperate to savor. Confused at first by her growing attraction, she understood it now. More than that, she needed to tell him how she felt.

Growing up in the unspoiled isolation of the

finca, surrounded by mostly male Shifters, Isabella had very few friends and confidants. Marco was a great brother, but he wanted her to be a baby forever. What she needed was a friend.

Something all teenage girls longed for. She had no idea how average girls of the time acted in this situation, and she didn't care. He would understand. He just had to!

She'd been drawn to Luis when he first came to them five years ago. A tall, quiet boy, with eyes so dark they looked black. It was his twelfth birthday the morning he'd arrived, and it had been raining.

He looked so sad, as many of the children who'd been selected by the universe to serve as Wardens did when they had to leave their families. Isabella naturally flocked to his side. Her nature demanding she comfort the older boy.

He'd been angry and sullen, but she'd held his hand and didn't let go no matter how hard he tried to pull away. From that day on, she became his shadow. Marco, following his little sister to keep her from harm, found an ally in Luis as well.

Isabella should have been annoyed at first by her brother's insertion into their group, but she wasn't. Instead, she was delighted with their sudden threesome.

The boys, being closer in age, tended to leave her out of the more dangerous things they did, but she was quick to catch on. And she followed them mercilessly.

Luis was sweet and caring with her. Just like Marco. Only, she didn't see him as brother. *Oh no, not a brother.* He was something more to her.

She loved teasing a rare smile from his lips. She brought him sweets and good things to eat from the kitchens. She showed him where he could Shift without being caught.

Her uncle had strict rules when the young Wardens were training. Shifting alone was not allowed, but Luis could not resist the pull of his other half any more than she could.

Marco was not like the two of them in that way. He could ignore his Fox. But not her and Luis. They indulged in their animal sides more often than not. Changing under the cover of the forest at night.

He'd told her often enough that he found true joy in his fur, unlike the awkwardness of his skin. It was a teenage boy thing, she guessed. But she didn't care. Fur or skin, he was special to her.

She wanted to wrap him up tight and keep him with her. *Always.* Luis was her best friend, but lately her feelings had evolved.

She was no longer wearing pigtails and running after him barefoot. The change had been subtle. Isabella had started caring about her appearance. She'd tamed the wild red locks of her hair. Took care with her clothes.

At first, it seemed normal. Something all teenagers did. But lately, she knew, she did it for him. So he would notice her.

Isabella stopped and scented the air. He'd passed by not fifteen minutes ago! She had to hurry.

It took her a while to admit her feelings to herself. She hadn't told anyone yet. Sure, Isabella thought of going to Marco first, but decided against it.

Her brother would not be happy with her if she told him of her new feelings for their friend. Her stomach clenched at the thought of confessing her love to Luis, but to a Shifter, honesty was as natural as breathing.

Sure, he was two years older than her, and probably the most handsome boy she'd ever seen, but none of that mattered.

They were destined for one another. She was sure of it. Isabella had picked tonight to tell him how she really felt.

She crept through the overgrown jungle and

followed her nose to the tangy scent of Luis' Jaguar. It was sharp and strong, with all the nutty flavors of his Latin American heritage. *Like home.*

He loved to free his animal at night despite the rules that stated all shifts would be monitored and for brief periods only until the young Wardens had mastered their ability to Change skins. Something she had in common with him.

Isabella had only started shifting this year, a process that was naturally occurring after puberty. Her Andean Fox was small and sleek, with reddish fur. As opposed to her brother who was a beefy sort of Fox, dark brown in color and hugely muscular.

Much larger than normal foxes, she stood almost four feet tall on four legs and weighed over ninety pounds of pure muscle when in her fur. She had wicked long teeth and nails and was as fast as she was stealthy.

Still, she didn't see the Jaguar hovering over her in the branches of the walnut tree. His beast was easily the size of a tiger, more than twice that of a wild jaguar.

His weight knocked her down as Luis dropped onto her back. He playfully tackled her from behind, careful to avoid slicing her with his razor-sharp claws. He chuffed and growled, and she barked in mock anger.

They tumbled and wrestled until they grew tired. Panting and carefree as only children could be for those precious few moments in the jungle. Her Fox gave his sleek Jaguar a run for his money!

They returned to the cave just behind the *finca* before Changing back. Dressing quietly in the clothes they had left there, with their backs to each other for a modicum of modesty that teenager Shifters found necessary. Isabella sucked in a deep breath steadying her nerves.

"What is it, Bella? I can feel you are tense. Where is Marco tonight? Studying as usual?" Luis asked in a quiet voice.

She turned to meet his quizzical stare. This was the moment she'd been waiting for all day. It would change everything.

"Luis, I, I don't want to talk about Marco."

"Okay. What's wrong, Bella?"

"Well, I visited the carnival today in town," she began.

"You went without me? *Por que?* Why?"

"I went to see the fortune teller. I know you said not to waste money, but it was important."

"And what did this seer tell you?"

"Well, she told me that I was special, lucky-"

"*Si*. You are. So, what else?"

"She told me I was one of the few Shifters to be lucky enough to meet their fated mates-"

"You told her you were a Shifter? Isabella! Does Marco know?"

"No! I didn't! And this has nothing to do with my brother. She just knew. Anyway, Luis, she said I met him already and she's right. I have. My Fox has been telling me this since the first day I Changed skins!"

"Bella, wait-"

"No, don't you see? It's you! Luis?"

"No. We are just friends, Bella, you and me, and your brother."

"Luis, I am right. Marco is my brother and your friend, but he has nothing to do with this."

"No. I am sorry, Bella, you are wrong!"

His eyes turned almost black as he looked down at her from his height. Isabella felt tears prick her eyes but before she could move closer, he turned away from her, shaking his head, and took off into the forest.

Isabella stared after him with her heart in her throat. She felt as if the entire world was closing in on her. *No! Luis!*

When she returned to the *finca*, Isabella headed

straight for her room. She knew without a doubt, they could work it out the next day.

Only, he was gone. Luis Fernandez left without saying goodbye and Isabella Fuente cursed the day she met him.

CHAPTER ONE

*P**resent Day*

"It's hot as fuck here," Luis Fernandez groaned aloud as he stepped outside of the hotel into the blazing sunshine of Orlando, Florida.

The entire town was a strip mall slash theme park designed to suck in tourists with the thrill of a special getaway that cost more for one week than most people could afford!

It was crowded and gawdy as hell. The noise and smells were a noticeable distraction, but he appreciated the sunshine after the gray rain and gloom that was springtime in Virginia.

He had to hand it to the folks at Stein Luxury Hotels & Resorts, they knew their shit. Set back from the regular hustle and bustle of the town, this hotel was different.

Run by folks like him, that is *supernaturals*. It catered to certain needs. One of them being peace and quiet, the other being a huge, secluded manmade forest built for the exclusive use of the guests.

Indeed. He couldn't wait to let his Jaguar out. The supernatural community needed more safe havens like this to escape the daily grind! When was the last time he went on vacation anyway?

Fuck. The last time he'd been out of the country had been back when he was a kid. In Ecuador. *With Marco and her. Rrrr.* His Jaguar hissed and roared inside if his mind's eye. Luis almost slammed his head into a brick wall just to get the blasted animal to shut up.

His Beast was still pissed off with him for walking out on Isabella Fuente all those years ago. But she'd been a child. Almost his kid sister for fuck's sake! And he'd been a teenager.

What were the choices anyway? He would never get between his best friend and the guy's little sister! That would be a complete dick move.

So Isabella had had a stupid crush. That's all it was. *Then why did you run when she called you fated mates?* He ran a hand through his thick black hair and straightened his clingy t-shirt.

Because. He answered his own question. Albeit rather immaturely. *Because it wasn't real.* He was smart to leave before things went too far. She was so beautiful. Especially that night.

Her hair was a wild tangle of red that always reminded him of fire. She was pale with plump lips and blue eyes, her skin like ivory with a smattering of freckles and yet she tanned in the sun like every other South American kid.

Damn. It broke his heart now to picture her petite frame and round face. She was a kid, but at the cusp of becoming a woman that night at just fifteen years old. He was in serious danger of falling under her spell.

She'd been warm and sweet and fresh. Loving and generous. Everything he'd ever wanted having come from a cold and distant family. He'd had no choice. Running was his only option.

He'd never have been able to explain to Marco that he and his sister had made out, *or worse*. And, let's face it, teenagers were not known for their restraint.

Only a crush, *yes*, but one he could not allow himself to indulge in. *We were children, not mates,* he told himself firmly. The hollow part in his chest begged to differ. As did his Beast.

Mates. Mine. Though he expected his Jaguar's reply, it didn't make hearing the guttural word any easier. Just lately his animal had gotten more and more demanding. Insistent even. The bastard was a real cockblocking son of a bitch.

Sure, Luis had looks and charm, but the truth was he'd not enjoyed a single one of the dozens of women who threw themselves at him regularly in the last year! Stupid cat could think of one woman only. *Isabella Fuente.*

The shame he felt at his behavior made his ears grow warm. He had not even seen her since then. That hurt the most. She seemed to avoid her brother whenever Luis was around. And yet he remained friends with Marco.

Luis was a loyal man. A good friend. Yes, they still kept in touch, Even worked together a time or two. He listened to tales of Isabella told by her brother with a practiced nonchalance over the years.

But lately, he couldn't handle it. He'd been avoiding Marco and anything having to do with his past. *With her.* His focus had turned to his Station and to building up his rep as a Warden and more.

The Latin Lover. He'd gotten that moniker after a

night on the town with his Station mates where he'd gotten twenty, that's right, twenty cell numbers in less than an hour. He hadn't used a single one despite the teasing.

Stupid nickname! And now here he was, at the centennial convention for the Wardens of Terra, in the sunshine state, and still his Beast longed for the one woman he hadn't seen in over a decade. Not one of the texts or emails he'd sent had been answered. *Not one.*

His human half wanted to rejoice in the fact that she'd been wrong. They weren't mates. If they were, how could she ignore him? *Nah.* He'd been right.

No. She is our mate. Mine. His Jaguar forced the words into his head. The animal was furious at his human half for believing his own bull shit. He'd been getting harder and harder to control over the past few months, but that wasn't unexpected.

Approaching thirty was a rough time for unmated male shifters. His Station Master, Rex, a big ass Bear Shifter, had sent him down to the convention after he'd gone a little too far apprehending a lone Warlock who'd been looking to stir up trouble near their base in Virginia.

Take a guy swimming and everyone gets a little antsy around you. Well, in their defense he'd taken the

Warlock to the pier in the middle of the night where he'd proceeded to dunk him headfirst into the water.

Luis avoided the liquid stuff, you know, being a cat and all. He'd tied the guy's feet with some industrial strength fishing line and hoisted him up over the water by tossing the line over a pole right on the far edge of the dock.

Damn line was strong as fuck. Designed for shark fishing, Luis wasn't surprised it held the Warlock's weight though everyone else seemed to be. Fucking sharks were big.

The Warlock, who'd screamed he couldn't swim repeatedly, also hadn't known about that. By the time the night ended, Luis had the location to the altar the Warlock had set up with the intention of calling to the Demons who waited on the other side of the veil for an invitation to cross over and run amuck. Dark artifacts bagged and stored, no harm no foul. But did Rex feel that way?

Hell to the no. And here he was, banished to a weekend of conferences with a bunch of stuffed shirts. Well, at least there would be a party tonight. Food, booze, maybe a pretty face or two to pass the time.

Who are you kidding? They mean nothing. He huffed out a breath and walked back through the doors into the hotel lobby. He stilled instantly. The air sizzled around him. *What the?*

The smell of mangoes and fresh air hit him right in the gut. He stopped dead in his tracks. One foot still in the air. His eyes grew wide. He hadn't smelled that perfect combination of sunshine and sweetness in years. *But how?*

Holy. Shit. She's here! Luis' dark gaze devoured her from the top of her wild red curls to the soles of her tiny little feet.

Isabella Fuente was still petite, a good foot shorter than he was. The surprise came in the womanly body he did not recognize.

Sleek and lean, she was fit as most Shifters were. Her toned athleticism easy to define, but what had him gasping for air was the ripe roundness of her breasts and hips. Isabella was a woman. *And he was fucked.*

Well, if he was lucky, anyway. She was more enticing than he'd imagined. And he'd done a lot of imagining. Isabelle Fuente was a Fox. Literally and metaphorically. And she was his. *Mine. Roar.*

"Hello, Bella," he said into her ear. He noted the shiver that pulsed through her body before he found himself holding the side of his face.

It was all he could do not to fall right on his ass after her fist smashed right into his cheek. *Fuck me!*

"What the heck?!" She yipped and turned to face him.

"*Mierda! Lo siento.* Sorry, Bella, I just wanted to say hello," Luis rubbed his stinging cheek and eyed her warily.

Her chest rose and fell with the force of her breath, but she gave nothing else away.

No other emotion. He didn't mean to startle her. Then again, he wasn't entirely sure she hadn't been aware of him before she went all Oscar De La Hoya on his ass.

He could have sworn he saw her nose twitch in recognition, but that was a split second before she swung that deadly left hook of hers. She'd always been a boxing fan. *Damn. What a woman!*

Being the smallest Shifter at the *finca,* Isabella had endured a lot of teasing. Teasing that Luis had helped put an end to when he'd started teaching her to box.

"I should have remembered the left hook," he smiled, hoping to smooth things over with the easy charm most women found irresistible.

Not Isabella. One look into her cold blue eyes told him charm was not going to work. *Fuck.*

"How are you, Isabella?"

"Go to hell, Luis."

She turned her back and walked away from him as if he was nothing to her. He cringed as her red high heels clicked across the tiled floor of the hotel as she made her way clear across the lobby to the elevators. He watched as many male heads turned to watch the sexy Fox Shifter. *Roarrr.*

He felt himself tense. Was that jealousy? *Fuck yeah.* Head held high, luscious backside swaying, she pulled her suitcase along, pressed the elevator button, and didn't look back. Not once.

He didn't need his Jaguar's roar in his head to know he was in deep shit this time. Isabella Fuente was here for the convention, he had no doubt. It was as if the universe had given him a gift. One chance to work things out. *And hopefully not fuck up. Again.*

One thing was certain, Luis was determined to settle things with her before the weekend was through.

Mine!

CHAPTER TWO

Of all the men in the world! *Por favor! No!* Isabella knew in the back of her mind that there was a possibility of running into the last Shifter in the world she'd ever wanted to see, but having to face him the second she arrived? That was one thing she hadn't counted on.

Luis Fernandez. Just thinking his name was enough to send shivers down her spine. The way he stood there, all lazy elegance and sex refined, made her mouth water. It wasn't fair! After all these years, to have him turn her insides to mush with barely a whispered *hello*.

No. NO. She was not doing this. Despite her months-long communication with Phoebe Bright, a Witch and Junior Station Master assigned to their Virginia branch, the woman who'd convinced her to attend this conference to meet with her about a transfer, Isabella had no intention of tangling with Luis again. Not after last time.

Sure, she had been a child. An innocent teenager in love for the first, and only, time in her life, but that hadn't made his complete and total rejection of her any easier.

On the contrary, she'd been devastated. Turning to her training, she graduated the *finca* at the top of her class and had been traveling through Stations across Latin America since then.

She'd inquired about obtaining a more permanent spot at a Station, but the ridiculously chauvinistic world of the Wardens of Terra had left her high and dry.

Until a certain Ms. Bright got in touch. She'd wrangled it so that Isabella would attend the highly secretive Wardens of Terra Centennial Convention.

Here, they would meet and discuss her permanent transfer to Ms. Bright's current assignment. The Virginia Station or Station Northeast as it was called, seemed perfect. She just had to make it through the next few days.

Meaning, she had to avoid Luis! Easier said than

done. She growled as she walked into her hotel room, slamming the door shut.

Later that night...

The ballroom was dimly lit, but what really astounded her was the thousands of twinkle lights that were set up all around the grounds outside. After spending the afternoon listening to one boring lecture after another, she'd looked forward to tonight's festivities with eager anticipation.

She'd expected to run into Luis again but was lucky to have missed him. *Lucky or disappointed?* Her Fox growled the answer. An answer she didn't want to hear. *Find him. Mate.*

No! She shushed her Vixen. She didn't want to go there. Not ever again. Luis had done enough damage. She was focused on her career now. Isabella would never risk her heart again.

She turned away from the pounding rhythmic music the DJ was playing and escaped through the double doors to the colorful carnival that was spread out across the grass.

"What is this?" She asked no one in particular, taking in the lights and noise with a childlike thrill she hadn't felt in years.

"The Heralds decided a real celebration was

warranted given we have been called back into action," the deep voice was familiar and yet foreign.

As a teenager, Luis Fernandez had been heartbreakingly handsome, as an adult, he was devastating. The timbre of his voice was rich and deep, his accent all but gone since his departure from Ecuador.

She'd been a Shifter long enough to know they picked up and dropped accents easily with their acute hearing. Also, as part of their training, Wardens had all but mastered the art of assimilation.

Still. She hadn't been talking to anyone in particular when she voiced her question. He must have been watching her. The thought left her stomach tightening in response.

She inclined her head, a thanks of sorts, and moved to turn away. The rustle of her skirt loud in the sudden silence between them.

"Isabella, please," he murmured placing a hand on her bare shoulder. She couldn't stop the shudder that racked her body. And hated herself for it.

"Luis, we have nothing to say to each other."

"Isabella, I was just a boy then, let me explain-"

"That is not necessary. I intend to enjoy the carnival before tomorrow's rounds of conferences. Good evening."

CHAPTER THREE

Luis watched her walk away from him. He grimaced as unexpected pain lanced through his heart. *Fuck.*

This was the only woman in the world who could wreck him so easily. *She always could.* He must have sensed that as a boy. *Maybe it was why he ran?* He watched her with covetous eyes.

She was unapologetically beautiful. Had been as a child, but as a woman her beauty surpassed every one of his expectations. The curve of her back as she swayed in and out of the crowds. She stopped and chatted with a few people.

Wardens he knew or would get the names of as soon as he was done following her! Her smile was still dazzling. He remembered how easily and readily she had smiled as a kid. Her inquisitive nature startled him back then. She'd been so open and honest. Now she was a stranger. *Or was she?*

His gaze never left her retreating form. The thick mane of her glorious red hair fell down her back in a careless tumble of waves that managed to look artistic, though he knew she'd have done nothing more than wash it before dressing.

Her shiny locks were enticing, begging for his nose to delve in between them and breathe in her scent. Luis practically drooled at the thought of smelling her, *everywhere.*

He bit his lip, silencing the growl that threatened to slip out. Not wise near so many Shifters. He watched as others looked their fill as she cut a path between vendors and revelers. *Back off fuckers!*

He closed his eyes and counted to five. *Chill out. You're acting like a caveman.* He opened them again and flicked his eyes over the people milling about. Where was she?

He breathed again when he spotted her, walking towards a row of games and miniature tents. This convention was truly a spectacle. The idea of hosting a carnival to celebrate the Wardens' return was unique if not a little daunting.

Still, through all the lights and noise of the party,

Luis could only picture Isabella and her deep blue eyes that always seemed to sparkle. She used to love rides, he wondered if she still did.

He sided up to her and took her hand, ignoring the way she tensed. Without words he pulled her alongside him to a line for some whimsical ride that was bound to spin them until he got sick. He hated spinning.

She raised an auburn eyebrow, but he just smiled. Giving her hand another squeeze and marveling at the zip of recognition that raced through him.

The strapless gown she wore was the color of midnight. The sheer material clung to her sleek curves, revealing the smooth length of her legs through strategically placed slits in the skirt. When they boarded the ride, her legs close to his as they squeezed in beside two other Shifters, Luis draped an arm around her.

Beautiful, tempting, and utterly fascinating to watch, Isabella bit her lip and closed her eyes as they began to spin.

"Ahh!" She screamed in delight. Unable to hold it in as they went faster and faster.

"You always loved rides, Bella," he whispered into her ear, taking in more of her sweet fragrance.

When the ride ended, she tucked her wild curls

back behind her ears and walked away. A nod of thanks was all he got. Not that he deserved more, he told himself.

His Jaguar growled as more heads turned, following her gorgeous figure as she went. *Shit.* He was helpless to resist. He should leave her alone. Really, he should.

But all he could do was follow in her wake. A slave to her whims. *No. I go to watch over her. Marco would expect at least that from me.*

He tried telling himself that his actions were self-less, but Shifters didn't lie. Even to themselves. The taste of it was abhorrent. The truth was simple. He was connected to Isabella, and he needed to face the truth.

Luis Fernandez was no stranger to sex or women. He knew the games they played and enjoyed mastering a few of them himself. But he was done with all of that.

His Jaguar and the human side of him were finally in agreement. Something had to change. He'd been seventeen when this glorious creature confessed to him that she believed he was her mate.

Seventeen years old, when his whole world tilted on its axis. He'd been ashamed of his feelings. The desire in his heart for his friend's little sister. And so, he'd refused her claim.

Seventeen and scared. Dumb as shit too. He'd scolded himself thousands of times since then. And what now of Marco? His best friend. A brother, really.

How could he betray his trust by drooling all over Marco's little sister like she was catnip?

Fuck if he knew. But one thing was for sure. Luis could no longer ignore the rage of emotions building up inside of him just from being near her.

CHAPTER FOUR

Isabella felt eyes on her as she walked among the carnival booths. She supposed the Wardens and Heralds had much to celebrate. This was sort of a coming out of retirement party for them, she thought with a silly little grin on her face.

A ride. He took me on a ride. Too bad she couldn't let herself go and simply enjoy it. Not with him at any rate, and the jerk was stalking her!

As if the constant reminder that he'd found her lacking wasn't enough. *Ugh.* She stopped at a booth depicting a large eye and some interesting runes. *Ah! A seer!*

Isabella pretended not to notice the huge man who stood right behind her. *Ignore the fragrance of him, the subtle rasping of his breath, the way heat seemed to radiate off his lithe frame.*

"Still looking to have your fortune read, little Bella?"

"Luis, haven't you noticed there's a party going on? Why don't you find some friend to chat with?"

"I have a better idea," he said and closed his long fingers over her elbow.

She stilled herself against the shock that came whenever he'd touched her. Years since the frequent occurrence and yet, bam, there it was. The electrifying *zap* that sent pulsing heat through her veins and moisture to her core.

"Let's go inside," his breath tickled her neck as he pulled back the curtain and gestured for her to go in.

"Really, Luis?" but before she could object, he was leading her through the purple velvet curtain by the small of her back.

That tiny part of her that still believed in magic stood awestruck at the decadently decorated tent. She'd expected to see a small, older woman dressed in skirts with gnarled hands and two teeth, much like the one she'd met years ago in Ecuador. The person who greeted them was anything but.

A young woman, in her twenties or so sat behind a table. She had stark white hair that seemed dyed but the fact that there were no dark roots gave Isabella pause.

She wore cut-off jeans that were raggedy around the edges and a Ramones t-shirt. Bright pink ear buds were stuck in her ears and her eyes were closed as she tapped out a drum solo on the wooden table.

Isabella watched as Luis grinned at her. He leaned forward removing one of the earbuds. The woman looked at him from head to toe in a way that made Isabella stand straighter.

"Excuse me," he said.

"Ahh! Hey! Well, at least you're cute for an old dude, and she's a hottie. So, what's up?"

Silver eyes turned to her, and Isabella gasped. She'd never seen anything like this woman.

"Um, hi."

"You know, you scared the shit out of me pulling out my earbuds like that!" A New York accent met her ears and Isabella grinned. She immediately liked this young woman.

"Forgive us, miss, is your mother or grandmother here?" Luis asked in that gentle tone of his he reserved for children.

Isabella grated her teeth against it. She'd always hated it when he'd used it with her. *I'm a woman dammit. Not a child.*

"No? Why would they be?"

"Well, we were interested in a reading, but we can come back-"

"Ah, you're one of those," the young woman eyed him with a bored expression.

"One of what?"

"You figured, fortuneteller must be some old woman with a kerchief on her head and a long skirt, big crystal ball, yada yada, you know that's like sexist or something!"

"Uh, no, I apologize, I didn't mean," Luis stuttered, and Isabella held back a grin.

"Sit down Luis, have your fortune read," Isabella gestured towards the chair, and he looked at her eyebrows raised.

"I thought you would enjoy this more," he said.

"And I will enjoy watching you, that is, Miss if you don't mind?"

"Nah, I don't hold grudges. Well, slick? What do you say?"

"Okay, I am game."

"Good, that'll be fifty. You pay upfront."

Luis lifted one perfectly arched eyebrow but reached into his pocket and pulled out a hundred-dollar bill.

"Do you have change?"

"Nope."

"I didn't think so,"

"Great, *jefe*! Let's get started!"

After the regular deck cutting and shuffling, the young woman with the crazy silver hair and eyes focused on her task. Isabella gasped as the room grew dark except for the table.

It was as if a silvery glow was pouring out of the young fortune teller and touching each one of them. She reached out with her Shifter senses but felt only purity and goodness. The Virgo in her approved and she relaxed.

Isabella arranged herself in the seat next to, but slightly behind Luis, but she was not excluded from the magic that wove itself around the room. In fact, she felt it gliding over hers in soft, feathery touches.

"Well, you're a retainer of Aquarius? The second one at your Station?"

"Yes, how did you know that?"

"I see things sometimes about my clients. And she is a retainer of Virgo. Interesting!"

"How so?"

"Cut the deck. Perfect! Okay, let's see. The Queen of Swords? Good card."

"Does it describe me?"

"You? No way. That there is your *fated mate*. I see

you struggling with this, but now that the Wardens are called back so are the legends. Your mates are out there and yours, well, she's a leader, *Aquarian.* Tough as nails, she's worked to prove herself. But a warning, you need to do something big to claim her. My advice is go for broke, you're either all in or you are O-U-T."

Luis nodded, his gaze flicking over to Isabella who'd been listening with intense focus though she tried to play it off. She'd heard the rumors surfacing. That a mated Aquarian was at the Virginia Station where she'd hoped to be transferred to, but she hadn't really thought about what it entailed.

"You both know the legends, yeah?"

"Legends?"

"Of the Wardens and their fated mates?"

"Of course."

"Okay, next card. See this here, the Six of Cups and the Seven of Swords reversed, you know this woman. Have a history together. One that involves a third party. Not kinky or anything, but this person is stopping you from fulfilling your destiny. You deny your feelings to please this person, but it hurts you both."

Isabella sat up, this was eerily close to the reading she'd had when she was a teenager in Ecuador.

Could it be? She had spent a long time pushing away thoughts of being mated, but here was Luis and he seemed almost open to the idea? Her heart raced in her chest and her Fox sat up in her mind's eye.

"The Six of Swords here, that is the key. The thing that solves your problems. You need to turn your back on your fear and take action. Your Queen needs this, the Knight of Wands, fierce and brave."

"Fierce and brave," he shook his head, but the seer continued.

"Aquarian, take heed. The tarot advises with these two cards, the Fool and the Sun. Be young again, like the children you once were. Woo her not with your words, but with that imaginative, passionate side that you hide from the world. The Two of Cups promises a good union. Together you will be the Warden you were destined to be, and she will find hers as well."

"That's it then?"

"Well, yeah, but really dude, you need to just go for it."

"Thank you."

"My pleasure. Remember. Sometimes being brave isn't all claws and battles, sometimes its admitting what's in your heart. If that don't work hope you know how to use your tongue! For something other than talking that is!" She winked and when Isabella looked again, she and the tarot deck were gone.

"Well!" He exclaimed, looking under the table for a trap door or something.

Isabella's head was whirling in a thousand different directions. She backed away from Luis and his exclamations over the seer's sudden disappearance.

Holy shit. What just happened? Did Luis really agree to have his fortune told? And had the seer spoken of Isabella? No way. But yes. It had to be her.

Fuck. She needed to get out of there. Without a word she shot past him. She fled out of the tent and moved towards the edge of the private woods that belonged to the hotel.

"Isabella!"

She ignored his call and whipped off her dress and shoes, and the scrap of lace she wore underneath. A second later, she felt her skin stretch and her fur sprout. She needed to run.

CHAPTER FIVE

Luis chased Isabella through the dense patch of trees and shrubs. He found her shoes and dress strewn across a bush about ten feet in. He didn't hesitate before shedding his own clothes and joining her.

Like when we were kids. His Jaguar salivated at the thought of a chase. His chest rumbled as he caught her sweet scent immediately. Like mangoes and the fresh air of the jungle back where they'd grown up.

He hadn't missed the sweaty, earthy scents of his former South American home. But he missed her. He could admit that now.

Somehow that little silver woman had dared him to face his own truths, and as Luis hunted her through the small patch of earth, he admitted it, if only to himself.

Isabella was everything. She always was, always would be. *Mine.* He cursed himself ten times the fool as he lost her scent only to pick it up again farther along the stream that cut across the woods.

There he found her, in nothing but her human skin. She was sitting on the bank of the stream. Her hair a wild tangle down her back. Like a swath of fire against her paleness.

Fuck. She looked like a goddess. Maybe more like the devil himself, sitting there, drinking up the starlight. All temptation and sin. Promising heaven.

Luis' Jaguar remained still behind her, his tongue sneaking out to taste her on the air. Sweetness and heat filled his senses. *Mine.* But even his stubborn cat realized he needed his human skin to do this right.

"Isabella?" his deep voice cut through the silence like a hot knife through butter.

"You followed me?"

"You knew I would."

"No. That's not true," she laughed deprecatingly, and he frowned.

He didn't like that sound on her lips. She should be full of happiness, like when she was a child. Not melancholy.

I did this. I made her sad. He wanted to punch himself for having caused her one iota of pain. For all the years they were apart.

"I mean, I hoped you would, hell, I fantasized about it for so long, but after a while, a girl just accepts it and moves on," she shrugged her shoulder, her blue eyes intent on the running water.

Comfortable in their nudity the way only Shifters could be Luis sat down next to her. Close enough to touch her, but he resisted. *Words.* She deserved to hear the words first.

"Have you then?"

"Have I what?"

"Moved on?" He was scared of her answer, but he needed to know before he went through with this.

"If you are asking if there have been men, Luis, I guess you should know I am not a virgin. There have been men. Not many, but a couple-"

He growled and she narrowed her eyes at him. Dammit. He was fucking this up.

"Sorry, please, go on," he said.

"You don't have a right to get all growly with me. I am a woman, have been for a while. I doubt you're a virgin either, so please, don't even try that."

"I said I am sorry. Look, I don't know if I can

handle thinking about you with men, but what I am asking is if you have a man in your life *now*."

"No. Not right now," she said it casually, but his sensitive hearing picked up the increased rate of her heart. Good. She wasn't as cool and collected about all this as she appeared.

Not that he wanted her anxious. No. he just wanted her. *Fuck.* That was the first time he'd ever admitted that to himself. And it felt damn good.

Like a burst of heat after a long, cold winter. A drink of water after a drought. *I want her.* His Jaguar roared within him, and he looked her over from head to toe quite blatantly. Not averting his eyes the way Shifters did out of mutual respect.

"You are so beautiful," his voice was deep, more growl than man. He could hardly help himself and raised a hand, but he stopped shy of touching her, instead running it just over the perfection of her skin.

She shimmered in the forest. Her petite frame was made of strong, supple limbs, pale skin, and a smattering of freckles as if she'd been kissed by the stars. She sat there still as could be, all pale and glowy. Her blue eyes and red hair poetry against the darkness.

"Isabella, I have something to say to you."

"Luis?"

"You were right, sweet Bella. All those years ago, you, my brave love, *knew*. At just fifteen you knew, and I've spent all the years since denying it."

"What are you saying?' her eyes narrowed, sparkling with emotion.

"I am saying, I feel you, in here," he pointed to his naked chest, a movement she followed and waited with bated breath.

"I need you, Bella, you are like air to me. I need you to live, to breathe. I thought I was protecting Marco. I thought I was honoring our friendship somehow by running away. I am sorry. So sorry. *Lo siento, mi amor.* Can you forgive me?"

"Oh, yes, Luis. I forgive you, but I still don't understand-"

"I am saying, I am asking you to acknowledge my claim," he sat up straighter, the power of Aquarius pulsed through him, recognizing this moment.

"My Jaguar recognizes you, my sweet Fox, you are part of my soul. We are fated and destined for each other. Will you walk this path with me? Together?"

"Do you mean this, Luis?"

"Yes. I know I messed up, but I've always meant it. If you accept my claim, we can begin here, the two of us, as equals. Destined by the *Parcae*, those sisters who wove our fate eons ago, I believe we truly are *fated mates*. And I want that future. With you, Isabella, only you."

"Are you sure, Luis?"

"I've never been more certain about anything, sweet Bella, my mate," he closed the distance between them and pressed his lips against hers.

"Yes, mate," she sighed and opened for him.

Luis lost himself in the sweet soft slide of their lips and tongues in a dance as old as time. And yet he remained fully aware, in the moment.

Their kiss went on, his lips melded to hers. He swallowed her flavors down, reveling in the sweet complexity that was his Isabella.

"Luis," she moaned as her naked flesh met his. She pressed against him underneath the light of the stars above them, determined as he was to seal their claim on each other.

"I accept your claim. *Mine. Mate.* And I claim you as well, under these stars and this moon. Here, now," she spoke with increased urgency.

Her hands guiding down his taught flesh and wrapping around his shaft in an all-encompassing grip that had him going cross-eyed.

"Bella," he growled pushing her down onto the

grassy bank of the stream and levelling himself up over her.

She was so beautiful. All silvery in the magical light from the stars, her heart in her luminous blue eyes as she gazed at him. She lifted up, her legs wrapped round his waist, encompassing him.

"I love you," he said and sucked in a breath as he sunk into her wet heat.

It was like coming home, the feel of her pulsing around him. *Fuck.* He'd never felt anything like it.

"Yes!" she moaned. Isabella writhed underneath him, meeting him thrust for thrust.

Their bodies wrapped around each other, melting into one another, moving in perfect synchronicity. As if he could read her mind, he touched and sucked and loved her on that shore like he never had before. Losing his soul to her with each thrust and press of their lips.

"Now!" She cried out and struck him just above his collar bone. Her bite sent him spiraling into an orgasm unlike anything he'd ever felt. A fucking volcanic eruption of emotion. *Love. Possession. Tenderness. Protectiveness. Hope. Passion.* A million things he couldn't name.

His answering bite had her channel squeezing his shaft, milking every last drop of cum from his throbbing cock. *Yes!* He roared into the night air. Reveling in her orgasm. Thrilled at the combination of their scents that seemed to permeate the air.

Isabella was his. Finally. And he was hers. There was no mistaking that.

Mine.

EPILOGUE

"Are you sure about this?" Luis asked as he unloaded the rental car and led her into the neat, two-story home that was his as long as he was part of the Virginia Station.

"Yes! I never did tell you that I was invited to join your Station here, did I?"

"No, you didn't, mate," he growled playfully and kissed her quickly before tugging her inside.

"It's why I was at the convention; your Junior Station Master is an acquaintance. She extended the invitation," Isabella said as she took off her spring jacket and turned to face her gorgeous mate.

"Ah, you mean Ms. Bright of the blonde curls?"

"What is this about blondes?"

"No worries, love, I prefer redheads, come let me show you," he growled and did just that.

The end...

WATERLOCKED

USA TODAY BESTSELLING AUTHOR

C.D. GORRI

*Water*locked

WATERLOCKED

Will Nathan Silvertongue, a cranky SeaDragon, change his attitude after he gets trapped by sassy Witch and Junior Station Master, Phoebe Bright?

Nathan Silvertongue is a Dragon Shifter, bound to the sign Cancer, and a Warden of Terra. Called into duty upon the disbanding of the Hounds of God, Nathan ignores the first few attempts of the Heralds to get in touch with him. Living on a tiny, unmarked island, the SeaDragon left mainstream life decades ago, preferring his isolation and solitude, but that all changes when *she* shows up.

Phoebe Bright has been promoted to the rank of Junior Station Master by the Heralds of Terra. Her job is to wrangle and confirm assignments for her charge. If only she could find him!

Tracking down the elusive SeaDragon hasn't been easy, but this Witch isn't about to give up. Not even when he slams the door in her face. Literally.

If he won't talk to her, he won't talk to anyone! Phoebe conjures a spell that leaves the two of them on his island without any means to communicate with the outside world until they come to an agreement.

Sparks fly as tempers and lusts grow wilder with each passing day, will they survive being waterlocked with only each other?

PROLOGUE

Present day, Roanoke, North Carolina.

The Heralds have gathered once again to discuss the upcoming events impacting the Earth they swore to protect. The Wardens have been reinstated, but are they all willing? That is the question at hand.

"Do you have the Scroll of the Parcae?"

"Aye."

"Let's hear it then."

"Here it is: 'Heed me, you Shifters of Terra, we are the Parcae, the three sisters whose needlework determines your lifespans. We, the Fates, have halved your souls, the missing piece of each of you lies within your one true mate. The Wardens of Terra have been thusly designed with the intention of balancing your powers and focus. You have been truly

blessed above all others. Your fated mates have been written in the stars. Your destiny spelled out across the heavens. Follow your path to your other half for you will not know truth until that mate is found. Your strength as Shifters of the Terra will increase when the claiming is complete. Power will flow in abundance in the veins of you Wardens, and your mates shall bask in the glow of such strength. You have only to speak your vows aloud and ask us for blessings, if granted you shall be bound for eternity. Stake your claim, but strike with care, for once complete, none can destroy your mate-bond. Blessings to you who embrace the powers of your Shifter soul and the one true mate fated for you.'"

The ancient Herald tucked the timeworn scroll back into its leather tube, where it had been encased for nigh on a thousand years. His almost completely white eyes fell on the nearest of his brethren before he opened his thin lips to speak.

"And this will aid us how?" Interrupted one of the younger Heralds. The Wolf had only two centuries but proved his loyalty beyond doubt.

"'Tis Simple. We must bring the Silvertongue back to the fold," the damp, brick walls of the darkened room seemed to swallow the sound of the ancient Herald's voice. Though, he did not worry that those gathered had any difficulty hearing his words.

It was once again time for the monthly meeting of *The Twelve*. The New Moon was upon them, and the Wardens of Terra had officially begun their chase to beat back the evil that threatened the Earth once again.

Yes, there was talk of a new leader rising to take over the Hounds, but the Heralds would not relent the position of the Wardens ever again. A meeting would have to be called. A truce to be made. But that could wait. There were other items that needed tending first.

The foremost being the new threat that loomed over the Earth like a dark, ominous cloud. And like all new threats, this one must be dealt with forthwith. The Twelve responded as they did, by selecting the Warden most equipped to deal with the evil that lurked.

"Silvertongue must return to active duty."

"The SeaDragon has renounced his responsibilities. He has closed himself off on that infernal island of his."

"It is not for him to shirk his duty. 'Twas placed upon him by the Three."

"Yes, the Parcae have chosen his path."

"And the Demon has chosen his puppet. Ao Guang is back, and he is gaining speed. He has already begun

creating storms and tempests near the SeaDragon's own dwelling."

"The Green Dragon of the East is not at peak strength yet, but Silvertongue must act soon! To wait is foolish."

"Aye, but still he denies both us and his calling."

"Fear not, Heralds. I am sending someone he cannot turn away as easily as he does us, old men that we are." The ancient one smiled with his thin, cracked lips. He had a surprise for the arrogant SeaDragon. One that had been revealed to him by the Parcae themselves! Those powerful *weavers of fate* have chosen the Wardens as their very own warriors, and he would not let them down.

"Praise to the Parcae, for showing us the way!"

"Yes."

"Good. He shall have no choice. The Silvertongue must accept his place."

"And he will, Heralds, for the Wardens of Terra are needed again."

CHAPTER ONE

A thousand years I have dwelled on this solitary rock. Completely alone on this deserted island. My own private paradise. Ha! Yet true. I am better off away from the tailless monkeys and their trivial lives. The last SeaDragon has survived this long unattended, and I shall continue to do so till I draw my last breath.

Nathan Silvertongue repeated the words to himself, inside the hollows of his brain, as he slowly woke to the familiar sounds of rushing water. His cave, well, *mansion* actually, was deep in the belly of the island he'd claimed centuries ago.

Shielded by a cloaking spell it'd remained undetected by normals and most supernaturals for as long as he'd been there. It was perfect for him. His own place where he could roam as both man and his beast, and more to the point, where he could live his life the way he wanted to.

Not as some puppet on a string answering the whims of those treacherous fates and their puppets! *The Heralds have done well to leave me alone these last thousand years,* he thought to himself as he stretched his enormous body.

Yes, he'd mostly slept the time away. Dragons did not hibernate exactly, but he was able to slumber for years, even decades if he chose to do so. This last sleeping spell was a few measly weeks, but what else was there to do when the sole purpose of your existence was taken from you?

Bloody Wardens and their bloody duties. Well, he'd more than done his duty! He frowned at his thoughts while he checked on his supplies. *Hmm. Need to place an order on Prime stat.* His last round of improvements to his manse were nearly complete. He'd needed to wait for the cement to cure to continue, so he'd napped away the time.

Life went on, he supposed. He began the process of making coffee and scrounging up some meat from his freezer before firing up his computer. *Who knew a SeaDragon would be so dang computer savvy?*

He loved the speed and infinite possibilities

surfing the internet gave him. He enjoyed placing orders and keeping an eye on the weather and such. *No need at all for anyone else. Not on my perfect island.*

Though, in truth, he did miss actual interaction. The comradery he'd had with the other Wardens. Heck, he even missed fighting with his Station Master when things got very dark out in the middle of nowhere. *No one knows where I am. I am forgotten.* The thought was damn depressing. *No. Not depressing. I like being alone.*

In his day, he'd defeated every water witch and demon that had tried to worm its way into the Earth. He'd done so for centuries. *I was really something back then.* But Nathan had lost himself somewhere along the long and winding road of his life. *I like my life how it is. Alone is better.*

True, he missed the activity of battle. The mental and physical preparedness that came with simply being a Warden. He sometimes wondered how he'd fair in a fight these days. *Note to self, start a morning work-out routine.*

Muscles notwithstanding, he hadn't engaged in anything resembling warfare in centuries. Nathan was not lazy exactly, but he simply hadn't had much contact with others in the past thousand years. Once upon a time, he'd spilled blood, sweat, and tears in the process of fulfilling his vows. *Sometimes his own.*

He'd used his powers of Cancer to control the water. An element that was as volatile as it was powerful. Aware with each moment that it could so easily turn on him. Nothing was as invigorating as invoking his powers!

Most Dragons did not swim. More comfortable in the air, were his brethren, where he'd always felt the seas were his true home. *What brethren?* They were all gone now.

He was the last. He'd been the last *SeaDragon* for eons. But now he was the very last Dragon Shifter as well. Sadness and fear gripped his heart, but he refused to give in to the panic as he stood and stretched his large body before sauntering forward.

It was a hard truth. Nathan had not heard the trumpeting sound of his kind in centuries. He would go on being the last Dragon Shifter on Earth until his final breath. Which would not come for a long, long while, provided he stayed on his island.

It was not like the Heralds of Terra had much use for a dried-up Warden like himself. *Hadn't for almost a millennium.* Not when the Christian God took over and the Hounds claimed the Earth their territory.

Those dogs had some serious issues when it came to territory.

Bastards had called his magic blasphemy. Declared all other supernaturals evil. The nerve of those shaggy flea-bitten mongrels! Nathan felt the fire of his beast rouse inside his chest. He took two deep breaths to calm himself then proceeded to get on with his day.

He scrolled along the website, double checking his order, and readying himself to read the world news while sipping the dark Italian roast he enjoyed so much. The dark, heavenly scent made even his Dragon growl in anticipation.

Being isolated didn't mean he didn't know anything about life. Hell, he did have a Prime account after all. *What am I, a barbarian?* He scoffed at the idea.

All Dragons loved their creature comforts. *Even SeaDragons.* His hoard consisted of many irreplaceable treasures and precious gems, gold bricks, stocks, and bonds, and all the usual wealth. It also happened to hold every techie gadget he could get his hands on. Something that was a little difficult considering he lived completely off the grid.

In the beginning, he'd mostly relied upon lost ships and later, airplanes for his supplies. His ability to traverse over both the water and the air made it easy for him to find such cargo.

With the revolutionary advancements in industry and other areas over the last century, it had become almost impossible for Nathan to simply ignore the world. So he did what he did best, *he adapted.*

Nathan had spent months setting up various accounts all over the world under several aliases. Using addresses in nearby islands, and some on the mainland, he'd ordered and shipped his goods to those isolated destinations every month or so. Then, after slipping into his other skin, he'd go pick them up.

Simple really. He always travelled in the dead of night, when there was little chance of being seen or heard, using his special cloaking magic, of course. Nathan had amassed quite the hoard over the years.

Not just material possessions and money, Nathan had also studied architecture and design. Building his own castle or manse, as it were, with his own bare, *er*, dragon hands. Just because he preferred his own company, didn't mean he couldn't live in luxury.

Not at all. In fact, he'd managed to set himself up rather nicely. His *cave* was more like a true *Dracan Castle* these days. The Castles of the Dragons of old were truly a sight to behold. In that tradition, the ways of the *Dracan*, he'd used both muscle and claw to carve his abode from the rough rock formations that made up his sandy isle.

Nathan had always had a gift for the artistic. Now, with over sixty thousand square feet of space, that is three full stories with floor to ceiling, hurricane proof glass facing outward to the seas, Nathan lived in his very own castle. He frowned at the thought that he, the last Silvertongue, had accomplished so much, and yet would never share it with anyone else.

Sipping from his mug, he perused the security cameras set up around the island from the monitors on his desk. From them he saw his castle, glittering like a diamond on the topmost peak of the volcanic mountain that made up the island.

He'd installed solar panels and wind turbines for electrical power, along with a large machine that utilized the current from the nearby waterfall to generate electricity. Satisfied, he set his gaze to the weather. The program beeped and glowed bright blue and green as it charted some unusual storms and winds headed his way.

"Damn, I'll need to head out sooner than I thought," he muttered to himself as he checked on the steak he'd just put in the broiler. Nothing better than a charred porterhouse for breakfast! Normally, he'd add sliced tomatoes, but he'd only just awakened. *Note to self, check the gardens.*

Nathan enjoyed every modern amenity, including plumbing, satellite, and a variety of extreme sporting equipment like his treasured ATVs and Jet Skis. He also had a greenhouse, several yards of outdoor gardens, a mini orchard, and a smokehouse. All he lacked was company.

He frowned hard at himself for the wayward thought. *I am not lonely. I like my life as it is.*

He poured himself a second cup of coffee, sweetened it with just a teaspoon of the dark coconut sugar he preferred and sat down to his steak. Famished, he finished without hardly skipping a beat and was just washing the dishes when a tinkling sound alerted him to something amiss.

He sat up, not bothering to dress as he followed the sound of the melodious chimes towards his front door. There was no lock. No doorbell either. *No reason to lock things when I am the sole dweller of this island,* he thought. Nathan scowled when, to his surprise, the handle began to turn.

He tensed as he readied himself for an attack. *Perhaps some animal thinks to break in?* Unlikely. He'd fought any predatory beasts off the land centuries ago. Besides, what beastie could open doors, much less, best a Dragon?

The tinkling sound grew louder as his door flew open to reveal a blinding yellow light. Nathan lifted a hand to shade his eyes against the brilliant light that momentarily blinded him. The brightness dimmed after a second, but he still had to blink to stop his eyes from watering. *Dammit!*

"Who dares enter my domain without permission?"

Nathan leapt forward, claws extended, and growled the question. Every cell in his perfectly honed body ready to defend his fortress. *Guess I don't need to work out after all,* he thought smugly as his muscle memory tensed in anticipation of the upcoming scuffle.

His Dragon rose to the front of his mind, ready to Shift at a moment's notice, until he inhaled. Nathan froze. He'd just tasted the most tantalizing bouquet on his forked tongue. He hissed as his body reacted rather unpredictably.

Silver eyes focused, he took in the shape of his mysterious visitor. *Not an animal.* Indeed not. A pair of shapely ankles teased his vision as he took in the curvaceous form before him. A very female form. *Grrr.*

He cut off the growl that had sounded from his chest without permission. *Frisky Dragon.* He would not succumb to temptation, no matter how lovely the woman who'd broken his solitude was. *And she was lovely.*

Large blue eyes opened wider, if possible, as she perused his naked body. He hardly bothered with clothing, especially when he slept. He'd only just woken. Her smooth, creamy skin seemed to go pink as she stared.

Suddenly abashed, Nathan wished he'd taken the time to don a pair of pants at least. But why should he feel that way? Why bother dressing when he was the only one there? He stood taller. Too bad if she was uncomfortable, this was his home. *And I live alone.*

"I said, who are you?" *Sniff.* Witch.

He sensed her powers instantly, along with a light citrusy fragrance that was simply *her.* Tempting, but he needed to focus. She might not be friendly after all. *We'll see about that.*

"Nathan Silvertongue?" Her voice rang out. It seemed to wrap around him like a sweet embrace, while setting him on guard at the same time. What did this temptress want with an old, solitary SeaDragon anyway?

"Who are you and why do you trespass on my isle?" He spoke with the authority that was innate in one as old and powerful as himself.

He was, after all, Nathan Silvertongue. Six-foot six inches of honed muscle and power. A SeaDragon Shifter who'd seen more than a thousand years on the Earth. Breather of fire, retainer of Cancer, and master of the oceans and seas. He was none to be trifled with.

"I'm Phoebe Bright, Mr. Silvertongue. I'm a Junior Station Master and I've been assigned to you by the Heralds of Terra-"

"Leave," he growled the word.

Nathan turned his back on her, struggling to keep control in her presence. His Dragon was pushing forward, trying to get out, but Nathan couldn't allow that. *What the heck was wrong with him?*

Breathing in and out, he forced his Dragon back down inside of him. He would deal with the tempting Witch swiftly and efficiently. Walking back to the slate countertop that he'd cut and polished himself; Nathan sipped his cooling coffee. Ignoring her gasp of surprise and defiant glare, he chose to act as if she were already gone.

"Mr. Silvertongue," she said, her short-heeled sandals clacking across the smooth stone floors grated on his nerves as she strode towards him. He had to admit he admired her determination to confront him, a six and a half-foot Dragon Shifter. *She is brave, this Witch, even if she works for those bastards.*

"Mr. Silvertongue, I don't think you understand, my job is to make you do yours. The fate of the world is at stake here-"

"The fate of the world is always at stake, away with you now before I get angry."

"Get angry then! I'm not leaving until you fully understand and complete your mission," she stood toe to toe with him, her blue eyes blazing. *So pretty,* he thought. Then, angry at himself for such a sentiment, Nathan grabbed the Witch by her hips, lifted her to his eye level and dropped a hard peck on her kissable lips.

"Oompf!" She pushed his shoulders and he laughed, dropping her back to her feet and walking around her.

"There now, seeing as how you aren't here for *other* forms of entertainment and as I have *no mission*, Witch, I will say it again. Leave. My. Island."

"No, you are a Warden of Terra! Sworn to protect the Earth-"

"The Wardens are no more. Why do you insist on dredging up a past best left forgotten?" He growled as he shrugged on a pair of pants, no longer comfortable flaunting his nudity.

It was that kiss. That pitiful excuse for a kiss, the one he'd pushed on her meaning to frighten the blonde beauty away, had stirred something inside of him. *Something best left hidden and alone.*

"I am afraid you're mistaken, Mr. Silvertongue."

She narrowed her ash blonde eyebrows at him, her frown caused a dimple to peek out on one otherwise smooth cheek. *Stubborn. No feisty. Grrr.*

His Dragon seemed to approve of her resolve. She was a plucky little thing indeed. Positively adorable. *Wait? What?*

Drawing himself up to his full height he turned his silver glare on her. Nathan Silvertongue did not think this pest was adorable! Or sexy. *Nope. Not at all.* He wisely ignored his SeaDragon's dramatic eye-roll. But what was it she just said?

"Mistaken? How am I mistaken?"

"Mr. Silvertongue, the Hounds of God have been disbanded by the Greyback Pack, the Wardens are once again needed-"

"Ha! Those mongrels were defeated then?"

"No, I am afraid corruption within weakened them. The Werewolves have a sort of new leader now, they are re-grouping and, we are now allied with them."

"Ah! I knew those dogs could not remain in power forever. Not that the Heralds would heed my warnings-"

"The point," she interrupted his tirade, "is that the Wardens of Terra have been called upon once more. We are back in business, as they say."

"You may be back in business, but I am not," Nathan bristled.

How dare she come into his home, intrude on his island, and order him about! *Not now.* Oh sure, he'd waited for a hundred years, *or three,* to be called back by the Heralds. Waited for the world to realize what he'd meant in the fight against the Dark. But no. He'd not been missed. All he'd sacrificed had been dismissed. Grossly discounted, in fact.

He'd had family once. A mate. A home. All gone while he was out doing his duty. *Arianna, how could you?* Pain squeezed his chest briefly as he recalled his greatest mistake with agony. *Forgive me, my brethren.*

The names of the fallen whispered across his mind. *Bluewing, Diamondscale, Onyxclaw,* and young

Ambereyes. Four of the finest Dragons he'd ever known. All Wardens of Terra. *Like him.* Though they'd carried no sign of their Dragon's powers, an extra blessing, as he did, they'd had other gifts. But still, they'd fallen under the betrayal of the one he vowed to protect above all. The elemental Arianna.

Nathan shut down the images of the past. His Dragon growled against the pain in his mind's eye. But like a steel door, he switched it off, focusing instead on the curvy little Witch who'd dared bring up his past.

"Leave," his voice was quiet. Dangerous. But did she heed his warning? No. Of course not. Stepping forward once more, she raised her hands as if in surrender and spoke.

"You have been called upon, Nathan Silver-tongue. Terra needs you," bright blue eyes bore into his and Nathan shuffled back.

No, he would not fall for her plea. He was wiser now. Stronger. He would not be fooled by the Heralds again. Standing up, tall and only half-nude, he stalked the shorter woman until she backtracked to the door from whence, she came.

The sun was just breaking out behind the storm clouds that had been passing more and more frequently overhead. *Not a good sign*, he acknowledged. The storms he'd seen on the weather tracker were coming. *Fast.* He needed to get his supplies, but first, he had this to deal with.

"The Wardens may have been recalled, but I am not one of them. Not anymore. Leave my island, Witch. You'll find no heroes here," he slammed the reinforced door in her pretty little face.

CHAPTER TWO

Phoebe Bright gasped in shock as she was unceremoniously locked out of the SeaDragon's home. *Pompous ass!* She couldn't believe what had just occurred.

Her charge, the Warden she'd come to supervise, was angry and distant at first. Then, he strutted around *naked* like he owned the place! Well, technically *he did* own the place, but that didn't matter!

It wasn't nearly the worst thing he'd done in her presence. *Oh no!* The jerk insulted her organization, interrupted her every time she spoke, and basically just ignored her! Did he not realize who she was?

Phoebe prided herself on being a White Witch born of the *Coven Clarum*. She was the daughter of the infamous Starr Bright, the high priestess for her Coven and renowned healer.

Phoebe was celebrated in some magic circles as hailing from one of the most talented Witch families of the age. Not as gifted as her mother perhaps, Phoebe herself had a certain knack for creating *shields* and other *protection* spells with her magic.

That gave her an idea. She smirked at the intricately carved door depicting a terrific scene of a Dragon rising from a turbulent sea, droplets of water raining down from his great wings. It was absolutely beautiful, but she had no time to admire it. Phoebe had work to do.

She shook her head. Perhaps she'd have time later to remark on the artistic abilities of her reluctant host. A reluctant host who would soon have no choice, but to listen to her.

Could she even reason with the beast of a man? Maybe. But only if she remembered her training! *You've doubted yourself for the last time, Phoebe.* Standing as tall as her short stature would allow, she sucked in a breath, straightened her shoulders, and knocked on the door. *Loudly.*

"Mr. Silvertongue! Mr. Silver-"

To her surprise, the heavy thing opened. Phoebe hid her startled expression and was only vaguely disappointed to see he had further covered himself with a tight cotton t-shirt.

The thin fabric did nothing to hide his impressive muscles from her covetous eyes. And boy did she covet. *Wowza.* Shifters were generally good-looking, but he was positively gorgeous. *Must be a Dragon thing,* she thought as she tried to appear unaffected by his nearness.

Not that it was easy. The man was practically a god. His black hair was shorn close to his skull, except for the top. Long, thick strands of his ebony hair flopped forward in the front, almost hiding his silver eyes from sight. *Oh boy,* he was truly breath-taking. A superb specimen of man, *er, Shifter.*

She shook her head. *Criminy, Phoebe, just do your job!* Her job. That's right. She was there to perform a duty, one that did not give her leave to indulge her fascination with the sexy SeaDragon. *Um. Yeah. Right.*

"I thought I told you to leave," his deep voice resonated with something inside of her, making her squirm under his glittering stare.

"Yes, well, I didn't," she had to run to catch up to his long stride.

This is ridiculous. Her lack of height had often given her fits in her youth, but she'd never felt positively tiny around anyone. *Not with all her curves.* But being called "Shortcake" and "Mite Bright" all her life had given her a slight chip on her shoulder. Hence her skills with certain spells. Spells she wasn't above using now, for that matter.

With a wave of her finger a heavy branch from a tall Palm broke off and fell right in Nathan's path. *Take that!* But the maddening man simply leapt over it without looking back. He didn't even have the race to break a sweat. *Drat!*

"You'll have to do better than that."

"Mr. Silvertongue, I have no intention of doing 'better than that.' My goal isn't to hurt you. I just need you to listen to me," she stumbled over a rock, but quickly righted herself as she jogged after him.

"Can't. I'm busy. Have to go get my supplies. Make sure you're gone by the time I get back," he said.

Phoebe was stunned to see a genuine smile cross his handsome face as the ocean waves splashed onto the shore. Her eyes followed the movement of his large hands. They moved to the waistband of his shorts, gathering the fabric, and getting ready to tug them off when he cleared his throat.

"I don't mind you watching, but I expect you'll return the favor then," Nathan cautioned, one perfect eyebrow raised mockingly. He laughed as her cheeks heated and she could only imagine her hideous blush.

"No need to be shy now. Look all you want, if you like, *Witch*, but I should warn you, you'll never be the same," he winked before yanking them off.

A moment later, a forty-foot SeaDragon with placoid scales, every color of the ocean stood mightily before her. He glittered in the sun like a gemstone, his tooth-shaped scales reflecting light making it appear as if he glowed. *Maybe he did.* She wondered at his coloring.

It seemed as if he were made of the sea. His scales were dark, a deep, rich blue green on his legs and back. Then they lightened to a pale, almost translucent, seafoam green on his neck and chest. He was unlike any beast she'd ever seen. Phoebe couldn't hide her gasp of pleasure. *Beautiful.*

Large, unblinking silver eyes flashed at her, the knowledge of who he was remained in his bright irises. She thought him regal, magnificent. Definitely inhuman. Then, he winked at her.

With a lithe flick of his tail, the SeaDragon tucked his short, powerful wings against his enormously muscled body. He crouched low, leaving his imprint on the sand beneath him, before vaulting high into the air, diving beneath the waves in a move that left Phoebe shocked and awed.

"Wow," she whispered to herself.

The man was truly magnificent. That is, his Dragon was. The man was a bit of an ass. *Don't you mean he has an excellent ass?* She shut her horny inner voice up as she gathered her nerve and headed back to his house. One thing she knew for sure, he wasn't chasing her away that easily!

"Just like a Dragon to build his home at the top of a hill," she grumbled. The climb back up to the SeaDragon's lair was much more daunting than the run down had been. *Go figure.*

For a Witch, whose love of chocolate cake and caramel fudge was obvious in her ample curves, Phoebe was actually very healthy. All in all, she was in excellent shape. Hiking, swimming, and bicycling were some of her favorite hobbies. It was just that she also liked food. *A lot.*

Despite all her athleticism, the steep incline was hell on her calf muscles. But ever the persistent little Witch, she pushed through. Thinking of the ways she'd get him back for leaving her on the beach like some washed up piece of junk.

"Ooh, I'm gonna filet that overgrown sea lizard, just you wait!"

Arrogant bastard. And to think she'd been thrilled when the ancient Herald had visited her back at the Virginia Station. Even Rex, her boss, had congratulated her on the assignment. Then again, the grumpy Bear was probably being sarcastic. *Sigh.*

Well, she was here now. and she was going to make the best of it, dammit. Even if it killed her. *Okay.* Maybe not killed. Maybe just left her out of breath.

For the time being, she was going to break into his house, take a shower, and settle in. And if Mr. Sexy-but-growly thought he was going to send her packing, she'd show him!

He had no idea who he was dealing with. Whatever was in his mind was one mystery that Phoebe did not care to unravel. He was just another stupid alpha male. Probably resented her for being a female in charge!

"Oof," stumbling over the tree limb she'd sent after him earlier, Phoebe growled in frustration. This was all his fault!

She never lost her cool like this. *Wouldn't talk to her? Wouldn't listen?* Well, she'd make sure he stayed put the next time he landed on this godforsaken island. Now, what did she need for that spell? Oh yes! A little hair, *I'll get that from a brush or comb.*

Next, she needed some sand, *she bent and scooped that up*, and lastly, just a touch of intention.

Nathan Silvertongue, you aren't going to know what hit you! She grinned as she pulled her *Spellbook* out of thin air. Well actually, it was her magical storage space which existed on another plane of reality. Most Witches had one. She was still grasping the book when she used her powers to open his front door.

He didn't even bother using his Dragon magic to seal the place! Clearly, he didn't see her as any threat. Well, she would have something to say about that! Phoebe might look sweet and cuddly with her baby blues and curvy figure, but she could be one tough Witch when the situation called for it, and this one did. Lucky for her, but unlucky for a certain grumpy SeaDragon!

Stepping over the threshold to his rather impressive home, Phoebe took a moment to compose herself after her hike. She flipped her hair over her shoulder, aware that the humidity had probably turned her soft curls into a huge frizzy mess. She puffed out a breath and turned to the correct page in her *Spellbook*.

Using rhythmic meditative humming, she called the objects she needed to her and began the circle.

Magic pulsed through the air, tickling her skin, and making her grin wildly. Like all true Witches, Phoebe was born with certain talents. She always had a special knack for calling upon her limited stores of magic and using it to create shielding spells.

Spreading out all her ingredients before her, she bit her lip and concentrated. This was unlike any shield spell she'd ever done before, but she was certain it would work. She was a *Bright* after all! Nodding her head, she began composing the words that would teach the big, bad SeaDragon not to mess with her.

Placing his hair together with a strand of her own and a pinch of sand, Phoebe drew a circle on the smooth stone floor with a piece of black chalk she withdrew from the pocket of her long skirt.

"East, West, North and South,

I bid you shield Nathan Silvertongue with me,

Until my heart's desire's revealed,

None shall find us, nor shall we leave,

As I will so mote it be."

"There. Now he just needs to cross the threshold and he won't have any choice. He will have to listen to me if he wants to get off this island."

CHAPTER THREE

Nathan flapped his strong wings, lowering himself on the rock lined pathway outside of his front door. He gently dropped the large wooden pallet filled with box after box bearing the smiling icon of his Prime membership before descending himself.

The whole idea of being able to simply one-click everything he could possibly desire was even better than some magic. Humans certainly were amazing if pesky little creatures.

Still, the free shipping alone beat the hell out of hunting down grounded ships for supplies. Satisfied with his haul, Nathan flexed his claws after releasing his heavy burden. His wings ached with the exertion, but it was a good ache. One of triumph and success.

Not quite the same as how he'd felt after battle centuries ago, but still content.

"Grrr," he growled as he rolled his muscles, still in his enormous other skin. *Who knew the material items he required could weigh so damn much?*

His Dragon grinned just thinking about the treasures he'd collected to add to his hoard. *Especially the hundred bricks of Callebout baking chocolate.*

A puff of smoke floated out of his nostrils at the thought. *Grrr.* Nathan couldn't help himself; he had a rather serious sweet tooth when all was said and done. *Perhaps he'd make a pan of fudge brownies after he showered.*

Speaking of a sweet tooth, it was a damn shame he'd gotten rid of that Witch so soon. Luscious and plump in all the right places, she was positively drool worthy. *A damn sight better than his own hand.* But what could he do? It'd been a good century since he'd last experienced anything remotely like lust for another being. And yes, he'd felt a powerful lust just looking at the tempting Witchy morsel.

Grrr, the woman made his Dragon practically tremble with some frenzied notion of mating. *As if.* He knew better than to believe there was someone out there in the world for him. Someone the universe had created for the sole purpose of providing solace to a lonely old SeaDragon. No. She simply didn't exist. But the Witch might have at least provided some distraction.

Too bad she was working for those pompous assholes. He'd been shunned by the Heralds for centuries. Retired from his commission far too early. Relieved of all duties. However you put it, it all boiled down to the same thing. Nathan was fired. *And now they want me back?* Too fucking bad.

Speaking of fucking. His Dragon grumbled as he walked towards the mountain of boxes. Lonely was not quite the same as horny. And he was both. She'd entertained him for the short time she'd been there.

Good to look at. Smelled divine. Sense of humor. Rockin' body. Yes. She was all anyone could want in a female. Nathan shook his head. This was getting him nowhere.

Still, should have asked the Witch if she fancied a fuck before kicking her out. He mourned the loss as he nudged the pallet with his serpentine head, pushing it closer to his abode. He'd have to do the rest as a man. No sense in risking any damage to his home by pushing the pallet through a wall with his Dragon strength. *Been there, done that.*

He shook off the tingling sensation that had been worming its way between his shoulder blades and contented himself with the thought that he was better off alone. Alone with an enormous amount of gourmet chocolate. *Yum. Mine!*

With barely a grunt he shifted back down to his smaller, though still large, human form. It wasn't exactly effortless, but he was well past the days of writhing in agony at the change from one form to another. Magic swarmed around him, like a million small electrical shocks buzzing along his skin.

Dragonlings, or young ones, did not experience their first Change until well after puberty. He recalled his first time with a winsome smile. He'd been assisted by an elder, one who knew the breathing and chanting techniques to get him through the sting and pain of the experience.

He'd even studied it himself so as to help his own young at some point in time. Not that there was a need of such knowledge. He had no mate. No kin. He was the last.

Before the familiar agony of being the last of a species could fill him, Nathan pushed the large pallet towards his treasure room barely straining his muscles in the process.

The first floor of his keep resembled a modern-day garage or storage shed than a traditional Dragon's treasure trove, but he was content with it.

Rather than bury it deep within his mountain where he'd concealed his other riches, he kept this area for his contemporary essentials. Mainly power tools, sports equipment, back-up appliances, and food.

He mostly stored dry goods in bulk. Imagine his shock when humankind began experimenting with grains and foods. He'd been affronted by most of the species' supposed success and now sought out only the top organic, non-GMO products to fill his stores.

He'd installed quite a few industrial sized freezers and refrigerators where he stocked his perishables. Meat, fish, most of which he'd caught himself, and a large selection of cheeses and curds. Nathan was a SeaDragon with quite the appetite despite his frequent hibernation sleeps.

A taste for fine things, Nathan built a wine cellar beneath the first floor with a generous assortment of liquors, wines, and case after case of his newfound love. *Craft beer*. Oh, how he adored IPAs! And finally, of course, his necessary supply of chocolate.

"A pan of brownies, and a six-pack of *Shipwrecked*," the craft beer was from a brewery in a place called Maccon City, New Jersey.

The Full Moon Brewing Company was located there and had earned his respect with their full-bodied bottled beers, though Shipwrecked was his favorite. Several cases were in his latest haul. *Just in time*, he thought as he inhaled the cool, salty air outside his island home.

Having carved most of his abode out of the mountain that sat in the center of the island over decades of time, it took both strength and skill to cross the steep incline leading to his door. He'd taken his time so that his home was invisible to the untrained eye. With the development of satellites and all sorts of spy tech, he'd found it necessary to remain hidden using his brains and brawn, as much as his magic.

The door to his storage chamber looked like any other side of the mountain-scape. Rocky and inhospitable despite the landing, it looked deserted enough. Until, with a complicated series of taps on the stones and shrubs growing out of the hill, the door opened.

Nathan smiled, pleased with himself as ever. He pushed the pallet and all its glorious contents inside, grabbing one of the chocolate bricks before closing that main door, shutting out the world beyond.

He did not need to turn on the lights. Dragons had excellent night vision, though of all the Shifter species, he supposed his hearing was on average. Not that he'd admit that out loud.

As a superior supernatural, he was perfect! *If not modest.* The beast inside of him *hmphed* at the criticism, but Nathan just laughed as he opened the connecting door that would lead to his large, expertly outfitted kitchen. *He did love to cook.*

He sniffed the chocolatey goodness of the paper wrapped bar and smiled greedily, not paying much attention to the citrusy notes that danced on the air as he stepped heavily onto the smooth stone floor. *Zap!*

"Ouch! What the hell was that?" Nathan roared.

His head shot up, silver eyes narrowing as he heard a familiar tinkling voice gaily laughing as he hopped from one bare foot to the other. *Dammit.* He really needed to start Shifting with some clothes on. *Shoes especially.*

"That was a spell, Mr. Silvertongue. And now that I have your attention, why don't we both sit down and have something to eat. Then we can discuss why I was sent here," the vision of a Witch in front of him smiled brilliantly, showing perfect white teeth as she swung her hips and sashayed away from where he stood dumbfounded. *Little minx!*

Nathan growled at the little blonde who just

zapped him a good one! And in his own home. The nerve of this woman, to simply smile at him like an imp and swing her perfectly rounded ass like so much temptation. *Hmph. No.* He would not fall for her wiles! He was a Dragon, and she worked for those bastard Heralds. *Need to show her to be properly afraid.*

His Dragon opened one teal-colored eye and snorted a bluish sort of flame erupting from his nostrils with a *dragony* laugh at his anger. *Silly man,* the beast seemed to say as he curled back up inside his mind's eye, undisturbed by the presence of the little Witch. *Wake up, fool! She is a threat.* But his Dragon simply went back to resting, and Nathan snorted in disbelief.

"Why don't you get dressed and sit?" She gestured towards him, seemingly undisturbed by his nudity, and back towards the beautifully set table.

His table. Though to be honest, he'd never seen it set so carefully or with so many dishes at once. His stomach grumbled. *Loudly.*

"Please," she tilted her head.

Nathan hated to be rude. He was hungry and the platters of roasted vegetables and baked fish filling the surface of his long table seemed to beckon to him. *Oh my,* were those yeast rolls? His stomach growled again.

He placed the chocolate on the counter and waved an impatient hand over his body, quickly summoning a pair of fine linen pants and a tank top. He took a plate and started to reach for a serving fork, keeping his eyes on her as he did. *Why does she disturb me so?*

"Give that here," she said, eyes dropping to his hands as she took his plate. He wanted to growl again. *Mine.* Only he wasn't so sure he meant the food, that alone kept him silent.

"Let me serve you," she said with a smile. *A too innocent smile.*

"As it should be," he grinned, playing the arrogant beast to perfection, if he did say so himself. He ignored her exaggerated eyeroll and focused on the wonderful scent of citrus, *her,* mixed with the rosemary and garlic infused grilled veggies and fish. *Yum.*

He sat down, leaning back in the chair, and watched as she gave him a sampling of everything she'd made in his absence. *She touched what is mine.* An offense that would result in death for most who'd dared touched a Dragon's hoard. But for some reason, he was not angry.

On the contrary, he liked seeing her there. Really

liked seeing her there. In his space. With his things. She looked as if she'd been born to it. Made for him and him alone. *Grrr.*

"No need to growl at me. There you go," she grinned and handed him the full plate.

Her big blue eyes hidden from him as she continued to look down. That annoyed him for some reason. He wanted to see her azure gaze. *On me. Yes, she should be looking at me.*

"You first," eyebrows raised, he watched as she rolled her eyes again before focusing on him.

Finally, he thought, *those stunning blues are on me. Perfection.* He watched as she lifted her fork and sampled each of the dishes herself.

"Now that you know I didn't spike the food with any poison, will you eat?"

"I doubt there is much that could harm me in this kitchen, Witch-"

"It's Phoebe."

"What?"

"My name," she said, blue eyes sparkling in a way that made Nathan drool, "is Phoebe. *Fee-Bee.*"

"Phoebe," he growled the word.

He liked the taste of her moniker all too much on his lips. Speaking of that delectable body part, his silvery gaze zeroed in on her plump pink lips. *So darn kissable.*

"That is a good name, *Phoebe.* It suits you. Please, call me Nathan," he looked forward to hearing her say it. *She would cry his name in ecstasy. Yes,* he could almost hear it.

She blushed prettily as she lifted her fork, bringing tender morsels of the sumptuous food she'd made to her mouth. He found himself watching her hungrily.

His guest seemed to enjoy eating. Something he could wholeheartedly understand. Food was meant to be consumed. It was the end result of a good and hard day.

A proper meal prepared with warm, loving hands-. He stopped himself from waxing poetic about her. Reading any more into this impromptu dinner would be hazardous. He was simply hungry. As a SeaDragon, Nathan had an enormous appetite.

"This is delicious," he exclaimed sampling the citrusy shellfish salad she'd placed on his dish.

Bits of jumbo lump crab meat and plump shrimp were tossed with thinly sliced celery, cilantro, and sprigs of parsley. The combination was dressed in fresh squeezed lime and lemon with just a dash of sea salt, crushed red pepper flakes, and olive oil. *Superb.*

"Thank you," her demure answer pleased him.

She was delightfully feminine to his eyes, despite being so thoroughly modern. He appreciated her differences and wondered what other mysteries the sexy as sin Witch was hiding. *I will find you out.*

"Maybe we can chat a bit? Get to know each other?" She forked a shrimp and ate it in tiny, precise bites. *So very tempting. Grrr.*

"Very well. I am a SeaDragon, Phoebe Bright. I like my meat charred, my vegetables crisp, and my women soft and receptive," he growled the last part, guiltily enjoying the way her cheeks blushed red.

"Well, I am sorry to disappoint you, Mr. Silver-tongue, but I am not on the menu," head high, she looked him squarely in the eyes as she responded to his barely disguised insinuation.

She had grit; he'd give her that. He allowed her to steer the conversation to safer waters as they ate their meal. A surprisingly good meal, he had to admit. Nathan couldn't recall the last time he'd dined with someone. Especially one so easy on the eyes.

"Allow me," he rose gracefully from the table just

as she finished eating. Refusing to have her clean up after the wonderful meal she'd made.

"Were you always a good cook?" He asked as he cleared away empty platters. His manners might be a bit rusty, but he knew enough to not make a complete ass of himself.

"I suppose I just always liked to cook," she shrugged as she handed him dishes, "I mean, you can tell I like to eat."

"You look fine, Phoebe, just fine," he said, his silver eyes piercing hers. For some reason, it bothered him to hear her say that about herself as if it were a bad thing. Liking food and oneself was healthy. Besides, she was stunning.

"Sit, please," he softened his tone.

She looked at him, her expression one of shock and he felt embarrassed by his earlier behavior. He'd been harsh, but she'd caught him off guard. Besides, one meal didn't change anything. She worked for the Heralds. Those who'd abandoned him. *My enemies. Those I've longed to hunt down and maim for centuries.* And yet, he felt compelled to treat her with honor and respect.

Pleasure flowed through him as she sat down, just as he'd asked. Taking a seat at the counter, she watched quietly while he loaded the dishwasher and placed the leftovers in a container. Not that there were many. The food had truly been marvelous. Cleaning the mess was the least he could do.

"I confess, I usually catch some fish and serve it grilled alongside a few basic vegetables. I never dress it up like you did-"

"I am spry if you didn't like it," she wrinkled her nose as she spoke.

"Quite the contrary, Phoebe. This was a real treat for me."

"Oh," she blushed prettily, tucking a stray strand of hair behind her tiny, seashell of an ear, "it's all in the herbs, actually."

Suspicion lifted his brows, but he dismissed it. *Witches brewed potions. Surely, she had not tried to poison me.* She'd said as much. Besides, no, he would have been able to tell if she were lying.

"I'm going to toss this in the compost outside," he gestured to some organic scraps.

"No!" She yelled and slipped off the stool to her sandal clad feet.

"Um, wait!"

"Why?" Nathan turned slowly, unsure of her sudden outburst, "Phoebe?"

"Well, actually. It is kind of a funny story-"

"Why don't you tell it then?"

"Okay. Like I said before, I am here at the command of the *Heralds*. You've been reinstated and there is an immediate threat-"

"No! I told you, I do not work for them any longer."

"But you're a retainer of Cancer! Do you know how rare it is to have a Shifter who can control water?"

"I don't care! They dumped me here in this place! Forgot I existed! I will not go back!" With that Nathan stormed to the front door.

He turned the knob and pulled, revealing a fresh storm brewing outside, but what did he care? A little rain couldn't hurt him. No water could. He was a SeaDragon after all.

Without looking back at her mumbled *wait*, Nathan stepped over the threshold. *Er*, well, he tried to. A sudden, shockingly strong force propelled him backwards, tossing him onto the cold, stone floor with more force than a normal electrical shock.

"What the-"

"Are you okay?" rushing to his side, Phoebe skidded to a stop just in front of him.

His eyes were level with her shapely ankles under her long, flowing skirt. He wondered if her skin was as soft as it appeared. *Grrr*. He bit his tongue to keep from growling aloud as he took in her appearance from his position on the floor. *Her not exactly surprised appearance at my being laid out like a Dragonling after his first thrashing.*

Guilt and apology lingered in her bright blue eyes and Nathan could have howled in disbelief. His little Witch cast a spell on him! *The nerve.* And what was the spell exactly? His head was about to burst as pain lanced through his body. Nathan was livid at the sheer audacity of the little Witch. *First, she feeds me, then she tries to kill me.*

"No, not kill, it's just-"

"Did you read my mind, Witch?"

"Um, no, you kind of said that other stuff out loud. But I promise I was not intending to kill you."

"Step back," he huffed.

With the utmost care, Nathan regained his feet. Stalking her to the long sectional couch in his living room, he almost laughed when she landed on her butt on one of the cushioned seats.

He leaned over, trapping her with his large arms on either side of her delectable little body. The Witch squirmed under his relentless stare. Her brilliant white teeth worried her lower lip, he used all his control to stop himself from licking the abused flesh. *She tries to maim me, and I still want her. Bloody hell.*

"What. Did. You. Do." More command than question, Nathan waited as she hemmed and hawed internally.

Finally, after a few seconds she raised her heart-shaped face, blue-eyes glistening with determination and more spunk than he'd given her credit for and met his angry stare. Inhaling a deep breath, she blurted words so fast he could hardly understand her.

"Isortofputaspellonyou-"

"Slow down," Nathan crossed his arms and glared at the Witch, his hackles rising with each second that passed.

"Okay," she inhaled another deep, deep breath. This one pushed her ample bosoms out, nearly calling them to spill from their flimsy confines.

Nathan's brain short-circuited for a second at the glorious sight. She was beautiful, there was no denying that. All pale, milky skin, pink lips, and blue eyes. Not to mention her hair, like spun gold. And that body of hers, *groan*, perfectly rounded for a Dragon's hands! *Grrr.*

"Okay," she started.

Fuck. Pay attention. He had to literally shake his

head to remind himself to listen to what the woman was saying. *I've been far too long without a woman.*

"Well, there's no easy way to do this without coming right out and saying it. So, *well*, um, I sort of put a teensy-weensy little spell on your house," she winced as the last word left her mouth and he almost smiled. *Almost.* She was really just so damn cute.

"What kind of spell?" Curiosity as to what the Witch had brewed up while he was off getting his supplies forced the question from his lips.

"A confinement spell. *Kind of.* Well-"

"Phoebe, what exactly did you do?"

Trepidation crept up his spine. And here he'd thought she'd stayed because she too felt the fierce attraction between them. Was he wrong? He could smell her arousal as it flared to life when she'd watched his naked form earlier. She was definitely interested. But then why all this subterfuge? Those blasted bosses of hers, that's why!

"Well, you wouldn't listen to me! I have a job to do, Nathan. An important one-"

"You did *this*," he gestured to the table then glared once again at her, "prepared all this food, flirted shamelessly, all to tempt me back into the fold?"

"I did not flirt with you!"

"What do you call batting those ridiculously blue

eyes then? And flaunting your delicious curves in my face? You took me for a fool!"

"No, that's not what I did!" She stomped her foot on the floor, anger making her cheeks redden.

He wondered if she'd flush that way under other circumstances. Anger flared to life, replacing arousal as he reminded himself that she was a spy come to trick him.

"Of course it is what you did! It's why *they* sent *you*. A woman after my many years in exile. The Heralds are using you to get to me."

"No, look, I realize you may have been cooped up here for centuries, but this isn't the freaking ice age, buddy! I am a fully qualified Junior Station Master! And yes, I cast a spell on this place to get you to listen to me!"

"Fat lot of good that will do you, Witch! I am a Dragon. Your powers can't hold me here."

He stalked back over to the front door, looking in the corners for any magical item she may have used to stop his entry earlier. Not finding any he grabbed some salt and tossed it over the threshold.

It wasn't much, but salt was known to neutralize some spells. Surely, this Witch had no real power. His beast would be agitated by her if she posed a serious threat. *Wouldn't he?*

"Nathan. Stop. I wouldn't try that-"

He snarled in her direction before he took a few steps back, attempting to stop him mid-sprint would require some powerful magic. He doubted she could hold a flea much less him, a powerful SeaDragon and retainer of Cancer!

Famous. Last. Words. A huge volt of electricity struck his body the second he came into contact with the doorway. Nathan realized that he might have been a little hasty in his appraisal of her powers as he flew across the room, back landing against the heavy stone mantle of his fireplace. He closed his eyes at the crack he heard and shuddered to think of the damage that little stunt had done to his home.

"I told you not to do that," the extended hand hovered above his face, but he couldn't move just yet.

It hurt to breathe at the moment. Not that he would admit it. *Fuck.* She was powerful. Of course she was. *And beautiful.* But he closed his mind off to that second thought.

He'd been foolish to think the Heralds would send someone who was weak to rouse him. *Interesting.* Even more interesting was the way his Dragon still did not stir despite the pain inflicted on his person.

What do you mean just lying about while I'm being attacked? He spoke to his Dragon in his mind's eye, but the beast merely curled up and slumbered on. Finally, he was able to breathe a little easier. He sat up, ignoring the concern in her gaze.

"Tell me *exactly* what it is that you did."

"I told you. It's a confinement spell. When you returned from your errands and stepped foot inside this house, you became bound to this space. Me too actually. The spell is on both us and your home. We won't be able to leave or communicate with the outside world until we come to an agreement."

"You did *what!*" He roared.

CHAPTER FOUR

Phoebe was proud of herself for not trembling in the face of a mightily pissed off SeaDragon the night before last.

She'd actually thought he was kinda cute. Until he started ignoring her and stomping around the house like a two-year old. *I mean, really?*

Forty-eight hours of dirty looks and a refusal to talk to her and she was going nuts. She was a bubbly person, she enjoyed long talks and even the occasional debate. This silent treatment was not gonna do.

She sat *crisscross-applesauce* on the gorgeous antique throw rug that graced his living room floor while she watched him as he once again emerged freshly showered from his private rooms. With an angry glint in his silver eyes and barely a glance in her direction, he walked round the whole first floor.

Room to room, like he had the past two days, and looked for a way out. For some weakness in her spell. *As if.* She cooked every night since she arrived, but he'd refused to eat the last two meals. Charring some plain meat for himself before returning to his room.

It hurt that he wouldn't partake of the food she'd prepared, but she tried not to let it show. After all, she was there for one purpose. To bring him back to the fold.

"*Om,*" she exhaled. Phoebe tried to focus on her meditation again. Distracted by the half-naked SeaDragon walking about what she now considered as her space. His ancient Dragon's markings glinted in the dim light from its place on the lower left side of his waist making her mouth water.

Focus, Phoebe. Running her hands along the soft carpet, she once again marveled of the feel of the rich fabric. *Must be Persian. Ooh. So soft.*

She'd changed into her comfiest pajamas before attempting to start her nightly meditation. The sky-blue short set was made of washable silk and felt great against her skin. The fit was loose and baggy, not that she worried about tempting the beast of a man. As she'd done the past two evenings, she'd set up her relaxation candle, bowl, and incense as she tried to release all the remaining tension of her day.

The peaceful scents of lavender and chamomile filled the air while she chanted to relieve the stress of the day. A crash sounded from the next room, but instead of rushing to his aid as she'd done the first night. *Six times the first night,* with no thanks from Nathan, she simply continued with what she was doing.

It was difficult given the rather colorful curses coming her way from what she now knew was his bedroom. *Oh well. That'll teach him to underestimate women!*

Heavy footsteps thudded her way pausing just in front of her. The sound of his forced breathing almost crept into her me time, but she wasn't about to give in to whatever tantrum he was about to throw next. Phoebe ignored them while she finished thanking *the Goddess* for all her blessings of the day and recited her vow to use her magic for good.

She opened her eyes only to be startled by the wild silver gaze of her new roomie. Her soaking wet roomie. He must have tried to leave through the *bathroom* window. *Yikes.* Maybe she should have warned him that her spell would do whatever it took to keep them both locked inside.

"Get. Rid. Of. It."

"Excuse me? I'm sorry, I couldn't understand you with all the growling."

"I said, remove the spell, Witch."

"Um, no."

"What do you mean no?"

"I mean, I can't. It won't work. The terms of the spell must be fulfilled, or it will simply go on forever."

Her answer was met with more growling, but Phoebe simply stood. Ignoring him, she waved her hand and cleared the area of her belongings. Moving objects to the storage space between realms where most Witches hid their goods was a snap. Breaking spells already in the works, not so much.

"Okay, well I've had a long day being ignored and I'm tired now. So, goodnight, Nathan. I'll try and get comfortable on this giant, hard lump you call a couch," she snarled.

Phoebe tried to walk past her host but found herself frozen in place. The sea air scent that clung to him tickled her nose causing tingles to race up her spine. The feeling only grew stronger as a large, feral smile spread across his handsome face. *Uh oh.*

"My couch is not to your liking, Witch? Well, we can't have that," Nathan stalked her across the room. His silver gaze raking her in from head to foot, penetrating her flimsy pajamas and suddenly she wished she'd worn something else.

Like that fuzzy, purple unicorn footie pajama her friend Isabella and her mate Luis had given her for Christmas last year as a gag gift. A low growl seemed to emanate from Nathan's throat as he crowded her. *Shit.* He was a predator.

Top of the food chain actually, but she forced herself to remain still as he moved in closer. Drops of water splattered loudly against the stone floor from his still soaked clothes. Her spell must have used the growing waves outside to force him back into the dwelling when he'd tried escaping. *Oops.*

"Um, look, Nathan, I realize we might have gotten off on the wrong foot-"

"Oh, what gave you that idea?"

"If you'll just listen to me-"

"You are the last person I want to listen to. If the couch doesn't suit you, I suggest you sleep on the floor, *Junior Station Master*," he flung her title at her like it was something obscene and she recoiled.

Shame filled her as he turned and walked away, slamming the door to his bedroom with a loud, resounding thud. Phoebe became aware of two things in that moment.

One, she was actually starting to care about the oaf. And two, she was going to have to sleep on the stupid rock-hard couch again. No matter what he said, she would not sleep on the floor like some sort of stray cat. *The jerk.*

Thank goodness the maddening SeaDragon stood over six and a half feet tall, she thought as she fluffed one of the few pillows on his overly big sofa and attempted to get snuggly. Unfortunately, it hadn't worked out well the past two nights, and she doubted she'd have much success this night.

Plus, she couldn't seem to find a thick blanket and didn't have anything other than a thin afghan in storage. *Damn.* She shivered a little, curving her body into a ball as she wiggled closer to the almost extinguished fire.

"Some gentleman. Taking the bedroom, leaving me out here alone, *again*," she muttered as she tossed and turned on the unbelievably uncomfortable couch.

Dammit. She was never going to get any sleep out there in the cold living room. Some island this turned out to be! After she'd spent weeks tracking the damnable SeaDragon to the remote, unchartered isle, she'd at least expected to be greeted with some tropical sunshine! But no, instead she raced ahead of the looming hurricane that was about to hit them.

Brought on by some maniac demon trying to get a foothold on the world! And to top it all off, the fool who was supposed to be her newest and first solo charge wouldn't even listen to one word about it! *Arghhhh!*

How was she going to get him to use his powers of Cancer to stop this threat? *That's it*, she thought, standing up much too quickly in the pitch-dark room.

"Oof!" she yelped, banging her shin on the marble coffee table, and hopping up and down in pain.

The little scream did some good at least. It sent a half-asleep Nathan running into the living room, in nothing but his skin. *Yummy, yummy, tanned skin.*

"What is it! Who's there?" He roared, looking around baffled and yet ready to tear apart the whole room. *For her?* Her heart warmed at the idea, but she didn't waste time thinking about it.

Phoebe did the only thing she could under the

circumstances. She slipped right past him and jumped in the bed, snuggling deep into the thick comforter that was still warm from his body.

"What the hell are you doing?"

"Look, I'm cold and I'm tired. I'm going to bed."

"Not in here you're not!"

"Oh, yes I am! Just try removing me from this bed, *cupcake*, and I'll turn every damn article of clothing you own into haircloth!" Her threat seemed to hold weight with him if the shudder that went through his powerful body was any indication. *Guess the rumors were true about Dragons, they loved their comforts!*

"I told you to take the couch," he grumbled.

"You take it. There's no blanket out there, the couch is hard as a rock, it's cold, and the wind is too loud," Phoebe bit her bottom lip.

She pulled the comforter up and around, covering her body from throat to foot. Still, she didn't miss the look of astonishment that crossed his handsome face once he figured out the reason for her behavior. *Damn.*

"You're afraid?!" Surprise laced his words as Phoebe sulked deeper into the pillows.

So what if she was a scaredy-Witch when it came to being in strange places alone at night? She hated the dark. She also despised being alone. That's why she had a roommate all lined up back home. That is she *had* one, until Isabella reunited with her old crush. She was now living happily-ever-after with her mate, a fellow Warden of Terra, Luis Fernandez.

Both Shifters dwelt and worked at the Virginia Station where Phoebe was Junior Station Master. Between them and the other mated pair, Troy and Andrea, things were getting kind of tense at the old quarters. What with the two pairs in a constant state of mutual admiration and the rest of the gang trying to keep their jealousy under wraps.

It wasn't easy, but mostly they just had to remember these were their friends. Rex wasn't happy of course. The Bear Shifter was used to being exceedingly powerful, but the mated Shifters certainly gave him a run for his money. But that wasn't the real reason why he was so averse to love, not that he actually confided in Phoebe or anything. Sometimes she had a sixth sense about these things.

The rumors of increased powers when a Shifter found his or her fated mate seemed to be true. The Parcae, those sisters who were responsible for weaving the fate of all Supernaturals, Shifter-kind included, throughout all time and universes, had decreed it. *Sigh.* A hopeless romantic, Phoebe loved those stories.

She'd even managed to find a copy of the recently revealed *Scroll of the Parcae*. She'd memorized it, having read the thing so many times:

"Heed me, you Shifters of Terra, we are the Parcae, the three sisters whose needlework determines your lifespans.

We, the Fates, have halved your souls, the missing piece of each of you lies within your one true mate.

The Wardens of Terra have been thusly designed with the intention of balancing your powers and focus.

You have been truly blessed above all others. Your fated mates have been written in the stars. Your destiny spelled out across the heavens.

Follow your path to your other half for you will not know truth until that mate is found. Your strength as Shifters of the Terra will increase when the claiming is complete. Power will flow in abundance in the veins of you Wardens, and your mates shall bask in the glow of such strength.

You have only to speak your vows aloud and ask us for blessings, if granted you shall be bound for eternity. Stake your claim, but strike with care, for once complete, none can destroy your matebond.

Blessings to you who embrace the powers of your Shifter soul and the one true mate fated for you."

Phoebe shivered as she recited the verse to herself. Though not a Shifter, was inclined to believe that such a bond was unbreakable and worthy of respect and devotion. Even if it meant she was now roommate-less. *Dammit.*

If only she could believe that the Parcae had gifted *her* with such a mate. One man in the entire universe designed specifically for her. *Who would desire and adore her, respect her independence and power, and would make her feel loved...?*

If she ever found such a man, he would be her entire world. She'd give him everything she had, happily. But she was not a Shifter and she seriously doubted she'd even register on the Parcae's list of things to do. *If only...*

"Alright, if you are really afraid then you can stay here, *but* I am not leaving my bed."

"Fine," she mumbled not about to let him see her shock.

"And." He continued with a sly grin on his face, "I prefer to sleep naked."

The last word was nothing more than a deep growl, the vibration from his chest hitting Phoebe right between her legs. *Uh oh.* It started an aching throb that she hadn't experienced in a while. *A very long while.* Biting her lip to keep from moaning, she scooted to the edge of one side of the bed.

She wasn't going to argue the point, after all, it was technically *his* bed. That and the fact that she was being both presumptuous and rude silenced her objections.

The mattress dipped disturbingly low as he settled in, and she realized he'd taken up residence further in the middle than she expected. She tried sticking to her side, forcibly hanging on to the outside of the mattress through the silky sheets, but it was no use.

Every time he moved, she slipped farther and farther back until she was right up against his enormous body. Good thing he'd fallen asleep almost as soon as his head hit the pillow. She didn't imagine he'd appreciate her being practically on top of him. *Oh dear Goddess! What was she going to do?*

She muttered a quick alarm spell and hoped she'd be up before the brutish Dragon opened his lethal silver eyes. Sighing, she took a moment to relish the heat coming off his ridiculously muscular body, as well as the softness of the sheets and blankets.

The couch had been fine to sit on, but it was grossly uncomfortable to sleep on without proper bedding. Sighing again, she snuggled deeper into the mattress, *and into him,* willing herself to relax against the stranger who'd suddenly rolled over. He now had one large arm wrapped around her middle.

Eyes wide she stiffened until his steady breathing reassured her that he was indeed asleep. *Great,* she thought, *I'm a freaking teddy bear to a SeaDragon!*

CHAPTER FIVE

Nathan's Dragon was holding on by a thread. The feel of the curvy little Witch up against his body was almost too much for him to bear. He'd been trying to avoid the minx the last few days, but tonight he'd had no choice. Not when she charged into his room and thought to commandeer his bed.

Truth be told, he liked her take-charge attitude. In fact, the very first second his SeaDragon had spotted the little Witch in her naughty short pajamas he'd wanted to get her in his bed. Imagine his delight when she jumped in all on her own! If only his beast would stop pushing him to claim her, to bite the sensitive skin at the base of her neck and make her his forever. *Es Meus.*

He reined in his beast, acknowledging that he

needed time to think more deeply about this new development. It had been decades since he'd had more than a few hours alone with a female. Perhaps he was just lonely? *Or horny?*

Grrr. His suddenly alert SeaDragon strongly disagreed. The Witch was his. His fated mate. Her natural fragrance, a tempting mix of lemon and mandarin-oranges with a hint of vanilla, was like ambrosia to him.

He recognized it as the scent of her *anima magicae,* the heart and soul of her supernatural powers. Sweet and light and tantalizing to his Dragon's nose. He wanted to breathe her in everywhere. To sniff and lick and taste each supple inch of her body.

Easy there. We need time, remember? His Dragon bristled at the command but agreed with his human half. Phoebe was not aware of the situation at all. Thought it was likely that she had been sent by the Heralds to use her wiles on him, she seemed genuinely unaware of her effect on him.

He was certain that she had been chosen for him. Perhaps by the Parcae themselves. But that didn't mean he had to fall in line so easily, did it? He certainly had no intention of following the Heralds commands simply because they willed it.

Why should this be easy for them? They'd abandoned him. Left him to rot alone without purpose. Did they even know what it is like to be a SeaDragon, *a retainer of Cancer,* and to have no purpose?

Anger surged through him, fast and fierce, but it was just as quickly doused when the Witch in his arms ran her petal soft hand over his forearm. The movement though rendered while she was asleep, made his Dragon want to roll belly up as she continued to pet and caress him. *Petting a Dragon?*

He should have been affronted by the gesture, but nope. He found himself leaning into her touch. Trying to prolong the moment. He bit back a moan as pleasure coursed through his blood. *Perhaps she uses her craft against me?* But Nathan knew better. His Beast was beyond thrilled at the feel of her body; her soft, gentle curves so close to him. The SeaDragon preened inside Nathan's mind's eye. *She touches us. She knows she is ours.*

Bloody hell. It had been so long since he even entertained the idea of a mate. Was he even worthy of such a blessing? For decades he'd blamed himself for the fall of the Wardens. Particularly for his final failure, just before the Hounds of God took over the Wardens of Terra as protectors of the Earth.

He'd been foolhardy and proud. He'd believed

her. The woman who'd turned out to be the greatest traitor of them all. Arianna, an *elemental,* had more power and more negative intentions than he was aware of.

He'd met her while fighting a mighty Sea Demon. She'd been captured by the creature and was being used to manipulate the weather, effecting the crops of the humans who inhabited the earth. The ones he'd sworn to protect.

So, Nathan rescued her. Brought her home with him, blinded by her beauty. She seduced him easily. And when she'd said, she was his mate, well, he believed her. She'd been so very beautiful and so very good at lying.

He'd been a young Dragon then. The last of his kind. He'd clung to the hope that Arianna was his true mate, though she would not let him mark her. He still hoped she would one day bear him young. Help him repopulate the world with SeaDragons. But she'd had other things in mind. Mainly killing him and using his blood for the Dark Magic that fueled the Sea Demon's rampages against humankind.

It had been bloody and painful, the battle that sealed his fate on this tiny rock. He'd spent the first century in mourning. Almost starving in his misery until he'd finally snapped out of it and decided to live again.

He was not so down as to try and kill himself. It took time, but he shook off his folly. Nathan worked hard to build a life on his private isle. Cut off from the other Wardens and the Heralds. Abandoned by them. *Yes.* He'd let bitterness fester in his heart for those he was once proud to be part of.

He would not go back to them so easily. Not just because they called him now. Still, he had needs. Needs the tempting little Witch in his bed could see to in the interim. He would not trifle with her, after all he was almost certain she was his fated mate.

A truly delectable and sultry vixen. The most gorgeous creature he'd ever seen, what with her golden hair and sapphire eyes. A true treasure for any Dragon's hoard. Laughter like the tinkling of bells, eyes like precious gems, skin pale and luminescent like the saltwater pearls he gathered from the deep.

Perhaps she'd like to see his treasures? *A good idea.* He'd show her soon. Well, as soon as he got her to remove this silly spell she put on his home. He could hear the winds raging outside and he wondered what damage they were doing to his crops. He could always replant, but it was unusual for such storms to present so early in the season.

Yes, he needed her to undo her magic immediately. Once she understood that she was his mate, she'd certainly give up on trying to get him to go back to the Wardens. She'd see her place was there with him. *Serving his needs, cooking his meals, bearing his young.* A fine place for a female! He'd be a good mate.

Nathan would protect her, see to her every material need, and come night, he'd make love to every inch of her willing body. *Yes.* Sounded perfect to him. Heck, he was looking forward to claiming her and solidifying the bond that had already started to form between them.

It wasn't love. *No.* He could never trust himself that far again. But he didn't need to offer love. He could offer riches, more material goods than she could possibly want, every protection a SeaDragon could afford, and guaranteed, mind-blowing sex.

How could she refuse?

CHAPTER SIX

P hoebe woke up to the scent of freshly brewed coffee. She moaned aloud wondering how quickly she could get a cup to her lips before she had to face the day.

It had taken her ages to fall asleep against the warm, *and very hard,* body that had clung tightly to her. All of her attempts to remove herself from his grasp were pretty much shot down as he simply tightened his vise-like grip around her soft middle. *Oh, who was she kidding?* She quite enjoyed being wrapped up in the gorgeous dark-haired, silver-eyed Dragon's embrace for the night.

Wouldn't mind a bit more actually. Not that he tried anything. He was a perfect gentleman. Kept his hands firmly on her abdomen. Not a single digit strayed out of bounds. *The jerk.*

Startled by the direction of her thoughts, she sprung up in bed. With a flick of her wrist she magicked the bed into making itself and hopped off to the bathroom. *Shower. Shave legs. Brush teeth. Get dressed.* A girl, even a Witch, had standards after all.

When she was finished with all the necessities, she threw on a long white skirt made of a light gauzy material with a simple scoop-neck tank top and headed out to meet the man himself.

Phoebe stopped in her tracks when she saw a shirtless Nathan standing at the kitchen counter with just a hint of sunlight outlining his body. He was positively ripped! With enormous, tanned muscles covering every solid inch of him. *So much sun kissed skin. Like cinnamon sugar. Yummy.* She licked her lips, wondering if he'd taste as sweet.

Oh no. Do not go there, I have a job to do, and it doesn't involve getting frisky with the hottie over there!

"Morning," he spoke first, breaking the silence. Phoebe turned away quickly, embarrassed to be caught staring at him.

"May I?" She gestured to the coffee.

"Of course," he replied, a smile on his perfectly chiseled features.

How could one man be so damn good-looking? *Ugh. Stop it,* she scolded herself. Phoebe straightened her shoulders and walked up to the counter. She jumped when he reached over her, filling her nostrils with his fresh sea air scent, to place a clean mug in front of her.

"Sorry. Didn't mean to startle you," his mouth was impossibly close to hers for a nanosecond before he straightened.

"No," she cleared her throat, "I mean to say, that's alright. Um, excuse me," she avoided his gaze as he poured the rich, hot brew into her mug. He offered her both cream and sugar, that same smile teasing the edge of his rugged mouth.

He was seriously handsome. Almost beautiful. Phoebe couldn't help but admire his uniquely masculine beauty. Though, she should probably admit she also found him endearing. Helping herself to both his offerings, she repressed a shudder as their fingers touched casually over the sugar bowl.

"Breakfast?"

"Sure. Did you want me to---"

"No, no," he answered.

"You have been cooking for days."

"Yes, but you haven't been eating it."

"A punishment for me I assure you. I have been a

lousy host, Phoebe. Allow me to make it up to you. It's only right I take care of breakfast."

"Alright then," Phoebe watched as he deftly moved about gathering a few pots and a cutting board. He opened the huge refrigerator and began taking out ingredients.

"Can I help at all?"

"No, please relax. I was thinking of whipping up a vegetable frittata. You just enjoy your coffee," he busied himself washing and chopping vegetables then set them in a pan to sauté, while he beat a dozen and a half eggs in a large stainless-steel bowl.

Phoebe was pleasantly shocked at the way he executed himself. He had all the confidence of a man who'd been living alone a long time, but none of the savageness she expected from someone cut off from civilization for so long. He obviously still enjoyed some kind of relationship with the world.

"What is it?" he asked while adding spices to the egg mixture.

"Nothing. You just surprise me is all."

"Ah, you expect me to be some sort of wild animal, then?"

She started to shake her head but stopped when he nodded and smiled instead.

"No, I get it. I do. A solitary SeaDragon living on

an unchartered island for a thousand years, I can hazard a guess at what your expectations of me were. You should know, stuck isn't exactly a word I associate with myself. I am a Dragon, you know, I have magic, and more recently, I have the internet," he winked at the last word, and she felt herself blushing in response.

She watched as Nathan placed the pan in the oven to finish. Then he began slicing long, thick pieces of bacon off a huge slab. They landed with a satisfying sizzle in the cast iron frying pan and Phoebe almost drooled at the delicious aroma.

"That smells amazing," she said.

"Thank you. I smoke the meat myself."

"Really? Is that some kind of a Dragon joke?" She smiled as his laughter flooded the kitchen.

"No, I'm afraid I use an old-fashioned smoking house, like ordinary *normals* used to. I built one on the other side of the mountain a few centuries ago. Of course, the wood needs to be replaced every few decades, salt air and all that, but I am pretty handy after all."

"Sounds interesting, I'd like to see it sometime."

"I could show you today, *flava meus.* That is, if you would remove your spell."

"I'm sorry, Nathan, but until you are ready to discuss business with me, the spell will remain."

"Well then, we will be stuck here," his fingers brushed the back of her hand sending tingles of awareness through her body.

"Alone," he continued as he dished out bacon and slices of the succulent frittata he made.

The concoction was practically bursting with fragrant onions, diced potatoes, tomatoes, mushrooms, and thick chunks of gooey, melted cheese. Freshly ground black pepper and sprigs of dill decorated the top, creating a divine flavorful experience. *Heaven on a dish!*

Phoebe was almost drooling, and it wasn't because of the delicious breakfast he'd cooked for her. *Oh no*. It was because of the way he seemed to touch her at every possible turn. Passing the salt, handing her a napkin, wiping a crumb of toast from her lips. He did all of that, and more, nonchalantly. As if he couldn't feel the sexual tension in the air. *Jerk*, she thought once again, blushing at the unkindness of her inner dialogue.

"Um, I'll clean up," she stood and tried to grab the dishes before he could, but he managed to move faster. His hand lingered on her wrist for a fraction of a second too long as he moved to gather the plates.

She quickly took over, shooing him out to the other room where she hoped to the *Goddess*, he would spend some time getting dressed before she was done loading the dishwasher and wiping down the counters.

She could've used magic, but the truth was she needed the time away from him to remind all her overactive little pink bits that she was there to do a job. *And not that kind of job.* Though she wouldn't mind dropping to her knees before that mountain of a man and exploring whether or not everything about him was fully proportional.

Sure, she'd gotten a glimpse the previous day when he was naked, but she hadn't really looked. And last night she certainly *felt* something large settle in behind her bottom, but she remained facing the other direction. She was not peeking, well, not without an invitation. No matter how much she wanted to.

He was definitely long and thick. *Sigh.* The hard evidence of his manhood that had snuggled against her buttocks during most of their time in bed had attested to the fact. Still, she'd sure love a long look at his marvelous cock up close and personal like. *Uh oh.* Moisture dampened her panties just thinking about him.

Damn. Okay, think of Math. Yeah, Math is hard. Like Nathan. Eep! No. Bad Witch. Okay, the formula to find the circumference of a circle is pi times the diameter, so if the diameter is six then, oh hell, I give up.

Utterly confused and doing her best to ignore the still shirtless SeaDragon, she approached him with both hands raised as if in surrender. She supposed *she was* surrendering in a way.

"Look, we need to discuss why I'm here."

"I know why you're here, but I told you already I won't discuss it. Now, tell me, does your spell confine us to these rooms on this floor?"

"Um, no, I bespelled us to be confined to your actual house. However large it is."

"Good. Will you come with me then? I have much to show you."

"Um, okay," she shrugged.

A curious Witch by nature, she wondered what Nathan had in mind. He didn't seem to want her there at all the past few days, and yet today he seemed anxious for her company. *Weird.*

She waited for him to return dressed in jeans and a clean white t-shirt. The starkness of the t-shirt only enhanced his generous tan which she knew covered his entire body. *Lots of sunbathing in the nude happening round here.* She only hoped she was around to see it next time. *Sigh.*

He looked mouthwateringly good. His short, black hair was combed away from his face, silver eyes flashing with heat whenever he looked at her. She wondered if the Dragon possibly found her attractive.

A short, chubby Witch from Virginia? Stranger things have happened she supposed. And it wasn't like she didn't think she was pretty or anything. He was just so *extra. Tall, tanned, muscular, sexy, handsome.* Just about everything the doctor, or in this case, Witch, ordered!

Phoebe was a sucker for a beautiful man. Though her rounded figure tended to attract a certain type of guy, she'd always preferred her men to be handsome and sculpted. *A girl has needs after all.*

She felt her blush creep along her skin and had to stop herself from swooning at his feet even if he did look like some kind of sex god with his muscles and exotic coloring. *Yum.*

"Come, *flava meus.* I want to show you my castle."

"Your castle?"

"Yes. All Dragons live in castles. This one is a little more modern than I recall them being, but I have embraced modern architecture and technology in this aspect. You should like it."

Nathan seemed concerned about that, so she nodded to assuage his anxiety. Of course she liked it. The house was amazing. A verifiable mansion on an island for the Goddess' sake!

He led her to an ordinary looking wall but surprised her yet again when he lifted a sconce to reveal a secret panel. After placing his palm on the security pad, another door appeared out of the natural rock wall, the stainless-steel portal slid open without making a sound. *High-tech indeed.*

"You know, I can't figure you out, Nathan. Sometimes you talk like someone out of the 12th Century, but then you have all these gadgets," she *tsked* and shook her head oblivious to his searching gaze.

"Is that a bad thing, *flava*?"

"No, not bad at all," she was about to ask him what that word meant when he placed one large hand on the small of her back.

Heat seeped through the fabric of her thin top as he guided her along the dark path to an area that seemed to glow with soft ethereal lighting. The temperature dropped a few degrees and she shivered, grateful for the natural heat that seemed to emanate from his powerful body.

"Come this way. Watch your step," he motioned towards the uneven floor, but his grip remained on her person.

For that, she was exceedingly grateful. Some Shifters had the ability to see in night vision, alas Witches did not share in that talent. Besides, Phoebe had always been a little clumsy. The last thing she needed to do was fall down in the dark!

"Thanks," she murmured and allowed him to lead her down an incline of about a hundred yards or so.

Another opening led to a large room that seemed more like a museum than what she'd imagined a Dragon's treasure room to look like. His hoard was certainly vast. Paintings and historical artifacts were placed along one side of the enormous structure.

Where she'd imagined a dank cave, she found herself standing in a very clean, climate-controlled room. The floors were highly polished, the walls finished, with vents on both the ceiling and floors.

As they neared the entrance, she noticed a force-field of some sort protecting the area. Nathan slowly exhaled a breath at the very center, and she went still. It was more than air that he breathed, it was *magic.*

Amazing, she thought. A deep blue flame leapt from Nathan's mouth and touched the forcefield allowing them temporary entrance. *Dragon fire*, she thought in awe of the miracle of him. She recognized the gift he bestowed upon her, allowing her to see his power. Dragons were rare after all, and very, *very* secretive.

"How did you do all this?"

"Partly sweat. I spent years clawing out the mountain and building my vault. I studied architecture and design, learned to utilize the island to maintain the climate needed for my treasures. Of course, later I installed more sophisticated means of security, ventilation, and so forth. And lastly, I called upon my *Dragon Magic*."

"I don't know much about *Dragon Magic*, I confess, but it fascinates me," she bit her lip as she looked at a pile of ancient scrolls.

The knowledge there! She'd love the opportunity to read them but wasn't so presumptuous as to ask.

"Of course you would not know about it. Our secrets were well hidden in my day, and I always thought they would die with me." *Until now.* She could have sworn he added those last two words, but she'd been watching him. His lips hadn't moved. *And yet.*

"Why do you say that?"

"I see you are interested in my scrolls. Some are

quite good. I have a few ancient Etruscan almanacs, and one rather racy Egyptian how-to book."

"A how-to what?"

"It's a manual on how to evoke extreme pleasure from your sexual partner," he leaned in closer.

"An ancient Egyptian sex book?" She gulped. Was it getting hotter in there or was it just her?

"Exactly. I imagine it was to instruct young virgins on how to keep their spouses satisfied," the last word was a guttural hiss that sent warm jolts directly to the juncture of Phoebe's thighs.

What would it be like to feel him there? To have that long tongue of his intimately involved with her needy sex. Swallowing lightly, she turned her head attempting to diffuse the suddenly tense situation.

"What's over there?" She pointed to another doorway and could have sworn his eyes flared when he turned to lead the way.

"Come, let me show you," he murmured grasping her hand and taking the lead once again.

Phoebe should protest really, but how could she when the view was so damn fine. His firm ass flexed in the tight jeans he wore as they weaved through the massive shelves of his hoard. She loved seeing this side of him.

He was neither haughty nor condescending, but

rather he seemed to enjoy showing her his treasures. She snickered as she imagined Matt Paxton, one of the hosts of Hoarders, the TV show, showing up here.

"What?" he asked, but she shook her head.

"Oh, nothing. please continue," Phoebe inhaled the whispery scent of saltwater with hints of smoke that reminded her of cozy bonfires on the beach late in the summer that seemed to surround him.

She breathed him in once more, sucking in the fragrance and holding it close before releasing it to their surroundings. She found it necessary to bite her tongue just to keep from sighing aloud and followed on.

Phoebe continued on with her musings, wondering where the SeaDragon was leading her until they came to a crystal-clear pool at the end of what looked more like a cave than the other part of his treasure trove. Steam rose from the water, and she turned wide eyes on him questioningly.

"This island was formed by a volcano many centuries ago. This pool is heated by the belly of the mountain, I found it a long time ago and claimed it as my own. It is one of my favorite treasures."

He spoke in a deep and growly voice. One that she felt all the way to her toes.

"It is so beautiful," she gasped as she looked around at the black volcanic rock that glistened in the dim lights that suddenly flared to life around them. *Like a million black diamonds. Beautiful.*

"Care to test the waters?"

Phoebe bit her lip as he smiled rakishly. He knew he was handsome. *Of course he did.* How was she going to resist making a fool of herself in this situation?

Just as she began to shake her head no, he stepped back, kicking off his shoes. Next, he drew his shirt over his head, exposing his cinnamon-colored muscles to her rapt gaze.

Heat sparked between them. Phoebe swore she heard a rumbling growl emanate from his chest. He seemed to fill the space. Larger than life, he had an innate charisma that she'd never encountered, and she found it very hard to resist. *Why should she try?*

Despite being in human form, she was keenly aware of his Dragon lurking beneath his skin. Tempted to ask to see his sea-beast, she was a little bit distracted by the impeccable shape of him in his human skin at the moment.

"You're not afraid, are you?" His taunt was full of jest, but she narrowed her eyes.

She never could take a dare. That trait got her

into oodles of trouble as a young Witch. Still, what harm could there be in a little friendly swim?

"No, of course not," she tugged her tank top free, whipping the fabric over her head and yanking down the gauzy skirt.

Standing there in her white bikini underwear and her lacy bra, Phoebe wondered if this was a wise decision. She was not exactly swimsuit model material, though truth be told, she was rather fond of her curves. But would he feel the same?

Looking up, she found herself mesmerized by the silver pools of Nathan's eyes. His chest was heaving with the force of his breathing as he stared. As if in a daze, the gorgeous Dragon Shifter walked closer to her. She held her ground, curious to see what he had in mind.

"Beautiful, *flava meus,* you are perfection," his hands reached out to touch her long blonde hair, gently tracing the column of her neck down to her bra strap.

The man clearly had no concept of personal space as he slowly invaded hers. She practically swooned under the intensity of his eyes. The silver depths glowed as he traced her hairline, fingertips skimming her skin, but not quite touching.

The near touch was more erotic than anything

she'd ever felt before. Breathing became difficult. She wanted so much more.

Phoebe braced herself for the impact of his kiss as his head bent. His chiseled features even more devastating up close. She licked her lips. The knowledge that this was surely going to change her world did nothing to prevent her from readying herself. Eyes closed, lips parted, she held her breath.

And *nothing.* She was left standing on the side of the pool. *Alone.* Nathan had pulled back rather abruptly with one last tug on one of her blonde curls. She blinked rapidly as he turned away from her.

Shucking his jeans, he did not look back as he jumped into the small pool. Around twenty feet across to the other side, it was small, but deep. Though, she was comforted by the fact that the water was perfectly translucent. She could see all the way to the bottom through the clear ripples he made as he sliced through the water.

Phoebe slowly stepped into the heated water, not moving beyond the edges of the soothing liquid. Worried about the sharpness of the rocks, she was pleased to find the bottom covered in soft, black sand.

Shaking off her disappointment at the near kiss

and his obvious lack of interest, Phoebe walked backwards to the edge of the water. The sandy shore was very small, next to it was a smooth rock formation. She sat down on a large, flat rock and looked nervously before sliding off, deeper into the translucent pool while keeping hold of the side of the rock.

The warmth of the water seeped through her flimsy underthings, rendering them completely see-through. But she didn't mind, it felt too good inside the pool.

The heated water relaxed her aching muscles. Releasing some of the tension she'd felt since the day before in a way she didn't know she desperately needed. Phoebe closed her eyes, head tilted back, unaware of the fiery silver gaze watching her from across the pool.

"Oh, this feels so good," she moaned.

"Does it?"

"Eep!" She squeaked and splashed, startled by how near Nathan was to her. How the heck did he get next to her so fast? *SeaDragon. Duh.*

"You swim fast," her inane comment earned her a dazzling smile.

"Thank you," he said hands fitted to her waist as he pulled her deeper into the pool.

"Oh, um, no. I can't really swim," she confessed biting her lip and clinging to his shoulders.

"You can't swim?"

"No," fear began to build inside of her as she clung to his massive body. He looked at her curiously, no judgement on his face as he continued to pull her deeper into the water.

"Actually, not at all. I've always been a little afraid of the water," embarrassed by her confession, she turned her head away from his penetrating stare.

"*Flava meus,* I swear I will allow no harm to come to you. Do you trust me?"

Nathan turned her to face him with two fingers on her chin. For some unfathomable reason, Phoebe believed him. She was a modern woman, a strong Witch, a Junior Station Master for the Wardens of Terra. She didn't need to depend on any man. *Or Dragon.* But she admitted to herself, it was rather nice to have the option. *For once in her life.*

He waited for her nod before continuing to swim with her until they reached the middle of the pool. The sensation of floating in made her tremble. She had no control out there. The water was so deep. *So very deep.*

The fear of drowning something most Witches got over once they understood those scary stories their peers told them about naughty little Witches sinking like stone in water were just to frighten them. *Jerks.*

Only Phoebe had never quite believed her parents when they'd said those stories were not real. What if she was a naughty little Witch who sunk like stone? She always tried to be a good person. But who didn't slip up now and then?

So, maybe she accepted too much change from the grocer because she forgot to check it at the time. And maybe, she ran a red light when no one was on the road every now and then. Did things like that make her bad?

Irrational as it might be, Phoebe clung to Nathan's shoulders with inhuman strength as he swam them both out to where she could not reach any rock or wall to help her stay afloat. *Eep!*

The water was even warmer in the center, the sandy floor so far away she couldn't see it. *Oh no.* Panic started to well up inside of her, but as if he could sense it, Nathan stroked her waist with his fingers and began talking.

"We are directly over the heat source now," his breath tickled her cheek.

"In a thousand years this pool has never cooled below seventy degrees. This is one of my favorite places. I have never shared this with anyone else, *flava*," he whispered the words, hypnotizing her with his steady tone.

Handsome face only an inch or so away from hers, Phoebe felt a ripple of awareness flash through her entire body. Mesmerized by his nearness, she could only stare in wonder as she felt the hardness of his body align with hers.

Was he getting even closer? Eyes widened, lips parted, Phoebe almost moaned when his hands brushed over the curve of her hips, bringing them flush against his.

"I've never wanted anyone else here. In this space. But here you are, Phoebe," he whispered.

His silver gaze was mesmerizing. Eyes glowing, he leaned in, and it was as if everything else faded away. She'd never been the center of attention for such an extraordinarily handsome man before.

It was dizzying, electrifying, enough to make her want to moan like a wanton and blush like a virgin at the same time. Biting her lip, Phoebe locked eyes with his. His hands moved, leaving her hips, and she gasped.

"I can't swim," she squeaked.

"Hold onto me, *flava meus*, you will be safe," his growly voice sent shockwaves of awareness through her body.

Head bent she closed her eyes, trusting him, waiting for the moment he would lay his claim. And it would be a claiming. He was strong and virile. Such power, her Witch's intuition was panting with the knowledge of what lay beneath his strong human façade. *Dragon. Mine.*

Shocked at her possessive thoughts, Phoebe blinked. She had no time to doubt, as his lips seized hers in a hard kiss unlike any she'd ever experienced. It was both a claiming and a surrender. How could it not be? A mutual take and give. His lips, firm, yet soft as velvet, found hers and demanded she part for him. She moaned under their strength, giving him the opening he was looking for.

Saltwater taffy. That was what he tasted like as his long tongue entwined with hers. She was taken back to bright sunny days roaming the Jersey Shore with bags of the sticky, salty, sweet snack as a child. *Delicious.* And safe. She felt safe with him, despite her current location.

As if sensing her trepidation, Nathan tightened his grip on her body. Bringing her womanly curves in line with his hardened musculature. Wrapping her arms around his neck, she plunged her tongue inside the warm cavern of his mouth, giving as good as she got.

Her breasts pressed against his chest in the water, and she cursed the constrictive bra she was wearing for separating them. As if he read her mind, Nathan's hands moved around her back, unhooking the blasted contraption and flinging it off her body.

He swallowed her moan as her nipples hardened and pressed into his chest. The sensation of his skin against hers was almost overwhelming. She writhed against him, searching for something *more*. More closeness, more friction, more *him*.

She'd never done this before. Never lost herself in a kiss with a man. *Not with any man, witch, beast, demon, or alien for that matter.* But she wanted to lose herself in Nathan. *Desperately so.* Perhaps that was why she pulled back.

"More," he growled angling his head for another assault.

"Wait," she replied, and he reared back, silver eyes blazing, "Why are you doing this?"

"What?

"Kissing me?"

"Isn't it obvious? I want you, *flava*, more than anything."

"You want me, but what are you offering me? A few minutes of no-string sex?"

"I assure you it would take much longer than a

few minutes, *flava*," he growled, hands gripping her ass, he pulled her into contact with the wondrously aroused flesh of his fully erect cock.

Phoebe sucked in a breath. Her entire body felt aflame despite being mostly under water. No stranger to attraction or the occasional tryst, this was something entirely different.

Her body was more than ready to receive any and all attentions from him. She marveled at the way he seemed to anticipate what she wanted and needed. But no. She couldn't do this with him, could she? *You have a job to do, Phoebe. One that doesn't involve doing him.*

"Nathan, I appreciate you feel attracted to me, but that isn't why I came-"

"No, *flava*, but I will make you come and then perhaps you will see. Afterwards, if you still don't understand, I'll simply have to try harder," he took her mouth on that last word.

Phoebe moaned into his mouth. Lost in his kiss, *in him*, once more, and she gave in. Goddess, did she give in. *Life was too short, too uncertain to turn your back on precious moments like this one.* Phoebe was Witch enough to know that. A child of magic, how could she ignore the chance to explore her wondrous response to his attentions? To truly be with him?

She felt deeply connected to the mysterious SeaD-ragon no matter how distant or out of touch he seemed. Their connection was worth exploring, wasn't it?

She didn't want to end up with regrets. Phoebe had promised herself a lifetime ago to always jump in and live life to the fullest.

No regrets, she told herself opening up for him as his lips travelled to her neck and throat.

"Yes," she moaned as the water itself seemed to buoy her.

She felt herself being lifted by the warm liquid until she was on her back, cradled safely while Nathan touched and explored every curve and dip of her lush frame.

"So beautiful," he whispered reverently as he worshipped every inch of her with his hands, mouth, and tongue until he reached her covered mound.

Silver eyes ablaze, he captured her gaze as he gripped both ends of her panties and pulled, tearing the fabric from her body, and baring her to his slow perusal. Phoebe's heart pounded as he let his desire be known. No one had ever made her feel so wanted before. She gasped, attempting to sit up, but he gently pushed her back against her watery bed.

"Let me look at you, *flava*. So pink, so perfect," he murmured, brushing his fingertips over her trim golden curls.

He spread her slick folds, watching her all the while with such intensity she felt pleasure spread through her veins. And he hadn't even touched her yet.

"What do you want, *flava meus*? My hands," he stroked her slit with one long finger, quickly withdrawing it as he waited for her response.

"Yes," she said, arching into his touch, trying to bring his hand in closer contact with her sex. Nathan *tsked* and withdrew.

"When I say, *flava*, not before. Now, where was I?"

His warm breath brushed against her skin, and she shivered in response. Tendrils of magic wrapped around her, hers and his mixed, and she sighed as pleasure beyond words began to tingle along her nerve endings.

"Please," she begged. She would surely die if he didn't do something.

Her pussy clenched on air as she writhed, her body on fire for him. Phoebe never felt so ready, *so needy*, in all her life. No past experiences could compare with the way she responded to this man, this Dragon.

As a Witch, she was a little more mature than she looked. She'd had lovers for sure, but none that set her on fire like this. *When would her Dragon take her already?*

Nathan's blood thrummed with need. *Mine. Mate. Flava es meus. ES MEUS.*

Both human and beast in complete agreement about this one fact. The beautiful, golden-haired Witch was his. His one, true, fated mate. His blood thrummed with the power of Cancer as it too recognized his other half.

Her vanilla-citrus flavor burst on his tongue as he stroked the cavern of her mouth with his long, agile tongue. Thank the gods he was a Dragon, for he was certain he would need every bit of his supernatural strength until he was fully satisfied that he had completely pleasured the intoxicating Phoebe Bright.

He would stand for nothing less than her total

surrender to his ministrations. Already, he could feel the *matebond* begin to pulse between them. In his element, the pool surrounding them moved to his command.

Cushioning and holding his sweet *flava* afloat above the clear waters, but still warming her with a steady stream of heated liquid around her luscious frame except for the places he was caressing and kissing. And he meant to sample them all.

He chuckled at her headlong response. Blue eyes flashed at him as he ran his fingers along the firm round globes of her ass before digging in and grinding her against his hard length trough her panties. Once furious, those baby blues were now glazed over with lust. A look he wholeheartedly approved of.

Nathan promised to keep that sultry expression on her face for the unforeseeable future. Pleasuring her was surely to be a lengthy process, as he desired to see her release again and again.

He captured her mouth, flicking his tongue against hers in slow, sensuous strokes that allowed him to taste her more completely. *Mandarins and vanilla,* like the sweetest *creamsicle* he'd ever had.

His little Witch was a fresh, bright burst of sweetness on his tongue. *More,* his SeaDragon growled inside his mind's eye, and he was quick to follow at his beast's behest.

He'd been alone for what now, centuries? Disconnected from society, without his calling, without any other Dragons left, Nathan had been close to despairing for some time now. And yet, all of it fell away. For the first time ever, he felt truly complete with her in his arms.

A Dragon with no purpose was a dangerous thing. He'd taken his rage and anger, his sadness and isolation, and had hidden himself away from the rest of the world.

And to his utter disgust, the world had continued without him, having no real use for a Warden unemployed. So, in turn, he'd shunned them all.

Except, he didn't need to be alone anymore. Not now that he'd found her. His mate. *Es Meus.* He recalled the lessons told by his father, a mighty SeaDragon who'd been the proud leader of their clan.

A SeaDragon's mate is a most treasured possession, my son. A jewel like no other found on land or sea. When you find yours, you must keep her safe, keep her protected, but most of all, keep her contented. For only then will you find happiness.

He moved his hands along her plush form, loving

the feel of her warm and wet within his pool. He skimmed his teeth over the soft part of her flesh just over her throat and ran his tongue over her rapid pulse.

Yes, she was affected by him. *Good.* Her mewls of excitement were like fuel to his already mile high flame. Everything about her intrigued him, kept him mystified. He wanted more and more of her. His appetite enormous, and he intended to sate himself wholly on her.

He moved down her neck and shoulders, to her full breasts. After freeing them from their rather sexy little confines, he lavished attention on each. Sucking one ripe berry into his mouth before switching to the other.

He massaged her mounds, kneading and pinching the hard pebbles that tipped her lovely breasts. He suckled and nipped, licked, and soothed both of them until she was moaning mindlessly, writhing her body in a bid for more. And he would give it to her. He'd give her everything she could ever ask for.

"Yes, that's it, *flava.* Moan for me," he growled, unable to keep the Dragon from his voice as he used his powers of Cancer to manipulate the pool.

Lifting her higher, like a tasty morsel on a platter

set out for his consummation. Nathan growled, looking his fill at her luscious body held by the crystal-clear liquid, *not pinned*, simply lifted before him. The distinction was important to him. She was there because she wanted this. *Wanted him too.*

"This feels so decadent," she whispered, her voice thick with emotion.

"As long as it feels good, *flava*," he returned.

"Yes, oh yes," she said, and only then did he settle himself between her soft thighs.

Nathan inhaled her sweet arousal as he pulled her legs up on his shoulders. Calling upon the waters again, he commanded they form a solid step under his feet. He couldn't trust himself to swim once he tasted her sweet nectar. Besides, he intended to be focused on her and her alone for the duration.

Phoebe mewled and moved her hips, a temptation he could not withstand. Nathan dipped his head, latching onto her clit and sucking, hard. His sweet Witch bucked and cried out, the unexpected attack on her sensitive nub brought on the first of what he hoped would be many orgasms for his beautiful mate.

She tasted incredible on his tongue. He continued to lap and suck, delving between her hot folds, determined to leave no inch unattended. *Yes, he thought as he drank down her sweet nectar.*

He felt her fingers in his hair, pulling the short strands while she thrust upwards, riding the wave of pleasure against his tongue and lips. *Fuck.* She was so earthy and sensual. The perfect mate for a SeaDragon!

He groaned against her clit, the tiny nub so damn lickable. He swirled over her sensitized flesh, then took long slow swipes with his tongue. She moaned his name, body growing taut as her pleasure built. *Explosive.* Yes, he felt as if he would explode just from tasting her! She was everything he'd ever wanted in a mate. Magnificent as she gave and sought pleasure with him. Unafraid to bask in her sexuality. *No shy maid. And thank the gods again for that.*

He'd never been one for simpering virgins. Though he loved being able to make his mate blush. Especially when that blush went all the way down to her pretty, plump breasts. *Grrr.*

The women of his youth had nothing on this gorgeous creature. And she was all his, in his care. All the women of his past were forgotten save for this one. She was it for him. His one and only, and he intended to hold on to her. *Forever. Es Meus.*

She struggled slightly, her movements getting jerky under his attentions. He could feel her sheath quivering around him. She was close. The Dragon inside of him sat up, demanding he do it now, pleasure her, then bite her. *Mark her. Es Meus.* And he would. *After*, he promised the beast.

"Now, *flava*, I want you to come with me inside of you," he growled, allowing the water to carry her sumptuous form down through the heated liquid to his awaiting hardness.

He wrapped her legs around his waist and waited for her approval. Phoebe did not disappoint. She grabbed his shoulders and pulled up before impaling herself on the rock-hard flesh of his cock.

Nathan roared at the feel of her. Hot and wet, she squeezed his cock. Stroking his erection with her velvet walls. The ferocity of emotions that thundered through his blood threatened to drown him.

Never before had Nathan felt so humbled, so blessed. Then again, he'd never been gifted a mate by the universe before. Never would again. She was his one and only.

His Phoebe wiggled her lush hips, enveloping him in her warm, tight flesh. Nathan loved having her wrapped around him, but he needed more. Something solid to lean on. He commanded the water to return them to the edge of the pool where he'd long ago carved a ledge some feet under the surface.

Perfect for this very thing. Firmly seated on the volcanic rock, yet still submerged in the heated pool, Nathan gripped her hips. Astride him, she was even more beautiful. A pale blonde goddess against his tanned self.

Already, he sank deeper into her slit. His senses heightened with the increased leverage. *Yessss.* She felt insanely good, and he didn't know if he could hold on to his Dragon, but he had to try.

"You have me now, *flava*, what shall you do with me?" He teased, nipping her bottom lip, and soothing the abused flesh with his tongue.

Wicked blue eyes sparkled at him as she rose high enough so that just an inch of his rather impressive length hovered inside of her warmth.

"I'm going to ride you," her sultry voice made him tremble in anticipation.

Her lips curved into a smile as she wrapped her arms around his neck, knees spread wide on either side of his trim hips. She used the ledge for balance as he wanted her to.

His Phoebe pulled on his hair, forcing his head back, so his gaze met hers. As if he needed reminding who he was with at the moment. Then, she slammed herself down, and Nathan couldn't think anymore.

She repeated the same sharp movement. Phoebe lifted her luscious body up until he almost slipped out of her slick heat before slamming back down on his thick cock. *Swivel, lift, slam, swivel, lift, slam.* Again, and again she moved.

Harder and deeper he went. *Fuck*, she was good. So very good. He kissed her neck, her shoulder, her breasts, anything he could reach. Forcing himself to allow her the freedom to take her pleasure as she would.

"Yes. Use me, *flava*, come on me, explode for me, gorgeous," he encouraged.

His hands sought out her secret places, whispering across her nub, tracing the globes of her ass to the sweet crack between that he couldn't wait to explore. He wanted her in every way. Could imagine taking her ass, her tits, her sweet pussy over and over again.

It would never be enough. Using telepathy, one of his many Dragon powers, Nathan shared the images with her. He noted her shocked gasp, and the residual lust that glazed over her face. Yes. She wanted that too.

"Nathan," she moaned his name as her movements began to grow unsteady.

Eyes wide, chest heaving, Nathan knew she was close. He gripped her rounded hips, loving the feel of her womanly shape under his large hands. He grunted as he lifted and dropped her down onto his cock. *Fuck.* It was good. So good.

Her pussy sucked and squeezed his length. Her velvety walls gripping him tightly, he continued to penetrate her, hard and fast. She was on top, but he was staking his claim. Their scents mingled, oranges and saltwater, musk, and smoke. Fucking delicious.

"Nathan, so close," she groaned, fingernails pricking the skin at his nape.

The added bite of pain only increased his pleasure. He had to fight to keep from coming before she did. *No. She will come first. Must pleasure my mate.*

He felt her climax before she vocalized it, screaming his name, and clinging to him in such a way that made his dick pulse and sped his release on. With one arm wrapped around her back and the other still gripping her hip he held her as she spasmed and shuddered over him. Each ripple of her cunt sent his cock into another spasm of ecstasy.

"Oh, Nathan," she murmured, slumping against him. He'd never tire of hearing his name on her lips.

Speaking of lips. Nathan brought his hands to her face, cupping her cheeks and forcing her to look directly at him.

"*Flava*," he moaned and dipped his head, capturing her lips in a possessive kiss the likes of which he'd never shared with anyone else.

He drank from her, sipping the heady wine that was her natural flavor. *Need more*, the Dragon inside of him growled. Nathan wholeheartedly agreed. Without warning he stood up, keeping her wrapped firmly inside of his embrace, legs tight around his waist.

"Nathan," she gasped.

"Hold on," he growled.

Using his supernatural speed and strength he brought them back through his secret treasure hoard, to his master bedroom.

"Now, *flava*, I shall take my time with you," he breathed the last word into her mouth.

Nathan growled as he lay down with her on the soft cover of his enormous bed. He settled on top, keeping his body from crushing her, but still firmly seated within her cleft.

"Es meus," he growled, nuzzling her neck, and kissing her again, thoroughly, and completely.

His mate's body opened for him, teasing him

with her ready submission. It was *teasing* only because his strong-willed Witch was anything but submissive.

Still, he couldn't help but be turned on by her seductive mewls and moans. By the way she sucked on his tongue and ran her fingernails down his back. Those naughty fingers grazed his buttocks, squeezing his cheeks and tracing his crack. Every touch, every lick, every sigh caused his shaft to harden and grow even more inside of her.

"Nathan," she moaned.

"What is it, *flava*?"

"Move. Please," she squeezed him with her thighs, and he hissed.

He'd been biding his time. Kissing his mate, tasting her in the comfort of his bed. The tension between them was tight, bodies glistening with sweat, Nathan reared back. Lifting himself to his knees, he brought her legs to his shoulders.

Yessss. His Dragon hissed the word in his mind's eye, beast more than prepared to mark her neck, claim her as his own. *Soon,* he calmed the Dragon.

It was easy enough to convince himself to wait. It might take some persuading, after all. And in the meantime, he got to pleasure his sweet *flava*. Hearing her moans and feeling her body tighten and clench with each glorious release was more than he could have ever hoped for.

She was *his*. Designed by the gods just for him, fated by the *Parcae* to come to his island and find him. *Yes*. He knew it to be true with every fiber of his being.

Thrusting his hips, he growled that one word against her mouth before he claimed her sweet lips with his tongue and moved in time with his cock.

Mine.

CHAPTER EIGHT

"Nathan?" Phoebe traced the glyph that marked his skin at his waist, the sideways "69" was a symbol of Cancer meant to represent the crab and claw of his Dragon's astrological affiliation and his prowess with water. It was not a tattoo but resembled one on his smooth tanned skin.

Makes sense that he was chosen by the water sign, him being a SeaDragon and all. She supposed his ability to control certain aspects of the sea was because of that connection. His SeaDragon's nautical nature was only enhanced by him being a Warden of Terra. A *former* Warden who was also her charge.

Tiny feelings of doubt and guilt pushed and wiggled, attempting to force their way into her head, but she urged them back. She refused to second guess what they'd just done. The entire experience had been so beautiful. *Too right to be wrong.*

"Yes, *flava meus?*"

"Hey, you said that before," she started.

"What's that?" He caressed her soft skin as he answered her questions, she could hardly focus. Her mind was already racing to the next time she could have him inside of her. His skills as a lover were beyond compare. Nothing had ever felt so right. *So perfect,* she sighed.

"'*Flava meus*', what does it mean?"

"Just a nickname in *Dracan*."

"What's that?"

"Dragon language."

"Ah. I've never heard it before-"

"And you won't from anyone else as I am the last Dragon this world will ever see," his silver eyes flashed with a deep sadness that shook her to her core. Then she realized what he'd said. *Last Dragon?*

"But you're not the last Dragon," Phoebe tilted her head, eager to meet his eyes. Surely, he knew others still roamed the Earth, though Dragons were still incredibly rare. He turned his face towards her, and she was surprised to find mostly anger mixed with a smidge of hope.

"Of course I am, I was there, at the last battle," he

returned.

Phoebe went still, her Witch's senses fully aware of his rising anger. Though not directed at her, his rage was a mighty force to be reckoned with. But she needed to confront him on this. She'd face his anger, but she'd rather he not believed himself alone in the world.

"You mean the *Battle of Blood*? The Wardens last Battle with the Sea Demon and the Dark Witch Arianna?"

Phoebe could not believe what she was hearing. Could Nathan really have been at that battle? Most supernaturals, but especially those affiliated with the Wardens of Terra, knew of the final showdown between the Wardens and an especially cruel elemental Witch named Arianna. The *Battle of Blood* was legendary and, as Junior Station Master, she'd studied it thoroughly in preparation for her position.

"Is that what they call it now? Much blood was spilled, I will give them that, half our force if not more," he snorted in distaste.

"Oh my Goddess! You're him! You are *the Silver Dragon* from the battle, aren't you?" Phoebe gasped covering her mouth with both hands as the implications hit her.

She'd been in the presence of *the Silver*! Lusted after him, bespelled him, and, *for fuck's sake*, she slept with him! *Oh shit. Shit. SHIT.* The man was a fucking legend.

"You're a hero, Nathan. I've read about the battle in depth. Where should I start? Can I ask you some questions?" Fangirling was probably not her best look, but it couldn't be helped. She knew all about his heroic exploits.

The way he'd sacrificed everything to right a wrong he'd committed by trusting the evil elemental. If only the Witch were still alive. Phoebe would gut the immoral slattern!

Jealousy coursed through her blood as she recalled how *the Silver* had been seduced by the Dark Witch. *In love,* some had said. He'd been blinded by her evil by his insatiable lust for the evil beauty. Phoebe had seen the paintings of Arianna and, yes, she had been beautiful. With hair dark as a raven's wing, eyes like emeralds, and a tall, lithe body.

The complete opposite of Phoebe. She cringed. Hating that her insecurities would flare up at a time like this. She had no time to deal with any of that.

Arianna is his past, she told herself firmly. Pushing her jealousy aside, she focused on him, on the present. He was hurting and she couldn't just stand there.

"Nathan, please, I want to talk to you-"

"No. I won't talk about it. Not even for you, *flava meus,*" he stood up from the bed they'd shared, running his hands over his head angrily.

Phoebe felt small and cold as Nathan stomped around and looked for his clothes. Eyes narrowed she tried again. This was too important to ignore. She wasn't about to let him dismiss what they'd shared with a temper tantrum of all things.

"Why? Why won't you talk to me?" Hurt at his refusal to look at her, she stood up.

Phoebe stepped towards him, but he raised a hand as if to ward her off and backed away. The action was more potent than a slap to the face would have been. She froze in her tracks, completely uncaring of her nudity, she met his eyes, silently pleading with him to stay and talk.

"Nathan. Please. Don't do this."

"Don't do what, Phoebe? Huh? What do you want to know? How I failed that day!"

"No, I-"

"I FAILED! I trusted the wrong person! I gave her the opening she needed and then poof, *all of my kind, gone!* More than half our force destroyed in one swoop of her evil powers. It was the greatest loss the Wardens had ever faced. It gave the Hounds the opening they needed to step in and shut us down forever."

"That was not your fault-"

"I FAILED! The Wardens were disbanded, and my kind gone FOREVER! What don't you understand? Damn you for making me remember!" He roared his agony, making her cringe. But that was nothing compared to how she felt watching him raise his fist and punching a hole clean through the stone wall.

"No," she moved forward regardless of the plaster and stone that littered the floor, "not forever, Nathan. We're back now. We can be of use again, and we need you," she whispered.

She bit back her sob. Her heart was breaking for him. It squeezed painfully in her chest as she watched the blood run from his knuckles. *What must he be thinking?*

She'd read thousands of retellings of *the Silver* and of his affair with the two-faced elemental Witch who'd tried to destroy him. The heartless bitch of a woman had betrayed him and taken out his entire clan.

"You think you know it all? You don't know how Arianna cut down my kin. She took their blood, the sacred lifegiving fluid of the Dragons, and used it to call forth a Demonic army the likes of which the world had never seen for her true lover," emptiness consumed Phoebe as he spoke, silver eyes staring at the floor.

She knew the tale well. Arianna's true lover was the very same Sea Demon who was currently trying to crawl back into the world through his puppet, *Ao Guang*. And he was headed straight for them.

"Nathan, I know you think I can't understand so much death and misery, but the blood is on her hands, not yours," she tried to reason with him, but he shook his head. His silver eyes were wide, panicky as he stepped back.

"No, don't you see, I am responsible."

Phoebe wanted to scream and sob for both the loss of life and his loss of purpose. The history books accounted for the death toll by blaming the plague, but she knew the truth. As did most supernaturals. Darkness had nearly destroyed the world. Using plague and pestilence, the maggot-riddled fiends working for the Demons had sucked the Earth dry of wheat and grain, of life and blood. The Darkness nearly overcame them all. And then *he* stopped it.

By all accounts, the *Silver Dragon* was the savior of the battle. He'd swept in, his fearsome fire glowing blue in the heat of the battle. He'd purified and cleansed the seas and fields of all evil. Sacrificing his *heart's flame* for the sake of the world.

"You," once more she walked towards him, "you gave them everything. You used the blue fire of Cancer, calling on the flames from the depths of the waters to cleanse the field of all Darkness. They say you gave your *heart's fire*, Nathan?"

Phoebe couldn't stop the rush of words from her lips. Couldn't stand to see the pain her words caused, but she was helpless to stop them. This complicated man, this strong, stalwart Dragon had endured so much.

He'd seen suffering the likes of which she could never imagine at the hands of true evil and at the behest of the Heralds and Wardens alike. No wonder he renounced them all. And there she was to remind him. *Oh Nathan, how you must despise me.*

"No. Not my *heart's fire*. For I am still here," he spoke as if he didn't deserve to be.

"Nathan, maybe-"

"No, I will not talk about it anymore with you.

You work for *them*. You're here at *their* bidding. Did you think to use your body to tempt me back to the fold? Well, I am sorry, but even one as fair as you can't make me return to those cold-hearted bastards."

Phoebe covered her mouth with her hand, stifling her gasp. She felt as though she were being stabbed right through her heart. Pain, intense and agonizing coursed through her. Those careless words he'd thrown at her eating away at her soul like acid.

Nathan turned away from her. He left the room and she almost fell to her knees. The vision of his tall back walking away remained with her and she bit her hand to stop herself from going after him.

She hated that she would still want to comfort him after he'd basically accused her of sleeping with him for her job. But he was hurting, and she'd been the reminder of a past too cruel to bear.

It took all of her strength, but she was finally able to see past the nasty accusation to the wound underneath. *Nathan Silvertongue was heartbroken and in trying to defend whatever remained of the organ, he'd broken hers.*

She didn't know it was possible to feel so helpless.

Phoebe didn't like the feeling at all. How stupid she'd been! Naïve and eager for this chance to prove her worth amongst her superiors and peers alike. She couldn't even make a hasty retreat! Oh no, she had to go and *bespell* them both to be *waterlocked* in his home!

Anger surged through her. Anger at him for speaking to her like that. At the Heralds for not telling her exactly who she was going after. And at herself, for allowing her heart to become involved. *Seriously involved. Am I thinking L-word?*

She stopped that thought almost as quickly as it popped up. Flicking her wrist, she used her magic to cloth herself quickly in a long, strapless dress that fit loosely. She stepped across the floor, barefoot, ignoring the mess he'd left after sending his fist through the wall. The pain of the stone shards on the soles of her feet only reminded her she was still there, alive, and well for the most part.

Broken heart aside. *Damn the man.* She'd had no idea the arrogant SeaDragon she'd been assigned could be *the Silver* of legend. Heck, she'd assumed he had died during the battle as a result of using his heart's flame. Never could have imagined she'd meet him in the flesh.

The bards had sung his praises for centuries, but

no one ever really said what became of him. Now she knew. He lived. *But not really.*

What kind of life was there to be had hidden away on a rock? She cried for him then. For what they could have had. Tears streamed unchecked down her face as she collected her wits.

I love him, she realized. Loved the big stupid man though it was hopeless. Pain lanced through her body from her very core. It was so unfair, but that was life, she supposed. *Okay, enough,* she told herself and bit her lip to keep from sobbing aloud.

She was a Witch and a Junior Station Master. She had a calling. One she couldn't give up just to ensure her heart's desire. *And I desire him. I love him. I really do.*

She acknowledged the truth of her feelings as she accepted the pain in knowing she could never act on them. Not until he could at least discuss the possibility of rejoining the world. She saw him standing by the door, unable to move through it and her heart wrenched.

"Okay, Nathan, look I know you don't think I could understand-"

"How could you?" He bellowed.

She jumped at the tone of his voice, trying to understand his rage for what it was. *Pain. Despair.*

Hopelessness. Abandonment. She'd just torn open his oldest wound and now he was caught up in the storm of his memories. Consumed with his regrets.

"How could you know what it is to be the last of a species? All because of a mistake! One that I made! I thought she was my mate. She betrayed me and they ALL DIED!"

"But you're not the last! I know more Dragons-"

"No! You lie to tempt me back to the fold."

The insult cut her deeply, and she glared at him, hands on hips. He might be the *Silver Dragon,* but she was Phoebe Bright. A well connected, if not mega powerful Witch, who was as honest as they came.

"I never lie!"

He harrumphed and turned his back on her. Frustration and pain rolled off of him in waves, tainting the air. She would have cringed at his suffering but was too angry to do anything but react.

Phoebe always was too volatile for her own good. But that was just the kind of person she was. She threw herself all in or nothing. It couldn't be helped. This SeaDragon needed someone to call him on his bullshit and she was just the Witch to do it.

"Listen here, you overgrown sea snake! There is a Clan of Dragons living as we speak off the coast of New Jersey. Four brothers actually. Before that, they lived somewhere called the Isle of Pain in the North. There are more Dragons, *Nathan*, but that fact is not important. No, what is important, *Mr. High and Mighty*, is that the Sea Demon you fought before has sent a minion to do his dirty work once again. And, in case you haven't noticed, he is occupying your neck of the Atlantic!"

"So, what do I care-"

"He's headed right here, you big buffoon!"

"What? Who dares come near my island?"

"Ao Guang, the Green Dragon of the East is headed straight here. Haven't you noticed the storms? Haven't you bothered questioning why your island has been hit by not one, but six almost-hurricanes in the last two months alone!"

Phoebe's rampage had only just begun. She moved towards him, stalking him across the cool stone floor with slow, measured steps.

"Look outside the window, Nathan. He is almost here! I've come at the behest of the Heralds to do my job. To get you back in the game. But I can see now you're too wrapped in the past to help. You've forgotten what it means to be a Warden."

He winced under her cruel words and her heart shattered. She turned her back on him, unable to stem this fresh flow of tears. She had no choice now. *It was over.*

"I'll work on breaking the confinement spell. And I will explain to the Heralds that I failed in my mission. You won't hear from me again."

With one final look at his turned back, Phoebe left the room. Heart around her ankles, she called upon her magic to aid her. She gathered all her belongings from his home and shoved them back to her storage space between realms, trying not to think about the angry Dragon in the next room. She had to focus now.

How to break the spell...

She knew of one sure way to break the spell she case, but she had no desire to do it. The ritual involved blood. *Hers.* And she'd vowed to never do blood magic, *but* this was an exception she'd have to make. Ao Guang was nearly upon them. The wild tempest outside alerting her to the Green Dragon's proximity. He had to be stopped. She might not be strong enough, but she had to try.

So little time. She wanted to cry out in her pain. From her youth she'd wondered if she'd ever find true love and up until a moment ago, she believed she had. Rolling up her metaphorical sleeves, Phoebe sat on the floor and recalled the steps to her spell.

A huge booming noise interrupted her. It sounded like thunder only amplified as it reverberated over the island. Then the thunder changed into something else. An evil, cynical laughter seemed to shake the very island. *Shit.* That could only mean one thing.

Ao Guang had found them.

The roar of the sea bashing against the far side of the island was loud even in Nathan's home. *Shit.* He'd fucked up and badly.

Phoebe had tried to explain, but he wasn't sure he believed her. Could she really have not known the Heralds would stoop to seduction to make him return? Hell, he didn't even know if her reactions to him were real!

No, that wasn't exactly true. His Dragon growled in his mind's eye, and he acknowledged there were some things he did believe. Like the fact that she was his fated mate.

And now, he knew that she spoke the truth about this as well. The echoing thunder and the evil laughter contained within it could mean only one thing. His old enemy, the Green Dragon was here. *Ao Guang* was his official title, but the Dragon King went by many names.

Jade Spring was one of his pseudonyms. That was how Nathan knew the Dragon who was King of the Eastern Seas. If you could believe it, Nathan had once studied with the Green Dragon. Had even counted him as a friend. *But that was many centuries ago.*

His *heart's fire* had been poisoned by the death of his mate, as a result Ao Guang became a puppet for the Sea Demon. And now he was back to hunt his old nemesis. *He endangers out mate.* Nathan growled. He remembered the pain he experienced that day, but it would be nothing compared to how he'd feel if Phoebe was hurt!

First, Arianna's betrayal had nearly crippled him. Then, he was made to watch the death of all the Dragons. *Clearly not all. Not if Jade was back.* His mate had spoken the truth.

He growled at his own stupidity and headed back to where he heard Phoebe moving around. The sight that greeted him almost petrified him in place.

Phoebe was sitting on the floor holding her arm

over a silver bowl. Her hair was still tousled from their lovemaking, her face flushed though stained with her tears. How he wanted to go to her and kiss the salty evidence of her pain away.

I caused her to hurt. His admission pained him, though he couldn't help but take her in. *A vision was his fated mate.* One that made every inch of him take notice. He felt his Dragon rise, even his powers of Cancer answer the call of her mere presence.

His Phoebe looked like an ancient goddess there on his stone floor. Like some flaxen, sacrificial angel on an altar. *Es meus,* growled his beast.

The loose gown she wore seemed to flow around her, *as if by magic.* She looked beautiful. But it wasn't those things that gave him pause.

No, it was the large, wickedly sharp athame in her other hand. She was chanting words he could not make out, but he didn't need to. It was clear she meant to harm herself.

"No," Nathan growled and leapt across the room using his inhuman speed to reach her before she could swing the blade down. Gripping the athame, he broke her grasp on the blade gently, sending the hateful knife slamming into the far wall.

Twin tracks of tears ran down her beautiful face

and Nathan's heart constricted in his chest. To think he was the cause of such pain shamed both man and Dragon. Fury rose in his blood, directed only at himself for causing her to almost harm her precious self.

"No, *flava*. I will never have you harm yourself," he growled as he pulled her into his arms. Rocking her precious body as she sobbed against his chest.

"No, Nathan, it's okay. I wasn't trying to hurt myself. I was only trying to break the spell-" she hiccupped as she spoke, but he simply held her tightly and smoothed a hand over her golden locks.

"Shh, it will be alright, *flava*, I will make it so," he whispered, leaving kisses on her forehead and cheeks. The feel of her safe and secure in his arms helped to somewhat soothe his Dragon, but it wasn't enough. *He could never get enough of her.*

"Seriously, Nathan. I was trying to break the spell. The only way to do it without fulfilling the terms are to draw my blood. At least, *I think* that should do it," she pushed against his chest, and he relaxed his hold, but still refused to let her go. He needed that connection to remind him she was alright. *He would never stop making it up to her*, he vowed to himself.

The confusion in her bright blue eyes wounded

him. That this beautiful, brave Witch should risk a single drop of her blood to release him from a spell was unthinkable.

"I am not so dishonorable as to ever wish to see a drop of your blood spilt on my behalf, *flava meus.*"

"I am sorry. But you refused your role, and now I have to meet the Green Dragon and fight him. I respect you, but it's my sworn duty to protect this world-"

"I understand sworn duty better than anyone, Phoebe."

"You don't have to say any of this, Nathan. I should have never let us get involved," she trembled, and he hated himself for doing that to her. For making her doubt them.

"Listen to me, *flava,* right now, *I* swear to you that *I* will meet Ao Guang, that *I* will defeat him, and that *I* will protect *you.* Always. *Es meus,*" the power of his vow rang throughout the room. The magic innate of his Dragon-self imbuing the very air with his promise, Nathan's eyes glowed with power as he made his oath to the only woman in the entire universe that mattered.

A *Dragon's word* when sworn was a sacred pact, that much he recalled from the days of old. A mate's oath was unbreakable. *And she was his. His one true, fated mate*. He knew that now.

The entire house, maybe the whole island, shook with the force of his promise to Phoebe. Then, as if the sun itself had heard his vow, it came out. Shining brightly through the floor to ceiling windows, and he felt her spell break as the front door slowly unlocked and opened.

Nathan smiled as Phoebe stared in wonder at him and at the heat that seemed to pulse between them. Need and desire rose up like the tide inside of him, swelling and growing with each breath they took. *Mine. Es meus*, growled his SeaDragon in his mind's eye.

He felt his true purpose for the first time in a millennium and it filled him with a righteous fire that burned brightly inside. *His heart's fire*. Nathan recognized it for what it was, awe filling him at the depth of his feelings. Rekindled in his chest with the love of his mate, *his heart's fire* was the source of his flame, the tie to his magic and the powers of Cancer.

True, she had yet to accept him as a mate, and he'd yet to claim her with his bite, but he would rectify that as soon as possible. There was no other recourse, she was his and he was hers.

"Phoebe, I speak from my heart when I say this week has changed me-"

"Nathan, we don't have time to discuss whatever this thing is between us now. Ao Guang is practically here," her wide, bright blue eyes met his, fear and longing in them.

"After then, after I defeat him, you and I must talk," he wanted to taste her lips, to give himself one more sweet reminder of his soon-to-be-mate, but before he could sweep in to steal a kiss, she seemed to fly away from him. A thick green limb wound round her middle as she screamed for him.

Nathan gave chase but was knocked to the ground by a deafening trumpet of a roar split the air, followed by a booming crash of thunder and lightning overhead. *Ao Guang!* Nathan growled as wind whipped palm trees and shrubs viciously outside and tore his front door right off its hinges.

"I see you have grown tired and complacent, old friend," a raspy voice hissed through the air a split second before a long, serpentine tail wrapped around Phoebe's waist and hauled her outside.

"Nathan!" She screamed.

"No!" Nathan roared. Fury and anger flooded his veins, but he could not allow them to cloud his thought process. Not when Phoebe's life depended on him.

"Jade? Is it really you?"

"*Yessss*. It is I, but you don't get to call me Jade any longer. I am the Green Dragon of the East, and you shall feel my wrath!"

"Jade! I thought you were dead!"

"Death would have been better than where I have spent the last thousand years, *Silvertongue*. And by the time I am finished with your mate here, you shall wish for death too!"

"No! You will release my mate at once!"

"Not a chance, old friend. This shit heap of a world is better off with one less Witch. Even *you* should recognize this," hissed the Green Dragon before turning his back on Nathan, a struggling Phoebe hovered high above the ground in the serpent's long, muscular tail.

"Nooo!" Nathan did not have time to think. He simply reacted, sprinting after the slithering beast.

His muscles burned as he leapt over fallen trees and rocks, but Nathan did not notice. The Green Dragon was a force to be reckoned with and he needed his wits about him to battle the great beast. His huge serpentine body wound through the rocks and greenery of Nathan's Island. All four of his muscular legs working to hasten his retreat to the fierce sea, where he was most at home.

Nathan had to use all his SeaDragon's strength and speed to follow the green-scaled sea serpent as he fled to the rocky shores below Nathan's home. The beast turned back, emerald eyes flashing as he taunted Nathan with his prize. *Phoebe.*

"What's wrong, *Silver*? Besides the fact that you've let another Witch wrap her treacherous lies around your foolish heart," Ao Guang roared with biting laughter as he dove beneath the waves, taking Nathan's mate with him.

Nathan's heart pounded ferociously in his chest as he looked into Phoebe's brilliant blue eyes a split second before she was taken from him. *Nooo!* His Dragon pushed to explode out of him, his powers of Cancer rising up like a storm, but he needed to control his baser instincts if he was to keep her alive. *Grrr.*

"Phoebe!" He roared to the skies, calling on his powers of Cancer. Nathan snarled at Jade.

No, he is only Ao Guang now, my enemy, Nathan thought. He concentrated on the pull of Phoebe's life force beneath the waters. She was still alive. He could feel her heart beating. *Flava meus,* his own heart screamed within him. The slithering serpent rose from the murky depths, lifting his body high above the waves with his long, muscular body as he advanced on Nathan once again.

"Your *mate* will soon be dead, *Warden*! She will sink to the bottom like the stone-hearted Witch she is! And then it will just be you and me. What do you say? A battle to the death, for old time's sake. You owe me that much, *Silver*," Jade hissed at Nathan.

"I owe you nothing," Nathan snarled, squaring off against the Green Dragon.

He was hesitant to take his SeaDragon shape, at least not until he tried to use reason one last time. He watched as, on his short wings, Ao Guang, hovered above the water holding a sputtering, drenched Phoebe above the tide with his long, muscular tale.

Her dress clung to her like a second skin, her golden locks were drenched, plastered to her head and face as she sputtered and coughed. Nathan wanted to fly to her aid, knowing her fear of the water. But he couldn't not without risking her life. He hated himself for not being quick enough to stop her capture. *Fuck!*

Stop it. You're not helping her this way, he told himself. He couldn't give in to his rage. Not now. Not when she was counting on him. The storm roared around them, but Nathan heard the Green Dragon loud and clear in his mind. Trepidation kept him frozen in his tracks for the moment.

Just looking at his frightened, soaked mate made him want to tear the world apart. She was his one true and fated mate. His other half. And he wanted her back at his side, safe and sound. The Green Dragon would pay for this. *Grrr.*

He'd never felt such an intense emotion. *Not even for Arianna.* The elemental of his past was nothing compared to the glory of his true mate. *Phoebe, I am coming. Hold on a bit longer.* He had to move fast. Nathan would not fail her. Not now. Not ever. *Es Meus.*

"Jade think for a moment. Remember who I am. You don't have to do this. Let my mate go, this is between you and me."

"No! I remember who you are, Silver. Do you? You let the Sea Demon take me, you showed no mercy for your childhood friend, you left me alone in hell for a thousand years!"

"We can still talk this out!"

"Talk? Ha! You left me to rot!"

"I did not know you were alive!"

"It matters not. If I kill your mate now, you will

feel the same hell I have been living for a thousand years!"

"Jade, don't you think I've been suffering too? And I will still. Look, you can have me. I won't fight. Take me in her stead, just put her down!"

"You don't get off that easy, Nathan! This world should be destroyed. The Sea Demon will see to it, but for now I will have my revenge on you!"

"No!" Nathan roared and felt his Dragon burst through his body. Human skin gave way to diamond hard scales. Rage at the danger to his mate and the powers of his SeaDragon and the sign of Cancer surged through him like a tidal wave.

Larger than the Green Dragon, Nathan, *the Silvertongue,* raced over the roaring waves and dove at the beast. He swam quickly to avoid the sea serpent's muscular coils as they tried to wrap around his sleek body.

Surprised at the sudden attack, Ao Guang dropped Phoebe. Her screams resounded over the booming thunder before she disappeared under the tumultuous waves. Nathan's heart froze for a split second, but he had no time to react as the serpent raked its claws across his neck and back.

Knowing she couldn't swim, but consumed by the battle before him, Nathan could do only one thing to save his mate. *Focus,* he scolded himself as panic threatened to overwhelm him.

He summoned his powers of Cancer. Concentrating on gathering his strength, he tried to block the Green Dragon's next blow, but missed, taking the hit to his left side. Nathan plummeted back to the shore, spitting saltwater and sand as he struggled to find Phoebe through their connection.

"You won't find her, Silver! She is dead!"

"Nooo!" He roared and inhaled. Digging dip inside himself, he pulled on his powers, sending a blast of saltwater straight at the Green Dragon. Like a rocket, the stream of water hit the serpent and knocked him to the side while Nathan called upon his powers further.

He commanded the water to calm beneath the waves while he searched for his scared mate. He sensed his *flava* drifting to the bottom, her heart was beating, but slowly. It was as if she was frozen in fear and worse, she was sinking fast.

His heart thudded in his chest, he had to act now. But it wasn't easy. Ao Guang lunged again, and Nathan was forced to dodge out of the way to avoid the sharp claws of his enemy that had been aiming for his one vulnerability.

The scales at the base of his throat were the

weakest on any Dragon, a blow there, especially with claws, could result in bleeding out. Nathan could not afford such a wound. He just couldn't die now. Not when Phoebe needed him. He concentrated on her once more. Her lifeforce was slowing down. *No!* He fought back the panic and focused on what she needed to survive.

As if he sensed his preoccupation, Ao Guang attacked. The sea serpent struck while he was vulnerable, wrapping his huge, muscular tail around Nathan's sleek body. Surprise threatened to interrupt his focus, But Nathan held strong. Phoebe was the only thing that mattered.

Ao Guang squeezed and tightened his coils around Nathan's SeaDragon's form. Sort of like a python, but with a million times more strength, he squeezed and crushed until Nathan thought he would pass out from the lack of oxygen. *Not yet*, his Dragon snarled. Despite the pain and the dots darkening his vision, Nathan understood one thing. He needed to save Phoebe before he blacked out.

Summoning all his strength, he made a concerted effort to focus all his powers on controlling a small section of the sea in front of him. The very section where he last saw Phoebe go down. *Grrr.*

He directed all of his attention towards saving

her, allowing his enemy to continue having the upper hand. Nathan hardly even felt it when Ao Guang raked a massive claw across his back. The move reopened the same wounds he'd inflicted on Nathan only moments ago. Shifters healed fast but with this type of onslaught, Nathan knew it wouldn't be long before he was bested.

He tried to breathe as Ao Guang squeezed again. The bastard thought to crush the life from him. Nathan simply grunted the pain away. He commanded the individual molecules of water in that section to break down and reshape. Thinking fast, he instructed them to form a circle under the thirty-foot waves, a sort of bubble around his mate's still form.

One more directive, he gasped as the darkness threatened to close in on him. *Push oxygen inside the bubble,* he told the molecules. *Refresh the air she breathes with each passing moment and form a hard shell to keep any activity up here from harming her. Please Phoebe, hold on.*

He prayed silently that he wasn't too late, that she could breathe in the protective bubble he'd made, and that she would remain hidden from the Green Dragon's wrath. Though it took moments for his plan to work, it felt like a lifetime. Fighting his lack of oxygen, Nathan did not waste one second worrying for himself.

The Green Dragon was on him. Had him wrapped tight, but he was too impatient. He must have wanted Nathan's death immediately, as he changed tactics. Ao Guang hissed as he hauled his *molten lava flame*, the blood of the deep ocean that was at his disposal as King of the Eastern Seas.

"I will end you now, Silver," he cried before loosing the power of his flame on Nathan.

"I don't think so," growled Nathan. Now that Phoebe's safety was ensured, *and she was safe*, Nathan could feel it through their bond, he was able to focus on the battle at hand.

He pushed out of the serpent's coils. Ducking and rolling, he avoided the burning liquid as best he could. When Ao Guang was spent, needing a moment to regain his strength. Nathan seized the opportunity.

He inhaled deeply. The briny air stung his burning lungs as he called upon his *heart's fire*. True, his mate was now safe, but the danger she had been in was still fresh in his mind. *Grrr.* His beast was furious. Only his *heart's flame* would do now.

The purification powers of the SeaDragon's flame were unparalleled. As was his unmitigated rage at the other Dragon's impertinence in taking his mate.

"Ao Guang, *Jade,* do not make me send you back to the pit. Surrender to me-"

"Coward! Fight me for your mate's honor! She is dead to the sea and still you don't attack? How you have changed, oh mighty *Silver,*" he hurled insults at Nathan.

"You leave me no choice," Nathan growled. He flexed his muscles, grabbing the long tail of the serpent in his claws.

"No, it can't be," cried Ao Guang as he tried to push out of his grip.

But Nathan did not let go. He rose from the water, droplets of the sea falling from his wings, his enemy tight in his grasp. He allowed the Green Dragon no time to speak or evade him. He'd crossed the line, attacking his mate, and now he would pay.

Nathan reared his serpentine head back, tossed Ao Guang down to the rocks below, and loosed a flame unlike any he'd ever used before.

Bright silver fire erupted from within him. A long, fierce battle cry sounded over the entire island with the onslaught. It drowned out Jade's wails as he continued to envelope him with the purification powers of his *heart's flame* made more intense by the powers of Cancer and his almost fully formed mate-bond. So intensely hot was his fire, that the entire storm, *born of Jade's Dark Magic,* ceased. Silence loomed over them both, except for the now natural waves that crashed behind him.

The Green Dragon's prone form was still on the rocky shore, his scales receded until he was human again. An unconscious one after all that. But still, Nathan wasn't taking any chances.

He called upon his powers of Cancer and encapsulated the unconscious Ao Guang in a prison of water. The same principle as the bubble he'd conjured for his mate, only this time the molecules hardened like diamonds around his body. *That should hold him until the Wardens come to collect his sorry carcass.*

Nathan sucked in a breath; his heart pounded in his chest. He faced the water with his silver dragon's eyes burning. *It was time.* He summoned the water to lift his still shielded mate up from the depths of the sea. All other thoughts left his brain as he focused on her and her alone.

He had not used his *heart's fire* since the *Battle of the Blood,* but he remembered how it worked. The land and sea that were damaged by the evil storm called out by Ao Guang were cleansed, purified, and rejuvenated once more. All evidence of battle washed away by his flame.

The Green Dragon himself would most likely remain unconscious for a while. He would not reawaken for some time, and when he did, he was sure to object to the unbreakable prison Nathan put him in. *Too fucking bad for him.* He stilled at the thought for a split second but pushed it away as his mate came into view.

"Phoebe!" He yelled as the air bubble he'd created rose out of the sea. Landing her unconscious form on the shore. Nathan ran to her, gathering her up in his arms. He roared aloud, begging her to wake up.

"Be at ease, SeaDragon, she is alive," a familiar voice spoke from the other end of the shore.

Nathan growled as he spied the ancient Herald move silently over the sand. His unsteady gait made more even by the aid of a large wooden walking stick.

"Lift her for me, Silvertongue," he asked, and Nathan was helpless but to obey.

She looked so small and still. Pale and soaked. Unlike the strong, demanding woman he knew and loved. *Yes. Loved.*

"She has swallowed some of the sea, I fear."

"Help her."

"And what of you, Silvertongue?"

"I need nothing from you, except for you to save her."

"Then it seems you need me sorely, old friend."

"You are more bastard than I thought if you think to use her as some kind of sick ransom over me, Herald. But it has been a long time, I am not the same Dragon I was-"

"No, you've learned more now, Silvertongue, and you have grown."

"I do not understand you, Herald, but you can have anything of me you want, *please*, you must *save* her."

"Why?"

"Because---" He swallowed, tears burning his eyes, "because, she is *everything*."

"Your mate?"

"Yes. And so much more. She is Phoebe Bright. Witch, woman, friend, mate, maddeningly beautiful and loving. There are not enough words, now help her! Please. I beg you."

"She has tamed you, Silvertongue. Not sure how useful you will be to us, a tamed SeaDragon at that."

"I will be anything you want, Herald, only heal her."

"And you will come back?"

"Anything. Heal her, Herald, please."

"Of course," the ancient one said and brushed his hand over his Phoebe's wan face.

She sputtered once, twice, then sucked in a great breath spitting out water and heaving as she struggled against his hold.

"Nathan?" she yelled

"It's me, *flava meus*, I've got you."

CHAPTER TEN

"No, you can't do this!" Phoebe's voice rose over that of the Heralds. Shocked and angry glares met her eyes, but still she refused to look at the once face in the room that mattered. *His.*

"You cannot ask Nathan Silvertongue to come back as a Warden of Terra because *you* saved *me*. It is not fair. He had been left alone for so long. Forgotten by your Council and all he wants is to be left alone-"

"Ms. Bright, the Silvertongue struck a bargain. The two of you were bound and waterlocked as had been fated before either of you were more than a notion to the gods who shaped the universe," began the ancient Herald to the nods and assent of the other Heralds in the room, "it is done now, Junior

Station Master, your life for his returning to the fold. That was the bargain struck. You must recognize the pact that was made with his vow."

"Yes, but-"

"But nothing, my dear. It is all settled. This meeting is adjourned, and your names shall be recorded in our ledger."

Frustration and anger at the Heralds welled up inside of Phoebe as she turned around and sped from the room. She was so ashamed! She'd failed to do her duty as a Junior Station Master and as a woman.

She was afraid to even look at Nathan. He must be so angry with her. All he wanted was to live his life on his island alone and away from the Wardens, and then she went and ruined it for him! His voice teased her senses as he called her name, but she hurried on. Wanting to avoid the confrontation that was sure to ensue if he caught up with her, she walked faster. Wiping her tears away as she unlocked the doors to her car.

"Phoebe!"

The sounds of heavy footsteps drew nearer and before she could climb in the front seat, he had her wrapped in his embrace. Nuzzling her ear, he inhaled her scent, his lips lingering on her neck for a split second before he turned her to face him.

"Three weeks, *flava*, I have been trying to call you for three weeks," he started.

"I know, I am sorry, I just didn't want a scene," she flattened her hands on his chest, trying hard not to shiver at the feel of his warmth beneath her fingertips.

So many muscles, all hard and strong, the perfect foil to her softness. By the Goddess, she loved how he made her feel. Safe, secure, protected, and tiny in his arms. Silly, but still. *No. You are not going down that road again.*

"Look Nathan, I am really sorry. I tried to make them let you go, but they won't. You don't have to stay in Virginia with me. I can ask them to move you to a different location."

"Why on earth would I want that?" He practically roared the question.

The sounds of people milling about made her look behind them. They weren't exactly in a private location, and she hardly wanted to have an audience for this, well, whatever this was exactly.

"There are too many people here, Nathan."

"Then let's go somewhere to talk."

"I can call you to schedule a meeting-"

"Not a chance, *flava*. I've been waiting weeks to get a hold of you and I'm not letting you out of my sight until we settle a few things," the deep timbre of his voice sent shivers down her spine, and she cursed herself for how easily he was able to arouse her.

Dammit. She hoped his super shifter senses didn't get wind of it, but it was too late judging by the smoldering gaze in his silver eyes.

"Fine. My place isn't far actually," she muttered as she got in on the driver's side and motioned for him to take a seat.

The black Mercedes was small, but comfy as she whizzed in and out of traffic until she reached the Station where she worked.

"That's my headquarters where I report. This entire community is shifter based and has ties to the Wardens."

"Yes, I was given a run down by the Heralds. So the Wardens are no longer strictly Shifters then?"

"Um, no. Given the rarity of Shifters, we have branched out to other *supernaturals*. Hence the Witch here," she said.

Phoebe continued making small talk as she pulled into the closed garage attached to her two-story home. It was nothing much from the outside.

In fact, it greatly resembled the other homes in the community. The inside, however, was different.

Using magic to create pockets of space where none seemed to exist on the outside, Phoebe's home was quite large. Decorated to be homey and comfortable with bright blues, whites, and yellows throughout, she smiled nervously as she led Nathan inside.

"Your home is beautiful, Phoebe," he said as if he sensed her nervousness. She stumbled over the rug when she thought she heard a whispered *just like you* following his sentence. *Must have imagined it.*

"Would you like some tea?"

"No, I just want to talk with you," he said.

"Um, okay. Please sit," she gestured towards a plush navy-blue sofa with yellow pinstripes and sat down in the chair across from him.

"Nathan-"

"Phoebe-"

They chuckled and he leaned forward taking her hand. *Oh damn.* He was so good-looking and after weeks of ignoring him, he was there in her home! She cared so much for the big, SeaDragon, but she didn't know if she could do this.

He wanted no part of her world. Had said so a million times. But there he was, in her living room, holding her hands, and her stupid heart was doing cartwheels.

"You first, *flava meus,* as it should be," he grinned, and her heart fluttered once more.

"Oh Nathan, I am so sorry you traded your freedom for my life," tears spilled down her cheeks, but she was unable to wipe them as he held her hands.

His silver eyes glowed as she tripped up her apology to him. How could she ever make him understand how she felt? She loved him too much to see him miserable forever.

"I swear I will find a way to free you of this obligation, Nathan, I-"

"Shhh, no more. I will not hear you speak like this for the whole world, *flava,*" he tugged her off the chair and into his willing arms. That's when she really lost it. Great, gut-wrenching sobs racked her body as he held her.

She couldn't make out his words over her own sobs, but she felt his lips as he pressed them sweetly to her hair and face, wiping her tears and rubbing her back. *Soothing her, tempting her.*

"Have I behaved so badly you would not believe I chose you freely?"

"But you don't want this, Nathan-"

"You are what I want, Phoebe. I will always choose you. No matter where or when or how."

"Your what? What are you saying?" Hope welled within her. Could he still want her after all she'd put him through?

"I said you are my fated mate, Phoebe Bright."

"But I am a Junior Station Master, and you don't want to be affiliated with the Wardens-"

"Calm yourself, *flava*, I was foolish and allowed my pride to speak for me before," he pressed his lips to hers briefly then continued with his eyes on hers.

"I am a Warden of Terra. Perhaps the oldest of all the Wardens. It is my true calling, as you are my one true mate. The idea of working with you is something I am anticipating, *flava*, but the Heralds have agreed to allow us time to settle in our life together first."

Phoebe couldn't believe her ears. Nathan wanted to remain a Warden. But what did he mean their life together? Confusion and hope rose within her. His strong thighs flexed under her buttocks. He squeezed her in his arms tightly before taking her face in his hands.

"These past three weeks without you have been unbearable, *flava*, please do not separate us longer."

"Nathan, I mean, I want you too, but are you sure? You aren't angry?"

"Of course I am not angry with you. And yes, I have never been surer of anything, my sassy little Witch. You are everything and more than I have ever wanted. Now, I ask you, and the Parcae above us to bear witness, will you accept my claim, *flava*? Will you take my bite, be my mate, fight side by side with me as Warden and Junior Station Master? Will you be mine forever Phoebe Bright?"

"Yes, oh yes," she said as his lips claimed hers in an all-consuming kiss.

"I vow to honor you, to love you and protect you with my mind, body, fire and soul. To cherish you and our young for all eternity under the watchful eye of the Gods and the Parcae. To exist for you, my sweet Phoebe," he said.

"Oh Nathan, I love you."

"I love you so much. It's been too long," he growled into her mouth. Lips and tongues tangled as his hands sought to remove her clothes.

"Yes. Too long," she agreed struggling to straddle his hips as she tugged on the hem of his shirt.

All her good intentions to send her SeaDragon away meted under that kiss. She simply had no willpower to resist him. And why should she? He was her mate. Chosen by the Parcae, fated to be together, they were a pair for better or worse.

Somehow, they ended up on the floor. In nothing but her silk panties, she felt no trepidation as his silver gaze raked her from head to toe.

"So beautiful," he growled as he grazed her skin with his rough fingertips. He parted her thighs and settled between them, using his long tongue to lick and taste the skin between her breasts.

"Oh Nathan," she murmured, loving the hint of pain as he nibbled on one pert nipple, rolling it between his teeth and tugging on the sensitive flesh.

He lavished attention on both her breasts, hands roaming over her soft flesh, leaving his mark everywhere. Her pulse fluttered wildly as he moved lower, his heated breath leaving her breathless as he sucked and licked a trail to her sex.

"You smell so good, *flava*, did I ever tell you? Like sunshine and oranges, and woman, my woman," he growled again and blew hot air through her damp panties.

He lifted her thick thighs, placing them on his shoulders as he met her eyes.

"Watch me, *flava*, I'm going to taste you now."

His eyes glowed with desire as he pressed his tongue against her undies and licked her through the thin material. *Fuuckkk.* She groaned, long and hard. Her body so wound up with missing him and the anxiety of the meeting earlier that day.

Yesss. She needed him, needed this. Phoebe moaned again when he sucked her through the silk, the friction of his tongue through the fabric felt so damn good. But it was not quite enough.

"More," he growled, reading her body expertly.

The ripping of fabric sounded loud in the room, but it was nothing compared to her moan of ecstasy when he sank his thick tongue deep inside of her. Moisture pooled beneath her as she frantically clutched at his hair, but Nathan was relentless.

He fucked her with his tongue, holding her still with his enormous hands as she tried to buck wildly against him. With his enormous shoulders holding her legs wide open, Phoebe was totally at his mercy. But she felt nothing other than love and trust for him and in him well up inside of her.

She felt his canines brush against her clit, and she lost control. Like a tsunami her orgasm crested, the wave of bliss going on and on until she felt as if she would break. But he didn't let her, *no,* not her Dragon. Nathan brought her back down again with tender licks and kisses.

"Please," she whimpered. Phoebe needed him inside of her. *Now.*

"Anything for you. *Es meus*," he growled the words as he moved up her body.

Phoebe moaned, locking her legs around his waist as his cock glided along her slick folds. *Fuck*, that felt good. He did it again, and again, teasing her with his thick velvety shaft.

"Nathan, inside me, now," she squeezed his ass and slapped the flesh there, earning her a growl from her soon-to-be mate.

She stroked his skin where she spanked him and bit her lip as she felt his huge head nudging her opening. Her cleft was soaked and ready for him. Desperate to have him.

"Please," she begged again, unashamed of her need for this one man. *Her mate, her SeaDragon.*

"*Es meus*," he growled the phrase and pushed himself, inch by inch, stretching her, until he was seated fully within her flesh.

Phoebe trembled at his slow, hard penetration. His salty smoky scent mingled with hers, creating something new and beautiful. Something her magic recognized as theirs.

She could feel the tendrils of their bond thickening as he began to move, stroking her from the inside out. He pumped harder, the slap of their skin echoing in the room.

"*Flava*," he growled, "so good, so perfect. Mine."

Their lips met and he plundered her mouth in time with his thrusts. Phoebe moaned, her skin humming with pleasure. Magic thick in the air, she welcomed their connection. Called it to her.

Her hands gripped his ass, squeezing the smooth tanned cheeks as he flexed and swirled his hips, grinding his pubis against her clit and creating the most delicious sparks of pleasure. Letting go of his mouth, she tilted her head, exposing her neck to him.

"Nathan, now," she moaned as her sex clenched. She wanted him to mark her during her next orgasm. Needed it like she needed air.

"*Es meus*," he growled and thrust his hips harder. Arms wrapped around her he pressed deeper and deeper until she thought she'd be crushed by his delicious weight, but she wouldn't let him go, not for anything. And then it happened.

Just as her pussy tightened around him with the first throes of ecstasy, he leaned his head closer. She felt his Dragon fangs break through her skin, reveled in his strength as he sucked on her flesh, cementing the bond between them.

Phoebe cried out as his cock jerked and he moaned as his hot seed spilled inside her, sending another wave of passion flowing through her veins. Tighter she milked his flesh, greedy for every single drop of him. Her orgasm lasted longer than she'd ever experienced. The incredible pleasure of belonging to him, of sharing in his *heart's fire* pulsed throughout her entire body.

Finally, mine forever, she swore it was his voice inside her head as he licked her wounds closed. She echoed the sentiment. *Wholeheartedly.*

"Mmm. That was incredible," she said pressing a kiss to his neck and smiling with pure joy as he lifted his face to look at her.

"Yes, *flava,*" he agreed and kissed her sweetly.

"Nathan?"

"What is it, my love?"

"You never told me what it means. All those things you say in *Dracan?*"

"Ah. I call you *flava* because of your beautiful flaxen hair. Like spun gold, so beautiful, my love. *Es meus* is something I can't help but say where you are concerned, roughly translated it simply means *mine.*"

"Yours? That's kind of caveman-ish don't you think?"

"A *caveman,* am I? Perhaps I should show you that

you are mine alone, *flava*, in case you have any doubts," he nipped her ear and she shivered in anticipation.

"Yes," she whimpered.

She felt his desire flare to life, echoing her own. One thing was sure, she would never tire of her making love to her SeaDragon.

"I love you, mate," he said and kissed her lips.

"I love you too," she wrapped her arms around his neck and yelped when he stood and lifted her clean off the floor.

"This time, I want a bed to properly love my mate on."

EPILOGUE

Months later...

"That was a long five hours," Nathan groaned as he stretched outside of his mate's Mercedes. He didn't mind that she insisted on driving all the time, but he sometimes wondered why they couldn't just fly where they needed to go. He did so enjoy flying. Especially with his little mate tucked against him. *Grrr.*

"We can't fly because someone might see you," she laughed and smoothed her hands over her hair.

She was so beautiful. Nathan smiled as she looked over her generous curves in the short blue sundress she wore for their day on the beach. He narrowed his eyes as he thought about the yellow two piece she wore underneath. That bathing suit was the reason they were two hours late to his first meeting with the Falk Clan Dragons of Maccon City, New Jersey.

What could he say? His *flava* was something to see in that high-waisted two-piece. *Hmm. Something he did not want anyone else to see.*

"Oh, can it with the caveman stuff already! These guys are all mated."

His mate had to remind him occasionally that it was an inappropriate use of his newly increased powers to send twenty-foot waves crashing down on anyone who happened to look upon his luscious mate with anything other than respect in their gaze. Not that he agreed, but he did try and please her these days, especially since she was expecting their first young.

It was months too soon for her to show, but he'd insisted on taking her shopping to buy her choice of maternity clothes and things for the baby. *A baby. Their baby.* Nathan was over the moon. And fiercely protective.

The Heralds had agreed to put him to work training other Wardens at their Virginia station while Phoebe could manage her Charges from her desk for the time being. They were both so happy with the news nothing else mattered!

He'd long since acknowledged that Phoebe who was right about most things, *okay, all things,* was probably right about there being other Dragons in the world. After a few phone calls, she set up today's little beach party as a way of introducing them.

Nathan walked around to the trunk of the car and lifted their bags and cooler before walking around to help his mate. She positively glowed as she smiled at him before lifting her sunglasses to sit atop her head.

"There," she said and smiled as she waved to a huge man with black hair and a small child high on his shoulders.

The man waved back, and a tall, blonde woman joined him and beckoned them forward. Nathan could see three other couples and an assortment of children frolicking in the waves and he sent a command to the waters to keep them safe for the young.

"Can you sense them?"

"Yes, Dragons. They are real *Dragons,*" tears stung his eyes as he walked closer to the family. The Dragons all looked at him curiously before smiling and nodding.

"Welcome, I am Callius, the eldest Falk brother. This is my mate, Winifred. Here are my brothers and their mates, Edric and Joselyn, Alexsander and Noelle, and Nikolai and his mate Melody."

Nathan nodded and shook his hand before turning to his own mate.

"Thank you. This is my mate, Phoebe, we are both pleased to meet you."

"Someone get little Ed before he goes too far," yelled Joselyn, but before she could step towards the water Nathan fixed the issue. He sent a gentle wave of water to lift the toddler and carry him back to the shore just as Edric reached him and scooped him up.

"That is a neat trick, friend, come tell us about it," said Callius motioning to the chairs they had set up.

"Sure, one moment," Nathan said and turned to Phoebe. His excitement at meeting other Dragons was nothing compared to the love he felt for her. A love that grew every single day.

"Thank you, for making this possible, and for choosing me as your mate," he said pressing his forehead to hers.

"Nathan, I love you. Come on, let's go talk to the other Dragons," she smiled and kissed his lips.

"I love you too, *flava meus*," he growled and nipped her lip. With her hand in his they walked to sit with the others and Nathan sent a prayer of thanks to the Parcae. Guess he wasn't forgotten after all. *Not at all,* he thought as he looked at his mate.

Es meus.

MOON KISSED

USA TODAY BESTSELLING AUTHOR
C.D. GORRI
Moon
KISSED

WARDENS OF TERRA

MOON KISSED

When a curvy human stumbles into the supernatural world, this Grizzly Warden has no choice but to make her his!

Station Master Rex Bastian is a Grizzly Bear Shifter and a retainer of Taurus. Running the Virginia Station for the Wardens of Terra has been his ultimate dream since he'd been recruited as an orphaned cub off the streets of Washington D.C.

He now has everything he ever dreamed of. Power and position. Everything except the one thing he never wanted, *a mate*.

When all the Wardens under his care are away with

other assignments, Rex finds himself designated to attend the annual Council of Shifters Halloween Ball.

The problem is he doesn't have a date or a costume. A trip to a magical pop-up Halloween store called *Hazel's Halloween Happenings* proves to have everything the Bear Shifter could ever hope for!

PROLOGUE

The group of large Shifters convened around one of the several desks that sat separated by partitions across the floor of the large workspace of the Wardens of Terra Virginia Station.

They had something serious to discuss. It wasn't a new danger or evil that had cropped up in their midst. No monster to fight or do battle with. Oh no. This serious matter was closer to home.

Huffing and puffing, they were all splattered with various shades of paint from the fierce training battle they'd just endured. As they slowly got their breaths back, several of them frowned, checking the hall every few minutes. All of them were on needles and pins watching out for *him*.

It had been another long session, a simulated

battle necessary to keep their skills sharp. None of them did well enough for him though. Oh no. Their leader had ripped them all new ones for not being attentive and alert enough.

He'd run twenty-six scenarios and they'd passed each and every one except the last. And that was simply not good enough for the grouchy grizzly.

Those paint balls hurt too! What did he do? Put BBs in them or something? The group of Shifters shared similar thoughts as they rolled their shoulders and stretched their sore bodies.

It was hard enough when your job was saving the world every other fucking minute and no one acknowledged it, but when you're a-hole of a boss was constantly riding your ass, *man*, it was enough to make anyone just up and quit! Only, being a Warden of Terra wasn't something you could just walk away from.

Fucking honor and duty.

"So, what do we do with this stubborn ass fucking Bear?" Luis Fernandez tipped back his bottle of cold water and looked over the partition that separated his desk from the next one.

Who knew supernatural warriors who fought evil on a regular basis had to have desks too? The South American native shrugged as he took another swallow of fresh spring water.

"Well, he's never gonna mellow the fuck out if he doesn't find *the one.* And he's never gonna do that if he stays cooped up in here all the damn time," Troy Waman, Thunderbird Shifter, and retainer of Aquarius, replied.

"*Oy*, I don't know what the big deal is. He doesn't want a mate, no skin off my nose, is it?" Cecil shrugged. The blonde giant was averse to wedded bliss just as their fearless leader.

"That's because you're too busy trying to dip your stick in everything that moves, Cecil, but Rex isn't like that. The guy's been alone a long time, and I'm thinking he needs a little *lovin'* to help him get off our asses," Luis retorted.

"And if he doesn't want to be tied to one female for the rest of his life, what then, eh? He's got a right to choose freedom. If the job is too hard for you mated pansies, you know what to do," Cecil taunted.

Cecil had been a bit of a fucking dick lately. Both Troy and Luis thought so. As if they'd read each other's minds, they both rolled their eyes. The fact they had mates of their own might have had something to do with their difference of opinions, but who cared. They all needed Rex to back off.

"You only think that way because you've never held your fated mate in your arms, Cecil. Let me tell you from experience, there is nothing like it in the entire world. It's as if you are whole for the first time in your life," Luis stated.

"Not to mention the power rush. The Parcae bless us with increased abilities and strength upon our *matings*, you know. And who doesn't want to be stronger?" Troy asked.

"I don't know, maybe you two are right. All I know is my fucking shoulder is killing me after he got me with that blue round. Rex is a tough nut to crack. How would we get him out of here anyway?"

"That's the million-dollar question," Luis said.

Movement to the right made the men quickly pretend to grab their tablets. Luis stepped up and held his as if presenting them with something. He just got his maps app to work when the big as fuck Grizzly Bear Shifter in question stopped in front of the trip.

"The fuck are you three assholes doin' standing around? Training session is over. Didn't you get your assignments?" Rex demanded.

"Yes sir, boss, Luis and I are just waiting on our mates, and Cecil here is just a dick," Troy smirked and ducked before the lumbering blonde could catch him with his fist.

"Alright," Rex grunted, "Knock it off and get the fuck out of here."

He was never one to mince words. As *Station Master* of the Wardens of Terra Virginia Station he had more responsibility than the rest of them.

Fuck modesty, he was in charge of the whole damn team. Sure they'd sent him help in the form of a *Junior Station Master*, but that was a little complicated these days.

With Phoebe Bright mated and expecting her first child with her SeaDragon husband, Nathan Silvertongue, a Warden whose job was to now train young Shifters recently accepted into the program, Rex was pretty much back to running things all alone.

As Junior Station Master and a powerful Witch, Phoebe was able to handle things just fine, but her overprotective and *twice as strong since they mated* husband refused to have her do anything that could put her or their child in danger.

Rex wholeheartedly agreed with him. If not for any other reason than the fact that when he'd tried to point out Phoebe was perfectly capable of taking care of herself, the fucking SeaDragon flooded his brand-new fully loaded Cadillac Escapade with enough briny seawater to kill the engine and transmission.

Asshole.

How the fucker managed to get that much liquid into his vehicle and nowhere else baffled the mind, but Rex was smart enough to stop arguing with the guy. Actually, he kind of liked Nathan Silvertongue. Not that he would tell the Shifter that.

As the leader of their crew, he couldn't afford to be too close to anyone in his Station. Maintaining his authority was of the utmost importance. Especially when he had to answer to that group of self-important old farts, the fucking Heralds of Terra.

Those ancient bastards whose job it was to call the Wardens to action were more than just a meddlesome bunch. They were a damn nuisance. The old timers hated every new idea him and the other Station Masters presented as options for increasing their efforts. They vehemently distrusted the advances that had been made in both normal and supernatural technology over the past hundred years and, therefore, made it virtually impossible for the Wardens to come into the twenty-first century.

In fact, he'd just come from a meeting with the fuckers and could not believe what they'd told him.

They'd given him assignments to send every single one of his Wardens out on the busiest holiday in the supernatural world. *Halloween.*

Of course, he'd sent them over text to each of his Wardens as soon as he'd gotten them. Which was why he was surprised when those three idiot Shifters were still fucking around after their session. Shouldn't they be following orders? What the fuck?

"Hey," Phoebe Bright-Silvertongue waddled towards him from her desk almost catching him off-guard, but he was not so lost in thought he couldn't hear her approach.

Rex paused long enough so she could catch up with him. The smart little Witch was entering her third trimester and the little bundle she was carrying was proving to be quite active. The idea of children made his tongue go dry and his hands itch. He couldn't imagine bringing cubs into this world. He'd seen too much darkness for that.

"Can I help you Mrs. Silvertongue?"

"Rex, you can still call me Phoebe," she smiled.

"Oh really? Have you met your mate?" He grunted.

"Oh, yes. Well, I am sorry about Nathan. He's just being protective of me," she practically glowed as she said those words and he wanted to roll his eyes. But he didn't. *Always respectful.*

"Was there something you wanted?"

"Yes, would it be okay if I left a little early tonight? Nathan is going to surprise me with a spooky movie and a foot rub," she said with a hopeful expression on her face, and he sighed. Normally he'd say fuck no, but how could he refuse?

"Fine. See you on Monday then," he nodded and tried to walk away but she thrust an envelope out towards him first.

"What's this?"

"Your tickets," she nodded. He stared blankly at the black envelope.

"My tickets for what?"

"For the *Council of Shifters Halloween Ball?* Remember you said you would go for me since I can't really stay on my feet too long anymore?"

"I did?" Rex went over their recent conversations in his mind before landing on the one they'd had a few weeks ago.

That was the day Cecil had cooked lunch for everyone. *Ugh.* Rex had been trying to make it to the men's room when Phoebe and her hubby had blocked his path. He'd had no choice but to agree without really paying attention or risk getting sick in front of everyone.

"Do you remember, Rex?"

Fuck.

He did.

"Uh, yeah. I didn't realize it was tonight."

"It's Halloween silly! Now remember, you will also need a date. It starts at midnight, so you have just enough time to run to the costume store to pick up the rental I'd ordered for Nathan. It should fit you just fine," she smiled again.

"A costume and a date? Shit, Phoebe maybe we can just skip it," he began, but her lip started to quiver, and Rex stared horrified before he found his tongue again, "Never mind! Seriously, it's okay."

"Oh, are you sure? Cause the Heralds told me how important this was for public relations and how we needed to attend to represent the Wardens and increase recruitment since we are not only a group for just any old Shifters anymore, but for other supernaturals as well, and, and I am so glad you changed your mind!" She expelled a large breath and Rex found himself doing the same.

The woman's emotions were all over the damn place lately! Rex thanked the Parcae she'd stopped before she started crying. He had no desire to deal with an angry SeaDragon. Not again at any rate.

"I'll text you the address to the store! It's called *Hazel's Halloween Happenings*," Phoebe shouted as he walked away and waved her off.

The less contact he had with all these crazy mated couples the better as far as he was concerned. What the fuck was wrong with these people? They were chosen among millions to be *the* Wardens of Terra! A group of elite warriors chosen to protect the entire fucking world from evil!

Who the hell had time to pick out curtains and shit when you had that kind of responsibility? And as for the extra strength and powers? Fuck that.

From what he'd seen, he was better off alone than flying off the handle every time someone looked or said something to some woman who was suddenly tied to him. He needed that like he needed a goddamn noose around his neck.

No thanks. Rex was a loner, and he was perfectly fucking okay with that. As for playing dress up, well, if it was part of the job, he'd do it. The one thing that stumped him was the whole *date* part.

He shot off a quick email to the secretary at the home office and was told that he absolutely *had* to bring a date. The Council did not allow unaccompanied persons to attend on account of Shifter emotions running high. His phone beeped and he looked down to see a text had just come through.

You must bring a date. Station Master. the Council has decided it is best for everyone to bring a mate or even a random date as sort of a shield from drama.

He blinked and looked twice at the sender. It was the *ancient herald* himself. When did he learn to text? Shit. Rex was truly fucked now. He couldn't ignore the powerful man who was essentially his boss. He sent a few texts out to women from the office who might be free to go with him to the event.

After that, he jumped in his repaired and *thankfully dry* Escalade and punched in the GPS coordinates Phoebe had sent him. The store was close by.

He would have just enough time get the costume Phoebe had ordered and put it on. Hopefully by then, one of the women from work will have gotten back to him. Or not. He wasn't exactly known as Mr. Friendly amongst his co-workers.

Shit.

"*Hazel's Halloween Happenings,*" he grumbled and started the engine.

Sure, they'd have his costume. But could they get him a date?

Fucking hell.

CHAPTER ONE

Candra Nichols hurried into the strange looking little shop that seemed to have sprung up out of nowhere. Rain had started to pour from the skies a second ago, and she wanted to avoid getting caught in it.

It was odd really, since the forecast had called for nothing but clear skies through to Monday. Weather apps weren't the most reliable things around though, she readily admitted to herself. In fact, meteorologists had to have the most forgiving bosses in the world given they were hardly ever accurate.

Oh well, she thought and wiped her face with a now damp napkin that she'd had in her pocket. The gloomy weather was sort of perfect for the time of year.

No matter what, she always found a way to look on the bright side of things. It was a holdover from her days in foster care. She'd been a lucky kid after her parents' death when she was a teenager. The foster family who'd taken her in were kind to her and unobtrusive.

She'd left there after one year and had the court declare her independent so she could attend college and begin her life. Sure things were hard without her parents, but she was generally a happy person.

She sighed and looked down at her black kitten t-shirt. The thing was soaked, and it was the closest item of clothing she'd had to a costume this year. There just hadn't been time with her work at the animal shelter and her web business to take care of. People loved her little handcrafted figurines and personalized signs especially around the holidays.

It was in the beginning stages, but she did okay. Enough to pay her bills and add some to her savings, she thought happily. Candra shivered as she stepped further inside the darkly lit store. The bell on her keys jingled and she thought about *Jingles*, the little black cat that had been adopted earlier in the day. *That was a win*, she thought proudly.

She'd done her best to make the dreary shelter a bit happier this Halloween by putting brightly decorated pumpkins on the desk and making orange and black bandanas for the animals there in an effort to make them cuter and more likely to get adopted. *Jingles* was one of the younger cats and the couple who'd gotten him for their daughter was tickled with the pumpkin printed kerchief he wore.

Poor old things, she thought about the other inhabitants of the shelter for just a second before she remembered she had finally convinced one of their volunteers to turn the various cats she'd fostered into permanent pets.

All in all, six cats were adopted that day alone! It made Candy, as she was called by her friends, feel just awesome inside. The world with all its darkness could be a pretty amazing place sometimes.

Sort of like this place, she mused as she shook the rain out of her long dark hair and gazed wide-eyed at her surroundings.

"Hazel's Halloween Happenings," she read the words etched into the glass door out loud, "Hello? Anyone here?" She called out before wandering through the semi-lit aisles.

It was one of those funky little costume shops better suited to Manhattan or D.C., not this decidedly untrendy part of nowhere Virginia. Still, what a find! *Lucky girl.*

Excitement bubbled up inside of her as she took in the rows of wigs and gloves, stockings, and faux jewelry. It was like she wandered into a fairytale or a time warp, she thought and sighed. She gasped as she picked up a package of lacey thigh highs that undoubtedly went with the French maid's costume to the left of them. *Ooh la la.*

Deciding she was too flat chested to pull off a costume like that she kept walking. *Not that I need a costume for any reason*, she thought with a sigh.

Wouldn't it be awesome to go to some super fancy masquerade ball somewhere and meet prince charming? Unfortunately, there were none of either of those things in sight. *Sigh.* Undaunted, she decided she could still have fun exploring the unique shop.

It would be like her own mini adventure, she decided! She'd always loved the idea of having her own personal, what was the word? Ooh! *Escapade. Yeah*, she liked that! A romantic fairytale escapade just for her! If only there was a *prince*, or maybe a *pirate*, at the end.

"Hello?" Candy called out again, wondering where the salesperson was hiding. Maybe he or she was dozing off in the back? *Oh well*, she'd get there eventually.

First, she wanted to check things out. Gory

displays of zombies and man-eating monsters took up an entire aisle and she thrilled at the idea that someone took the time to set up such intricate realistic scenes for a seasonal shop!

Swords, wands, axes, throwing stars, and dozens of other blood curling weapons and accessories guaranteed to dazzle any Halloween reveler filled shelf after shelf. There was even a certain scary as hell glove with knives where the fingers should be. *Shiver.* Candy let out an excited giggle as she continued to browse.

"So spooky! It's perfect," she said to herself and laughed again.

Her excitement level continued to grow as she passed the horror stuff in favor of the more fairytale themed displays.

"Oh wow!" She exclaimed.

A huge toadstool sat against one wall with fairy wings in all colors and glittery tiaras next to it. Super cute, but not *her*, she thought as she ran a hand over the flower crowns and vials of fairy dust. *So cool!*

Finally, she reached the very back wall where dozens of dresses and suits from every time period hung decoratively from wires. A devourer of period romance novels, she gasped in surprise as she took in the beautiful gothic dresses and sexy vampire costumes.

They were simply beautiful. Something of an artist herself she recognized the custom work and was astonished to find it on display in such an out of the way shop. *Must do the bulk of their business on the internet,* she thought.

Candy *oohed* and *aahed* over the sumptuous gowns and rakish heroes' costumes even as she wondered why this place was still open since most trick-or-treaters would be home by now.

Her cell phone confirmed her suspicions. It was after ten already. Her shift at the animal shelter had run later than usual and then, she'd gotten caught in the rain. But who cared about wet hair and soaked sneakers when there was all this cool stuff to explore!

"Hello! Anyone here?" She called out again dutifully, though at this point she secretly hoped the store was deserted so she could look some more and maybe even try on some stuff without being hassled by a salesperson!

Biting her bottom lip, she walked behind the counter. A clear dress bag hung from the rack next to the register. Curiosity got the best of her, and she picked up the two costumes that bore the same ticket number. Candy shrugged and read the invoice. Her smile wide as she read the name.

"*Phoebe Bright.* Hmm, nice name," she said and looked over the intricate costumes.

Whoever Phoebe Bright was, Candra suspected she'd ordered one of the two costumes for a boyfriend as it was a man's gladiator rig.

A simple loincloth or *subligaculum,* as she recalled the thing was named, with a matching cloak hung from a hanger. There were brass wristlets, reminiscent of shackles that went with it and leather sandals with laces that went around one's calves. *Hmm, cool.*

The silky dress next to it was made of some sort of pale material that clasped over one shoulder with a golden leaf. Layers of that fabric made up the long flowing skirt and Candy sighed. It looked like a dream. Several gold bangle bracelets and smaller lace-up sandals were tucked inside a bag next to it.

Ooh! It was a *Gladiator* and a *Roman Noblewoman*! Maybe she was having a careless fling with the slave warrior her husband owned? Or maybe she was trying to buy the freedom of her gladiator lover despite her family's objections. Candra's imagination ran away with her as she stared at the complimentary outfits.

She became mesmerized by the costume as she

ran her fingers over the layers of silky, sheer fabric. The dress seemed to grow warm in her hands. It pulsed and glowed as she held it. Eyes wide, Candy bit her lip and smiled.

It was as if destiny was calling out to her. A small fire had begun inside of her with hope and expectation fanning it on. Perspiration dotted her brow or was that the rain? Nope, she was definitely sweating. Her heart thudded in her chest. The store itself seemed to hold its breath as she waged an internal war within herself.

Could this be for me, she wondered as she fingered the material. What were the odds another woman somewhere was her exact size and coloring?

She had to admit that the silvery pale shade was perfect for her pale skin, steel-colored eyes, and ebony hair. Candra was an artist first after all, and she deeply appreciated the complimentary way the dress would enhance her features.

But it was more than that. She truly felt as if she'd just begun some amazing adventure. Or at least, she would, if only she wore that dress!

She couldn't help herself. Candra had to try it on.

R ex tapped on the steering wheel of his Escalade and grumbled as he drove into the cold rain. *When the fuck did that start?* He hadn't even noticed the change in weather since he'd taken off from the Station.

He'd never heard of *Hazel's Halloween Happenings* until Phoebe had brought it up. *Must be new*. Fucking place was in a nasty part of town, but that was Virginia for you. Plenty of pretty suburbs, but every now and then there was a fucked up little section that no one liked to talk about or acknowledge. *Like every other fucking city, I'd ever travelled to*, he thought grumpily.

After he passed his third boarded up *bodega*, Rex shook his head. No way would that fucking SeaDragon have let his mate step foot into this derelict of a fucking town. On the corner sat a group of young men, riled up and looking for trouble. Out to prove something or other to the world, not that Rex gave a fuck.

Whatever they thought about themselves or the concealed weapons they carried, a fact he could scent in the air, they were no match for his Grizzly Bear. *Hell no*, growled the beast inside of him.

Rex was a giant in his human form, but as his Shifter, filled with the mega dose of testosterone and general bullheadedness thanks to his affiliation with Taurus, he was one unstoppable fucker. His Grizzly Bear was massive. almost one-ton of furry and *fangy* fury. Speaking of which, the animal inside of him was getting antsy as he continued to drive to the programmed coordinates.

Rex rolled his shoulders and shot a glare at the thugs on the corner. Smartly, they turned away. At seven-feet tall with a dozen tribal tattoos swirling over his hulking muscles and his hair and beard cropped closely to his rugged face, Rex was a scary looking dude.

He snorted. He long ago accepted he was not like *normals*. Hell, he wasn't like other Shifters either.

Blending in was a little bit harder for him, but he rolled with it.

Made his job as Station Master a little easier. He doubted he'd have the respect of many of his Wardens if he looked like the boy next door. He grunted at the thought. They were a loyal bunch; he'd give them that.

He passed more dilapidated looking houses, some with wrought iron bars over the windows. Imagine all this just twenty minutes from their neat looking, secure little Station. *Shit.* Was the GPS fucking with him? There was nothing around here! Well, not true. If he wasn't mistaken there was an animal shelter somewhere in the vicinity, but other than that *nada.*

Finally, he found the place. A small neon signed blinked the word "open" making it stand out on the otherwise dark sidewalk. He growled as he turned off his vehicle. *Fuck.* It was raining heavily. Rex grunted. He wasn't going to just sit around bitching about it. *Get moving fucker,* he told himself.

As soon as he pushed the door open, he noted a change in the atmosphere. It was as if the very air grew thick and heavy around him. That sixth sense he had relied on in battle so many times before started tingling. Only it was different. Not a warning per se, more like anticipation filled his veins.

What the fuck is that heavenly smell? The Bear within him pushed at his skin, urging him on. The scent of strawberries and sunshine filled his nostrils. His Bear rumbled loudly in his chest.

The animal inside him demanded he hurry the fuck up and seek out the source of that tantalizing aroma. Stomping loudly on booted feet, Rex stalked to where his nose led. The sound of a distinctly feminine giggle reached his ears. He stopped in his tracks. *Fuck no.*

His heart pounded and the roar inside of his head grew louder, more demanding. Everything inside him cried out for him to move. *Now.* He needed to find the female who belonged to that seductive little giggle and stake his claim before someone else did. *Mine,* growled his Bear. *Back the fuck off,* countered the man.

There was no way Rex Bastian, Grizzly Bear Shifter and Warden of Terra, was about to get pussy whipped by some nutty fucking female who was giggling all by herself! He knew instinctively the shop was empty save for the strawberry scented woman and himself. Despite the blood thundering in his veins, Rex held himself still. *Maybe he could still sneak out?*

"Is someone there?" A voice that rang of bells and sweet melodies reached his ears and the Bear inside him went wild. *Shit.* She'd heard him.

"You have an order waiting for me," he said as he approached the back counter.

He still hadn't seen the woman belonging to the magical scent and tempting voice. He didn't want to. *Maybe she'd be butt ugly then he could tell the Parcae thanks, but no thanks for this mate of his?*

Long black velvet curtains hung behind the desk, to some back room he imagined. He waited as they were parted by long slender hands. *Pale hands tipped with long fingernails*, he groaned. He fucking loved women with long nails.

As more of her was revealed through the black curtain, Rex felt his entire body grow taut with anticipation. Every Shifter he knew had grown up with the fairytales of fated mates and finding "the one". Every single one of them waited for this day. Some for what seemed like their entire lives. Others never achieved such blessings from the universe.

He should be counting himself lucky, but Rex hesitated. He wasn't like other Shifters. He was a leader. A good one too. But that was only because he never allowed himself to get too close to those under his command.

He'd remained aloof and apart. How could he learn to care for a mate when he'd never had one serious relationship in his entire life? *No.*

She stepped through the curtain completely and every single thought he had left his mind. The female was swathed in a silky confection that left one creamy shoulder bare. Gathered at her indented waist with a golden, tasseled rope, the dress flowed to her ankles in sheer layers that gave him glimpses of the sumptuous flesh beneath.

She was tall for a woman. *Deep breath,* for a *normal* woman, he thought shocked at the revelation. High, tip-tilted breasts thrust out from the gathered fabric of the bodice. *Shit,* she wasn't wearing a bra. Rounded hips flared out from her tiny waist and his fingers itched to touch, to test the skin he instinctively knew was soft as silk.

Her smile was infectious. Intelligent silver eyes sparkled from beneath thick black lashes. Her hair was the same shade of ebony and hung low on her back in a straight midnight curtain that he wanted to bury his face in. She was strikingly beautiful. *Oh, I am in serious trouble.*

"Hi! My name is Candra Nichols," she said and held her hand out in front of her.

That smile wavered when he didn't accept said hand. She recovered immediately. Dropping the proffered hand, she shrugged that beautiful pale shoulder and tilted her head.

"*Rex*. My name is Rex," he said, *like a fucking moron*. "Uh, an order? You have my order."

"Oh, um, the only one here is for a *Phoebe Bright*," she winced as she said it and he scented a touch of guilt in her answer. He tilted his head as he waited for her to explain.

"I'm so sorry. I, uh, tried this one on, couldn't resist," she said as she handed him the bag and gestured to her costume. He nodded and glimpsed at what was obviously the male counterpart to the costume she wore.

"The order was for two costumes?"

"Yeah, I am so sorry. Please tell your girlfriend or wife that I apologize, let me just get this thing off," she took a step back, but he reached out and caught her hand before she could retreat.

Sparks ignited between the place where their skin touched. Rex sucked in a breath. He'd been unprepared for the powerful shot of lust that shot straight to his groin at such platonic contact.

"Uh, no, no need, *Candra*," just saying her name was fucking with his senses. Making him feel all sorts of naughty things for the stranger in front of him. Her eyes widened and he caught a whiff of her own arousal. *Shit.*

This was not good. If this kept up, he'd have her bent over the counter and his dick buried inside of her faster than he could say his own name.

"Look, uh, I'm headed to a ball, and I need a date. Why don't you close up shop and come with?"

He winced as he said it, his voice gruff and demanding. *Fuck.* If he was Luis or Cecil, he could get away with shit like that. Those two smooth talking fucks were better at this type of thing. But not him. He was awkward and stiff in his mannerisms and speech. Just part of that *stay the fuck away from me* attitude he exhibited.

"Really?" She said and he could practically taste her excitement.

"Uh, yes?" He said though it sounded more like a question to his own ears.

"Wow! Really? Is it a Halloween ball?"

"It is."

"Great!"

"So you'll come with me?" He couldn't hide his shock.

"Sure," she nodded.

"Um, okay then. Is there a place I could change?" He asked hurriedly so she couldn't change her mind.

"Sure, back here," she pointed to the curtain, and he frowned at her willingness to go. Did the woman have no sense of self-preservation? He could be an axe murderer for fucks sake.

"Look you don't know me-"

"Yes, I do. You're Rex," she laughed, and he swallowed, "Go get changed and I'll try to find the person who runs this place."

"What? It's not you?"

"Who me? No," she tucked her hand behind her ear and laughed a little self-consciously, "I just kind of wandered in out of the rain on my way home from work. This place is great though, isn't it?"

"Uh, yeah, sure. Give me a second to get dressed then," he grunted and wandered off to the back with his costume.

"My phone is on the counter if you want to get it and call some of my contacts to make sure I'm not some crazy guy off the street who's just kidnapping you or something," he said and was rewarded with another of her sweet, wholehearted laughs.

Damn, this woman was about as free, open, and honest as air. *Like sunshine personified*, he thought.

For the first time in his life, Rex found himself wanting to get to know someone.

He wanted to know *her. What made her tick? Would he be able to make her smile like that?* The realization that he wanted her was like a punch to the gut. It would change everything, he knew, but it was worth it just to bask in the warmth of *her.*

"Oh, I trust you, Rex, but if it makes you feel better, I'll call someone. How about Phoebe Bright herself?" she said.

"Sure," he grunted and unlocked the cell phone for her with a swipe of his thumb.

He dressed quietly, listening to her phone call. Lucky for him, his supernatural hearing picked up on Phoebe's voice as she picked up her cell.

"Hi, my name is Candra Nichols. I'm calling because Rex here has just asked me to attend a ball with him and he wanted to make sure I knew he wasn't a crazy axe murderer, so, is he?"

Rex let out a hoarse chuckle at her speech. The little minx! *Ha!*

CHAPTER THREE

Candy's eyes lit up the second she spotted the tall god-like man step up to the counter. *Uh oh.* Sure that she'd been caught, she waited for him to bust her, but much to her surprise he didn't. In fact, he asked her out! *My own mini romantic adventure,* she thought with wonder.

Nothing like that had ever happened to her before. Not that she wasn't always hoping and looking out for some amazing opportunity to find her. She sighed and ran a hand over the butter soft leather of the luxury SUV.

"You sure you're comfortable?" Her gruff escort asked turning brilliant blue eyes on her. Like lasers they glued her to her seat, and she found herself wishing all sorts of naughty things. *Why Candy, your inner slut is waking up! And isn't it delicious.*

"Oh yes, I'm comfortable," she said and bit her lip. True he made her want naughty things, but she couldn't help it. She was simply drawn to his animal magnetism. He was so big and strong and just *wow*.

"So, the place we're going to is a bit *different*," his roughened voice tickled her senses, and she closed her eyes to savor it.

"Like *bdsm* different? Cause I am telling you now if anyone is getting spanked it's gonna be you," she smirked, and he nearly swerved off the road.

"No! Not like *that*," he looked her way, and she swore those crazy eyes of his were glowing. Like magic. *Yummy.*

"You into spanking?' he asked wide-eyed.

"Not sure. I never tried it. So what about you?"

"Am I into spanking?"

"No, well yeah I guess, but I meant what do you do for a living Rex?"

"Oh," he cleared his throat, "I run a group of *security guards*, you could say," he mumbled.

"Oh, that's why you look like that then," she said and raised her dark eyebrows as she tried not to stare at the large mass of muscles on view in his tiny gladiator outfit.

Not that she could help it. The red cloak that went over his shoulders was open so he could use his arms to drive, gifting her with a perfect view of sculpted pecs and abs. It was all she could do not to reach out a hand and run them over his amazing physique.

"Look like what?"

"You know, so *athletic* and all," she answered.

"Athletic?"

"You're completely ripped! Rex, your muscles have *muscles*. You do know that, right? I mean women must fall at your feet when you walk into a room," she laughed as he continued to look out the window with the cutest little confused expression on his oh-so-serious face.

She must have embarrassed him though cause his neck turned a deep shade of red as she spoke. *Oh wow! Cute and shy*, she thought and reached out with a hand to skim his bicep.

"Yup, hard as a rock!" She exclaimed and thought she heard a grunted *you have no idea*, but she wasn't sure, so she didn't mention it.

"So, uh, what do you do Candra?"

"You can call me Candy," she answered and turned in her seat to face him. "Well, right now I work at the Animal Shelter over on Belvidere, but really, I'm sort of a professional *crafter*!"

"A what?"

"I'm an artist. I craft things, sell them at local art shows and street fairs," she smiled and itched to reach out to wipe the frown off his face.

What was it about the big man that made her just want to curl herself around him? Besides his good looks, that is. Maybe it was because of the way he seemed so guarded?

"Oh," he grunted his frown deepening, "How can you live off that?"

"You'd be surprised. People love handmade things and I have a website and everything. I make the cutest little animal figurines. Bears are my specialty. Not teddy bears, more like little clay versions of the real thing. I sell my crafts year-round."

"*Bears?*" He seemed to choke on the word. "Uh, maybe I can see them sometime," another mumble.

Happiness radiated through her at that one sentence. Without thinking about it she leaned over and kissed his cheek. Always a demonstrative person she relied on tactile ways to express herself. It was part of what made her a good artist.

Still, Candy wasn't prepared for the smoldering heat in his blue eyes when he turned his head at the last second and caught her lips with his. It was like kissing a volcano. She could feel his power and heat slowly bubbling to the surface, threatening to consume her.

Would that be so bad? She thought as she opened her lips for him, giving him entry to her deepest secrets. The sound of a horn blaring behind them turned his expression from smoking hot desire to fury in an instant. His eyes even seemed to glow in the dark cabin of the SUV, and she swore she heard a growl.

"Sorry," he said, "I didn't mean for that kiss to get so out of hand."

"That's alright. I wasn't complaining," she smiled and felt warmth spread over her face.

She wasn't embarrassed exactly, but here she was in a stranger's car going to a fancy Halloween Ball and getting kissed. What a night! Like a fantasy out of one of her beloved novels. You know, the ones you read once or *five times* cause they were just that good.

Candy was a firm believer in repeating things that made her feel good. And she planned on getting a repeat of that kiss. *Soon.*

They arrived at their destination shortly. She gaped in wonder at the huge seemingly abandoned warehouse that was surrounded on all sides by vehicles of every shape and size. Men larger than her date blocked the entry doors and she watched in wonder as Rex handed the men two tickets. They nodded and he maneuvered them both smoothly through the throng of party goers.

"Wow! Look at these costumes!" she exclaimed.

Her eyes were going to explode at the sheer amount of gorgeousness in the room! Every single person there was movie star beautiful and beyond. The stunning physical perfection made her itch for a sketch pad, but no one caught her attention like the mountainous man beside her.

He moved gracefully for someone so big. She noted the careful, yet possessive hand he placed at the small of her back while he greeted the people who seemed to be throwing the event. Oddly enough, Candy noted several of the revelers sniffing the air and watching her with eyes that seemed to glow.

"Come on," he said and lead her to a small table, "I need to go talk to that man there. Will you be alright for a minute?"

"Sure."

Candra watched her date walk to the bar where he bowed in a rather old-fashioned sort of greeting. Maybe cause of his costume? She shrugged and watched the byplay before realizing she was no longer alone.

"Greeting this Hallow's Eve, young one," a tall, thin man with an equally slender woman took the seats opposite her and gazed at her with dark predatory eyes. He was handsome in his own way, she supposed, but he didn't appeal to her on a personal level.

"Hi! Happy Halloween," she smiled.

"You are unaccompanied? Perhaps looking for some *entertainment*," the woman leaned forward and ran a long black fingernail down Candy's arm, making her shiver.

"Who me? No, my date is just over there," she nodded to where Rex was standing with his back to her.

"You are with the Warden?" The woman looked alarmed and squeezed her companion's arms. Candy couldn't help wondering her ancestry as she had the most unique features she'd ever seen.

Exaggerated eyes, big and luminescent like some anime doll, they were like liquid ink, slanted at the ends. She had a tiny nose and a wide mouth, when she spoke, Candy could've sworn she saw at least three rows of sharp little teeth. Her date was equally foreign looking.

Not beautiful, not really, with his green tinted skin. *Cool makeup*, she thought as she took in the rest of his features. His aristocratic nose was interesting, but it was the same three rows of pointy teeth that made her shiver again.

"But I like this one," he said in a low voice, "she is fat and ripe."

"Hey! Watch it buster," she argued.

Candy was not exactly sensitive about her weight, but no girl liked to be called fat! At a hundred and seventy pounds she was hardly skinny, but she worked out and she was tall for the women in her family!

"Yes, spicy too, but *the Warden*," the female hissed.

"He should not have left her alone then," the man continued but Candy was incensed.

"Would you like to meet some people?"

"I haven't even met you yet," Candy frowned.

"Forgive us, sweet. My name is Cornelius, and this is Simone," he nodded at the thin woman whose skin had also taken on a greenish hue.

"I'm Candra," she took his hand and was amazed at the strength behind the thin man's grip. *Whoa. Must be a fitness buff like Rex.* Where the hell was her date anyway?

"I really should wait for Rex," she began.

'We will take you to him, no worries, dear. But wouldn't you like to meet the host?" Simone spoke over the band that had just begun to play.

The music was jazzy and soulful, nothing like anything she listened too, but it seemed to fit the atmosphere and Candy was too curious to sit still for long. She shrugged and stood up, following the couple in their matching black suits, and wondered if they were supposed to be cat burglars or ninjas.

"Hey, where are we going?"

"Somewhere very interesting," Simone said and gripped her hand tighter as she pulled her through the crowd, further away from the direction she'd last seen Rex go in.

Her survival instinct must have kicked in because she stopped in her tracks, startled by the sudden angry hiss that came from both Cornelius and Simone.

"No stopping now, sweet, we are *sooo* hungry," he purred softly and pulled her against him in a tight embrace when she would have struggled to get the attention of passersby.

What the hell had she gotten into? One second, she was having a fantasy date with the most handsome man she'd ever seen, then this?

CHAPTER FOUR

R ex growled in frustration as he listened to one of the Shifter Council members drone on and on about their continued relationship with the Wardens and what the future meant. He knew this was why he was here, but he felt antsy leaving his mate alone for so long.

Candra, he couldn't call her Candy without images of eating her floating through his mind and that was not a good thing in this fucking costume, was probably bored as hell. He was going to kill Nathan. The gladiator costume was little more than a miniskirt for fuck's sake, with a hip length cloak to cover the rest of him and a pair of shackle bracelets. *The fuck?* He felt like a stripper.

Candra, thoughts of her invaded his mind taking

the place of the dull whine of the Councilman. He still hadn't explained anything to her about what he was and what she was.

As a powerful Shifter and a Station Master, Rex had a great deal of responsibility thrust upon him. He could handle that. But what was he going to do with a delicate normal mate who was too trusting with strangers and full of bubbling warmth, honesty, and curiosity? *He would make her happy*, his Bear insisted. But would she even want him to try?

She was a logistics nightmare for someone like him. He never did anything on the fly. Always a planner, he was in charge of organizing and orchestrating assignments for the most elite team of Shifter warriors on the fucking planet. What were the Parcae thinking tangling his life with someone who just jumped into the car with a stranger?

Okay, so she did call Phoebe as a reference, but still, Phoebe could have been part of his devious plans to kidnap her or worse! He needed to get back to Candra, to explain things so she wouldn't misunderstand.

"Excuse me, Councilman. I must return to my date," he said.

"Looks like you already lost her, Station Master," was the wry reply.

"What?" Rex roared and turned around earning the shocked stares of many of the partiers.

Shit. He should have remembered where they were, who it was that attended these things. The Shifter Council invited many species of supernaturals to these events to foster the spirit of cooperation.

Some that might not know how very serious the rules were. *Yes,* they were all warned to keep their hands to themselves, hence the mandatory date, but he was unsure of whether or not that extended to innocents or persons out of the know. *Shit.* Candra could be in trouble. As Troy like to say *fuck and damn.*

He tipped his head back, allowing his Bear out a little bit more than he'd intended, to try and pick out her scent among the crowd of people and, *er,* things. From the far end of the room he caught the faintest whiff of sunshine. *Grrr.*

"Excuse me!"

"Watch it!"

Rex ignored the shocked gasps as he pushed people aside to follow the trail his mate had left through the dark room. There had to be five hundred potentially deadly *supernaturals* there already. And his little normal mate. *Fuck and damn* again.

The music was loud and pulsating. He couldn't pick up her voice even with his supernatural hearing. She could be calling out for him! *Grrr.* He increased his pace. Never had he felt so helpless.

The sight of a small door slightly ajar caught his attention and he raced towards it. Sure enough, the scent of strawberries and sunshine grew stronger with every step he took.

"Hey! I said no buddy, I am not interested! I told you before-"

That voice. It was his Candy, and she was in trouble from the sounds of things. Rex burst through the door not knowing what to expect. He cursed himself ten times the fool for not telling her to stay put or warning her about what kind of place they were in. *Fuck and damn.*

"Rex!" Smiling silver eyes landed on him and his breath caught in his throat. She was safe, unharmed, but his Bear was still pissed as hell.

"It's the Warden!"

"I told you this was a bad idea, Cornelius," hissed the female of one of the most devious pairs of supernatural creatures he'd ever come across. The *Succubus* and it's male companion, the *Incubus*. These two had a most unusual yet entirely symbiotic relationship.

Related to Vampires marginally, the two creatures fed on *sex*. His eyes quickly jumped back to where Candra sat primly on a stool with her arms crossed over her stomach. She didn't appear to be harmed or molested in any way, *but still.*

The idea of her being hurt on his watch was too unthinkable. He'd only just met her, hadn't had a chance yet to explain what he was or what she meant to him. What if these two assholes had hurt her? Anger shot through his blood, thundering in his ears and he growled again.

Fur sprouted along his arms and face, claws tipped his fingernails, the Bear pushing to let loose. A slow, unending rumble reverberated from his chest making the two incubi hiss and move nearer to each other.

Not especially built for battle, these two had other means of fighting. Mainly to bite with their needle thin teeth, inducing a coma-like state among their victims. Their venom was like supernatural *Rohypnol.* They were no better than fucking rapists in his book.

"We saw her alone," the male parted his hands as if to explain, but Rex was beyond reasoning he growled loudly and shoved the slender man. His Bear pushed against his skin, begging for release, wanting to do all manner of gory things to this *thing* who dared touch his female.

"Mine," he bared his teeth and snarled in the direction of the one who dared speak.

"Rex, you found me!" He turned and watched an unmolested Candy slip off her stool with a great wide smile on her beautiful face.

She walked up to him and laced her arm with his soothing his beast, "Hey, what's with the fur? Anyway, this is kind of embarrassing, but these guys thought I was up for some kind of three way with the two of them," she giggled.

"What?" he bellowed.

"Yeah, I know. So completely forward of them, and flattered, but that is a hard pass. No harm, no foul, right guys?" Candy said in her happy voice, soothing his Bear's fur and claws into receding. *Just like that.*

"Um, right," Simone said and smiled, revealing several rows of tiny sharp teeth. Rex growled again, fur and claws threatened to re-sprout his Bear taking the sight as a challenge to which the Succubus squeaked and hid behind her male counterpart.

"I know what you are and what you were about to do-"

"No! We have mended our ways, *Warden*, I swear it. We were not going to bite her, merely to ask if she was interested in a little, *um, well, er,*" Cornelius stuttered and backed up a step nearly knocking Simone down.

"We weren't going to bite her," blurted Simone.

"Why bring her here then?" He growled. His anger palpable.

"To ask and maybe t-to *show,*" stuttered the Succubus.

It took everything in him to rein in his Bear who wanted nothing more than to tear the two vermin apart. They dared bring his mate, *his mate,* to this fucking closet where they intended to what? Entice her to sex. *With them?* Fucking hell no. *Mine!*

"I'm fine, Rex, really. They thought that maybe if I saw them, you know, *getting it on,* that I'd want to join in, but I refused really," she held one hand up high like she was testifying in court, and he wanted to scream. The woman had no idea how much danger she was in.

"Get out before I lodge a complaint with the Council or *worse,*" he whispered surprising himself and the two Incubi.

"What?" Cornelius asked.

"Get out!" Bellowed Rex, eyes closed he focused on the sound of the two running out the door of the small eight by ten room before he turned to find Candra looking at him with concern in her pale silver gaze.

"Are you alright?"

"Am I alright? Do you have any idea how dangerous those two are? No, of course you don't! You go behind counters in weird shops and jump into cars with strange men!" He growled and took a step away from her kicking one of the several boxes on the floor of the storage closet clear across the room. The resounding crash wasn't nearly as satisfying as he needed it to be.

He exhaled and closed his eyes, willing himself to calm down, but it was no good. She stood there, her sweet strawberry sunshine scent wrapping around him like chains. *Fuck.*

His dick hardened under the flimsy gladiator costume he wore. Rex thanked the Parcae he chose briefs that morning instead of free balling it like he usually did. She was driving him wild with her fucking delicious scent and bright smile.

"Rex, are you okay?" The feel of her small hand on his naked bicep made him shiver.

He opened his eyes and pinned her with his stare, fully aware his Bear was showing in them. She opened her mouth and gasped. He could hear her heart rate speed up. *Finally*, he thought, *she's afraid.*

"Candra," he growled her name, tasting each syllable against his tongue like he wanted to taste her.

She swayed towards him, eyes wide, breathing heavily as he placed his hands gently on her waist. Not afraid, *aroused,* he realized as he breathed in the subtle addition to her fragrance.

He pulled her slowly towards him, until her tall, lush frame was nestled against his. *It was now or never,* he decided. He had no patience for games or a slow courting, but still, he would try to give her what she needed. *Always.*

She was his fated mate. Even he couldn't fight the entire universe. Just being near her made his blood sing and his soul cry out to get closer. *Yes*, he would give her anything she wanted, he realized.

"Rex," she whispered his name, hands moving up his arms to rest on his shoulders.

"Mine," he growled and dipped his head.

A ray of silver shone down on them from a small skylight, and he thought he'd never seen anything as beautiful as his mate, kissed by the moon and *soon,* by him as well.

His lips met hers, slowly, steadily at first. Taking his time to absorb the softness of her skin he allowed her to test their connection, to nibble at his lower lip before he crushed his mouth to hers. Her berry bright sweetness burst on his tongue, the Bear in him craving more of her flavor with every swipe of his tongue. *Bears loved berries. Grrr.*

As far as first kisses went, this one was a record breaker. Never before had he been possessed of a desire to do anything and everything within his power to please the woman he was with. But with her, he'd do it all. Anything to make her moan like that again.

"Rex," she sighed his name. He caught her looking at him while the moonlight danced in her long dark hair and across her pale skin giving her an unearthly glow. *Magic. She is magic.*

"Beautiful," he said, the words foreign to his tongue, but right as his eyes devoured her heart-shaped face and lust glazed eyes.

"Candra, I need to explain a few things to you," he said continuing to rub small circles on her lower back. The sheer fabric hid nothing from his roaming hands. He ran them up and down from her supple hips to her shoulders. Soothing her while indulging in his need to touch and claim.

"*Mmm*, okay," she said and dropped kisses on his chin and neck, working her way down to his bare pecs.

"Can-Candra," he groaned as her mouth closed over one flat male nipple, her tiny teeth nipping the bud and causing a serious reaction in his briefs.

"Feels so good, Rex, I don't want to stop," she moaned the words as she pushed herself closer to him, rubbing her soft, tender flesh against his rock-hard body.

"I'm trying to do the right thing, baby," he said and gasped as she ran her hand down his abs, slipping it under his gladiator's costume and over his too-fucking-tight briefs.

"Me too," she smiled against his mouth and drove her tongue inside.

"Candy," he growled her name unable to resist. He lifted her up in his arms crushing his mouth to hers, loving the way she instinctively wrapped her long legs around his waist. The scent of her arousal was driving him completely fucking nuts.

He backed her up against the wall using it to support her as he slid one hand beneath the layers of sheer fabric, up her silky legs to that secret hidden place that was made just for him.

"Fuck," he groaned, "You're so wet for me baby."

"Yes," she answered.

He slid her panties aside and moved his long fingers along her slick folds. Heat and moisture greeted him as he slid first one than two digits inside her. She bucked against his hand wildly and the beast in him preened over the fact that he could bring such frenzy to his mate. *As it should be.*

The sounds of the party going on behind the closed door seemed to float away. Everything did. Everything except *her*. Using his thumb to circle her small bundle of nerves as he pumped his fingers, Rex soon brought his mate to her first climax.

She moaned against him, grinding her pelvis into his hand until she arched her back and opened her mouth in a long, drawn-out moan. He kept stroking her until she was breathing normally, kissing her lips and neck, her bare shoulder. *Everywhere* he could reach.

"What about you?" She asked and his heart squeezed.

"What about me, baby?"

"That was all for me," she said and shook her head as he stilled her hand.

"No, that was for me, baby."

Rex wanted nothing more than to feel his mate's soft fingers stroking him, but he didn't think he could take her without claiming her. And he needed to explain things first.

CHAPTER FIVE

"*H*oly *shit!*" Candra had almost lost it completely when Cornelius and Simone had explained to her what they were and what this party actually was. The *Council of Shifters Halloween Ball. Whoa!*

Apparently, all the fairytales and fantasy romance stories she loved were actually real! Her two strange looking friends here were actually a breed of *Vampire.* And not the sparkly kind.

Nope. These guys *fucked to feed* or *fed on fucking. Whatever.* They got their nourishment from sex and, well, they thought Candy looked like an all you can eat buffet. *Flatterers! But no. Ew.*

Still, they did give her the 4-1-1 about her date. Rex, the big hottie, was something called a Shifter and a Warden of Terra. She wasn't exactly sure what that meant, but the Shifter part, heck yeah. The hunk of a man was a *Shapeshifter. So cool!* From the looks of him, she thought he must be a Bear. *Imagine that!*

Oddly enough Simone and Cornelius kept asking her if she was "claimed" or "mated" to him and, though she wasn't sure what the hell they were talking about, she knew they weren't any of those things since she and Rex had just met.

True, she'd felt an overwhelming connection with the serious man from the second she saw him with his gorgeous blue eyes and amazing body. The way he looked at her made her toes curl. Hot guys did not dig fluffy chicks where she came from, but he didn't seem to mind her wide hips and soft belly. In fact, he seemed quite fond of them if the way he was kissing her a second ago was any indicator.

She couldn't believe she'd kissed him, and well, did other things. But it all made sense now. At least to her it did. She could hardly keep from smiling as she sat down in the stool that he'd procured for her from the wall. Poor guy, he looked like a pirate about to walk the plank as he ran his fingers, *those oh-so-talented fingers,* through his short hair.

"Candra, I need you to keep an open mind-"

"Sure, I can do that," she smiled.

"Good. I, uh, am not like other men you know-"

"You can say that again," she said and bit her lip. He was so deliciously yummy. And so caring and concerned for her!

What other man would have charged into a room without knowing what to expect for a virtual stranger? What other man would have given her such pleasure only to take none for himself? Just him and if she was lucky, he was all hers!

"Candra, I'm not just a man. Please don't be afraid, but I'm a *Shifter*. A Bear Shifter to be exact-"

"Cool! I was hoping you were a Bear! Aren't you a Warden or something though?"

"Yes. I am a Bear and a rare retainer of the Sign of Taurus, that means I have extra strength and powers. Wait, why aren't you freaking out? And why do you know what a Shifter is?" His eyebrows raised in shock was so darn cute, but not as cute as the confusion that soon took its place.

Standing up, Candy beckoned him forward and pushed him down on the stool. She straddled his lap and was thankful when his big strong hands gripped her waist as she almost slid off. Those sheer skirts were slippery!

"Okay look, big guy, I'm not as dumb as you think."

"I don't think your dumb," he said seriously.

"Good. Because I'm not. Just because I am impulsive doesn't mean I am careless," she began and wrapped her arms around his neck. For security. *Uh huh.*

"Okay," he said in that low growly voice she was starting to love.

It might have had something to do with the place that she'd wiggled ever so slightly on that hardened part of him that was currently residing under her butt. Either way she loved it when he got all *grrr* on her.

"I feel drawn to you, Rex. Safe in your arms-"

"You are safe. I'd never hurt you," he interrupted with the sweetest most earnest expression on his face. Her heart melted at the sight.

"I know that," she bit her lip and continued, "I trust you. I think fate brought us together tonight. That empty store, these costumes, this spooky and yet awesome ball with its strange guests. All of it was designed to bring us right up to this moment."

"This moment? And what happens now," he said, his large hands cupped her ass as she spoke, those eyes of his riveted to her mouth.

"Now is when you tell me that you're *my* Shifter,

Rex Bastian. Now is when you tell me you want to claim me as your mate."

"Is it now?"

"*Yes*," insecurity threatened to rear its ugly head, but Candy pushed it back down. She wasn't that kind of woman. Confidence had always been a friend of hers, so she waited patiently, a small smile in her eyes as he seemed to mull things over.

"Okay. You got me, Candra. Since the second I walked into *Hazel's Halloween Happenings,* I've been fiercely drawn to you. Your beautiful face, those silver eyes, that scent, like strawberries and sunshine, not to mention your gorgeous body, every single thing about you is perfect. Designed especially for me by the Parcae, *the Fates*. Meeting you is a miracle and being with you would make me complete in ways I can't even imagine, and I don't want to-"

"You don't want me?" Her heart threatened to stop beating if he confirmed those words.

"No! Baby, *I want you*, believe me. I was going to say I don't want to just imagine being with you. You are my mate. *My fated mate.* And I want to claim you. I will claim you. As soon as you say the word."

"*Word,*" she said and pressed her lips against his. Their tongues tangled and he held her face where he wanted it with one strong hand on her neck. She quivered with need. Wanting him, all of him. *Now.*

"Let's go home," he groaned against her mouth.

To a girl who'd never had a real home, that sounded pretty damn good.

EPILOGUE

Rex carried her into his house like a conquering hero and why the fuck not. He was bringing his mate home for the first time.

She smiled enticingly at him as he dropped her gently onto the bed and removed her silky costume from her lush body. The soft gray of his comforter seemed to emphasize the silver in her eyes. He thought he'd never seen anything as beautiful as the sight of his mate naked on his bed with only the moonlight touching her pale ivory skin.

He stripped before her, his predatory gaze not missing the sudden widening of her eyes as she caught sight of his naked form for the first time. His cock thrust out from its nest of dark curls, proudly it pulsed wanting her attention. *Not yet*, he told himself.

First, he needed a taste. Starting with her feet he circled her toes with his fingers, stroking the soft skin of her ankles, up to her calves. He knelt on the bed, placing himself between her legs, gently pushing her knees until they fell apart.

Her plump lips parted as she watched his hands trail slowly up her sensitive thighs until they reached her core. Parting her silky folds, Rex breathed in deep, her sweet and heady musk driving him to lose control. *Mine.*

He dipped his head, taking long, slow laps with his tongue until she was mindless beneath him. Candra bucked and moaned. Sensing her urgency, he slid his fingers inside of her sopping wet pussy.

Rex groaned loving the squeeze of her tight channel on his digits. He couldn't imagine how good it was going to feel on his dick. *Soon.*

"You taste so good, baby," he growled before latching on to her clit.

Her pussy throbbed around his fingers and his balls tightened in response. Yes, he wanted to fill her, but first she had to come. Since the second he'd seen her, he wanted this, wanted her in his bed. Could hardly believe she accepted it so readily, but that was his mate.

Sweet and impulsive, completely trusting him to do right by her and he would. He fucking swore it as he made love to her with his mouth. Rex might have been a grumpy bastard before he met her, but he would spend every minute from now on making her happy.

Their lovemaking took on a frantic tone as her climax took over. Rex slid up her body, making sure he touched every single inch of her glorious skin before stopping with the tip of his thick cock kissing the entrance of her wet heat.

"Candra, you have to be sure you want this, I can't stop once I start, baby," he growled, his Bear showing through his eyes.

"I want this. I want you, Rex. Only you," she said. He closed his eyes for a second. *Thank the Parcae!* Then he pushed.

Stars burst behind his eyelids as he slid home. Pure ecstasy, the likes of which he'd never had before filled him as he filled his one fated mate.

"I need you, mate," he growled the words as he flexed his hips.

"Yes," she answered, wrapping her legs around his waist, and holding him to her.

He tugged her closer nipping her lips with his teeth and sucking on them as he continued to thrust and grind. He'd been careful not to crush her under his weight, but she pulled him to her, seeming to need more of it, of him. So he gave it to her.

"Mine," he growled as her sheath tightened around him. He felt hot and tight and ready to explode. *But not without her.* No fucking way.

Up. Down. Faster. Hotter. He worked his way in and out of his Candra in a rhythm old as time and yet all their own. She began to tremble, her core tightening, and he knew she was almost there. *Pivot. Swirl. Grind.*

"Rex!" She screamed his name, raking her nails down his back and the Bear in him roared.

He wanted her to mark him. The primal instinct to wear his mate's claim ingrained in him. And he would mark her too. *Now.*

His teeth sliced through the skin of one soft, creamy shoulder and the pleasure increased tenfold. Rex was hardly prepared for the jolt of pure satisfaction that racked through his hard body.

He rammed his cock one final time into her heat and bathed her womb with his seed, marking her on the inside too. The magical tendrils of their *matebond* wove around them. Almost complete.

"Mine," he purred against her flesh, licking the wounds he'd made until they closed. She would wear the mark now, always, as a sign of their mating.

He gazed into her eyes still breathing harshly from their shared ecstasy. Their hearts pounded in a symphony of heat and sex, and *could it be love? Yes,* his Bear answered. Even as he admitted it to himself, he felt his entire body fill with joy.

"Candra Nichols, I swear by the Parcae, those sisters who control our destiny, to protect, honor, and love you until the end of time. Will you accept me and my claim?"

"Yes," she sighed the word and lifted up to nuzzle his neck with her nose and lips.

"*Thank you,*" his voice was rough and deep, his Bear making himself known as their *matebond* pulsed all around them. "I will be a good mate, Candra, I promise you."

"I know you will, Rex and I know it is too soon, but I love you," she whispered the words, silver eyes bright with tears as he looked down at her.

"I love you too," he said and proceeded to show her how much.

The end...

P. S

Don't forget to tell me how you liked this story by leaving your honest review! *No pressure.* 😉

A review can be one or two brief sentences where you simply state whether you enjoyed the story and would recommend it to someone! It is an enormous help to authors and the best way for us to reach larger audiences so we can keep writing the stories you love!

Thank you so much!

Xoxo!

Del mare alla stella,

C.D. Gorri

P.S.S Don't forget…

GRAB THEM IN AUDIO HERE!

The Falk Clan Tales are my stories surrounding four Dragon Shifter brothers and how they find their one true mates.

Each brother's chest is marked with his rose, the magical link to his heart and his magic. They each have a matching gemstone to go with it.

She's given up on love, but he's just begun.

In *The Dragon's Valentine* we meet the eldest Falk brother, Callius. He is on a mission to find a Castle and his one true mate, one he can trust with his diamond rose....

His heart is frozen; can she change his mind about love?

In *The Dragon's Christmas Gift* our attention shifts to Alexsander, the youngest brother of the four. He has resigned himself to a life alone, until he meets *her*.

Some wounds run deep, can a Dragon's heart be unbroken?

The Dragon's Heart is the story of Edric Falk who has vowed never to love again, but that changes when he meets his feisty mate, Joselyn Curacao.

She just wants a little fun, he's looking for a lifetime.

We finally meet Nikolai Falk and his sexy Shifter mate in *The Dragon's Secret*.

**Now available in a boxed set.*

Look for The Dragon's Treasure in 2022!

CONNECT WITH C.D. GORRI

To learn more about me please visit:

https://www.cdgorri.com

https://www.facebook.com/Cdgorribooks

https://twitter.com/cgor22

https://www.bookbub.com/authors/c-d-gorri

TikTok

Visit my website to find out more about my supernatural world also known as the Grazi Kelly Universe and sign up to be a subscriber!

https://www.cdgorri.com/newsletter

HAVE YOU MET MY BEARS?

Looking for a Paranormal Romance series that is loads of growly fun?

Meet the Barvale Clan first in the Bear Claw Tales! A complete shifter romance series about 4 brothers who discover and need to win their fated mates!

Followed by two more spin off series, the Barvale Clan Tales and the Barvale Holiday Tales!

No cliffhangers. Steamy PNR fun. Go and read your next happily ever after today!

Other Titles by C.D. Gorri

Young Adult Urban Fantasy Books:

Wolf Moon: A Grazi Kelly Novel Book 1

Hunter Moon: A Grazi Kelly Novel Book 2

Rebel Moon: A Grazi Kelly Novel Book 3

Winter Moon: A Grazi Kelly Novel Book 4

Chasing The Moon: A Grazi Kelly Short 5

Blood Moon: A Grazi Kelly Novel 6

*Get all 6 books NOW AVAILABLE IN A BOXED SET:

The Complete Grazi Kelly Novel Series

Casting Magic: The Angela Tanner Files 1

Keeping Magic: The Angela Tanner Files 2

G'Witches Magical Mysteries Series

Co-written with P. Mattern

G'Witches

G'Witches 2: The Hary Harbinger

Paranormal Romance Books:

Macconwood Pack Novel Series:

Charley's Christmas Wolf: A Macconwood Pack Novel 1

Cat's Howl: A Macconwood Pack Novel 2

Code Wolf: A Macconwood Pack Novel 3

The Witch and The Werewolf: A Macconwood Pack Novel 4

To Claim a Wolf: A Macconwood Pack Novel 5

Conall's Mate: A Macconwood Pack Novel 6

Her Solstice Wolf: A Macconwood Pack Novel 7

Also available in 2 boxed sets:

The Macconwood Pack Volume 1

The Macconwood Pack Volume 2

Macconwood Pack Tales Series:

Wolf Bride: The Story of Ailis and Eoghan A Macconwood Pack Tale 1

Summer Bite: A Macconwood Pack Tale 2

His Winter Mate: A Macconwood Pack Tale 3

Snow Angel: A Macconwood Pack Tale 4

Charley's Baby Surprise: A Macconwood Pack Tale 5

Home for the Howlidays: A Macconwood Pack Tale 6

A Silver Wedding: A Macconwood Pack Tale 7

Mine Furever: A Macconwood Pack Tale 8

A Furry Little Christmas: A Macconwood Pack Tale 9

Also available in two boxed sets:

The Macconwood Pack Tales Volume 1

Shifters Furever: The Macconwood Pack Tales Volume 2

<u>The Falk Clan Tales:</u>

The Dragon's Valentine: A Falk Clan Novel 1

The Dragon's Christmas Gift: A Falk Clan Novel 2

The Dragon's Heart: A Falk Clan Novel 3

The Dragon's Secret: A Falk Clan Novel 4

The Dragon's Treasure: A Falk Clan Novel 5

Dragon Mates: The Falk Clan Complete Series Boxed Set Books 1-4

<u>The Bear Claw Tales:</u>

Bearly Breathing: A Bear Claw Tale 1

Bearly There: A Bear Claw Tale 2

Bearly Tamed: A Bear Claw Tale 3

Bearly Mated: A Bear Claw Tale 4

Also available in a boxed set:

The Complete Bear Claw Tales (Books 1-4)

<u>The Barvale Clan Tales:</u>

Polar Opposites: The Barvale Clan Tales 1

Polar Outbreak: The Barvale Clan Tales 2

Polar Compound: A Barvale Clan Tale 3

Polar Curve: A Barvale Clan Tale 4

Barvale Holiday Tales:

A Bear For Christmas

Hers To Bear

Thank You Beary Much

Purely Paranormal Pleasures:

Marked by the Devil: Purely Paranormal Pleasures

Mated to the Dragon King: Purely Paranormal Pleasures

Claimed by the Demon: Purely Paranormal Pleasures

Christmas with a Devil, a Dragon King, & a Demon: Purely Paranormal Pleasures (short story)

Vampire Lover: Purely Paranormal Pleasures

Grizzly Lover: Purely Paranormal Pleasures

Elvish Lover: Purely Paranormal Pleasures

Hot Dire Wolf Nights: Purely Paranormal Pleasures

Christmas With Her Chupacabra: Purely Paranormal Pleasures

The Wardens of Terra:

Bound by Air: The Wardens of Terra Book 1

Star Kissed: A Wardens of Terra Short

Waterlocked: The Wardens of Terra Book 2

Moon Kissed: A Wardens of Terra Short

*Now in a boxed set and in audio!

<u>The Maverick Pride Tales:</u>

Purrfectly Mated: Paranormal Dating Agency: A Maverick Pride Tale 1

Purrfectly Kissed: Paranormal Dating Agency: A Maverick Pride Tale 2

Purrfectly Trapped: Paranormal Dating Agency: A Maverick Pride Tale 3

Purrfectly Caught: Paranormal Dating Agency: A Maverick Pride Tale 4

Purrfectly Naughty: Paranormal Dating Agency: A Maverick Pride Tale 5

Purrfectly Bound: Paranormal Dating Agency: A Maverick Pride Tale 6

Also available in 2 boxed sets:

The Maverick Pride Volume 1

The Maverick Pride Volume 2

<u>Dire Wolf Mates:</u>

Shake That Sass: Sassy Ever After: Dire Wolf Mates Book 1

Breaking Sass: Sassy Ever After: Dire Wolf Mates 2

Pinch of Sass: Sassy Ever After: Dire Wolf Mates 3

Also available in a boxed set:

Dire Wolf Mates Volume 1

Doubly Tied

<u>Hearts of Stone Series</u>

Shifter Mountain: Hearts of Stone 1

Shifter City: Hearts of Stone 2

<u>Accidentally Undead Series</u>

Fangs For Nothin'

<u>Moongate Island Tales</u>

Moongate Island Mate

<u>Mated in Hope Falls</u>

Mated by Moonlight

<u>Shifters Unleashed Boxed Sets</u>

Check out these amazing anthologies where you can find some of my books

and the works of other awesome authors!

<u>Coming Soon:</u>

Ash: Speed Dating with the Denizens of Hell

Hungry Like Her Wolf: Magic and Mayhem Universe

Shifter Village: Hearts of Stone 3

Midnight Magic Anthology (Water Witch)

Mouse and the Ball: A FUCN'A Book

Tiger Claimed

For Fangs Sake

Tiger Denied

Werewolf Fever: A Macconwood Pack Novel 8

Moongate Island Captive

Witch Shield: Guardians of Chaos 5

Sweet As Candy (as seen in Once Upon An Ever After)

Taming Magic: The Angela Tanner Files 3

Rituals & Runes Anthology (Air Witch)

EXCERPT FROM CODE WOLF

"Are you fuckin' with me?"

"No, Randall, I assure you I am not fuckin' with you," Rafe Maccon eased his immense frame back into his oversized, black leather chair and narrowed his ice blue eyes at his Third and one of his oldest friends. How long had he known the man sitting in front of him?

Randall had come to Maccon City when Rafe was about ten, he looked the same then as he did now. Tall at six foot three inches, muscular, and more than a little intimidating to the Wolves under him with his long beard and equally long dark brown hair.

Rafe, however, was the Alpha. He was more amused than intimidated by his surly friend.

"A vacation?! What the fuck am I gonna do on a vacation? Come on, Rafe, this is bullshit!"

The door to Rafe's private office flew open and in strolled a very happy, very pregnant Charley Maccon, Rafe's wife. The Alpha's eyes glowed as they landed on his positively glowing mate. She wore a long, flowy dress. The shade was a pale-yellow color that, Randall admitted to himself, looked damn good with her creamy complexion and curly dark hair.

Their Alpha Female was quite something. There wasn't a Wolf Guard in the place who wouldn't lay down his/her life for her.

"Well, maybe you should consider a vacation to be a relaxing experience, Randy," she dropped a kiss on Randall's cheek and walked past him, over to her husband whom she kissed full on the mouth.

The way his Alpha's eyes homed in on her when she opened the door was nothing compared to the hungry gaze that followed her across the room.

Randall had noticed it took a while for Rafe to get used to his mate's habit of greeting everyone with a kiss or hug. Wolves were protective of their mates, but Randall thought his Alpha was doing an exceedingly good job of hiding his tension. Werewolves did not share very well.

Charley; however, had stood firm. That was the

way she was raised, and she wasn't going to change for any, how had she put it? Neanderthal brow-beating husband, regardless of how cute his ass was!

Randall had no direct knowledge if the "cute ass" statement was true or not. And he didn't want to know. He liked Charley though, had from the beginning. He was musically inclined and often took to one of the common rooms to strum his guitar or play a few keys on the piano.

Keeton's Mountain Lion hissed angrily as he boarded the plane for the States. Three months on Moongate Island did nothing to repair his faith in people. Shifter or human, they pretty much sucked.

True, he was no longer being blackmailed by the sniveling cretin who'd been part of his last black ops assignment. Fucker had stepped on a landmine deep in the jungles of a place Keeton was not at liberty to name. Not even in his own head.

Fucking hell.

Yeah, it meant he could return home now, but to who? Keeton had no family waiting for him. His few friends were back on the island, but that was no place for his inner feline. The beast craved the hills and valleys of the New Jersey forests he called home.

He'd bought a hundred acres of forest off the beaten paths of New Jersey's Panther Mountains years ago. Even commissioned the building of a cabin deep in the woods. The design was environmentally conscientious and entirely sound. Two stories high, it had its own generators, additional solar paneling, and wind turbines for power, and indoor plumbing.

He wasn't an animal, for fuck's sake. But even if Keeton was going to avoid people, he didn't have to be uncomfortable doing it. Eyes closed, he sat seemingly at ease, but he was keeping tabs on every living thing around him on the plane.

Once a soldier, always a soldier, his two commanders, Callan McGregor and Landry Smyth, had said that often enough. Both men were Shifters, a unique Alpha and Omega pair who'd completed their Triad once they'd found their mate in Sage Freeman, a smart mouthed human female. That had been Keeton's cue to leave the island he'd called home for eighty-nine and a half days.

They hadn't kicked him out or anything. On the contrary. But he was restless and antsy. The island could no longer contain his need for isolation.

Memories of the disgust on Bruce Taylor's face when he'd seen Keeton lose control of his shift during a particularly bloody battle were forever ingrained in his brain. The human male had been a new recruit in the special ops task force where Keeton had served his country for the last five years in secret.

Dismantling dictatorships and stopping atrocities the likes of which he could hardly put a name to before they could ever see the light of day had been his job, and blackmail was his reward.

He'd kept the fact that he'd unwittingly told the secret about Shifters to the human from Callan and Landry until the night Bruce had died believing Keeton was the only one of his kind. The two men had investigated his claims, making sure that he never downloaded or emailed the proof he'd recorded with his phone the night Keeton lost control.

The half a million dollars he'd sent to Bruce's offshore bank was nothing. He didn't care about the money. It was simply the point of it all. The man had not trusted Keeton because of his dual nature. And he'd lost his life as a result.

"We need to stick to this route, Bruce," he growled at the human who'd become increasingly toxic to their two-man operation.

"Think I'm gonna trust a fucking animal. I'll go this way," the man argued.

After a few more minutes of trying to convince him, Keeton threw his hands up. His beast scratched at his skin, the animal sensing something was not right. The sounds of the explosion and Bruce's bitter cry rang in his ears, but he died before Keeton could ever hope to reach him.

It was his fault. He was the reason Bruce had died. After pledging his life to help save lives, he'd brought death instead.

Keeton was better off on his own.

"Are you out of your mind?"

Xavier DuMont, Vampire and Prince of the Tenebris Clan out of DuMont, New Jersey, ran a hand over his face. It was almost five in the morning on Wednesday, and he was still going over the weekly requests and complaints.

He could not believe it. One after the other, he'd received dozens of requests for formal introductions for most of the eligible young females in the Clan by their parents or some family matchmaker or other. It was the 21st Century, and yet, the Vampires of the Tenebris Clan still thought he needed an arranged marriage to run things!

"No, Lucius, I assure you my mind is sound."

"How can you be thinking of going away? To some retreat? At this time of year! You know, the whole Clan is up in arms over the tax laws your father had set into motion before his demise. Some are questioning your right to rule. Then, there is still the matter of your mating—"

"Lucius, for the love of fuck! I know what is going on in my own Clan. I am even now revoking those tax laws, people will just have to be patient."

"And what about meeting with these young females? Maybe that will quell some of the unrest—"

"No! I am not inclined to take a mate at this time. My father's grave has barely begun to grow grass. There is no rush!"

"There is pressure though, sire," Lucius Redwing insisted.

He was Xavier's oldest and most reliable friend. At nearly three hundred years old, they'd known each other for a considerable length of time. Lucius had been his childhood companion when they'd fled France for the New World. After settling the town of DuMont, his father had not only been the most productive of the local normals, but he had taken over their branch of the Clan.

Breaking ties with the old regime, and establishing their own rule, the DuMonts had done exceedingly well. Of course, coming into the new century had been difficult for some, but Xavier was determined to do it, to breathe new life into the old-fashioned world of Vampires. He would see them succeed and blossom in this age that was simply exploding with technology.

"I know you have plans, sire. But the anxious mamas are already parading their daughters resumes as if they were applying for a job." Lucius grinned. He waved a manila envelope bursting with applications for audiences with him from the most prestigious Vampire families in all of DuMont.

"For fuck's sake, Luc. Get rid of them," Xavier growled, and ran a hand over his face.

"Now, now. Surely, you know enough not to disrespect tradition and courtesy. These families are your staunchest supporters. Without their aid, your ascension to leadership could be challenged. The right mate would stop all of that—"

"I will not be forced into this, Luc. If anyone wants to challenge me for the right to lead, then he or she can face me out in the open. Not hide behind some political game."

"But sire—"

"No. I will not be manipulated. You should know that of me, old friend."

"Yes. Of course." Lucius nodded, placing the hefty envelope on the corner of Xavier's desk.

Vampires did not always inherit the right to lead. Princes were not born but made. Wasn't that what his father had always said? And yet, royal blood flowed in his veins. And it was because of that blood —*his royal DuMont blood*—that so many hungry mamas yearned to tie one of their young to him for eternity.

Fortunately, Xavier had avoided them. He refused to be pressured to take any of the hungry misses for his mate, as of yet. But with his recent ascension, that pressure was now on full keel.

Shit and fuck.

"I've got an idea," Lucius said, thrusting a copy of *The Nightly News* at him.

"What is it, Luc? I am in no mood."

"Read there," his friend said, pointing at an article on the bottom left.

"A retreat? I haven't been on one of those since I was ninety."

"Yes, but remember the fun? I brought my *sheep* at the time, and you pouted because I wouldn't share her!"

"As I recall, she came quite willingly to my bed when summoned, Luc. Why do they still call them sheep? My gods, that is positively medieval!" he replied.

"In case normals see the newspaper, of course."

"Impossible. The Covens bespelled the paper to only go to supes."

"It has happened, Xavier. You know this as well as I."

"True. And Luc, I am sorry about Temple. That was your donor at the time, was it not?"

"Temple? Yes. Not to worry, sire. You always did woo the ladies without trying. Besides, now they have their own donors on hand. You do not need to bring one."

"You don't have to do that, you know."

"What?"

"Calling me sire."

"I do have to call you sire, *sire*. You are my Prince."

"Oh, do shut up. I am your friend, Luc. You've known me my entire life."

"Yes, sire."

"Luc," he growled his friend's name.

"Shall I make the arrangements then?"

"Fine. I will go to this retreat for the weekend if

only to shut you up. And to get away from all this." He indicated the pile of correspondence.

"Very good, sire."

EXCERPT FROM THE ENFORCER
BY C.D. GORRI

The moon would soon be full. Isabeau looked at the night sky and pulled the hood of her ivory sweater up over her fiery red curls. She passed between the red and sugar maples, a few tall beech trees, and a lonely pine when a low growl sounded next to her. She reached out to touch the thick fur of the adult she-Wolf who walked beside her through the forest trail.

"It's okay Artemis, let's finish our rounds and get home."

As she walked around the perimeter of her land she chanted an ancient language that few would be able to identify fortifying the wards around her large animal sanctuary. That was what the mortals around her thought it was, and for the most part they were correct.

To them, Isabeau Rose had just arrived in town a few years ago with the deed to five-hundred acres of Northern New Jersey farmland. Within a few months, she'd transformed the abandoned horse farm and the woods around it into a series of habitats for wild animals that were injured or discarded. Creatures that needed a haven for rehabilitation.

She had a main house for herself that boasted ten-bedrooms and six-full baths, an indoor pool and spa, two stables, one for her horses, the other for more exotic wildlife, two large red barns, and a state of the art veterinary clinic on the grounds.

"Out late, aren't you?" Beau turned around to find the source of the unfamiliar voice. She lifted her hand to calm Artemis who was ready to pounce on the intruder.

"Who are you?" she demanded.

"The real question is what are you doing out here so late? Surely your wards don't need reinforcement at this time of night, not out in this quiet New Jersey forest, Sorceress Rose?" The dark stranger spoke with an unearthly calm to his voice that put Beau on edge.

This was no mere mortal. She used her keen sight

to see him despite the darkness and almost gasped aloud. His face was perfect, except for a thin silver scar that ran from his left eyebrow to his chin. His eyes blazed cerulean blue fringed with impossibly dark lashes. They were carefully masked to hide his emotions.

ABOUT THE AUTHOR

C.D. Gorri is a USA Today Bestselling author of steamy paranormal romance and urban fantasy. She is the creator of the Grazi Kelly Universe.

Join her mailing list here: https://www.cdgorri.com/newsletter

An avid reader with a profound love for books and literature, when she is not writing or taking care of her family, she can usually be found with a book or tablet in hand. C.D. lives in her home state of New Jersey where many of her characters or stories are based. Her tales are fast paced yet detailed with satisfying conclusions.

If you enjoy powerful heroines and loyal heroes who face relatable problems in supernatural settings, journey into the Grazi Kelly Universe today. You will find sassy, curvy heroines and sexy, love-driven heroes who find their HEAs between the pages. Werewolves, Bears, Dragons, Tigers, Witches, Romani, Lynxes, Foxes, Thunderbirds, Vampires, and many more Shifters and supernatural creatures dwell within her worlds. The most important thing is every mate in this universe is fated, loyal, and true lovers always get their happily ever afters.

Want to know how it all began? Enter the Grazi Kelly Universe with Wolf Moon: A Grazi Kelly Novel or pick up Charley's Christmas Wolf and dive into the Macconwood Pack Novel Series today.

For a complete list of C.D. Gorri's books visit her website here:

https://www.cdgorri.com/complete-book-list/

Thank you and happy reading!

del mare alla stella,
    C.D. Gorri

Follow C.D. Gorri here:
    http://www.cdgorri.com
    https://www.facebook.com/Cdgorribooks

https://www.bookbub.com/authors/c-d-gorri
https://twitter.com/cgor22
https://instagram.com/cdgorri/
https://www.goodreads.com/cdgorri
https://www.tiktok.com/@cdgorriauthor

www.ingramcontent.com/pod-product-compliance
Lightning Source LLC
Chambersburg PA
CBHW061048210726
48294CB00001B/60